IT STARTED WITH A KISS

IT STARTED WITH COLLECTION

October 2015

November 2015

December 2015

January 2016

Miranda Lee is Australian, and lives near Sydney. Born and raised in the bush, she was boarding-school educated, and briefly pursued a career in classical music before moving to Sydney and embracing the world of computers. Happily married, with three daughters, she began writing when family commitments kept her at home. She likes to create stories that are believable, modern, fast-paced and sexy. Her interests include meaty sagas, doing word puzzles, gambling and going to the movies.

Published in Great Britain 2016
by Mills & Boon, an imprint of Harlequin (UK) Limited,
Eton House, 18-24 Paradise Road, Richmond, Surrey, TW9 1SR

ISBN: 978-0-263-91746-8

011-0116

Harlequin (UK) Limited's policy is to use papers that are natural, renewable and recyclable products and made from wood grown in sustainable forests.The logging and manufacturing processes conform to the legal environmental regulations of the country of origin.

Printed and bound in Spain
by CPI, Barcelona

THE SECRET LOVE-CHILD

MIRANDA LEE

CHAPTER ONE

'PLEASE, Rafe. My reputation for reliability is on the line here.'

Rafe sighed. Les had to be really desperate to ask him to do this. His ex-partner knew full well the one job he'd hated when they'd been in the photographic business together was covering weddings. Where Les enjoyed the drama and sentiment of the bride and groom's big day, Rafe found the whole wedding scenario irritating in the extreme. The pre-ceremony nerves got on *his* nerves, as did all the hugging and crying that went on afterwards.

Rafe was not a big fan of women weeping.

On top of that, it was impossible to be seriously creative when the criterion was simply to capture every single moment of the day on film, regardless. Rafe, the perfectionist, had loathed having to work with the possibilities that the weather might be rotten, the settings difficult and the bridal party hopelessly unphotogenic.

As a top-flight fashion and magazine photographer, Rafe now had control over everything. The sets. The lighting. And above all…the models. When you shot a wedding, you had control over very little.

'I presume you can't get anyone else,' Rafe said, resignation in his voice.

'The wedding's on Saturday, exactly a fortnight from

today,' Les explained. 'You know how popular Saturday weddings are. Every decent photographer in Sydney will already be booked.'

'Yeah. Yeah. I understand. Okay, so what do you want me to do?'

'The bride's due at your place at noon today.'

Rafe's eyes flicked to the clock on the wall. It was eleven fifty-three. 'And what if I'd refused?'

'I knew you wouldn't let me down. You might be the very devil with women, but you're a good mate.'

Rafe shook his head at this back-handed compliment. So he'd had quite a few girlfriends over the years. So what? He was thirty-three years old, a better-than-average-looking bachelor who spent his days photographing bevies of beautiful women, a lot of whom were also single. It was inevitable that their ready availability, plus his active libido, would keep the wheels turning where his relationships were concerned.

But he wasn't a womaniser. He had one girlfriend at a time, and he never lied or cheated. He just didn't want marriage. Or children. Was that a crime? It seemed to be in some people's eyes.

Rafe wished his married friends—like Les—would understand that not everyone wanted the same things out of life.

'Just give me some details before the bride actually arrives,' he said a tad impatiently, 'so I won't look a right Charlie.'

'Okay, her name is Isabel Hunt. She's thirtyish, blonde and beautiful.'

'Les, you think *all* your brides are beautiful,' Rafe said drily.

'And so they are. On the day. But this one is beautiful all the time. You're going to enjoy photographing Ms Hunt, I promise you. Or should I say, Mrs Freeman. The lucky girl is marrying Luke Freeman, the only son and heir of Lionel Freeman.'

'Is that supposed to mean something to me? Who the hell is Lionel Freeman, anyway?'

'Truly, Rafe, you're a complete philistine when it comes to subjects other than food, the Phantom and photography. Lionel Freeman was one of Sydney's most awarded architects. Poor chap was killed in a car accident a couple of weeks back, along with his wife, so tread easily with the groom when you finally meet him.'

'Poor bloke. What rotten luck.' Rafe's own father had been killed in a car crash when Rafe had been only eight. It had been a difficult time in his life, one he didn't like dwelling on.

'Oh-oh. I just heard a car pull up outside. The bride-to-be, I gather, and right on time. I hope she's just as punctual on her wedding day. Now what about money, Les? What do you charge for a wedding these days?'

'A lot less than you could command, my friend. But I'm afraid you'll have to settle for my fee. It's already been agreed upon and the full amount paid up front. If you give me your bank account number, I'll...'

'No, don't bother,' Rafe broke in, not caring about the money this once. Les might need it. He wouldn't be running around covering too many weddings with a broken leg. 'You can owe me one. Just don't ask again, buddy. Not where a wedding is concerned. Must go. The doorbell's ringing. I'll call you back after the bride's gone. Let you know what I thought of her.'

Rafe hung up and headed downstairs, then hurried along towards the front door, curious now to see if Les was exaggerating about the bride-to-be's blonde beauty.

She'd have to be something really special to surprise him. After all, he was used to beautiful blondes. He'd photographed hundreds. He'd even fallen madly in love with one once.

He'd been twenty-five at the time, and had just started climbing the fashion photographic ladder. Liz had been an up-and-coming cat walk model. Nineteen, nubile and too nice to be true. Only he hadn't realised that in the beginning. He'd become so besotted with her he'd actually begged her to live with him. Which she had. But only till she'd milked him for everything he was worth, both personally and professionally. Within a year she'd moved on to an older, more influential photographer, leaving an emotionally bruised and embittered Rafe behind.

He was no longer bruised, or bitter. That had all happened years ago. But he hadn't lived with a girlfriend since, no matter how much he might occasionally be tempted to. And he didn't date blondes any more. Experience had taught him blondes often played sweet and vulnerable and not too bright, when they were actually smart as a whip, sneakily manipulative and ruthlessly ambitious.

Photographing them, however, was another question. A blonde was still his model of choice.

Rafe wrenched open the front door to his inner-city terrace home and tried not to stare. Wow! Les hadn't exaggerated one bit.

What a pity she was going to be married, he thought as his male gaze swept over his visitor. Because if ever there was a blonde who might make him reassess his decision never to date one again, she was standing right in front of him.

Talk about exquisite!

Ms Isabel Hunt was the epitome of an Alfred Hitchcock heroine. Classically beautiful and icily blonde, with cheekbones to die for, cool long-lashed blue eyes and what looked like a perfect figure. Though, to be honest, she would have to remove the fawn linen jacket she was wearing over those tailored black trousers for Rafe to be sure.

'Ms Hunt?' he said, smiling warmly at her. What had been an irksome task in his mind now held the prospect of some pleasure. Rafe liked nothing better than photographing truly beautiful women. Of course, only the camera would tell if she was also photogenic. It was perverse that some of the most beautiful women in the flesh didn't always come up so well on film.

'Mr Saint Vincent?' she returned, her own gaze raking over him. With not much approval, he noted. Maybe she didn't like men who hadn't shaved by noon.

She looked the fussy type. Her make-up was perfection and her clothes immaculate. That white shirt she had on underneath her jacket was so dazzlingly white, it could have featured in one of those washing-powder ads.

'The one and only,' he replied, his smile widening. Most women, he'd found, eventually responded to his smile. Rafe liked his photographic subjects to be totally relaxed with him. Being stiff in front of a camera was the kiss of death when it came to getting good results. 'But do call me Rafe.'

'Rafe,' she said obediently, but coolly.

Ms Hunt, Rafe realised ruefully, was not a woman given to being easily charmed. Which perhaps was just as well. She was one gorgeous woman. Those eyes. And that mouth! Perfectly shaped and deliciously full, her lips were provocative enough in repose. How would he react if they ever smiled at him?

Don't smile, lady, he warned her silently. Or we both could be in big trouble!

'Would you object if I called you Isabel?' he said recklessly.

'If you insist.'

Was that contempt he saw flicker in her eyes? Surely not!

Still, Rafe decided to pull right back on the charm for now and get down to tin tacks.

'Les rang me a little while ago with just the barest of details,' he informed her matter-of-factly, 'so why don't you come inside and we can discuss a few things?'

He led her into the front room where he conducted most of his business. It wasn't an office as such, more of a sitting room, simply and sparsely furnished. The walls, however, were covered with his favourite photos, all of women in various states of dress and undress. None actually nude, but some were close, and all were in black and white.

'I don't see any wedding photos,' the bride-to-be noted curtly as he led her over to the nearest sofa.

'I no longer work as a wedding photographer,' he admitted. 'But I was once Les's partner, so don't worry. I know what I'm doing.'

She gave him a long hard look. 'I suspect you're more expensive than Les.'

Rafe sat down on the navy sofa opposite hers and leant back, stretching his arms along the back.

'Usually,' he agreed. 'But not this time. I'm doing this job as a favour to Les.'

'What about the actual photos? Will I have to pay more for them?'

'No.'

She glanced up at the prints on the wall again and almost rolled her eyes. 'You do take coloured snaps, don't you?'

Rafe was not a man easy to rile. He had a very even temper. But she was beginning to annoy him. Coloured snaps, indeed! He wasn't some hack or hobby photographer. He was a professional!

'Of course,' he returned, priding himself on sounding a lot calmer than he was feeling inside. 'I do a lot of fashion photography. And fashion wouldn't be fashion without colour. But wedding photographs do look fabulous in black and white. I think you'd be pleased with the results.'

'Mr Saint Vincent—' she began frostily.

'Rafe, please,' he interrupted, determined not to lose it. My, she was a snooty bitch. Mr Luke Freeman was welcome to her. Rafe wondered if the poor groom knew exactly what type he was getting here. Talk about an Ice Princess!

'The thing is, *Rafe*,' she said in clipped tones, 'I wouldn't have chosen a wine-red gown for my maid of honour if I wanted all the photographs done in black and white, would I?'

Rafe simply ignored her sarcasm. 'What colour is the groom wearing?'

'Black.'

'And yourself?'

'White, of course.'

'Of course,' he repeated drily, his eyes holding hers for much longer than was strictly polite.

She flushed. She actually flushed.

Rafe was startled. She *couldn't* be a virgin. Not at thirty. And not looking like that. It was faintly possible, he supposed. Either that, or sex wasn't her favourite pastime.

Rafe pitied the groom some more. It didn't look as if his wedding night was going to be a ball if his bride was this uptight about sex.

'I'm sorry but I really don't want my wedding photos done in black and white,' she pronounced coldly, despite her pink cheeks. 'If you feel you can't accommodate me on this, then I'll just have to find another photographer.'

'You won't find anyone decent at this late stage,' Rafe told her bluntly.

She looked frustrated and Rafe found some sympathy for her. He *was* being a bit stubborn, even if he *was* right.

'Look, Isabel, would you tell a painter how to paint? Or a surgeon how to operate? I'm a professional photographer. And a top one, even if I say so myself. I know what will look good, and you won't look just *good* shot in black and white. You'll look magnificent.'

She was clearly taken aback by his fulsome compliment. But he'd never had the opportunity to photograph a bride as beautiful as this. No way was he going to let her muck up his creative vision. With the automatic cameras now available, any fool could take colour snaps. But only Rafe Saint Vincent could produce black and white masterpieces!

'There will be any number of guests at your wedding taking coloured snaps, if you want some,' he argued. 'My job, however, is to give you quality photographic memories which will not only be beautiful, but timeless. I guarantee that you'll still be able to show your wedding photographs to your grandchildren with great pride. They won't be considered old-fashioned, or funny, in any way.'

'You're very sure of yourself, aren't you?' she threw at him in almost scornful tones.

'I'm very sure of my abilities. So what do you say?'

'I don't seem to have much choice.'

'You won't be disappointed if you hire me. Trust me on this, Isabel.'

She half rolled her eyes again.

Trust, Rafe realised, was something else Isabel Hunt did not do easily.

'Why don't you look at some of my more conventional black and white portraits?' he suggested, pushing over the album portfolio which lay on the coffee-table between them. 'You might find them reassuring. I confess the shots on my walls are somewhat…avant-garde. Meanwhile, I'm dying for a cup of coffee. I haven't been up all that long. Late night last night,' he added with a wry smile. 'Would you like one yourself? Or something else?'

'No, thank you. I've not long had breakfast.'

'Aah…late night, too?' he couldn't resist saying.

She looked right through him before dropping her beautiful but chilly blue eyes back to the album. She began flicking through it, insulting him with the little time she spent over each page.

He glowered down at the top of her head, and had to battle to control the crazy urge to bend over and wrench the pins out of her oh, so uptight French roll. His hands itched to yank her to her feet and shake her till her hair spilled down over her slender shoulders. He wanted to pull her to him and kiss her till there was fire in her eyes, not ice. He wanted to see that blush back in her cheeks. But not from embarrassment. From passion.

He wanted… He wanted… He wanted *her*!

Rafe reeled with shock. To desire this woman was insane. And stupid. And masochistic.

First, she was going to be married in two weeks. Second, she was a blonde. Third, she didn't even like him!

Three strikes and you're out!

Now go get your coffee, dummy. And when you come back, focus on her simply as a fantastic photographic subject, and not the most challenging woman of the century.

CHAPTER TWO

ISABEL did not look up till she was sure she was alone, shutting the photo album with a snap.

The man was impossible! To hire him as her wedding photographer was impossible! Rafe Saint Vincent might be a brilliant photographer but if he wasn't capable of listening to what *she* wanted, then he could just go jump.

Truly, men like him irritated the death out of her.

And attracted the devil out of her.

Isabel sighed. That was the main problem with him, wasn't it? The fact she found him wickedly sexy.

Isabel closed her eyes and slumped back against the sofa. She'd thought she'd finally cured herself of the futile flaw of fancying men like him. She'd thought since meeting and becoming engaged to Luke that she would never again need what such men had to offer.

Luke was exactly what she'd been looking for in a husband. He was handsome. Successful. Intelligent. And extremely nice. A man who, like her, had come to the conclusion that romantic love was not a sound basis for marriage, that compatibility and common goals were far more reliable. Falling in love, they'd both discovered in the past, made fools of men—and women. Passion might be the stuff poems were written about, but it didn't make you happy in the long run. Mind-blowing sex, Isabel now believed, was not the be-all and end-all when it came to a relationship.

Not that Luke wasn't good in bed. He was. If her mind sometimes strayed to her own private and personal fantasies while he was making love to her, and vice versa, then Isabel hadn't been overly concerned.

Till this moment.

It was one thing to fill her mind with images of some mythical stranger during sex with Luke. Quite another to go to bed with him on her wedding night thinking of the likes of Rafe Saint Vincent.

And she would, if he was around all that day, looking her up and down with those sexy eyes of his.

Isabel shook her head with frustration. She'd always been attracted to the Mr Wrongs of this world. The daredevils and the thrill-seekers. The charmers and the slick, smooth-tongued womanisers who oozed the sort of confidence she found a major turn-on.

Of course, she hadn't known they were Mr Wrongs to begin with. She'd thought they were interesting, exciting men. It had taken several wretched endings—especially the disaster with Hal—to force her to face the fact that her silly heart had no judgement when it came to the opposite sex. It picked losers and liars.

By her late twenties, desperation and despair had forced Isabel's brain to develop a fail-safe warning system. If she was madly attracted to a man, then that was a guarantee he was another Mr Wrong.

So she didn't have to know much about Rafe Saint Vincent to know his character. She only had to take one look at him. Les *had* provided her with some brief details about him—namely that he was a bachelor, and a brilliant photographer—but to be honest, aside from the warning bells going off in Isabel's brain, Mr Saint Vincent's appearance said it all, from his trendy black clothes to his earring and his designer stubble. The fact he lived in a terraced house in Paddington completed the picture of a swinging male single of the new millennium whose priorities were career, pleasure and leisure, and who was never going to buy a cow when he could have cartons of milk for free. Rafe might not be a criminal or a con man, like Hal had been, but he would always be a waste of time for a woman who wanted marriage and children.

Actually, *every* man Isabel had ever fancied had been a waste of time in that regard. Which was why, when she'd found herself staring thirty in the face, still without the home and family of her own she'd always craved, Isabel had decided enough was enough, and set about finding herself a husband with her head, not her heart.

And she had.

Isabel knew she could be happy with Luke. Very happy.

But the last thing she needed around on her wedding day was someone like Rafe Saint Vincent.

Yet she needed a photographer. What excuse could she give her mother for not hiring him? The black and white business wouldn't wash. Her mother just *loved* black and white photographs, a hangover from the days when that was all there was. Her mother was not a young woman. In fact she was seventy, Isabel having been the product of a second honeymoon when Doris Hunt had turned forty.

No, there was nothing for it but to hire Rafe God's-gift-to-women Saint Vincent. Isabel supposed there was no real harm in fantasising about another man while your husband was making love to you, even on your wedding night. Luke would never know if she never told him.

And she wouldn't.

Actually, there were a lot of things about herself she'd never told Luke. And she didn't aim on starting now!

Her eyes opened and lifted to the photographs on the wall again and, this time, with their creator out of the room, Isabel let her gaze linger.

They really were incredibly erotic, his clever use of shadow highly suggestive. Although the subjects were obviously either naked or semi-naked, the lighting was such that most private parts were hidden from view. There was the occasional glimpse of the side of a breast, or the curve of a buttock, but not much more.

Tantalising was the word which came to mind. Isabel could have stared at them for hours. But the sound of footsteps coming down the stairs had her reefing her eyes away and searching for something to do. Anything!

Fishing her mobile phone out of her bag, she punched in her parents' number and was waiting impatiently for her mother to answer when her nemesis of the moment walked back into the room, sipping a steaming mug of coffee.

She pretended she wasn't ogling him, but her eyes

snuck several surreptitious glances as he walked over and sat down in the same spot he'd occupied before. He was gorgeous! Tall and lean, just as she liked them. Not traditionally handsome in the face, but attractive, and oh, so sexy.

'Yes?' her mother finally answered, sounding slightly breathless.

'Me, here, Mum.' No breathlessness on Isabel's part. She sounded wonderfully composed. Yet, inside, her heartbeat had quickened appreciably. Practice *did* make perfect!

'Oh, Isabel, I'm so glad you rang before we left for the club. I was thinking of you. So how did it go with Mr Saint Vincent?'

'Fine. He was fine.'

Isabel saw his dark eyes widen over the rim of his coffee-mug. Clearly, he'd been thinking she wasn't going to hire him.

'As good as Les?' her mother asked. Les had been hired by her parents before, for their recent golden wedding anniversary party.

'Better, I'd say.'

'That's a relief. I've waited a long time to see you married, love. I would like to have some decent photographs of the momentous event.'

Isabel's eyes flicked up to the two most provocative photos on the wall and a decidedly indecent thought popped into her mind. What would it be like to be photographed by him like *that*? To be totally naked before him? To have him arranging filmy curtains or sliding satin sheets over her nude body? To have to stand—or lie—perfectly still in some suggestive pose for ages whilst he shot reel after reel of film, those sexy eyes of his focused only on her?

Just the thought of it sent her heartbeat even higher.

Fortunately, Isabel was not a female whose inner feelings showed readily on her face. She could look at a man and be thinking the hottest thoughts and still look cool. Sometimes, even uninterested. Which perhaps was just as well, or she'd have spent half of her life in bed.

She didn't flirt easily. Neither was she capable of the sort of coy sugary behaviour some men seemed to find both a come-on and a turn-on. Most men found her slightly aloof, even snobbish. They often confused her ice-blonde looks and ladylike manner with being prudish and undersexed. Which perhaps explained why most of her lovers had been men who dared to do what a gentleman wouldn't, men who simply rode roughshod over her seeming uninterest and simply took what they wanted.

Isabel looked at the man sitting opposite her and wondered what kind of lover he'd be.

Not that you're ever going to find out, her conscience reminded her harshly.

'I have to go, Isabel,' her mother was saying. 'Your father and I were just having a bite to eat before we go down the club. When will you be home? Will you be eating with us tonight?'

Isabel had been living with her parents during the last few weeks leading up to the wedding. She'd quit her flat, plus her job as receptionist at the architectural firm where Luke worked, content to become a career wife and home maker after their marriage. She and Luke were going to try for a baby straight away.

'As far as I know,' she told her mother whilst she continued to watch the man opposite with unreadable eyes. 'Unless Luke comes back today and wants to go out somewhere. If he happens to ring, you could ask him. And tell him I'll be back home by one at the latest.'

'Will do. Bye, love.'

'Bye, Mum.'

She clicked off the phone then bent down to tap it against the album on the coffee-table. 'Very impressive,' she said, giving him one of her super cool looks, the ones she fell back on when her thoughts were at their most shocking. Pity she couldn't have rustled one up earlier when his barb about her wearing white at her wedding had sent a most uncharacteristic flush to her cheeks. Still, she was back in control now. Thank heavens.

She put down the phone and opened the album to a page which held a traditional full-length portrait of a woman in an evening gown. 'I liked this portrait very much. If you feel you could reproduce shots like this, then you're hired.'

'I don't ever *reproduce* anything, Isabel,' he returned quite huffily. 'I'm an artist, not a copier.'

Isabel's patience began to wear thin. 'Do you want this job or not?' she threw at him.

'As I said before, I'm doing this as a favour to Les. The question is...do *you* want *me* or not?'

Isabel's eyes met his and she had a struggle to maintain her equilibrium. If only he knew...

'I suppose you'll have to do,' she managed to say.

'Such enthusiasm. When and where?'

How about here and now?

'The wedding is at four o'clock at St Christopher's Church at Burwood, a fortnight from today. And the reception is at a place in Strathfield called Babylon.'

'Sounds exotic.'

It was, actually. Isabel had a secret penchant for the exotic. Though you'd never tell by looking at her. She always dressed very conservatively. But her favourite story as a child had been Aladdin, and she'd often dreamt of being a harem girl, complete with sexy costume and gauzy veils over her face.

'Do you want me to come to your house beforehand?' he asked. 'A lot of brides want that. Though some are too nervous to pose well at that stage. Still, when I was doing weddings regularly, I developed a strategy for relaxing them which helped on some occasions.'

'Oh?' Isabel tried to stop her wicked imagination from taking flight once more, but it was a lost cause.

'I'd give them a good...stiff...drink,' he said between sips of his coffee.

How she kept a straight face, Isabel would never know.

'I don't drink,' she lied.

'Figures,' he muttered, and she almost laughed.

He obviously thought she was a prude.

'Don't worry,' she went on briskly. 'I won't be nervous. And, yes, I'm sure my mother will want you to come to the house beforehand. I'll jot down the address and phone number for you.' She pulled out a pen from her bag, plus a spare business card from her hairdresser, and wrote her parents' details on the back.

'What say you arrive on the day at two?' she suggested as she handed it over to him, then stood up.

He put down his coffee, stared at the card, then stood up also.

'Is this your regular hairdresser?' he asked.

The question startled her. 'Yes, why?'

'Did they do your hair today?'

'No. I did it myself. I only go to a hairdresser when I want a cut. I like to do it myself.' Aside from the money it cost, she wasn't fond of the way some hairdressers had difficulty following instructions.

'So you'll be doing your hair on your wedding day?'

'Yes.'

'Not like that, I hope,' he said as he slipped the card into his shirt pocket.

Isabel bristled. 'What's wrong with it like this?'

'It's far too severe. If you're going to have it up, you need something a little softer, with some pieces hanging around your face. Here. Like this.'

Before she could step away, or object, he was by her side, his fingers tugging at her hair and touching her cheeks, her ears, her neck.

It was one thing to keep her cool whilst she was just

thinking about him, quite another with his hands on her. His fingertips were like brands on her skin, leaving heated imprints in her flesh and sending quivery ripples down her spine.

'Your hair seems quite straight,' he was saying as he stroked several strands down in front her ears. 'Do you have a curling wand?'

'No,' she choked out, knowing she should step back from him but totally unable to. She kept staring at the V of bare skin in his open-necked shirt and wondering what he would look like, naked.

'I suggest you buy one, then. They're cheap enough.'

Her eyes lifted to find he was studying not her hair so much, but her mouth. For one long, horribly exciting moment, Isabel thought he was going to kiss her. She sucked in sharply, her lips falling apart as a shot of excitement zinged through her veins. But he didn't kiss her, and she realised with a degree of self-disgust that she'd just been hoping he would.

But what if he had? came the appalling thought. What if he *had*?

Just the *thought* of risking or ruining what she had with Luke made her feel sick.

'I must go,' she said, and bent to pick up her bag, the action forcing his hands to drop away from her face. By the time she'd straightened he'd stepped back a little. But she had to get out of there. And quickly.

'If I don't hear from you,' she added brusquely, 'then I will expect you to show up at my parents' home at two precisely, a fortnight from today. Please don't be late.'

'I am never late for appointments,' he returned.

'Good. Till then, then?'

He nodded and she swept past him, her bag brushing against him as she did so. She didn't apologise, or look down. She kept going, not drawing breath till she was in her car and on the road home.

Relief was her first emotion once his place was well out of sight. Then anger. At herself; at the Rafe Saint Vincents of this world; and at fate. Why couldn't Les have recommended a photographer like himself, a happily married middle-aged conservative bloke with three kids and a paunch?

When a glance in the rear-vision mirror reminded her she had bits of hair all over the place, courtesy of her Lord and Master, she pulled over to the kerb and pulled the pins out of her French roll, shaking her head till her hair fell down around her face like a curtain.

'Maybe you'd like me to wear it like this!' she stormed as she accelerated away again. 'Lucky for me it isn't longer, or you'd be suggesting I do a Lady Godiva act at my wedding. I could be the first bride ever to be photographed in the nude!'

She ranted and raved about him for a while, then at the traffic when it took her nearly twice as long to get home as it had to drive into the city. She was feeling more than a little stressed by the time she turned into her parents' street, her agitation temporarily giving way to surprise when she spotted Luke's blue car parked outside the house. She slid her navy car in behind it, frowning at Luke who was still sitting behind the wheel. When she climbed out, so did he, throwing her an odd look at her hair as he did so.

She felt herself colouring with guilt, which really annoyed her. She'd done nothing to be guilty about.

'Luke!' she exclaimed, trying not to sound as flustered as she was feeling. 'What on earth are you doing here? I wasn't expecting you. Why didn't you call me?'

'I tried your mobile phone a while back,' he said. 'But you didn't answer.'

'What? Oh, I must have left the blasted thing behind at the studio. I took it out to ring Mum and tell her how long I'd be.'

Isabel wanted to scream. How could she have been so stupid as to leave it behind? Now she'd have to go back for it. And she'd have to see that man again, *before* the wedding.

'Oh, too bad,' she muttered, slamming the car door. 'It can stay there till tomorrow. I'm not going back now.'

She could feel Luke's puzzled eyes on her and knew she wasn't acting like her usual calm self. She shook her head and threw him a pained look. 'You've no idea the dreadful day I've had. The photographer I booked for the wedding's had an accident and he made an appointment for me to meet this other man who's not really suitable at all. Brilliant, but one of those avant-garde types who wants to do everything in black and white. I pointed out that I wouldn't have selected a wine-red gown for my maid of honour if I'd wanted all the shots done in black and white, but would he listen to me? No! He even told me how he wanted me to wear my hair. As if I don't know what suits me best. I've never met such an insufferably opinionated man.'

Isabel knew she was babbling but she couldn't seem to stop.

'Still, what can you expect from someone who fancies himself an *artiste*. You know the type. Struts around like he's God's gift to women. And he wears this earring in the shape of a phantom's head, of all things. What a show pony! Goodness knows what our photographs are going to turn out like, but it's simply too late to get someone else decent. His name's Rafe—did I tell you? Rafe Saint Vincent. It wouldn't be his real name, of course. Just a career move. Nobody is born with a name like Rafe Saint Vincent. Talk about pretentious!'

Isabel finally ran out of steam, only to realise that Luke was not only staring at her as if she'd lost her mind, but that he wasn't looking his usual self, either.

Always well-groomed, Luke was the sort of man who kept 'tall, dark and handsome' at number one on every woman's most wanted list.

'Luke!' she exclaimed. 'You look like you've slept in your clothes. And you haven't even shaved. That's not like you at all.' Unlike other men she would not mention. 'What are you doing here, anyway? I thought you were going to stay in your father's old fishing cabin up on Lake Macquarie for the whole weekend.' And do some proper grieving, Isabel had hoped. The poor darling had to have been through hell this past fortnight since his parents' tragic deaths. Yet he'd been so brave about it all. And so strong.

'The cabin wasn't there any more,' he said. 'It had been torn down a few years before.'

'Oh, what a shame,' she murmured. But it explained why he was looking so disconsolate. 'So where did you stay last night? In a motel? Or a tent?' she added, hoping to jolly him up with a dab of humour.

'No.' He didn't crack even the smallest of smiles. 'Dad had built a brand-new weekender on the same site. I stayed there.'

'But…' Isabel frowned. 'How did you get in? You didn't break in, did you?'

'No. There was a girl staying there for the weekend and she let me in.'

Isabel was taken aback. 'And she let you *sleep* the night?'

Luke sighed. 'It's a long story, Isabel. I think we'd better go inside and sit down while I tell it to you.'

She tried not to panic. 'Luke, you're worrying me.'

When he took her arm and propelled her over to the front gate, she pulled out of his grip and lanced him with alarmed eyes. 'You're not going ahead with the wedding, are you?'

Isabel waited in an agony of anxiety for him to speak.

'No,' he finally answered, his expression grim. 'No, I'm not.'

CHAPTER THREE

ISABEL stared at him, aghast. 'Oh, no. No, Luke, don't do this to me!' Bursting into tears, she buried her stricken face in her hands.

'I'm so sorry, Isabel,' Luke said softly as he tried to take her into his arms.

'But why?' she wailed, gripping the lapels of his suit jacket and shaking them.

His eyes held apology. 'I've fallen in love.'

'Fallen in love!' she gasped. 'In less than a *day*?'

'No one is more surprised than me, I can tell you. But it's true. I came back straight away to tell you, and to call our wedding off.'

'But love's no guarantee of happiness, Luke,' she argued in desperation. 'I thought we agreed on that. It traps and tricks you. It really is blind. This girl you've supposedly fallen in love with—how do you know she'll be good for you? How do you know she won't make you miserable? You can't possibly know her real character, not this quickly. She could be playing a part for you, pretending to be something she's not. She might be a really bad person. A gold-digger, perhaps. A…a criminal even!'

'She's not *any* of those things,' he returned, looking

shocked by her arguments. 'She's a good person. I just know it.'

Isabel shook her head. One *day*! One miserable *day*! How could he know anything for sure? 'I would never have believed you could be so naïve,' she pronounced angrily. 'A man like you!'

'I'm not naïve,' he denied. 'Which is why I'm not rushing into anything. But I can't marry you, Isabel, feeling as I do about Celia. Surely you can see that.'

Isabel was not in the mood to see anything of the kind. She wanted to cry some more. And to scream. She'd been so close to having her dream come true. So darned close!

'Maybe I do and maybe I don't,' she grumbled, letting his lapels go. '*I'd* still marry *you*. I haven't much time for the highly overrated state of being in love.'

And she'd thought he felt the same way.

'Maybe that's because you've never really been in love,' Luke said.

Isabel's laugh was tinged with bitterness. 'I'm an expert in the subject. But that's all right. You'll live and learn, Luke Freeman, and when you do, give me a call. Meanwhile, let's go inside, as you said. I need a drink. Not tea or coffee. Something much stronger. Dad still has some of the malt whisky I gave him for his birthday. That should do the trick.'

Isabel let herself into the house, Luke following.

'But you don't drink Scotch,' he pointed out with a frown in his voice.

'Aah, but I do,' she threw over her shoulder at him

as she strode into her parents' lounge room, heading straight for the drinks cabinet in the corner. 'When the occasion calls for it,' she added, pouring herself half a glassful. 'Which is now. Today. This very second.'

She knocked back half of it, steadfastly refusing to shudder like some simpering female fool while it burnt a red-hot path down her throat. 'Ahh,' she said with a lip-smacking sigh of satisfaction once it reached its destination. 'That hits the spot. You want one?' she asked Luke, but he shook his head.

Swirling the amber liquid in her glass, she walked over and settled in one of her mother's large comfy armchairs, her feet curled up under her. Hooking her hair behind her ear with her left hand, she lifted the whisky to her lips and took another deep swallow. She glanced over at Luke, who was still standing near the doorway, looking startled by her behaviour.

Isabel supposed she wasn't living up to the image he obviously had of her. Up till today it had been easy to play the role of the super-serene, super-sensible fiancée who was never fazed or upset by anything he did. Because he'd never done anything to really upset her.

Clearly, he didn't know what to make of her as her real self, instead of Lady Isabel, the unflappable.

But did he honestly think he could roll up and tell her their wedding was off at this late stage with no trouble at all? Did he imagine she wouldn't be hurt by his obviously being unfaithful to her last night?

The realisation that she had been mentally unfaithful to *him* today tempered her inner fury somewhat, and brought some sympathy and understanding for Luke's actions. Marriages made with the head and not the heart might have worked in the past, she appreciated. But in this modern day and age, with all the abounding sexual temptations, such a union was a disaster waiting to happen.

Still, she would be surprised if it was true love compelling Luke to do this. More likely that good deceiver *lust*!

'I suppose she's beautiful, this Celia,' she said drily.

'I think so.' Luke finally sat down as well.

'What does she do?'

'She's a physiotherapist.'

A physiotherapist. Not only beautiful but clever and educated as well.

Isabel hadn't embraced tertiary studies after leaving high school. Her exam results hadn't been good enough. Oh, she wasn't dumb, just not focused on her school work. She'd been far too interested in boys at the time, much to her parents' dismay.

She had managed a brief receptionist course at tech. That, combined with her looks, had meant she'd been rarely out of a job. Over the years she'd become a top receptionist, computer literate and very competent.

Yet she'd never really been interested in a career as such. She'd always wanted marriage and motherhood. It irked Isabel that this Celia, however innocently, had stolen the one man who might have given her both.

'And what was she doing, staying in your father's weekender? Did he rent it out?'

'No. She's his mistress's daughter.'

'His *what*?' Isabel's feet shot out from under her as she snapped forward on the chair.

'Dad's mistress's daughter,' Luke repeated drily.

Isabel gaped. 'No! I don't believe you. Not *your* dad. With a *mistress*? That's impossible. He was one of the best husbands and fathers I've ever met. He was one of the reasons I wanted to marry you. Because I believed you'd be just as good a family man.'

'As I said…it's a long story.'

'And a fascinating one, I'm sure,' Isabel mused. 'It seems the Freeman men have a dark side I don't know about.'

'Could be,' Luke agreed ruefully.

'I wish I'd known about it sooner,' she muttered, and swigged back the last of the whisky in her glass.

Luke shot her a puzzled look. 'What do you mean by that?'

'Oh, nothing. Just a private joke. I have this perverse sense of humour sometimes. Come on, tell me all the naughty details.'

'I hope you won't be too shocked.'

She chuckled. 'Oh, dear, that's funny. Me, shocked? Trust me, darling. I can never be seriously shocked by anything sexual.'

Luke frowned at her. 'Did I ever really know you, Isabel?'

'Did I ever really know *you*?' she countered saucily.

Their eyes met and they smiled together.

'You'll find someone else, Isabel,' Luke said with total confidence.

'I dare say I will. But not quite like you, darling. You were one in a million. Your Celia is one lucky girl. I hope you'll be very happy together.' Privately, she didn't think they would be, but who knew? Maybe Luke was a better picker than herself when it came to falling in love. *If* he was really in love, that was.

'Thanks, Isabel. That's very generous of you. But we won't be rushing to the altar. Which reminds me. I will, of course, be footing the bill for any expenses your parents have encountered with the wedding. I'll send them a cheque which should cover everything, and with some left over. And I'll be doing the right thing by you, too.'

She shook her head, then slipped the solitaire-diamond engagement ring off her finger. 'No, Luke. I wasn't marrying you for your money. I know you might have thought I was, but I wasn't. I was just pleased you were successful and stable. I wanted that security for my children. And for myself.'

When she went to give him the ring, he refused to take it. 'I don't want that ring back, Isabel. It's yours. I gave it to you. You keep it, or sell it if you want to.'

Isabel came close to crying again. He really was the nicest man. He'd have made a wonderful father.

She shrugged and slipped the ring onto her right hand. 'If you insist,' she said, using every bit of her will-power to keep it together. 'But I won't sell it. I'll wear it. It's a beautiful ring. Fortunate, though, that I didn't find any wedding rings I liked yesterday, so at least we don't have to return *them*.'

Isabel was still amazed by the fact that less than twenty-four hours ago Luke had been very happy with her. But, as they said in the classics, there was many a slip 'twixt the cup and the lip.

She sighed, then stared regretfully into her now empty glass. 'I'd better go get you your credit card while you're here.' And while she could still stand. That whisky was *really* working now.

'That can wait,' Luke said before she could get up. 'I want to finish discussing the rest of my financial obligations first.'

She frowned. 'What other financial obligations could you possibly have?'

'I owe you, Isabel. More than a ring's worth.'

'No, you don't, Luke. I never lived with you. I have no claim on you other than the expenses for the wedding.'

'That's not the way I see it. You gave up your job to become my wife. You expected to be going on your honeymoon in a fortnight's time and possibly becoming a mother in the near future. Aside from that, married to me, you would never have had to worry about money for the rest of your life. I can't help you with the honeymoon or the becoming a mother bit now, but I can give you the financial security for life that you deserve.'

'Luke, truly, you don't have to do this.'

'Yes. I do. Now listen up.'

Isabel listened up, amazed when Luke insisted she

have his town house in Turramurra, as well as a portfolio of blue-chip stocks and shares which would provide her with an independent income for life. It seemed his father had been a very rich man. And now so was Luke.

She thought about refusing, but then decided that would just be her pride talking. At least now she wouldn't have to worry about having to live here under her parents' roof till she found another job. Her mother was going to be very upset when she found out the wedding was off.

She smiled a wry smile at this wonderful man she had hoped to marry. 'I always knew you were a winner. But I'd have preferred you as my husband rather than my sugar-daddy.'

'You've no idea how sorry I am about all this, Isabel,' Luke apologised again. 'I wouldn't have hurt you for the world. You're a great girl. But the moment I saw Celia, I was a goner.'

Isabel's mind flew straight to the moment she first saw Rafe Saint Vincent today. She hadn't been a goner. But she might have been, if he'd come on to her. Thank heaven he hadn't.

'She must be something, this Celia.'

'She's very special.'

And very beautiful, no doubt, Isabel deduced, with a body made for sin and eyes which drew you and held you and corrupted you. Just as Rafe's eyes had today.

He'd fancied her. Isabel hadn't liked to admit it to herself before this, but she'd sensed his male interest at the time. She'd sensed it from the first second they'd looked at each other. She always sensed things like that.

You could go back for your phone after Luke leaves. You could tell Rafe the wedding's off. You could…

No, no, she screamed at herself. Not again. Never again!

'Okay, so tell me all,' she demanded of Luke, desperately needing distraction from her escalatingly dangerous thoughts. 'And don't leave out anything…'

CHAPTER FOUR

RAFE noticed the phone she'd left behind almost immediately. He snatched it up from the coffee-table and was running out after her when he stopped and waited to see if she remembered and came back for it herself.

But she didn't, and he just stood in the hallway and listened to her drive off.

It was crazy to want to see her again this side of the wedding. Crazy to force her to return.

She wasn't the type to let him have his wicked way with her. She wasn't the type to let *any* man have his wicked way with her without a band of gold on her finger.

Maybe not a virgin, but close. The way she'd frozen when he'd dared touch her hair. The way she'd bolted out of his place, probably in fear that he might do more.

And he'd wanted to. Oh, yes. Being that close to her—actually touching her—had turned him on something rotten. When her bag had hit him as she'd hurried out, he'd just managed not to visibly wince. Luckily, she hadn't stopped and looked down at where her bag had hit him, or she'd have been in for one big fright!

That was another reason why he hadn't run out into the street after her just now. Looking a fool was not his favourite occupation.

Hopefully, by the time Isabel realised she'd left her phone and turned round to come back, he'd have himself under control again.

And then what, Rafe? What is the point of this exercise? Is it some form of sexual masochism?

Even if you were the kind of man who seduced other men's fiancées—which you're not, usually—you haven't one chance in Hades of defrosting *this* one.

So, if and when she does come back, have the damned phone handy near the front door, give it to the lady and send her on her merry way.

His decision made, Rafe dropped the metallic-blue cellphone on the hall table and headed upstairs for some breakfast. After that, he came back downstairs to his darkroom, where he set about developing the rolls of film he'd shot last night at Orsini's summer fashion parade, and at the after-parade party, which had gone well into the wee small hours of the morning. The women's magazines would be ringing first thing Monday morning, wanting to see the best of them.

Two hours later, Rafe was still in his darkroom, going through the motions, but his mind simply wasn't on the job. The object of his distraction hadn't come back, and he simply could not put her out of his head.

The truth was, she intrigued him. Not just sexually, but as a person. He wanted to know more about her.

In the end, Rafe stopped trying to put her out his mind. He abandoned his work, pulled the business card she'd left him out of his pocket, went back upstairs, picked up his phone and punched in the number she'd written down.

The line rang and rang at the other end, with Rafe about to hang up when someone finally picked up.

'Hello there.'

Rafe frowned. It was a woman, but he wasn't sure if it was Isabel. She sounded…odd. 'Isabel?'

'Yep? To whom do I have the pleasure of speaking?'

Rafe couldn't believe his ears. She was drunk!

'It's Rafe. Rafe Saint Vincent. The photographer.'

Dead silence. Though he could hear her breathing.

'You left your mobile phone at my place.'

More silence.

'I thought you might be worried about it.'

She actually laughed.

'Isabel,' he said with concern in his voice. 'Have you been drinking?'

'Mmm. You might say that.'

'I am saying it.'

'So what?'

Rafe was taken aback. This wasn't the woman he'd met today. This was someone else. 'You said you didn't drink,' he reminded her.

She laughed again. 'I lied.'

His eyes widened with shock, then narrowed with worry. 'Isabel, what's wrong? What's happened?'

'I guess there's no point in not telling you. You'll have to know some time, anyway. The wedding's off.'

He couldn't have been more taken aback, both by the news *and* her manner. 'Why?' he asked.

'Luke's left me for someone else.'

Rafe experienced a small secret thrill at this news, but his overriding emotion was sympathy. He knew what it was like to be left for someone else, and he wouldn't wish the experience on a dog.

'I'm so sorry, Isabel,' he said with genuine feeling. 'You must be feeling rotten.'

'I was, till I downed my third whisky. Now, I actually don't feel too bad.'

He had to smile. That was exactly what he'd done the day Liz had left him. Hit the bottle. 'You should never drink alone, you know,' he warned softly.

'Oh, I'm not drunk,' she denied, even though her voice was slurring a little. 'Just tipsy enough so that my pain is pleasantly anaesthetised. Why, you offering to drink with me, lover?'

Rafe's smile widened. It seemed Isabel's ice-princess act melted considerably under the influence of three glasses of Scotch.

'I think you've had enough for one day.'

'That's not for you to say,' she huffed.

'Maybe not, but I'm still saying it.'

'Did anyone ever tell you that you are the bossiest person alive?'

'Yeah. My mother. She threw a party the day I left home.'

'I can well imagine.'

'But she loves me all the same.'

'I doubt other people would be so generous.'

Her alcohol-induced sarcasm amused him. 'Did anyone ever tell you you're a snooty bitch?' he countered.

He liked it when she laughed. Being drunk suited her. No more Miss Prissy. How he wished he was with her now.

There again, perhaps it was wise that he wasn't. When and if he took her to bed, he didn't want her drunk. Or on the rebound. He wanted her wanting him for himself, and no other reason.

'I guess you won't be needing my services now,' he said.

'As a photographer, you mean?'

Rafe sucked in sharply. What a provocative reply! Perhaps she didn't disapprove of him as much as he'd thought she had.

Or perhaps it was just the drink talking.

'Actually, I'd still like to photograph you,' he said, truthfully enough.

'Really? Why?'

'Why? Well, firstly, you are one seriously beautiful woman, and I have a penchant for photographing beautiful women. Secondly, I just want to see you again. I want to take you out to dinner somewhere.'

'You mean…like…on a date?'

'Yes. Exactly like that.'

'You don't waste much time, do you? I've only been dumped for two hours. And you've only known about it for two minutes! What if I said I was too broken up over Luke to date anyone for a while?'

'Then I'd respect that. But I'd ask you out again next week. And the week after that.'

'I should have guessed you'd be the determined type,' she muttered.

'Being determined is not a vice, Isabel.'

'That depends. So why is it you don't already have a girlfriend? Or *do* you? Don't lie to me, now. I hate men who lie to me,' she added, slurring her words.

'I'm between girlfriends at the moment.'

'Oh? What happened to the last one?'

'She went overseas to work. I wasn't inclined to follow her.'

'Why?'

'My career is here, in Australia.'

'Ahh. Priority number one.'

'What does that mean?'

'It means no, thank you very much, Rafe. I've been down that road far too many times to travel it again.'

'Now I'm confused. What road are you referring to?'

'Dating men who want only one thing from me. You do only want one thing from me, don't you, Rafe?'

Rafe considered that a loaded question.

'I wouldn't say that, exactly.' He liked talking to her, too. 'But I have to confess that marriage and kiddies are not on my list of must-do things in my life.'

'Well, they're on mine, Rafe. And sooner, rather than later. But I appreciate your telling me the truth. That's a big improvement on some of the other men I've become involved with in the past.'

His eyebrows shot up. It sounded as if there had been

scads. Any idea that she might almost be a virgin went out of the window. It just showed you first impressions weren't always right.

'Did your fiancé lie to you?'

'Luke? Oh, no…no, Luke was no liar.'

'But he was obviously two-timing you,' he pointed out.

'No. He wasn't. Look, it's rather difficult to explain.'

'Try.'

So she did, explaining the circumstances which had led up to Luke's meeting Celia.

'So he hasn't been two-timing me,' she finished up. 'He only met Celia yesterday.'

'Perhaps, but he didn't tell you the truth about why he was going up to his dad's fishing cabin on Lake Macquarie in the first place, did he?'

'No, but I can understand why. He'd been thrown for a loop when the solicitor told him his Dad wanted to leave his weekender to some strange woman.'

'You make a lot of excuses for him, don't you? He was still unfaithful to you. And he hurt you, Isabel.'

'He didn't mean to. Look, I'm sorry I told you about it now. It's really none of your business. Thank you for ringing and for making me feel a little better, but I think we should leave it right there, don't you? As I said, we want different things in life. I wonder…could you possibly post my phone back to me?'

'I'd rather drop it off to you.'

'And I'd rather you didn't.'

'You're afraid of me,' he said, startled by this realisation.

'Don't be ridiculous!'

Oh-oh. She was definitely sobering up. And returning to her former stroppy self.

'Just tell me one thing.'

'What?'

'Did you love him?'

'I was marrying him,' she snapped. 'What do *you* think?'

'I think that's a very evasive answer. For a person who demands the truth from others, you're not too good at delivering it yourself.'

She sighed. 'Very well. I liked and respected Luke, but, no, I did not love him. Satisfied?'

'Not even remotely,' Rafe said ruefully. 'Did you think *he* loved *you*?'

'No.'

'What on earth kind of marriage was *that* going to be?'

'One that lasted.'

'Oh, yeah, right. It didn't even get through the engagement. For pity's sake, Isabel, what did you expect? Men want passion from their wives. And sex. At least in the beginning.'

'You think I didn't give Luke sex?'

'Not the kind which his new dolly-bird obviously does.'

'You don't know what you're talking about. Look, I'm sorry I started this conversation. You simply don't have the capacity to understand what Luke and I had together. How could you? You're one of those men who lives for himself and himself alone. A woman is just a passing pleasure to you, a bit of R&R from your work. You don't want a real relationship with one. As for children, you probably see them as inconveniences, little ankle-biters who'd get in the way of your lifestyle. Luke wasn't like that. He wanted a family. Like me. He wanted for ever. Like me. We might not have been madly in love but we were good friends and extremely compatible, *in* bed as well as out. We could have had a happy marriage. I don't believe he's in love with this new dolly-bird, as you call her. He only met her yesterday. I think it's just sex, the kind that obsesses you so much sometimes that you can't think straight.'

Rafe's eyes widened. It sounded as if she'd been there, done that. She was becoming more interesting by the minute.

'That kind of physical affair never lasts,' she finished bitterly.

Yep. She'd been there, done that, all right. Rafe didn't know if he felt tantalised by this knowledge, or jealous. Either way, the thought of Isabel in the throes of an all-consuming sexual passion was an intriguing one.

'Is that what you're hoping?' he suggested. 'That maybe this thing your Luke is having with this girl won't last? That maybe he'll wake up on Monday morning, realise he's made a big mistake and beg you to take him back?'

'Well, actually, no. I hadn't been hoping that. But now that you've mentioned the possibility…'

Luke could have kicked himself.

'Don't start grasping at straws, Isabel.'

'I'm not. But I'm also not going to repeat the mistakes of my past. So, thank you for thinking of me, Rafe. But find someone else to photograph, and to take to dinner, because it isn't going to be me.'

'Isabel, please…'

'No, Rafe,' she said sternly. 'I realise you have difficulty in accepting that word, but it's definitely no. Now I must go. Goodbye.'

And she hung up on him.

Swearing, Rafe slammed down his end of the phone. He'd handled that all wrong. Totally abysmally wrong!

Still, perhaps it *was* for the best. Isabel wanted marriage. Whereas he most definitely didn't.

But she was wrong about what he wanted from her. It wasn't just sex.

Oh, come now, the voice of brutal honesty piped up. It's always just sex you're looking for these days. All that other stuff you offer a female is nothing but foreplay. The chit-chat. The photographing. The dinner dates. All with one end in view. Getting whatever pretty woman has taken your eye into bed and keeping her there on and off till you grow bored.

Which you always do in the end. Admit it, man, you've become shallow and selfish with women, exactly as Isabel said you were. You haven't been worth two bob since Liz left you. She stuffed you, buddy. Took away your heart. Isabel was right not to get involved with you. You're a dead loss to someone like her. Go back to work. That's the only thing you're good for. Creating images. Anything real is just too much for you.

He stomped downstairs, still muttering. Till he saw Isabel's shiny blue cellphone on the hall table. How odd that just seeing something she owned gave him a thrill.

Did he dare still take it back to her?

No, he decided. She'd said no. He had to respect that. He'd post it to her on Monday, as she'd asked.

Feeling more empty and wretched than he had in years, Rafe returned to his darkroom and tried to bury himself in the one thing which had always sustained him, even in his darkest moments.

But, for the second time that day, his precious craft failed to deliver the distraction he craved.

CHAPTER FIVE

ISABEL groaned. She'd handled that all wrong; talked too much; revealed too much.

Alcohol always made her talkative.

She thanked her stars that she'd pulled herself together towards the end—and that she'd had enough courage to resist temptation.

But oh, she'd wanted to say yes. To everything he'd offered. The photography. The dinner date. Sex afterwards, no doubt.

Isabel closed her eyes at the thought.

They sprang open again at another thought. Her mobile!

Would he still post it to her after all she'd said to him? Her assassination of his character had been a bit brutal, even if correct. He hadn't denied a single word. Okay, so the man did have a sweet side. But how much of that was real? Maybe he'd just learnt that you caught more with honey than with salt.

If he was really sweet, then he'd post her phone back. If not?

Isabel shrugged. She couldn't worry about a phone. If she never got it back, then she'd report it lost and get another one. After all, she didn't have to watch her pennies any more. She was an independently wealthy woman now. Or she would be soon.

Luke would be as good as his word. That, she knew.

Isabel wandered down the hallway to her mother's kitchen, thinking about Luke. Was it possible he might change his mind about this Celia? Or was she simply looking for an excuse not to tell her parents the wedding was off when they came home?

Just the thought of their reaction—especially her mother's—made Isabel shudder. If she hadn't been over the drink-driving limit, she'd pack up her car right now and make a bolt for the town house Luke had given her. She had her own set of keys.

Unfortunately, as it was, there was nothing but to stay here and face the music.

The music, as it turned out, was terrible. Her father recovered somewhat after Isabel explained Luke was going to recompense them for everything they'd spent. But her mother could not be so easily soothed, not even when Isabel told her what Luke was doing for *her* in a financial sense. When Isabel repeated Luke's suggestion that her parents go on their pre-booked holiday to Dream Island, her mother's face carried horror.

'You think I could be happy going on what should have been your honeymoon?' she exclaimed. 'No wonder Luke left you for another woman. You have no sensitivity at all! I dare say he worked out that you were only marrying him for his money. So he gave you what you wanted, then looked elsewhere for some genuine love and warmth.'

Isabel was stunned by her mother's harsh words. 'You think I was only marrying Luke for his money?'

Her mother flushed, but still looked her straight in the eye. 'You weren't in love with the man. *That*, I know. I've seen you in love, girl, and what you felt for Luke wasn't it. You cold-bloodedly set out to get that man. I didn't say a word because I thought Luke would make a fine husband and father, and I hoped that you might eventually fall in love with him. You played false with him, Isabel. And you got what you deserved.'

'Dot, stop it,' Isabel's father intervened sharply. 'What's done is done. And who knows? Maybe it's all for the best. Maybe someone better will come along, someone our girl can like *and* love.'

Isabel gave her father a grateful look. But she was close to tears. And very hurt by her mother's lack of sympathy and understanding. 'I...I have to go and ring Rachel,' she said, desperate to get away from her mother's hostility. Rachel would at least be on her side.

'What about everyone else?' her mother threw after her. 'Who's going to make all the other phone calls necessary to cancel everything?'

'I'll do all that, Mum.'

'On *our* phone?'

Isabel closed her eyes for a second. Phones. They were her nemesis today. 'No,' she said wearily. 'I'll be moving into the town house Luke gave me tomorrow. I'll make all the calls from there.'

'You're moving out?' Suddenly, her mother looked wretchedly unhappy.

Isabel sighed. 'I think I should.'

'You…you don't have to, you know,' her mother said, her voice and chin wobbling. 'I don't really care about the phone bill.'

Isabel understood then that her mother had been lashing out from her own hurt and disappointment. She'd always wanted to see her only daughter married. And now that event seemed highly unlikely.

Because her mother was right, Isabel conceded. She *had* set out to get Luke rather cold-bloodedly, and she simply couldn't do that again. Which left what? Falling in love with another Mr Wrong?

No! Now that was on *her* list of never-do-again.

'It's all right, Mum,' Isabel said, giving her mother a hug. 'Everything will be all right. You'll see.'

Her mother began to cry then, with Isabel struggling not to join in.

She looked beseechingly at her father over her Mum's dropped head and he nodded. 'Go ring Rachel,' he said quietly. 'I'll look after her.'

Rachel, who was Isabel's only real female friend and now the owner of an unused wine-red bridesmaid dress, answered on the first ring.

'Can you talk?' was Isabel's first question. 'Have I rung at a bad time?'

Rachel's life was devoted to minding her foster-mother who had Alzheimer's. She'd been doing it twenty-four hours a day, seven days a week, for over four years now. Despite being a labour of love, it was a grinding existence with little pleasure or leisure.

Rachel's decision to take on this onerous task after her foster-mum's husband had deserted her, had cost her her job as a top secretary at the Australian Broadcasting Corporation, and her own partner at the time. Sacrifice, it seemed, was not a virtue men aspired to.

Nowadays, Rachel made ends meet by doing clothes alterations at home. Her only entertainment was reading and watching television, plus one night out a month which Isabel paid for and organised. Last night had actually been one of those times, Isabel taking her friend to Star City Casino for dinner then a show afterwards. It was a pleasing thought that she'd have the time and the money to take Rachel out more often now.

'It's okay,' Rachel said. 'Lettie's asleep. Thank goodness. It's been a really bad day. She didn't even know me. Or she pretended not to. She's always difficult the day after I've been out with you. I don't think she likes anyone else but me minding her.'

'Poor Rachel. I'm sorry to ring you with more bad news.'

'Oh, no, what's happened?'

'The wedding's off.'

'The miserable bastard,' was Rachel's immediate response, which rather startled Isabel.

'What makes you think it was Luke's doing?'

'I know you, Isabel. No way would you opt out of marrying Luke. So what was it? Another woman?'

'How did you guess?' Isabel said ruefully.

'It wasn't hard. Men are so typical.'

'Mum blames me. She says Luke looked elsewhere because I didn't love him.'

'You *confessed* it wasn't a romantic match?'

'No, she guessed.'

'Oh, well, you have to agree she had a few clues to go on. Luke wasn't your usual type. Too traditionally good-looking and far too straight-down-the-line.'

'Mmm. It turned out he wasn't quite the Mr Goody-Two-Shoes I thought he was. Not once he met the sexy Celia.'

'So who is sexy Celia? Where and when did he meet her?'

'He only met her yesterday, and she's his father's mistress's daughter.'

'*What*?' Rachel choked out. 'Would you like to repeat that?'

She did, along with the rest of Luke's story. Isabel had to admit it made fascinating listening. It wasn't every day that a son found out his high-profile hero-status father had been cheating on his mother for twenty years. Or that the same engaged and rather strait-laced son would jump into bed with the mistress's daughter within an hour or two of meeting her.

Isabel still did not believe that Luke was in love with this Celia, but he obviously thought he was after spending all night with her doing who knew what. Even now he was speeding back up to his dad's secret love-nest on Lake Macquarie for more of the same!

It sounded like an episode from a soap opera.

No, a *week* of episodes!

Rachel's ear was glued to the phone for a good fifteen minutes.

'You didn't tell your mother all that, did you?' she asked at the end of it.

'No. I just said he'd met someone else, fallen in love with her and decided he couldn't go through with the wedding.'

'At least he was decent enough to do that. A lot of guys these days would have tried to have their cake and eat it too, a bit like Luke's father did with this Celia's poor mother for twenty years.'

'Yes. I thought of that. But I also wondered if Luke might eventually realise it wasn't love he felt for Celia, but just good old lust.'

'Could be. So you'd take him back if he changed his mind?'

'In a shot.'

'Maybe I shouldn't alter my bridesmaid dress just yet, then.'

'Maybe not.'

'And maybe you shouldn't cancel the reception place, or the cake, or the photographer. Not for a couple of days, anyway.'

Isabel wished Rachel hadn't mentioned the photographer. She didn't want to think about Rafe.

'Oh, dear, I think Lettie's just called out for me,' Rachel said. 'Amazing how she's remembered my name now that I'm on the phone. I must go, Isabel. And I am sorry. But…'

'Don't you dare tell me it's all for the best,' Isabel warned.

Rachel laughed. 'All right, I won't. Keep in touch.'

'I will.' When Isabel got off the phone, she realised she hadn't told Rachel about her financial windfall. But she would, the next time she rang her.

Meanwhile, she set about packing her clothes. She was emptying the drawers in her old dressing table when her mother came into the bedroom, looking miserable and chastened.

'I feel terrible about what I said to you earlier, Isabel. Your father said I should have my tongue cut out.'

'It's all right, Mum. You were upset.'

'What I said. I…I don't think you were marrying Luke just for his money. I know you liked him a lot, too.'

'Yes, I did.'

'Do…do you think he might not have fallen for this other girl if you'd slept with him before the wedding?'

Isabel turned to stare at her mother. Truly, what world did she live in? 'Mum,' she said with a degree of exasperation, 'I did sleep with him. Quite often.'

'Oh…'

'And he liked it. A lot.'

'Oh!'

'Sex wasn't the problem. It was passion.'

'Passion?'

'Yes, that overwhelming feeling you get when you look at a person and you just have to be with them.'

'Jump into bed, you mean?'

'Yes. Luke and I never really felt like that about each other.'

'I used to feel that way about your dad,' her mother whispered, 'when we were first married. And he felt that way about me, too.'

Isabel smiled at her. 'That's good, Mum. That's how it should be.'

'Maybe your dad's right. Maybe you'll find someone nicer than Luke, someone you'll fall deeply in love with and who'll feel the same way about you.'

'I hope so, Mum. I really do.' It would be cruel to take away her mother's hope. She'd always had this dream of seeing her daughter as a bride. Isabel had had the same dream.

But not any more.

'You're still going to move out?' her mother asked a bit tearily.

Isabel stopped what she was doing to face her mother. 'Mum, I'm thirty years old. I'm a grown woman. I have to make my own life away from home, regardless. I only moved back in for a while because it was sensible and convenient, leading up to the wedding.'

'But I…I've liked having you home. You are very good company.'

Isabel thought the compliment came just a bit late.

'You're a good cook, too. Your dad and I are going to miss the meals you've cooked for us.'

Isabel relented and gave her mother another hug. 'What say I come over and cook you a meal once in a while? Will that do?'

'Just so long as you come over. Don't be a stranger.'

'I won't. I promise.'

'And you've forgiven your old mum?'

Isabel smiled a wry smile. 'Have you forgiven me for not giving you some grandchildren by now?'

'Having children isn't everything, Isabel.'

Isabel gave her a dry look. 'Said by a woman who had five.'

'Then I should know. What you need to do is find the right man. Then the children will follow.'

'Don't you think I've been trying to do that?'

'Don't try so hard. You're a beautiful girl. Just let nature take its course.'

Isabel was tempted to tell her that nature always led her up the garden path into the arms of men who'd never give her children.

But it was too late to confess such matters. She'd never told her mother the bitter truth about her boyfriends. She hadn't wanted to shock her. To reveal all now would only make her look even worse than she already did in her mother's eyes.

'Are you sure you don't want to go on that Dream Island holiday, Mum?' she asked, deciding a change of subject was called for.

'Positive. I'm too old that for that kind of holiday, anyway. Look, why don't you go yourself?'

'It's not a place you go alone.'

'Then ask a friend to go with you.'

Isabel thought immediately of Rafe... He'd jump at the chance of going with her, all expenses paid!

It was a tantalising idea. Did she dare? Could she actually *do* something like that without getting emotionally involved?

Perhaps she could. Her experience with Luke had changed her, made her stronger and much more self-reliant. She'd gone after what she wanted for once, listening to her head and not her heart. She'd actually gone to bed with a man she didn't love, and quite enjoyed it. Her mind no longer irrevocably linked sexual pleasure and being in love.

Just because Rafe was more like the type of man she'd used to fall in love with willy-nilly, that didn't mean she would fall in love this time. She also had the added advantage of knowing in advance that he wasn't interested in marriage or children. There would never be any fooling herself that she had a future with him.

He'd just be a passing pleasure. A salve to her pride and a comfort to her bruised female ego. Not to mention a comfort to her female body!

By the time she got through the next fortnight, cancelling everything and putting up with everyone's condolences, she'd need comforting. And what better way than on a balmy tropical island in the arms of a gorgeous man you fancied like mad, and who seemed to fancy you in return?

'Isabel?'

Isabel shook herself out of her provocative thoughts.

'Yes, Mum?'

'Well, what do you think about finding a friend to go

away on that holiday with you? If you can't get your money back, it does seem a shame to waste it.'

'We'll see, Mum.' She'd better sleep on the idea. She'd been knocked for a couple of sixes today. And she *had* been drinking. The booked holiday on Dream Island didn't start for another fortnight and she doubted Rafe was going anywhere in a hurry. Maybe if she felt the same way in the cold light of Monday morning…

A shiver ran down Isabel's spine at the thought of doing something that bold. It was one thing to deliberately go to bed with a man like Luke, when your intention was marriage. Quite another to contemplate a strictly sexual affair with the likes of Rafe Saint Vincent!

CHAPTER SIX

RAFE didn't sleep well that night, which wasn't like him. Usually, he was out like a light soon after his head hit the pillow.

But not this time. He tossed and turned. Even got up on one occasion and poured himself a stiff drink.

The trouble with that, however, was it reminded him even more forcibly of the reason for his insomnia.

Had she drunk some more after hanging up on him? Was she also up, wandering around the house in her nightie with another glass of whisky clutched in her hands?

He carried that image of her back to bed with him and tossed and turned some more, his hormone-revved head wondering what kind of nightie it might be. Short or long? Provocative or prissy?

Various alternatives came to mind. She'd look delicious in long creamy satin, and wickedly sexy in short black lace. Better still in nothing at all.

His groan was the groan of a man suffering from a case of serious sexual frustration. Which would never do if he wanted to get some sleep. And he did. He hadn't finished his work today and he'd have to beaver away at it all day tomorrow. No Sunday brunch down at

Darling Harbour with his mother. No slouching around watching the cooking shows on satellite.

Dragging himself up again, he made his way into the bathroom, where he had the hottest of hot showers, a technique he'd found worked much better on him than cold. The heat sapped his energy, and relaxed his tense muscles and other aching parts. After a good twenty minutes of sauna-type soaking, he snapped off the water, dried himself with one of his extra-fluffy white bath sheets, then fell, naked and pink-skinned, back into bed.

An hour later he was still wide awake.

Swearing, he rose, pulled on his black silk robe, made himself some very strong coffee and trudged downstairs to his darkroom where he surprised himself by working like a demon for several hours. It was light when he emerged, but by this time he was too exhausted to care. He went upstairs, switched off his mobile, took his other phone off the hook, closed the roller shutter which he'd recently installed on his bedroom window and collapsed into bed.

If his oblivion was ravaged by erotic dreams, he certainly didn't recall them, but he was embarrassingly erect when he was wrenched out of his blissful coma by the sound of his front doorbell ringing. It was just as well, Rafe decided as he struggled out of bed, that the robe he was still wearing provided discreet coverage. Because he had no intention of getting dressed. He was going to get rid of whoever was at the door, then go back to bed for the rest of the day.

It was Isabel, looking as if she was on her way to afternoon tea with the Queen.

Cream linen trouser suit. Blue silk top. Pearls. Pink lipstick. And that lovely blonde hair of hers, slicked back up in that prissy roll thing.

Her perfect grooming highlighted his own dishevelled appearance. Why couldn't he have any luck with this woman?

'I presume you've come for your phone,' he grumped.

She looked him up and down with about the same expression she had when she'd first arrived yesterday. 'Sorry to get you out of bed,' she said drily. 'But it *is* two in the afternoon.'

Rafe decided there was no point in telling her the truth, that he'd worked most of the night because of her.

'Yeah well, we party animals do get tired. And last night *was* Saturday night. I didn't get to bed till dawn.'

'Alone?'

He crossed his arms. 'Such a personal question for a lady who's just come for her phone.'

'*You* said I'd just come for my phone. *I* didn't.'

Rafe stared at her. Was he about to get lucky here?

'Do you think I might come inside?' she went on in that silkily cool voice of hers, the one which rippled down his spine like a mink glove.

'Be my guest,' he said eagerly, stepping back to wave her inside.

'I need to go to the bathroom,' she said straight away. 'I've just driven straight down from Gosford Hospital.'

Rafe frowned as he swung the front door shut behind

him. 'What were you doing up there?' And, even more to the point, what was she doing *here*? The suburb of Paddington was not on the way from the Central Coast to her address at Burwood. So she wouldn't have dropped in just to use his toilet!

His heart was already thudding with carnal hopes.

'Luke was in a car accident on the F3 freeway yesterday,' she said.

'Is he all right?'

'A few bumps and bruises. Nothing too serious. But he knocked his head and was unconscious for a while. The police found my number in his car and contacted me early this morning, so of course I had to go and see how he was.'

'He's having some rotten luck on the road lately, isn't he? First his parents and now him. Does his new girlfriend know about this?'

'Yes, I was there when she arrived. With her mother.'

'The infamous mother. What was she like?'

'The bathroom first, please, Rafe?'

'Oh, yes—yes, of course. This way.' He had the presence of mind to take her upstairs, instead of to the small downstairs toilet. The main bathroom upstairs was quite spacious and luxurious, another recent renovation. He'd been steadily renovating his terraced home since he'd bought it a couple of years back. It had cost him a small fortune, despite being little more than a dump. But, as in all big cities, you paid for position.

After showing her where the bathroom was, he dashed into his bedroom to dress. Hurrying into his walk-in robe, he ran his eye along the hangers, wondering what to wear. The day wasn't hot, but neither was it cold. Lately they'd had typical spring weather in Sydney, fresh in the morning but warming up as the day progressed, provided it wasn't cloudy. And it wasn't today, judging by the sunshine on his doorstep just now.

By the time Isabel emerged from the bathroom Rafe was looking and feeling a bit better in his favourite black jeans and a fresh white T-shirt. But his face still sported a two-day stubble and his feet were bare.

There was only so much a man could achieve in just over three minutes, the time it took for Isabel to emerge. Clearly she wasn't a girl who titivated.

'Nice bathroom,' she said crisply.

He'd known she'd like it. It was all white, with glass and silver fittings. Cool and classy-looking, like she was.

'You might not like this room as much,' he said as he led her into his main living room, which was decorated for comfort rather than style. No traditional lounge suite, just huge squashy armchairs to sit in, functional side tables, far too many bookcases and an old marble fireplace which he never used, although the mantelpiece was good for leaning on and holding glasses during a party. He had a hi-fi set in one corner and a television and video in the other.

'I like the doors,' Isabel said, as she sat in his favourite armchair, a reclining one covered in crushed claret-coloured velvet.

He glanced at the white-painted French doors which led out onto the small terrace. 'They're purely decorative,' he said. 'I never open them because of the traffic noise.'

'What a pity.'

He shrugged. 'You can't have everything.'

'No,' she agreed with a touch of bitterness in her voice. 'You certainly can't.'

Rafe sank down in a cream leather armchair facing her, and tried to guess at why she'd come to see him.

'The mother was stunningly good-looking for a woman of forty plus,' she said abruptly. 'And the daughter was…well, let me just say that I don't think Luke is going to have a change of heart and marry me after all.'

'Were you seriously hoping he would?'

'Stupidly, I think I was beginning to. Which is really pathetic. But on the drive back to Sydney today I decided I had to stop hoping for some man to come along and give me what I want out of life. I have to go out and get it for myself. And if it's not quite what I've dreamt about all these years, if I have to compromise, then that's just the way life is.'

'That sounds sensible,' Rafe said, even though he had no idea exactly what she meant. 'So what is it you're going to do? And where do I come into the equation?'

She smiled. She actually smiled. Only a small, wry little smile, but it was even better than he'd imagined. Or worse. He'd do anything she asked of him, *be* anything she wanted him to be. If only she'd let him make love to her.

'The thing is, Rafe, I've always wanted a baby,' she announced baldly and Rafe nearly died of shock.

Hold it there, buddy, he reassessed. Now that was one thing he *wasn't* going to do, even if it did mean he'd get to do what he wanted to do most at that moment.

'Naturally, I would prefer to have a husband,' she went on, with an elegant shrug of her slender shoulders, 'or at least a live-in partner before having a child.'

'Naturally,' he said with heavy emphasis.

'But that's simply not going to happen in my case in the near future, and time is running out for me. So I've decided to opt for artificial insemination from a clinic which supplies well-documented but anonymous donors.'

Rafe was both relieved and confused. Why was she telling him all this?

'Now that Luke is going to make me an independent woman of means, I don't need a man's financial support to have a child,' she elaborated. 'I can well afford to raise one on my own. I could put the child in daycare and go back to work, if I so desired. Or hire a nanny. Of course, I do realise it's not an ideal situation, but then, it's not an ideal world, is it?'

'No,' Rafe agreed. 'But why are you telling me all this, Isabel?' he finally asked.

'I'm just filling you in on my plans so you can understand the reasons behind the proposition I am going to make you.'

'And what proposition is that?'

'I want you to come to Dream Island with me on the honeymoon Luke and I booked.'

Rafe tried not to gape. 'Er…run that by me again?'

'You heard me,' she said in a straight-down-the-line, no-nonsense fashion.

Rafe stared at her. Wow. Talk about a shock.

He might have been ecstatic if he hadn't been just a tad wary. The thought that she might have some sneaky plan to use his sperm to impregnate herself without his knowing did not escape him. Though, if that was the case, why tell him about her intention to have a baby at all? Better to keep that a secret if that had been her hidden agenda.

'Why?' he demanded to know.

'Well, it isn't because I don't want to waste money,' she threw at him with a measure of exasperation. 'Even though the honeymoon package was all prepaid and it's too late to cancel. I *want* you to come with me because I want you to come with me.'

Rafe had difficulty embracing the possibility that she just wanted him for sex, even though it was the most exciting thought. All his fantasies of the night before coming true!

'As what, exactly?' he persisted. 'If you think I'm going to pretend to be your husband as a salve to your pride, then you can think again.'

'Don't be ridiculous. I wouldn't insult you like that. You'll be with me as my…my lover.'

Mmm, she'd choked a bit over that last word. He stared deep into her eyes and tried to see what was in her mind.

'Yes, but is my role as lover just a pretend one, or do I get to have the real thing with you?'

She blushed, and it enchanted him as much as it had the first time. It also didn't gel with her wanting him as little more than a toy boy. She just didn't seem to be that kind of girl.

'Spell it out for me, Isabel. I might be being dense but I'm still not getting the full picture here.'

She sucked in deeply, then let the air out of her lungs very slowly, as though she was gathering the courage to say what she had to say. He watched her, fascinated and intrigued.

Isabel hadn't thought it would be as difficult as this. When she'd made the decision on the drive down to ask Rafe to come away with her, she'd thought it would be easy. He'd just say yes and that would be that. She hadn't anticipated that he'd question her so closely, or make her confess her desire for him quite so bluntly.

It was embarrassing, and almost…shameful.

Yet why *should* she be ashamed? came the resentful thought. Had Luke been ashamed, taking what he wanted? At least she wasn't guilty of jumping into bed with Rafe the same day she met him, or while she was engaged to someone else. They wouldn't be breaking anyone's heart by going away together.

Not that Luke had broken her heart exactly. But he'd certainly shattered her dreams.

Isabel cleared her throat, determined not to start waffling, and doubly determined not to feel one scrap of shame!

'The bottom line is this, Rafe. Just because I've decided to have a baby alone doesn't mean I always want to be alone. I happen to like sex. Actually, I like it a lot. Perversely, I seem to like it most with men like you.'

Rafe's eyebrows shot upwards, then drew darkly together. 'Hey, hold it there. What do you mean by men like me? That sounded like an insult.'

Isabel winced. She hadn't worded that at all well. 'It wasn't meant to be an insult. It was just a fact. I'm always attracted to men who aren't into commitment. That used to be a big problem, given I wanted marriage and a family. It was the main reason I decided on a marriage of convenience with Luke, because I was sick and tired of falling in love with Mr Wrong. Now that I've made the decision to have a baby on my own, I don't have to worry about the intentions of the men I sleep with, because I won't want to marry them. I just want to have sex with them. Is there some problem with that? I thought that was what you wanted, too.'

Rafe frowned. He'd thought that was what he wanted, too.

'I guess I still like my girlfriends to think I'm an okay guy, not some selfish sleazebag who uses women for one thing and one thing only.'

'Oh, but I don't want to be your girlfriend, Rafe. After the honeymoon holiday is over, I don't want to ever see you again.'

He was truly taken aback. 'But why not?'

Isabel was not about to tell him the truth on this occasion—that she didn't want to push her luck by spending too much time with him. It was one thing to live out a fantasy fortnight with him on Dream Island, quite another to have him popping around all the time after they came back to Sydney. He really was too nice a guy to allow that. She was sure to end up wanting more from him that he could give.

Right at this moment, however, she just wanted him for sex, and nothing more. One look at his gorgeously rakish self on his doorstep this morning had confirmed that. Isabel didn't want to risk changing that status quo.

'I have my reasons, Rafe,' she said firmly. 'This is a take-it-or-leave-it proposition. I'm sure I could find someone else to go with me if you turn me down.'

The thought of her going with someone else made up Rafe's mind in a hurry. 'No need to do that,' he said hurriedly. 'I'd love to go with you.'

'On my terms and no questions asked?' she insisted.

'None except essentials. Firstly, how long will I be away?'

'Two weeks.'

Two weeks. Fourteen days and fourteen nights. Fantastic! 'And it's on Dream Island.'

'Yes, you've been there before?'

'No, but I've heard about it.' It was the newest and most exclusive of the tropical island resorts off the far North Queensland coast, specialising in romantic holidays for couples and honeymooners. He wondered if they would have one of the special bures overlooking their own private beach. That would be really something. To be totally alone with her with nothing to do but eat, sleep, swim and make love. His kind of holiday!

'When, exactly, do we fly out?' he asked eagerly.

'Today fortnight, at ten in the morning. I'll pick you up here at eight. Be ready.' She stood up abruptly.

'Hey.' He jumped up also. 'You're not leaving, are you?'

'I have no reason to stay any longer,' she returned, her manner firm. 'You said yes. We have nothing more to discuss.'

'What about contraception?'

She stared hard at him. 'I presume I can rely on you to see to that.'

'You're not on the pill?'

'No, and even if I was I would still want you to use condoms.'

He supposed that was only sensible, but he still felt mildly insulted. Which was crazy, really.

'Fine,' he said. 'But there's still no reason to rush off, is there? I mean…fair enough if you don't want to see me afterwards, but it might be nice to spend some time together *before* we go off on holiday together. Get to know each other a little better.'

'I'm sorry but I don't want to do that.'

'Why not, for pity's sake?'

'Look, Rafe, may I be blunt?'

Did she know any other way? 'Please do,' he bit out.

'We both know what the term 'getting to know you' means in this day and age. No, please don't deny it. I'm being brutally honest with you and I would appreciate the same in return. Aside from the fact my period is due this week and I'm suffering considerably from PMT right now, I simply don't want us to go to bed together beforehand.'

'Why not?'

She gave him another of those small enigmatic smiles. 'Maybe I don't want to risk you finding me a disappointment in bed and running a mile.'

Never in a million years, he thought. She only had to lie there and he'd be enchanted. Anything more was a bonus. But, since she openly confessed to liking sex, then he figured she was going to do more. How *much* more was the intriguing part.

'Don't *you* want to try before you buy?' he said with a saucy smile, and she laughed.

'I've seen all I need to see. You really shouldn't come to your front door half asleep and half dressed, Rafe darling. Now, show me where you put my phone, please. It's high time I went home.'

CHAPTER SEVEN

RAFE paced the front room, waiting for Isabel to arrive. She'd said she'd pick him up right on eight. But it was eight-ten and she hadn't shown up yet.

Maybe she wasn't going to. Maybe this had all been some kind of sick joke, revenge against the male sex.

This ghastly thought had just occurred to Rafe when he heard a car pulling up outside. Peeping out through the front window, he was relieved to see that it was her. Snatching up his luggage, he was out of the door before she could blow the horn. By the time he'd reached her car she'd alighted and was waiting beside the hatchback for him, looking gorgeous in pink pedal-pushers, a pink and white flowered top, and sexy white slip-on sandals. Her lipstick was bright pink, her hair was bouncing around her shoulders and her perfume smelt of freshly cut flowers.

'Sorry I'm a bit late,' she apologised as she looked him up and down. Without contempt this time. 'I had this sudden worry that you might have forgotten some essential items so I stopped off at a twenty-four hour chemist on the way.'

He grinned at her. 'Not necessary. They were the first thing I packed. But no worry. We won't run out now, will we? Which might have been a possibility if you're going to look as delicious as you look this morning all the time. Love the pink. Love the hair. But I especially love that perfume.'

Isabel tried not to let her head be turned by his compliments. Men like Rafe were always good with the charm.

At the same time, she'd come here today determined to enjoy what he had to offer. Cancelling everything for the wedding had been infinitely depressing, as had Luke's call telling her that he and Celia were now officially engaged. Isabel was in quite desperate need to be admired and desired, both of which she could see reflected in Rafe's gorgeous brown eyes.

'It's new,' she told him brightly. 'So are the clothes. I splashed out.'

That had been the only positive thing to happen during the last fortnight—Luke coming good with his promise to set her up financially. To give him credit, he hadn't let the grass grow under his feet in that regard. Guilt, no doubt.

Still, she was now the proud owner of a brilliant portfolio of blue-chip stock and shares, the deed to the Turramurra town house and a bonus wad of cash, some of which she'd recklessly spent on a wild new resort wardrobe. She'd given the more conservative clothes she'd bought to take on her honeymoon with Luke to Rachel, who was grateful, but wasn't sure where she'd ever get to wear them.

'You should splash out more often,' Rafe told her. 'I like the less formal you.'

'And I've always liked the less formal you,' she quipped back.

He was wearing fawn cargo slacks and a multi-coloured Hawaiian shirt, his bare feet housed in brown sandals. He must have shaved some time since she last saw him, but not that morning. Still, he looked and smelt shower-fresh, his silver phantom earring sparkling in the sunshine.

He smiled and rubbed a hand over his stubbly chin. 'You could have fooled me. So you like it rough, do you?'

'No lady would ever answer such a question,' she chided in mock reproof.

'And no gentleman would ask it,' he said, smiling cheekily. 'Happily for you, I'm no gentleman.'

'I'm sure you have your gentle side. Now, stop with the chit-chat and put your bag in here. If we don't get going we'll miss the plane.'

'Nah. At this hour on a Sunday morning we'll be at the airport in no time flat. The plane doesn't go till ten, does it?' he asked as he swung his one suitcase in beside her two.

'No,' she said, and slammed the hatchback down.

'Then we have time for this.'

When he pulled her abruptly into his arms, Isabel stiff-ened for a second. But only for a second. What was the point in making some silly show of resisting? This was why she found him so attractive, wasn't it? Because this was the kind of thing he would do.

Not like Luke. Luke always asked. He never took. Luke was a gentleman.

Not such a gentleman with Celia, however. He'd whisked her into bed before you could say Bob's your uncle! A matter of chemistry, Isabel realised.

As Rafe's lips covered hers, Isabel knew the chemistry between *them* was similarly explosive.

Sparks definitely flew and her head spun.

This was what she craved! Forceful lips and an even more forceful tongue. She leant into him, wanting more. She moaned before she could stop herself.

Rafe was startled by her response. The way she melted against him. The way she moaned. Wow, this was no ice princess. This was one hot babe he had in his arms!

When his head lifted, she made a small sound of protest.

He gave her one final peck on her wetly parted lips before putting her away from him. 'I can see this is going to be one fantastic holiday, honey,' he murmured throatily. 'But perhaps you're right. Perhaps we should get going before we really do miss that plane.'

Isabel hoped she wasn't blushing. She'd done enough blushing since meeting this man. Blushing was for female fools. And wishy-washy wimps. Not for a woman who'd decided to fashion her own destiny in every way.

So Rafe turned her on with effortless ease. Good. That was his job for the next fortnight.

But what about after that? she wondered, throwing him a hungry glance as she climbed back in behind the wheel. Mmm, she would see. Maybe she would keep his number in her little black book for the occasional night of carnal pleasure. Depending on how good he was at the real thing. If his kissing technique was anything to go by, she was in for some incredible sex.

Rafe didn't know quite what to make of the smug little smile which crossed that pink mouth.

Frankly, he didn't know what to make of Ms Isabel Hunt at all!

But he wasn't going to worry about it. He'd lost enough sleep over her this last two weeks. The next fortnight was going to be a big improvement, particularly in the insomnia department. He always slept like a log after sex.

'So, who did you tell your mother you were going away with?' he asked as soon as they were on their way.

She slanted him a curious look. 'What makes you sure I told her anything?'

'I have a mother,' he said drily. 'I know what they're like. They want to know the ins and outs of everything. Often, you have to resort to little white lies to keep them happy. I keep telling my mother that the only reason I haven't married is because I haven't met the right girl yet.'

'And that works for you?'

'I have to confess it's losing its credibility. I think by the time I'm forty she'll resort to taking out ads for me in the newspapers. You know the kind. "Attractive single male seeks companionship view matrimony from attractive single female. Must be able to cook well and like children."'

'If she does, I might answer. I cook very well and I adore children.'

'Very funny, Isabel. Now answer the question. Who is supposed to be going with you?'

'Rachel.'

'Who's Rachel?'

'My best friend. The one who was going to wear my wine-red bridesmaid gown.'

'And your mother *believed* you were taking a woman to Dream Island with you?'

'Yes.'

'Wow. My mother would never have believed that.'

'That you were taking a woman to Dream Island?'

'My, aren't we witty today?'

She smiled. 'Amongst other things.'

'What other things?'

'Excited. Are you excited, Rafe?'

He stared over at her. What was he getting himself into here? Whatever it was, it was communicating itself to that part of himself which he'd been trying to control for fourteen interminable days and nights.

'That's putting it mildly,' he confessed.

Her head turned and their eyes locked for a moment. He'd never felt a buzz like it. He could hardly wait.

But wait he had to. For two hours at the airport when the plane to Cairns was delayed. Then another short delay at Cairns for the connecting helicopter flight to Dream Island.

It was almost five in the afternoon by the time they landed on the heliport near the main reception area of the resort, then another hour before they were transported by luxury motor boat to—*yes*! Their own private bure on their own private beach!

Rafe was over the moon. Talk about fantasies coming true!

As he helped Isabel from the boat onto the small jetty, he glanced up at where the bure was set, on the lushly covered hillside on a natural terrace overlooking the water. Hexagon-shaped, it looked quite large, with what looked like an outdoor sitting area, a fact confirmed as they came closer. There was even a hammock strung between two nearby palm trees. Rafe eyed it speculatively when they walked past, wondering what it would be like to make love in a hammock.

The young chap named Tom who'd brought them there in the boat took them through the place, explaining all the mod cons which were state of the art, especially in the bathroom. The spa was huge. There was no expense spared with the white cane furniture and linen furnishings either, all in bright citrus colours with leafy tropical patterns.

No air-conditioning, Tom pointed out. Apparently that didn't work well in the humidity. But the bure had a high-domed ceiling and quite a few fans. Rafe wasn't sure how comfortable visitors would be in the height of summer, but at this time of year the climate was very pleasant, especially with the evening sea breeze which was at that moment wafting through the open doors and windows.

The bed, Rafe noted, had a huge mosquito net above

it on a frame which they were warned should be used every night. If they wanted to sit outside in the evenings, they were to spray themselves with the insect repellent provided and light the citronella-scented candle lamps dotted around.

Holidaying in the tropics, it seemed, did have some hazards.

'Because of all your travelling today,' Tom told them, 'the manager thought you'd be too tired to return to the main resort for dinner, so he had the chef pack you that special picnic dinner.' And he nodded towards the large basket he'd placed on the table in the eating nook.

'The refrigerator and cupboards are well stocked with more food and wine. The bar in the corner over there has every drink on its shelves you could possibly imagine. As I'm sure you are aware, all drink and food is included in the tariff here, so please don't stint yourself. Each day, you can either eat in the various restaurants in the hotel on the main beach or have something sent over. You only have to ring for service. Cigarettes are included also, if you smoke.'

'We don't smoke,' Isabel said for both of them, before frowning up at Rafe. 'You don't, do you?' she whispered and he shook his head.

'I'll be going, then,' Tom said crisply. 'There are brochures on the coffee-table explaining all the resort's facilities. You have your own little runabout attached to the jetty which I will show you how to operate before I leave. You must understand, however, that you can't walk to anywhere from here, except up to the top of the hill we're on. The path is quite steep from this point, but the view's pretty spectacular, especially at sunrise. Worth the effort at least once. I think that's all, but if you have any questions you only have to pick up the phone and ring Reception. Now, if you'd like to come with me, sir, I'll show you how to start the runabout's motor and how to steer.'

Isabel watched them leave, then walked over and sat down on the side of the bed, testing it for comfort. It was firm. Luke's bed had been firm, she recalled.

Luke…

He'd rung her yesterday and told her he and Celia were getting married in a couple of months. For a honeymoon, he was going to take her around the world. For a whole year. After that, they were going to start trying for a baby.

Isabel didn't envy Celia the trip. She'd travelled a lot herself. Saved up during her twenties and gone to those places she'd always thought exotic and romantic. Paris. Rome. Hawaii.

But she envied her that baby. And Luke as its father. He was going to make a truly wonderful father.

Suddenly, all her earlier excitement faded and she wanted to cry. Before she knew it she *was* crying, tears flooding her eyes and overflowing down her cheeks.

Isabel dashed them away with the back of her hands, angry with herself. If only she hadn't let Luke go racing off to Lake Macquarie that Friday. If only she hadn't been so darned reasonable she would have been here tonight, with him. They would have been married, and she would have been making a baby in this bed. Or at least trying to.

Instead, she was here with Rafe!

Throwing herself onto the bed, Isabel buried her face in the mountain of pillows and wept.

Rafe was taken aback when he walked back in and found Isabel crying on the bed. He hated hearing women cry. His mother had cried for a long time after his Dad had been killed. It had upset Rafe terribly, listening to her sob into her pillows every night.

'Hey,' he said softly, and touched Isabel's trembling shoulder.

With a sob, she turned her back to him and curled up into a ball on the green-printed quilt. 'Go away,' she cried piteously. 'Just go away.'

Rafe didn't know what to do. He hadn't a clue what was wrong. She'd said she hadn't loved her fiancé. Had she lied? Had she taken one look at this place and this bed and wanted not him, but Luke?

Dismayed, Rafe went to leave, but then decided against it. She shouldn't be left alone like this. She needed him, if only to comfort her for now.

He lay down on the bed and wrapped his arms around her from behind. 'It's all right, sweetheart,' he soothed, holding her tightly against him. 'I understand. Honest, I do. I'll bet you've been holding your hurt in this last fortnight, and now that you're here, where you should have been with Luke, his dumping you for that Celia girl has hit you hard. Look, I know what it's like to be chucked over for someone else. And it's hell. So cry all you want to. I did.'

Talking to her and touching her seemed to do the trick. Her weeping subsided to a sniffle and she turned over in his arms to stare up at him. 'You did?'

'Yep. Maybe it's not the done thing for a bloke to blubber, but I was like Niagara Falls for a day or two. Heck, no, longer than that. I was a mess on and off for a week. I didn't dare go out anywhere. It was most embarrassing. I drank like a fish too, but that didn't help at all. Made me even more maudlin.'

'Why did she dump you?'

'Ambition. And money. And influence. Be assured it wasn't because the other chap was better in bed,' Rafe added with a grin, and she laughed. It was a lovely sound.

He took advantage of the moment and kissed her. Not the way he'd kissed her back in Sydney this morning, but slowly, softly, sipping at her lips, showing her with his mouth that he *did* have a gentle side. He kept on kissing her, nothing more, and gradually he felt her defences lower till finally she began to moan, and move against him. Only then did he start to undress her—and himself—still taking his time, touching and talking to her as he went, reassuring her of how much he admired and desired her.

It wasn't easy, keeping his head, especially when he uncovered her perfect breasts and sucked on their perfect and very pert nipples, but he managed, till they were both totally naked and she was trembling for him.

It almost killed him to leave her and go get a condom. But a man had to do what a man had to do.

He was quick. Real quick. After all, he'd been slipping on condoms for years. Though rarely when he'd been as excited as this. Had he *ever* been as excited as this, even with Liz?

Maybe his memory was defective but he didn't think so. This was a one-off experience, perhaps because Isabel had made him wait two weeks to consummate what she'd evoked in him the first time he'd looked at her. This was lust at its most tortuous. And frustration at its most fierce.

He was thankful she felt the same way.

Or so he'd thought, till he hurried back to the bed and saw her looking at him with something like fear.

But why would she be afraid of him?

'What is it?' he asked as he joined her on the bed once more and drew her back into his arms. 'What's worrying you?'

'Nothing,' she said, shaking her head. 'Nothing.'

'Is it still Luke?'

'No. No!'

'Is it me, then? You're worried I might hurt you.'

She blinked her surprise at his intuition.

'Oh, honey, honey,' he murmured. 'I would never hurt you. I just want to make you happy, to see you smile and hear you laugh again. I want to give you pleasure. Like this,' he said as he stroked her legs apart, his fingers knowing exactly where to go and what to do.

She gasped while he groaned. How wet she was. It

was going to feel fantastic, being buried to the hilt in that.

Waiting any longer was simply not on. And possibly counter-productive. He would feel safer inside her. Less tense. He might even relax a bit.

As though reading his mind, she shifted her thighs apart and bent her knees, inviting him in, murmuring yes in his ear over and over. His fingers fumbled a fraction as he sought to push his suddenly desperate flesh into hers.

Rafe sighed with relief, then just wallowed in blissful stillness for a few seconds. But any respite was short-lived.

As soon as he began to move, her legs were around him like a vine. Or was it a vice? She was squeezing him with her heels and with her insides, rocking backward and forward.

Rafe felt a wild rush of blood along his veins, swelling him further, compelling him to pump harder as he sought release from his agony.

And he'd thought he'd be more relaxed inside her.

Foolish Rafe!

'Rafe,' she cried out, her arms tightening around his neck, her lips breathing hot fire against his throat. 'Rafe…'

Her first spasm sent him into orbit, to a place he hadn't known existed. Was it pleasure or pain as his seed was wrenched from his body? Agony or ecstasy as her almost violent contractions kept milking him dry, making him moan as he'd never moaned before.

Rafe didn't know if he was experiencing happiness, or humiliation. All he knew was that no sooner did he feel himself falling away from that place she'd rocketed him to, than he wanted to be there again.

'You're right,' she murmured, kissing his throat and stroking his back, his shoulders, his chest. 'You didn't hurt me.'

His eyes opened to stare down at her.

'You looked so big,' she explained breathily. 'I haven't been with a man that big before.'

Rafe was startled. He'd always thought of himself as pretty average. What she'd been seeing was mostly *her* doing. Still, he was secretly flattered.

'I'd thought you were worried I might hurt you emotionally,' he said.

'Oh, no,' she said, shaking her head. 'No, that won't happen. I won't ever let that happen.'

Now Rafe felt piqued. Which was crazy. She'd spelled out what she wanted when she'd propositioned him and he'd agreed. Sex on tap for a fortnight without any strings and without any follow-up.

He'd thought such a set-up was every man's fantasy come true. Now, for some reason that he hadn't anticipated, Rafe wasn't so sure.

Oh, for pity's sake, stepped in the voice of cold reason. What's got into *you*? This *is* every man's fantasy come true. Stop playing the sensitive New Age guy and start being exactly what she thinks you are. Rafe the rake!

The trouble was Rafe wasn't really a rake. Never had

been. Still, it might be fun. He could do every outrageous thing he'd ever wanted to do and get away with it. Make the most wicked suggestions. Play Casanova to the hilt, with a bit of the Marquis de Sade thrown in.

He had to smile at that. Him, into bondage and stuff? Wasn't his usual cup of tea, but that hammock had possibilities…

'Why are you smiling like that?' she asked.

'Like what?'

'Like the cat who got the cream.'

'Perhaps because I just did. You are the best in bed, sweetheart. Simply the best.'

She looked slightly uncomfortable with his compliment, as though she didn't like her performance being rated. Yet she must know she was good at sex.

She was a complex creature, and a maze of contradictions. Cool and ladylike on the surface whilst all this white-hot heat was simmering away underneath.

Rafe aimed to keep her furnace well stoked for the next fortnight. She wasn't going to be allowed to retreat into that ridiculous touch-me-not façade, not for a moment. She might think she'd hired him as her private toy boy, but in fact *she* was the one going to be the toy, to be played in whatever way he fancied.

Rafe might have been shocked by the wickedness of his thoughts under normal circumstances. But these were hardly normal circumstances, and it was what she wanted, after all.

'Hey, but I'm hungry,' he said. 'Aren't you?'

'A little. But I could do with a shower first. We've been travelling all day.'

'Mmm. Me, too. But why have a shower when there's that lovely big spa? We could pop in together. What say we take that picnic basket with us as well, kill two birds with one stone?'

'But…'

'But, nothing, honey. You just do what good old Rafe tells you and you'll have the time of your life.'

CHAPTER EIGHT

RAFE was right, Isabel thought two days later. She *was* having the time of her life. He was exactly what she needed just now.

Oversexed, of course. He never left her alone.

But she wasn't complaining. If she was brutally honest, she wanted him as much as he wanted her. He was wonderfully flirtatious and fun, with just the right amount of bad boy wickedness to his lovemaking which she'd always found exciting.

'So what do you think?' she said as she modelled her new red bikini for him.

Rafe was still sitting on the terrace in the morning sunshine, partaking in the slowest, longest breakfast. He was naked to the waist, a pair of colourful board shorts slung low around his hips. He was all male.

His eyes lifted and he stared at her. She hadn't worn this particular swimming costume for him as yet and it was scandalously brief. All the swimwear she'd bought with Luke's money was scandalous in some way, selected in a mood of rebellion and defiance.

And with Rafe in mind.

The white one-piece she'd worn yesterday went totally transparent when wet. Swimming had come to a swift end on that occasion, which was perhaps just as well, since her fair skin couldn't take too much sun. As it was, she was slightly pink. All over.

'Turn round,' he ordered.

She did, knowing full well what the sight of her bottom in nothing but a thong would do to him. Still, that was the general idea. She'd been like a cat on a hot tin roof since he'd come up behind her as she'd been setting out breakfast on the terrace an hour ago, and proceeded to have her right then and there, out in the open. No foreplay whatsoever. Just him, whispering hot words in her ear as he lifted the hem of the sarong she was wearing, then commanding her to stand perfectly still whilst he quite selfishly took his pleasure.

She'd nearly spilled the jug of orange juice she'd been holding at the time. She hadn't come, of course. He'd been much too fast and she'd been much too tense. It had left her terribly turned on, though. She was still turned on an hour later. Hence the red bikini.

Isabel hadn't brought Rafe along with her to remain frustrated for long.

When he said nothing, she spun back round and glared at him, her hands finding her hips.

'Well, what do you think?'

'I think you should come over here,' he said, and downed the rest of his orange juice.

A quiver ran all through her as she walked towards him. What was he going to do to her? Or make her do to him?

When he handed her the empty glass, she just stared at him.

'What's this?' she said.

'I've finished. I thought you might like to clear the table.'

'Then you thought wrong,' she snapped.

'In that case, what do you want to do? Or should I say, what is it you want *me* to do to *you*? If you tell me in minute explicit detail, Isabel, I'll do it exactly as you describe. Anything you want, honey. Anything at all.'

Her mouth had gone dry. '*Anything*?'

'Uh-huh.'

'I…I don't know what I want…'

He took the empty glass out of her hands, put it back on the table, then drew her down onto his lap. 'Yes you do,' he murmured as he moved aside the tiny triangles which barely covered her breasts and began playing with her nipples. 'You know exactly what you want.'

'I…' She could hardly think with him doing what he was doing. Her nipples had tightened into twin peaks of heightened sensitivity, and he was rolling them with his fingertips in exquisite circles.

'Tell me,' he said, his breath hot in her ear. 'Tell me…'

She shuddered and squirmed. 'No,' she croaked. 'No, I can't.'

'Why not?'

'It's…it's too embarrassing.'

'Then I'll tell you what you want. You want me to give you a climax first. With my tongue. You want *me* to wait this time, till I'm climbing the walls like I was our first time together. Even then, you want to torment me some more with this sexy mouth of yours.'

His right hand lifted from her aching nipples to touch her lips, making them gasp apart. She automatically sucked in when he slipped a finger inside.

'Yes, just like that,' he said thickly, sliding his finger in and out of her mouth. 'You'd like to do that to me, wouldn't you, Isabel?'

She shuddered all over.

'And then,' he went on in a low seductive whisper, 'you want me to do it to you like there's no tomorrow. You want me to scatter your mind, to make you feel nothing but the wild heat of the moment, and the beautiful blissful oblivion that will follow afterwards.'

When his hot words finally stilled, so did that finger. A charged silence descended, with no sounds but the heaviness of his breathing and the waves on the beach.

Isabel wasn't breathing at all!

Suddenly, his chair scraped back and he was up and carrying her, not over to the bure and the bed, as she was desperately hoping, but down the path which led to the beach. She was startled when he dumped her into the hammock on the way past then continued on himself to run across the sand and plunge into the ocean. Meanwhile, she had to clutch wildly at the sides of the swinging hammock to stop herself from falling out.

When he returned less than a minute later, all wet and smiling, she threw him the blackest look. 'You did that deliberately, didn't you?' she growled, still clutching at the hammock. 'Turned me on, then made me wait some more.'

'Nope. It just happened that way. Perversely, I turned myself on even more than I was trying to do to you. I had no idea just talking about sex like that was so powerful. Had to go cool myself off before things became downright humiliating. But I'm back now, ready and able to put my words into action. So where shall we begin, lover? Right here in the hammock?'

'Don't be silly. The darned thing won't stay still. And you don't have a condom with you.'

'I wasn't going to have actual sex with you here, Isabel,' he said drily. 'If you recall, that doesn't come till much later in the scenario I outlined, by which time I'm to carry you back to the bure.'

Her mouth gaped open. 'You...you mean you're going to do what you...d...d...described?'

'Every single bit of it. And so are you.'

Her face flamed.

'You'll like it, I promise,' he purred as he pulled her round crosswise and began peeling off her bikini bottom.

She did like it. Too much. Way too much.

But he was wrong about afterwards. He might have fallen into blissful oblivion on the bed afterwards, but she lay there wide awake, her thoughts going round and round.

She wasn't going to be able to give him up after a mere fortnight. That was the truth of it. She was going to want him around for much longer than that.

Why? That was the question. Was it the way he *could*

make her forget everything but the moment? Was it for the brilliant and blinding climaxes he could give her? Or was it something more insidious, something she'd vowed never to do, ever again?

Fall in love…

Rolling over onto her side, she looked at him lying there, sprawled naked on the lemon sheets, his arms flung wide, his silky brown hair. Leaning forward, she lifted one heavy lock from across his eyes and dropped it onto the pillow, then removed another which was covering his nostrils and mouth.

As if sensing that he could now breathe more easily, he sighed a deep, contented sigh, his mouth almost smiling in his sleep.

Isabel found herself smiling as well. Maybe she wanted to keep him around because she just liked him. And because he seemed to really like her in return.

Liking was good, she decided. She could live with that.

Finally, Isabel's worries calmed, she curled up to Rafe and went to sleep.

CHAPTER NINE

'NO RINGING for a dinner drop tonight, Isabel,' Rafe told her. 'We need to get up, get dressed and get away from here for a while. Do something else for a few hours. Have a change of scene.'

Isabel's head lifted and she smiled at him. 'Yes, Rafe darling, but surely you don't want me to get up and get dressed right at this precise moment.'

He stared back down into her cool blue eyes and wished he had the strength to tell her, yes, stop. Stop tormenting me. Stop enslaving me. Stop making me addicted to your body. And to you.

It was Wednesday, and they were back in bed, not long awake from an afternoon nap after a rather rigorous morning. They'd gone for a dawn swim after minimal sleep the night before and hadn't bothered with swimwear. There was no one to see them, after all. No one to see what they did in the water. Or on the wet sand. Or in the hammock again.

The hammock...

Rafe swallowed as he thought of what he'd done to her in the hammock last night, how he'd used the silk sarong she'd been wearing to bind her hands to the rope up above her head. He'd never done anything like that before. And neither had she, if he was any guess.

But what a sight she'd been stretched out there, naked, in the moonlight. Rafe had been incredibly turned on. And Isabel…Isabel had been beside herself. She'd come so many times he lost count. In the end, she'd begged him to stop.

But he hadn't been able to stop, not for a long long time.

And now he wasn't able to stop *her* as she drew him deep into her mouth once more.

He moaned at the heat of it. And the wetness. It was like being sheathed in molten steel. He was going to come. He knew he was going to come.

His raw cry of warning stopped her, leaving him dangling right on the edge.

'You have a problem, lover?' she drawled huskily as she reached for one of the condoms they kept beside the bed.

He choked out a rueful laugh. 'You're cruel, do you know that?'

'Now you know how I felt last night,' she said as she protected them both. 'Just as well my perfume acts as an effective insect repellent or I'd have been covered with insect bites.'

'Instead, you have a few bites of another kind.'

'Beast.'

'You loved it.'

'And you're loving this. So why don't you just lie back and enjoy?'

He sucked in sharply when she bent to take him in her mouth once more.

'No, don't,' he groaned, and her head lifted, her eyes surprised.

'No?'

'No.' He shook his head. 'Not like that.'

He reached down and pulled her up and onto him, spreading her legs outside of his, then pushing his tormented flesh inside her once more. With a primal groan he grabbed her buttocks, kneading them as he rocked her quite roughly up and down on him. They came together, backs arching, mouths gaping wide apart, bodies throbbing wildly in unison.

'Oh, Rafe,' she cried, collapsing face down across his chest, her insides still spasming.

He held her to him till she stopped, though a shudder still ran through her every now and then.

Too much, he began thinking. This is all getting too much.

'I have to go to the bathroom,' he told her a bit brusquely.

'No, don't leave me,' she begged, clinging to him.

'Sorry. Nature calls.' He was out of her and off the bed in a flash, lurching across the sea matting floor and into the bathroom. Closing the door, he leaned against it for a few air-sucking seconds before staggering over to the toilet, not really needing it except to do some essential personal housekeeping.

When he went to do just that, he stared down at himself in horror.

'Oh, no…' he muttered.

Not once had Rafe had a condom break before on him. Not once!

Till now…

His heart sinking, Rafe inspected the damage and it was the worst scenario possible. The darned thing had totally failed. Ripped asunder. Right across the tip.

Immediately he thought of Isabel and in his mind's eye he could see millions of eager little tadpoles careering through her cervix and into her womb, swimming around with more energy than the Olympic water-polo team, watching and waiting to score a home goal.

What were the odds of their doing just that? he wondered frantically, his mind scouring his memory to recall what Isabel had said to him that Sunday just over two weeks ago. Something about her period being due that week. Probably early on in the week, he guessed. She'd said something about suffering from PMT that day.

Rafe did some mental arithmetic and worked out that if Isabel was a normal regular female with a normal monthly cycle, then she had to have already entered, or be entering, her 'most likely to conceive phase' right now.

Rafe sank down on the side of the spa bath. He might have just become a father!

His head whirled. So did his stomach. She was going to kill him when he told her.

Then don't tell her, came the voice of male logic. It will only spoil everything. And there's nothing you can do about it now. Besides, it might not happen. It might not be the right time. Even if it was, couples sometimes tried for years—hitting ovulation day right on the dot—and the woman didn't fall pregnant. Let's not be paranoid about this.

But what if Isabel *had* fallen pregnant. What then?

Cross that bridge when you come to it, Rafe.

Right. Good advice.

Rafe stood up, jumped into the shower and turned on the water. Picking up the shower gel, he poured a generous pool into his hands and slapped it onto his chest.

But a *baby*, he began thinking as he washed himself. *His* baby. His and *Isabel's* baby.

Talk about the best plans of mice and men.

Isabel lay there listening to Rafe in the shower and thinking she could do with a shower herself. She felt icky. But no way was she going to join him in there, not after the way she'd just carried on, clinging to him and pleading for him to stay with her like some lovesick cow.

How typical of herself! And how humiliating!

No wonder he'd bolted out of the bed.

Rafe was right. It was high time they did something else instead of have sex. She was beginning to fall into old ways.

Isabel sighed. If only he was less skilful in the love-making department. If only he didn't know exactly the sort of thing which excited her unbearably. If only he didn't always turn the tables on her such as just now.

She'd thought she was being the boss in the bedroom, as she'd used to be sometimes with Luke, but in a flash Rafe had whipped control out of her hands and she'd become his willing little love slave again, as she'd been last night.

Isabel's face flamed as she thought how crazy it had been of her to let him tie her up like that. But, ooh, it had been so deliciously thrilling. And really, down deep, she'd never felt worried. There'd been no fear in her, only excitement.

It had been a game, an erotic game. Just as this holiday together was a game. Rafe knew that. And she knew that.

So why did she keep forgetting?

No more, she resolved. From now on she would stick to the rules. And to the agreed agenda. As for any silly idea she'd been harbouring of seeing Rafe occasionally after this fortnight was over… That was not on. Experience warned her if she saw Rafe outside of this fantasy setting she was sure to fall in love with him, or start relying on him for her day-to-day happiness. She'd been there, done that, and she wasn't ever going there again. Heaven help her, if she couldn't learn from her past mistakes!

Isabel was lying there under a sheet, feeling relatively in control once more, when Rafe emerged from the steaming bathroom, rubbing his brown hair dry with a bright orange towel, a lime-green one slung rather hazardously low around his hips.

Wow, she thought as her gaze ran hungrily over him. He really was gorgeous, even more so now that he was sporting an all-over tan. She loved the long lean look on a man, loved broad bronzed shoulders which tapered down to a small waist. *Loved* tight little buns.

Not that she could see his buns at that moment. But she had an imprint in her memory bank.

'It's time you got up, lover,' he said, draping the orange towel over his shoulder and finger-combing his hair back from his face. 'It's just gone five. I want to be gone from here by six.'

'Fine. I was just waiting for you to finish,' she replied, but, when she swung her feet over the side of the bed and sat up, Isabel hesitated. There wasn't anything for her to put on at hand. She hadn't worn any clothes all day and the sarong she'd been wearing last night was still tied to the hammock. The rest of her clothes were in the walk-in wardrobe, and it was actually further to walk over there than it was to the bathroom.

It was silly that walking around naked in front of Rafe should bother her. He'd seen every inch of her up close and personal. Too silly for words!

Gathering her courage, she tossed aside the sheet she'd been clutching and stood up, wincing a little once she started walking. Oh dear, she *was* icky. That was another thing she found a bit embarrassing. How wet she was all the time.

Not that Rafe minded. He said it was a real turn-on.

Still, once Isabel reached the shower she lathered herself up down there with some degree of over-enthusiasm, as if by removing the evidence of her ongoing heat, she could better keep her cool around him. A waste of time, she realised on remembering she had nothing to wear to dinner tonight but the choice of three highly provocative outfits, all bought to tease and tantalise, herself as well as Rafe.

Which one would do the least damage? she wondered. The little black dress?

No. It was way *too* little, halter-necked with no back and a short tight skirt which looked as if it was sewn on, owing to the material being stretchy.

What about the blue silk petticoat-style number with the swishy skirt?

No. Not with her nipples standing out all the time like ready-to-fire cannons. The material was too thin and the bodice too clingy.

It would have to be the emerald and gold trouser suit. Although still provocative, she at least got to wear a bra, of sorts. But the outfit did have other hazards. Such as the fulfilling of an old fantasy of hers to look like a harem girl. The pants were harem-style, and the emerald material semi-transparent, shot with gold thread. The outfit was only saved from indecency by being overlaid with a thigh-length jacket. The bra of sorts was a strapless corselette, heavily beaded in green and gold glass beads and designed to manoeuvre even the smallest of breasts into a cleavage. Isabel's breasts, though not large, were not small either. The result was eye-catching to say the least.

Once dressed and made-up, Isabel stared at herself in the floor-length mirror which hung on the back of the walk-in wardrobe door and thought she'd never looked sexier. Her hair was up, though not in its usual French roll. She'd just bundled it up loosely in a very casual topknot, leaving strands of various lengths to fall around her face. The long green and gold crystal earrings in her ears would swing when she walked. *If* she could walk, she amended as she squeezed her feet into the outrageously high gold sandals she'd bought to go with the outfit.

'Shake a leg in there, lover,' Rafe called out. 'It's gone six.'

With a shudder which could have been excitement or apprehension, she dragged on the gauzy green jacket, sprayed on some perfume, then went to meet her master.

Rafe was out on the terrace, admiring the view in the dusk light and thinking that this place really was a fantasy come true when Isabel emerged from the bure, looking like something out of the Arabian Nights.

'Well,' he said, smiling wryly to her as he scraped back the chair and stood up. 'If ever there was an outfit designed to turn a gay man straight, then you're wearing it tonight.'

She laughed a slightly guilty-sounding laugh. 'I didn't bring any let's-do-something-else clothes with me, I'm afraid.'

'I see,' he said drily. And he did. She was only here with him for the sex. She'd made that quite clear from the start.

And he'd been with her all the way. Till their little mishap this afternoon. Now, suddenly, everything had changed. Now, suddenly, when he looked at her, he didn't see a delicious bedmate but a possible pregnancy.

Not that he didn't still desire her. He'd have to be dead not to. It was just that other thoughts were now overriding his X-rated ones. Such as perhaps he should still tell her what had happened. It wasn't too late for her to get the morning-after pill. They had a doctor on the island, he knew. And a chemist shop. He'd read the list of services available in one of the coffee-table brochures.

But, oddly, he hated the idea of her ridding her body of his baby—if his baby *was* in there. Peculiar, really, when he'd never wanted to be a father before. He still didn't.

But *she* did. Want to be a mother, that is. She wanted one enough to have one on her own. So why not his? Better than having herself artificially inseminated. Bad idea, that.

'Rafe! Why are you just standing there, frowning at me like that? What on earth are you thinking?'

'What am I thinking?' He took her arm and started propelling her down the path towards the jetty. 'I was thinking that your idea of having a baby all by yourself is not a good one. In fact, it's a very bad one. My mother found it extremely difficult raising me by herself, and she had help for the first eight years.'

'Yes, well I can understand how raising *you* would have tried the patience of a saint,' Isabel said. 'But my baby won't be having your impossible genes, Rafe, so hopefully my job won't be quite so difficult.'

'Is that so?' Rafe smiled. He couldn't help it. Irony always amused him.

'Yes, that's so!' she pronounced haughtily.

'But if you go through with this plan of yours to be artificially inseminated with some unknown donor, then you won't have any idea what kind of genes your baby will inherit from its father. Surely even *my* genes would be better than the lucky-dip method.'

'All that will be unknown is his name and address,' she informed him somewhat impatiently. 'I will know a lot of information about the donor. A complete physical description, all aspects of his health, his level of education, plus other personality traits such as his sporting interests and hobbies. That's how I aim to choose him. I will look at the list of available donors and select the one which best fits my prerequisites.'

'Fascinating. Here, I can see you're having trouble walking in those heels. I'll carry you.' She went to object but he just swept her up into his arms and carried her across the sand towards the jetty.

'Mmm. You're as light as a feather. You know, I think you've lost weight since coming to this island. Too much exercise and not enough eating,' he said, at which she pulled a face up at him.

'We have to make sure you're in tippy-top health, you know, if you're planning to have a baby soon. Three good meals a day, and no silly dieting.'

'Yes, Dr Saint Vincent,' she mocked.

'Just talking common sense. Of course perhaps you're not serious about having a baby soon, or on your own at all. Maybe that was just talk.'

'I'm deadly serious. We're on the jetty now,' she said curtly. 'Please put me down.'

Rafe stared down into her eyes, suddenly aware of how stiffly she was holding herself in his arms. It hadn't occurred to him when he picked her up that she might be turned on by it. Whilst her vulnerability to his closeness was very flattering, taking advantage of it wasn't a priority of his at this precise moment.

He lowered her carefully onto those wicked-looking shoes. 'So tell me, Isabel, what *are* your prerequisites for choosing the father of your child?'

'No.'

'No? What do you mean, no?'

'I mean no, Rafe,' she said firmly as she marched on ahead of him out along the jetty. 'I am not going to have this conversation with you,' she threw over her shoulder. 'I wish I hadn't told you about my plans now. Why you're even interested is beyond me.'

He hurried after her. 'Oh, come on, don't be like that. If we're going to sit across the table and have dinner for a couple of hours we have to talk about something. And I'm curious.'

She spun round to look him straight in the eye. 'Why?'

'Why not?'

For a moment her eyes flashed with frustration, but then she shrugged. 'I might as well give in and tell you whatever you want to know, because you won't give up, will you? You'll get your way, like you did with the black and white photos. You're like that Chinese water torture.'

He grinned. 'I've been told that before.'

'I can imagine. But you can't have it *all* your own way *all* the time. If I'm to answer such highly personal questions then I have a few of my own I want answered.'

'Fair enough.' He had nothing to hide and, frankly, was intrigued over what she might want to know. More than intrigued. Rather pleased. Maybe she didn't want him just for sex. Maybe she wanted more, whether she admitted it to herself or not.

The prospect of having a more permanent relationship with this beautiful and spirited woman brought a rush not dissimilar to sexual arousal. He'd never been entirely happy with the thought of never seeing Isabel again after this fortnight was over, but had brushed aside any qualms over the rather cold-blooded terms she had set down because he wanted her so much.

But things were different now.

If she was carrying his child, then going their separate ways was simply not on.

Rafe couldn't stop his eyes from drifting down her body, first to her breasts—his baby was going to be very happy with *those*!—and then to her stomach—athletically flat at this moment. But he could imagine how it would look in a few months' time, all deliciously soft and rounded.

Isabel's insides contracted when she saw the direction of Rafe's eyes. He was thinking about sex again. She could tell. The way he'd just gobbled up her cleavage, and now he was undressing her further. He was making her all hot and bothered inside again, like he had when he'd been carrying her just now.

'Now you stop that!' she snapped, and his eyes jerked up to her face.

'Stop what?'

'You know what, you disgusting man. Now help me into this darned thing.'

The runabout rocked wildly when Isabel first stepped down into it, with Isabel almost tipping into the sea. 'Maybe we should have called Tom to take us over,' she said in a panicky voice as she clutched at the sides.

'If you'd just sit down in the middle of the seat, Isabel,' Rafe pointed out calmly, 'everything would be fine.'

Isabel did just that, and everything was fine, with Rafe starting up the motor as though he'd been doing it all his life, then steering her safely back to the main beach where he eased the small craft expertly into another jetty. His confidence and competence at things marine and mechanical reminded Isabel that men like Rafe *did* have their uses in life, other than to give women mind-blowing climaxes.

If she kept him coming around occasionally, he could also be called upon to change light-bulbs, put new washers in leaking taps and even mow the lawn. Now that she was a home owner she'd have to do things like that from time to time.

When he climbed up onto the jetty with his back to her she ogled his body quite shamelessly, especially those tight buns, housed as they were tonight in tight black jeans.

'Now you stop that,' he said, turning and grinning down at her.

'Stop what?' she managed to counter, but her cheeks felt hot.

'You know what, you disgusting woman.'

'I have no idea what you're talking about,' she parried. 'Now, help me out of here, and don't let me fall in the water.'

'Might do you good. Cool you down a tad.'

Isabel decided she really couldn't let him get away with mocking her. Her glance was cool as a cucumber. 'I thought you liked me hot and wet, not cold and wet.' And she swept past him.

Rafe watched her stalk off up the jetty and smiled. She was a one all right. More sassy and sexy than any woman he'd ever met.

But he had her measure. She liked him. She didn't want to but she did. That was why she was going to such great pains to put him in his place all the time. What she didn't realise was that fate might have already propelled him out of his role as temporary lover into possibly something far more permanent. Father of her child.

Mmm. That was another thing he had to check up on. What the odds were of that.

'Where are we going for dinner exactly?' she asked him when he caught up and took her arm.

'To the Hibiscus Restaurant. This way.' He guided her

along the planked walkway which connected the jetty to the main resort buildings which sat in several acres of tropical gardens just behind the beach.

Aside from the reception area, which also encompassed the island store, there was a five-star hotel nestled amongst the palms which boasted two à la carte restaurants, a buffet-style bistro, a couple of bars, a casino games room and a pool which, from the brochures, had to be seen to be believed. One of the restaurants was called the Hibiscus, named no doubt after the lovely tropical flower which grew in abundance on the island.

'I booked a table there while you were in the shower,' he told her. 'The woman on the other end of the phone said it was the most romantic of the restaurants here. I gather she thought we were honeymooners.'

'And you didn't tell her we weren't,' Isabel said drily.

'Goodness, no. That way, we were assured of a good table. She said since it was a balmy night she'd give us one of the ones on the terrace overlooking the pool.'

'Con artist,' Isabel scorned.

'Just being my usual clever charming self.'

'Arrogant and egotistical, that's what you are.'

'You like me arrogant and egotistical.'

'Only in bed.'

'People spend a third of their lives in bed. Except when they're on a pretend honeymoon. Then, they spend nearly *all* of it.'

Isabel laughed. And why not? Rafe had to be one of the most entertaining men she'd ever been with. It was impossible not to surrender to his charm, or be amused by his wit, which was wicked and dry, just the way she liked it.

'I love it when you laugh,' he said. 'You look even more beautiful when you laugh.'

'Do stop flattering me, Rafe. I might get used to it.'

'Ooh, and wouldn't that be dreadful?'

'Not so dreadful. Just unwise.'

'Why?'

She sighed as her good humour faded. 'I told you once before, Rafe. I don't want to have another relationship with a man whose idea of a relationship begins and ends in the bedroom.'

'And you think that's all I'd ever want from you?'

'Isn't it?'

'That depends.'

'On what?'

On whether you're carrying my child...

'On how good you can cook,' he quipped.

Her eyebrows shot up. 'You're saying the way to your heart is through your stomach? I don't believe it.'

'I *do* like my food. This way to the Hibiscus,' he directed on seeing an arrowed sign veering off to the right through the gardens. 'Mmm, I wonder what their wine list is like? Since there's no extra charge, I'll order a different bottle with each course.'

'I'm not going back in that tin-can with you if you've been drinking heavily,' she warned.

'Me, neither. If I feel I'm over the limit, we'll get someone else to take us back. Okay?'

'Okay.' She nodded. 'And don't encourage me to

drink too much, either. I still haven't got over the hang-over I had from my last binge.'

'Yes, but that was hard liquor. A few glasses of wine won't hurt.'

'Mmm. You'd say that. You're probably trying to get me drunk so that you can have your wicked way with me.'

He laughed. 'Honey, I don't have to get you drunk to do that.'

Isabel winced. 'I asked for that one, didn't I?'

He gave her an affectionate squeeze. 'Don't be silly. I love the way you are.'

Isabel didn't doubt it. Men had always been partial to whores.

Her stomach turned over at this last thought. She wasn't a whore, but maybe, in Rafe's eyes, she was acting like one. There again, maybe not. Rafe was not a narrow-minded man, and he didn't seem to be afflicted with that dreadful set of double standards which some men dragged up to make women feel guilty about their sexuality.

Her mother, however, wouldn't be impressed with the way she'd been behaving.

Isabel suppressed a groan. Why, oh why did she have to think of her mother? The woman was out of the ark when it came to her views on such things. She didn't appreciate that the world was a different world now. Marriage couldn't be relied upon any more to provide a woman with security for life. And men…men couldn't be relied upon at all!

'You've gone all quiet on me,' Rafe said worriedly.

'Just thinking.'

'Thinking can be bad for you.'

'What do you recommend?'

'Talking is good. And so, sometimes, is drinking. You could do with a measure of both.'

'You conniving devil. You just want to find out all my secrets.'

'You mean you have some?'

'Don't we all?'

'My life is an open book.'

'Huh! Any man with designer stubble and a phantom's head in his ear has to have *some* secrets.'

'Not me. What you see is what you get. If you think I'm indulging in some kind of pretentious arty-farty image with the way I look, you couldn't be more wrong. The phantom's head belonged to my father. I wear it all the time because when I look in the mirror I'm reminded of him. I don't shave every day because it gives me a rash if I do. As far as my clothes are concerned, I dress strictly for comfort, and in colours which don't stain easily. I am who I am, Isabel. And I like who I am. Can you say the same? Aah. Here we are. The Hibiscus.'

CHAPTER TEN

THE Hibiscus lived up to its recommendation, with even the indoor tables having a view of the spectacular pool, courtesy of glass walls on three sides of the restaurant.

Still, given the balmy night, it was going to be very pleasant sitting outside under the stars, and the table they were shown to *did* overlook the pool directly.

Round and glass-topped, the table was set with hibiscus-patterned place-mats, superb silverware and crystal glasses to suit every type of wine. The menus were printed with silver lettering on a laminated sheet which matched the place-mats.

After seeing them seated, the good-looking young waiter handed Rafe the wine list, then lit the lantern-style candle resting in the circular slot in the middle of the table, possibly where an umbrella would be inserted during daylight hours. The wine list was small but select, and Rafe ordered an excellent champagne to start with whilst Isabel silently studied the menu.

Even after the waiter departed she didn't glance up or say a word, leaving Rafe to regret the crack he'd made about her perhaps not liking who she was. She'd looked down-in-the-mouth ever since.

But if she was going to keep firing bullets, then she had to expect some back.

Still…he hated seeing her sad.

But what to do?

'Find anything there to tempt your tastebuds?' he asked lightly on picking up his own menu. A quick glance showed there were three choices for each course, rather like a set menu.

'I'm not that hungry, actually,' she murmured, still not looking up.

Rafe put down his menu. 'Look, I'm sorry, all right? I didn't mean to offend you.'

Now she did look up. 'Don't apologise. You're quite right. I don't think I do like who and what I am. I suspect I never have.'

'What rubbish. What's not to like, except the way you used to do your hair? I hated that. And it wasn't the real you at all.'

'The real me? And what's that, pray tell? Slut of the month?'

Rafe was truly taken aback, then annoyed with her. 'Don't you *dare* say that about yourself. So you're a sensual woman and enjoy sex. So what? That's nothing to be ashamed of.'

'If you say so,' she muttered unhappily.

'You should be jolly well proud of yourself. A lot of females would have folded after what you've been through just lately. But not you. You lifted your chin, squared your shoulders and went on. I might not agree with your decision to have a baby all alone, but I do admire the guts it took to make such a decision.'

Isabel was taken aback, both by his compliments and

his apparent sincerity. He liked her, and not just because she was good in bed.

'Good grief, Isabel, don't you ever go putting yourself down like that again. You have to be one of the most incredible women I've ever met, so stop that self-pitying nonsense and choose something to eat, or I'll lose patience with you and not even want to play sheikh to your harem girl at the end of the night.'

She laughed, her eyes sparkling with returned good humour. 'I knew I did right to ask you to come here with me. You are so…so…'

'Sensible?' he suggested when she couldn't find the right word.

She smiled. 'I was thinking more along the lines of refreshing.'

'Now, that's something I haven't been called before. Refreshing.'

'Take it as a compliment.'

'Oh, I will, don't worry.'

Her head tipped to one side as her eyes searched his face. 'You really are a nice man, Rafe Saint Vincent. And a very snazzy dresser. Love that black and white shirt. Can I borrow it some time?'

'You can borrow anything of mine you like. Sorry I can't return the compliment. I have a feeling I wouldn't look too good in any of your clothes.'

They were both smiling at each other when the waiter materialised by their side again with the champagne, which he duly poured, then asked if they'd like to order. Rafe did, with Isabel surrendering the choice to him, saying she liked the look of everything on the menu anyway and had recently used up all her decision-making powers.

He grinned and chose a Thai beef and noodle dish for an entrée and a grilled barramundi for the main, with a salad side plate.

'And mango cheesecake for dessert,' he finished up. 'We'll also be ordering more wine with each course. Do you have any half-bottles?'

'I'm sorry, sir, but we don't. However, you can order any of the wines listed by the glass.'

'Really? What happens to the rest of the bottle if no one else orders it?'

The waiter gave a small smirk as he whisked the menus away. 'It doesn't go to waste, sir. Be assured of that.'

'I'll bet,' Rafe said drily after the waiter departed. 'I'd like to be a fly on the wall of the kitchen every night after closing.'

'There are always perks to any job,' Isabel pointed out.

'Oh? And what were the perks of being a receptionist at a big city architectural firm?'

Isabel frowned. 'How did you know that was my job?'

'I found out when I rang Les and told him your wedding was off. We had quite a chat about you. He thinks you're a dish and wanted to know what I thought of you.'

'And you said?'

'I was suitably complimentary but discreet. Not a

word about this little jaunt, since it was obvious he knew your family fairly well.'

'Fancy that. Rafe Saint Vincent—the soul of discretion.'

'I have many hidden virtues.'

'Some not so hidden,' she said saucily.

'Naughty girl. But back to the original question. What perks were there in your job beside meeting multi-millionaire architects?'

'Not too many, actually. Free ball-point pens? And we won't count meeting Luke, since that didn't work out. I don't have to ask you what the perks of *your* job are. I've seen them on the walls of your office.'

Rafe frowned. 'What do you mean?'

'Oh, come now, lover, those photographs speak for themselves. They have foreplay written all over them.'

'You think I slept with all those women?'

'Didn't you?' Isabel picked up her crystal flute of champagne and began to sip.

'Heck, no. There were at least one or two who held out.'

Isabel spluttered into the glass.

'But they were lesbians.'

Isabel had to put down her glass.

'Stop it,' she choked out, and mopped up around her laughing mouth with her serviette.

'Would you like me to photograph you like that?'

Isabel swallowed. 'In the nude, you mean?'

'Good heavens, no. You saw my photographs. I never take full nudes. You can wear earrings, if you like. And those shoes.' One eyebrow arched wickedly as he peered at her sexily shod feet through the glass table. 'Oh yes, *definitely* those shoes.'

'You're teasing me.'

'Yep. I didn't bring my camera with me. Unfortunately.'

Thank Heaven, she thought. Because no doubt she would have let him photograph her *just* like that. Her behaviour with him since arriving on this island had been nothing short of outrageous.

'So!' she said, and swept up her champagne glass again. 'Tell me why you're opposed to my decision to have a baby alone.'

He smiled a wry smile. 'A change of subject, I presume. A wise move.' Just *thinking* about photographing her in nothing but earrings and those shoes was making him decidedly uncomfortable, especially since he was wearing rather tight jeans.

Rafe picked up his champagne, took a couple of sips and put his mind to answering her very pertinent question. If she hadn't brought up the subject of having a baby herself, he would have worked his way round to it. He hesitated to tell her what he *really* thought of her decision to have a baby alone by artificial insemination. She was determined anyway, and they'd just end up arguing. What he needed to know was the likelihood of her having conceived *his* child today.

'I just think it was a hasty decision, and one made on the rebound after Luke. You're still a young woman, Isabel, with well over a decade of baby-making capabilities left. You have more than enough time to find a suitable father for your baby before launching into motherhood alone. I think you should wait and see if he turns up.'

'Look, I told you. I tried finding Mr Right both with my heart and then my head and I bombed out both ways. No. I can't keep on waiting. And you're wrong about my having a lot of time. A woman might be theoretically capable of having a child right up until menopause, but the odds of her conceiving and carrying a healthy baby full term start to go downhill after she reaches thirty. No, Rafe, my biological clock is ticking and, knowing my luck, it's probably about to blow up. The time for action is now.'

Rafe had a bit of difficulty keeping a straight face. Little did Isabel know but the time for action might very well have been this afternoon!

'I see,' he muttered, dropping his eyes towards his champagne for a few seconds before looking up again. 'So if your marriage to Luke had gone ahead, you were planning to get pregnant pretty well straight away, then?'

Isabel sighed. 'Yes.'

'On this honeymoon?'

'Uh-huh. I had it all worked out, right to the very hour and the day.'

'Hard to pinpoint ovulation with that kind of accuracy, isn't it?'

'Not when you're as regular as I am, and when you've taken your temperature every day for three months.'

'And?' Rafe prompted. 'When would the critical time have been?'

'What? Oh, not till tomorrow, I think. Yes, Thursday. I do everything on a Thursday. Ovulate and get my period. Regular as clockwork, I am. Twenty-eight days on the dot. My girlfriends at work always used to envy the fact I was never taken by surprise, which was true. I used to pop into the loo at morning tea on P-day because I knew, come noon, the curse would arrive.'

'The curse?'

'That's what we women call it. You don't think it's a pleasure, do you? Oh, but this is a depressing topic. Would you mind if we changed the subject again? Let's talk about you.'

'Fine,' Rafe said, his head whirling. Thursday. Did sperm live for a full day? He was pretty sure it was possible, but she'd got up and had a shower soon afterwards. The odds weren't on his side.

Weren't on his side! Was he mad? He should have been relieved. He didn't really want to be a father, did he? *Did* he?

He looked at Isabel and realised he did. With her, anyway.

The realisation took his breath away.

He reefed his eyes away and stared down at the pool. Stared and stared and stared. And then his eyes flung wide. Who would have believed it?

'Rafe? Rafe, what's wrong? You look like you've seen a ghost or something.'

His gaze swung back to her and he almost laughed.

'I have. In a way. See that blonde frolicking down in the pool?'

'The one with the really big bazookas?'

'Yes, well she didn't have such big bazookas when I knew her. She must have had a boob job. Anyway, that's Liz—the girl I told you about. The one who dumped me.'

'Really?' Isabel was close enough to see the buxom blonde quite well, even better once she swam over and hauled herself up to sit on the edge of the pool. When she lifted her hands up to wring out her hair, her boobs looked like giant melons pressed together. Truly, they were enormous!

The grey-haired man she'd been canoodling with in the water climbed out via the ladder and walked over to where he'd left his towel. Whilst Liz looked in her late twenties, her companion was sixty if he was a day.

'Let's go, honey,' Isabel heard the man say with a salacious wink as he walked by. 'Time you earned your keep.'

'Coming, darls,' the blonde trilled back, though her face behind his back was less than enthusiastic.

'Is that the man she threw you over for?' Isabel asked, unable to keep the distaste out of her voice.

'No. I have no idea who that is, although I presume he's rich. No, the man Liz left me for was a fellow photographer. A more successful one at the time, though I'd heard rumours he had associations with some less than savoury video productions. I wondered what had become of Liz when I didn't see any more of her in the fashion world. I think the answer lies in those double D cups. A lot of models, especially ones who want fame and money too quickly, get sucked into doing things they shouldn't do. Pity. She could have been really someone. Instead, she's turned into *that*.' And he nodded towards the sight of her hurrying after her sugar-daddy, her gigantic breasts jiggling obscenely.

'You seem slightly sorry for her,' Isabel said, rather surprised.

'Oddly enough, I am.' He sounded surprised, too. 'Seeing her again, in the flesh so to speak, has given me a different perspective. And it's laid quite a few ghosts to rest.'

'You loved her a lot once, didn't you?'

'Yes. Yes, I did. Stupid, really. In hindsight, I can see she wasn't worth it, but love is blind, as they say.'

'I know exactly what you mean. I couldn't count the number of creeps and losers I've fallen for over the years. But, dear heaven, the last fellow I was involved with before Luke made the others look like saints. Still, I didn't know that when I first met him.'

'And where was that?'

'I was working my way around Australia and had taken this job as a salesgirl in a trendy little boutique on the Gold Coast which sold Italian shoes. One day, this sophisticated guy came in and I served him. He bought six pairs of shoes, just so he could spend more time with me, he said. Naturally, I was impressed.'

'Mmm. A bit naïve of you, Isabel, falling for a line like that.'

'That's me when I fall for a man. Naïve.'

'You weren't with me.'

'I was *attracted* to you, Rafe. I didn't fall for you.'

Terrific. Well, he'd asked for that one, hadn't he?

'So what happened next?'

'What do you think? He took me out to dinner that night, then straight home to bed afterwards.'

Rafe decided not to pursue that conversation further. He felt decidedly jealous of this Hal and his instant sexual success. Isabel had given him icicles the first day they'd met. Still, she *had* been a bride-to-be at that stage, and possibly still suffering from the once-bitten twice-shy syndrome after this fellow.

'So how did it end? Did he dump you?'

'No. Actually, he didn't. In a weird way I believe Hal did love me. As much as a man like that is capable of love. No, something happened and I could no longer pretend he was Mr Right.'

'Oh-oh, sounds like you found out he was already married.'

She laughed. 'If only it were as simple as that.'

'Now I'm seriously intrigued. What happened?'

'He was arrested. For drug importation and dealing. He got fifteen years.'

'Wow. And you never suspected?'

'Not for a moment. He didn't use drugs himself, and he never did any dealing in my presence. Even when he made numerous trips to Bangkok I didn't suspect. He said he was an importer. Of jewellery. I should have known by past experience that he was too good to be true, but as you said…love will make a fool of you every time. I thought all my dreams had come true. Hal was handsome, successful, exciting, masterful. Materially, he had it all as well. The mansion on the water. The car. The yacht. He swept me right off my feet, I can tell you. Told me he adored me. It was just a matter of time, I thought, till he proposed. I was on cloud nine till I picked up the paper one day and saw his photograph on the front page.'

'Must have been one bad day.'

'That's an understatement, I can assure you. I was devastated.'

'Did you have to testify at his trial?'

'No. Which was fortunate. Also fortunate that this all happened in another state. I hadn't told my parents about Hal, you see. But I was going to, once we were engaged. I thought he'd be a pleasant surprise after all the going-nowhere men I'd been with in the past. Some surprise he'd have turned out to be!'

'Just as well he was arrested when he was, then.'

'I didn't quite see it that way at the time,' Isabel muttered.

'No. Just as I didn't see I was better off without Liz. But we're both better off without both of them, Isabel. Much better off. And you're better off without Luke, no matter what you think now. He didn't love you.'

'Love I can do without from now on.'

Rafe looked at her. 'Oh, I don't know. Love still has a certain appeal.'

'I can't see what. It makes you do things. Stupid things. Irrational things.'

'Mmm. You could be right there.' Because for the next two days he was going to do the stupidest, most irrational things in his life!

'Where on earth is that food?' Isabel said irritably.

'It'll be here soon. Meanwhile, have some more champagne,' he added, and topped up her glass. 'Good, isn't it?'

'Yes. But if I don't eat soon it'll go straight to my head. I have a very low intoxication level with champagne. It can make me tipsy quicker than anything else.'

'Is that so? Well, there's no worry in being a bit tipsy, is there? It won't make you do anything later that you wouldn't be doing anyway.'

The eyes she set upon him over the rim of her glass were very dry. 'My, aren't we full of the sauce tonight?'

I hope so, Rafe thought ruefully. Because my sauce is going to have to work very hard to do the job from now on. He didn't dare cut the whole top off every condom he used during the next two days. She might notice. He really could only risk a pin-prick or two. Except perhaps tonight…

Isabel's powers of observation could very well be limited if she got well and truly sloshed. If he was clever with what position he used, he might get away with not using anything at all.

The thought excited, then worried him.

It was a stupid thing to do, as she said. Stupid and irrational. She didn't love him. She wouldn't marry him.

At best, he would be a father to their child at a distance, having limited access.

But so what? he thought recklessly. He was still going to do it, wasn't he?

CHAPTER ELEVEN

ISABEL woke with a moan on her lips. The sun was shining in through the open doorway of the bure, indicating Rafe was already up, probably having his early-morning swim.

'That man must have a constitution of iron,' she muttered as she dragged aside the mosquito net and tried to sit up. But the room spun alarmingly and there was a bongo drummer—complete with drums—inside her head.

With a low groan, Isabel sank back carefully onto the pillows then ever so slowly rolled onto her side. The room gradually stopped spinning.

It was then that she saw the tall glass of water sitting next to the bed, alongside a foil sheet of painkillers.

'What a thoughtful thing to do,' she murmured, though not yet daring to move. In a minute she would take a couple of those pills Rafe had left her. Meanwhile, she would close her eyes and just do nothing.

Isabel closed her eyes and tried to do nothing, but her mind was by now wide awake. She began thinking about last night after dinner. In the end, they hadn't got anyone else to run them back to their jetty. Rafe had said he was fine to operate the boat and she'd been far too tipsy to worry.

Tipsy! Hardly an adequate word to describe her state of intoxication. She'd been seriously sloshed. Not Rafe though, yet he'd consumed as many glasses of wine as she had. Or had he? Perhaps not. He'd talked a lot between courses, and she'd just sat there, sipping her wine and listening to him like some fatuous female fool, thinking how gorgeous he was and how stupid Liz was to dump him.

No, Isabel finally conceded. Rafe hadn't consumed nearly as much wine as she had. If he had, he wouldn't have been able to make such beautiful love to her as he had after they'd come home.

Not that she could remember it all. Some bits were pretty hazy. But she could remember the feel of his hands on her as he undressed her and caressed her. So gentle and tender. The same with his kisses. His mouth had flowed all over her and she had dissolved from one orgasm to another.

She'd never known climaxes could be like that. Blissful and relaxing. Her bones had felt like water by the time he'd rolled her onto her side, rather like she was lying now. Only last night Rafe's naked body had been curled around her back.

Isabel's stomach contracted at the thought. That was one thing she hadn't forgotten. How he'd felt when he'd first slipped inside her. She moaned at the memory. It had felt so good. Even better when he'd begun to move.

Never had she been so lost in a man's arms, her mind and body like mush. She hadn't come again. But, Rafe must have. She had a vague recollection of his crying out. But after that, all memory ceased. She must have fallen asleep. And now here she was the next morning with a parched mouth and a vicious headache, whilst Rafe was down at the beach, no doubt bright-eyed and bushy-tailed.

A shadow fell across the corner of her eye and she rolled over just enough to see Rafe walk through the sun-drenched doorway. His dark silhouette eventually lightened to reveal that she'd been right. He had been swimming, thankfully dressed in board shorts. She couldn't cope with him in full-frontal nudity this morning.

'How's the head?' he said as he walked towards the bed.

'Awful. Many thanks for the tablets and the water.'

'My pleasure. And it *was*,' he added with a devilish grin.

'Don't be cocky. I was pretty plastered.'

'So I noticed. You know you're very agreeable when you're plastered.'

'I really couldn't say. Last night is somewhat hazy.'

'You mean you can't remember anything?'

Isabel caught an odd note in Rafe's question. Was he pleased or offended? 'I didn't say that. I said hazy, as in…hazy.'

'Ahh. Hazy. Hazy word, hazy.'

'You were pretty good, if that's what you're waiting for.'

He smiled. 'That's nice to hear.'

'Different, though.'

Rafe's stomach flipped over. 'Different?' he asked, trying not to panic. 'In what way, different?'

She shrugged. 'Gentler. Sweeter. Different.'

Rafe smiled his relief. 'Well, I didn't need to rush it. You weren't making any of your usual control-losing demands.'

Isabel was taken aback. 'What do you mean, control-losing demands?'

'Honey, you have a very impatient nature when it comes to sex. It's always faster, Rafe. Harder. Deeper. Again. More. No more. Stop. Don't stop. The list is endless.'

'That's not true!' she denied hotly.

'Perhaps a slight exaggeration on my part. But it was still a rather nice change to know I could take my time and do exactly what I wanted to do with your total co-operation. I really enjoyed it.'

And how! Rafe thought.

Any apprehension over his bold decision not to use any protection had disappeared once he'd put his plans into action. Knowing that a child could possibly result from his lovemaking had added an emotional dimension Rafe hadn't anticipated. When he'd felt his seed spilling into her he'd thought his heart would burst with elation. And when she'd gone to sleep in his arms afterwards he'd been consumed by feelings so powerful and deep that they'd revolutionised his ideas on what loving a person was all about.

Seeing Liz last night was the best thing that could have happened to him. What a fool he'd been, choosing a solitary life for fear of being hurt again. Fair enough to withdraw into his cave for a while. But it had been years, for pity's sake. Years of keeping women at a distance, except sexually, and telling himself—and everyone else—that he didn't want marriage and a family, when the truth was he'd become too much of a coward to risk his male ego a second time. He'd been afraid of being dumped again, afraid of rejection.

Not any more. He was going to take a leaf out of Isabel's book and go after what he wanted. Which was *her* as his wife as well as the mother of his child. Or children. Heck, he wasn't going to stop at just one. He'd hated being an only child.

But he couldn't tell her all that yet. He couldn't even tell her how much he loved her. She wasn't ready for such an announcement. But she would be, in time. And when Mother Nature eventually took her course.

It was to be hoped that last night had done the trick. But if it hadn't, he'd already doctored a few more condoms for today. If at first you don't succeed, Rafe, then try, try again.

Trying again had never looked so pleasurable. Pity she had a hangover. Still, that would pass.

'God, I can't stand people looking perky when I'm dying,' Isabel grumbled.

'What you need is a refreshing swim,' Rafe suggested.

She groaned. 'My head is already swimming, thank you very much. Do you think I could con you into getting me a cup of coffee?'

He jumped up off the foot of the bed. 'One steaming mug of sweet black coffee coming up!'

Isabel groaned again. Not only perky, but energetic. He even started whistling.

Still, she had to concede Rafe wasn't anything like she'd first thought. Oh, she didn't doubt he was a bit of a ladies' man. And marriage and children were not part of his life plan. But he wasn't at all arrogant, or selfish. He was actually quite considerate, and highly sensitive. That Liz female had really hurt him, stupid greedy amoral woman that she was.

His dad's death had scarred him as well. Isabel had been moved last night when Rafe had told her how his father had been a country rep for a wine company, travelling all over New South Wales, selling his products into hotels and clubs and restaurants. Rafe had been just eight when his dad's car had hit a kangaroo at night and careered off the road into a tree, killing him instantly. Unfortunately, his father hadn't been a great success as a salesman—a bit of a dreamer, though in the nicest possible way—and money had been tight for his widow and son after his demise.

But he'd been a great success as a dad. Clearly, Rafe had adored him. His voice had choked up when he'd told Isabel that the only things his father had left him in a material sense were a camera and a pair of phantom's-head cuff-links. Father and son had had a real thing for the Phantom, his Dad always bringing Rafe home a *Phantom Comic* after he'd been away. They would always read it together that night. Isabel had been moved to hear that, when one of the prized cuff-links had been lost during a house move Rafe had had the other made into an earring and never took it off for fear of losing it as well. How he must have loved that man!

It was a pity he shied away from being a father himself. With his dad's example to go by, he'd probably be a very good one.

She sighed. That was the incorrigible romantic in her talking again. Next thing she'd have him returning with her coffee and saying he'd changed his mind about what he wanted in life, after which he'd declare his undying love and beg her to marry him.

Fat chance!

'Here's your coffee, lover. Now, stop all that sighing and drink up. Oh, for pity's sake, you haven't even taken your headache tablets yet. Or drunk the water. How do you expect to feel better unless you rehydrate yourself? No, no coffee for you till you've done the right thing. And there'll be no more drinking to excess in future. It's no good for you.'

Isabel glared at him. 'And there I was, thinking you weren't the bullying bossy pain in the neck I'd first met. But I was deluding myself. The only reason you want me to feel better is so that you can have more of what you got last night.'

He grinned the cheekiest sexiest grin. 'You could be right there.'

Isabel glowered at him as she popped two tablets into her mouth and swallowed the water.

'A shower or the sea?' he said, eyeing her rather salaciously where the sheet had slipped down to her waist.

Isabel didn't have to look down to know what he was seeing. Maybe *she* wasn't too perky this morning, but her nipples still were.

And she was so wet down there it wasn't funny.

'I think a spa bath is in order,' she said. 'Alone,' she added firmly.

'I could scrub your back,' Rafe offered.

'No.'

'Spoilsport.'

'And then, after breakfast, I'd like to do something unenergetic. I noticed there was a pack of cards in the cupboard over there.'

'Cards,' he repeated drily. He hated playing cards. His mother was a fanatic at euchre and cribbage, and used to rope him in when she couldn't find another partner. She always won so there hadn't been much fun in it for him.

'There's plenty of other games in there as well, if you'd prefer,' she went on, no doubt hearing his reluctance.

Rafe eyed her with determination. The only games he aimed to play today were those of the erotic kind. He couldn't afford to waste the whole of this very critical twenty-four hours. She might be ovulating at this very second.

But then an idea came to him.

'Okay,' he agreed. 'But, to make it interesting, let's bet on the outcome of each game.'

She frowned. 'For money, you mean?'

'Don't be silly. What would be the fun in that?'

'What, then?'

'If I win, you have to do whatever I want. And vice versa.'

Her eyes widened. 'Are we talking sexual requests here?'

'Not necessarily. I might ask you to go for a swim with me. Or cook me a meal. Or give me a massage.'

Yeah, right, she thought ruefully.

'I won't agree to *anything*, Rafe, especially sexually. There has to be limitations.'

'Nothing too kinky, then. Nothing you think the other person wouldn't like.'

That was far too broad a canvas! 'I…I don't want to be tied to that hammock again.' Not in the daylight. That would be just too embarrassing for words.

'Fair enough. What would you rather be tied to?'

'Rafe!'

'Only kidding.' Hell, he didn't want to tie her up. He just wanted to make her a mother.

Isabel could feel the heat spreading all through her body. This was just the kind of thing which turned her on. Oh, he was wicked.

'Let me have that bath and some breakfast first, then,' she said, trying not to sound too eager. 'You find whatever game you think you would prefer.' And hopefully one that he was darned good at playing. Because she didn't want to win, did she? She wanted him to win.

He chose an ingenious little game called Take It Easy,

and by eleven they were sitting on the terrace, playing. The trouble was luck rather than skill played a large part and, even if you didn't try, sometimes you still won. Each game didn't last all that long and the rules suggested you play three games then totalled up the scores to see who won.

Isabel won the first round, by one point, despite not concentrating at all.

'Oh,' she said, trying not to sound disappointed by the result.

Rafe eyed her expectantly across the table. 'Well? What cruel fate awaits me, oh, mistress mine?'

'You said nothing kinky,' she reminded him.

'No, I said nothing *too* kinky.'

'You also said it didn't have to be a sexual request.' Surely she would lose next time and then she would be forced to do what *he* wanted. That would be much more fun. She would wait. 'So I'd like a toasted ham, cheese and tomato sandwich, please. And a tall glass of iced orange juice.'

'What?' he snapped, his face frustrated. 'You just had breakfast half an hour ago.'

'I'm sorry but I'm still hungry,' she said blithely.

When he just sat there, scowling at her, she crossed her arms. 'Are you welching on your bet already?'

'You'll keep, madam,' he muttered, then went to do her bidding.

Five minutes later he returned with the sandwich on a plate and a very tall glass of frosted orange juice. The fridge and freezer really were very well stocked, especially with the ingredients for easy-to-make snacks. Honeymooners and illicit lovers—who were the likely bookers of the private bures—apparently didn't surface back at the main resort for meals all that often.

Isabel accepted the toasted sandwich and ate it very slowly, pretending to savour every bite. In actual fact, she wasn't at all hungry. She just hadn't been able to think of anything else to ask for. The orange juice was nice, though, and she drank it down with deep gulps. Her hangover had long receded but she was still probably a bit dehydrated.

'Ahh,' she said, and placed the empty glass on the empty plate, pushing them both to one side. 'That was lovely, Rafe. Thank you. Shall we get on with the next round?'

'By all means.'

Rafe won. Easily.

'Oh, dear,' Isabel said.

'My turn, it seems,' Rafe said with cool satisfaction in his voice, and a smouldering look in his eyes.

Isabel began to tremble inside.

'Take off your sarong,' he commanded.

When he didn't add anything else, she just looked at him. 'That's it? Just take off my sarong?'

'Yes. Do you have a problem with that?'

She gulped. It was far less than she was expecting. And yet…

It suddenly hit her that he meant for her to sit there, playing the next round of the game, in the nude. The deviousness of his mind excited her, as did the idea.

Isabel felt her blood begin to charge around her veins as she stood up and slowly undid the knot which tied her sarong between her breasts. Their eyes met and she was just about to drop it down onto the terracotta flagstones when the phone rang.

'Leave it,' Rafe commanded thickly. 'It's probably just Reception wanting to know if we want a picnic lunch brought over.'

Isabel tried to do what he said. Tried to ignore it. But she couldn't, especially when it just kept on ringing.

'I can't,' she blurted out and, retying the sarong, she hurried in to answer it.

'Hello,' she said breathlessly.

'Isabel?'

'Rachel!'

'I'm so s…sorry to bother you,' she cried, her voice shaking.

'Rachel, what's wrong?'

'It's Lettie. She…she's gone, Isabel.'

'You mean…passed away?'

'She wandered out of the house a couple of nights back when I was asleep and got a chill. She…she wasn't wearing any clothes, you see. She often took them off. Anyway, by the time I realised she was gone and the police found her, wandering in some park, she was shivering from the cold and it quickly developed into pneumonia. Her doctor put her in hospital and pumped her full of antibiotics, and they said she was going to be all right, but last night she…she had a heart attack and they couldn't save her.'

'Oh, Rachel, I'm so sorry.'

'You know, I thought I'd be relieved if and when she died,' she choked out. 'You've no idea what it's been like. The endless days and nights. The utter misery and futility of it all. Because I knew she'd never get better. She was only going to get worse. And worse. I used to lie in bed some nights and hope she wouldn't wake up in the morning. But now that she has died, I…I'm not relieved at all. I'm devastated. I look at her empty bed and just cry and cry and cry. I…I can't function, Isabel. I needed to talk to you. That's why I had to call. I needed to hear your voice and know that somewhere in this world there was someone who loved me.' At that, she broke down and wept.

'It's all right, Rachel. I'll ring Mum and Dad straight away and get them to go and bring you home to their place. And I'll be back in Sydney as soon as I can.'

'But…but you can't,' she cried, pulling herself together. 'Your mum will know, if you do that.'

'Know what?'

'That you didn't go to Dream Island with me. She'll know you went with…with some man.'

'Oh, never mind that. What does that matter? So she'll think I'm wicked for a while. She'll get over it. Now, you hang in there, Rach, and don't go doing anything silly.'

'Such as what?' Rachel sniffled.

'Such as drinking too much of Lettie's sherry. Or sleeping with the gardener.'

'I don't have a gardener,' she said mournfully. 'But

if I did I would sleep with him, no matter what he looked like. I'm so lonely, Isabel.'

'Not for long, sweetie. Just hang in there. I'll ring Mum straight away and get her to ring you.'

'All right.'

'You are home, aren't you?'

'What? Yes, yes, I'm home.'

Isabel's heart turned over. The poor darling. She sounded shattered. 'Okay, don't go anywhere till Mum rings you.'

'Where would I go?'

'I don't know. Shopping, perhaps. Or back to the hospital.'

'I don't want to ever go near that hospital ever again.' And she started to weep again.

'Oh, Rachel, please don't cry. You'll make me cry.' Isabel's chin was already beginning to quiver.

'S…sorry,' Rachel blubbered. 'Sorry.'

Isabel swallowed. 'Don't be sorry. Don't you ever be sorry. I'll try to get a flight back today. At worst, it will be tomorrow. Meanwhile, you do just what Mum tells you to do. She'll bombard you with cups of sweet tea and plate-loads of home-made lamingtons but don't say no. You could do with fattening up a bit. Do you realise you've lost most of those fantastic boobs of yours? You know, I used to be jealous of those at school. You've no idea. But they'll bounce back. And so will you, love. Trust me on that.'

'I knew I was right to ring you,' Rachel said with a not so distressed-sounding sigh.

'If you hadn't, I'd have been very annoyed. Now, I must go. Loads to do. See you soon, sweetie. Take care.'

Isabel hung up with a weary sigh. Rachel was right about one thing. Her mother was not going to be pleased with her little deception over this holiday.

But that was just too bad. Squaring her shoulders, Isabel swept the receiver up again, and asked Reception for an outside line.

'I gather the honeymoon's over.'

Isabel spun round to find Rafe standing in the doorway.

'How much did you hear?'

'All of it.'

'Then you know I have to go home. You can stay for the rest of the fortnight if you want to.'

He stared at her as though she were mad. 'Now, why would I want to do that? Without you here with me, Isabel, it would just be a waste of time. No, I'll be coming back to Sydney with you. If you find there aren't any available seats going back this afternoon, you could have Reception offer the rest of this pre-paid jaunt to all the couples on the island whose holiday ends today. Someone is sure to take you up on it.'

'That's an excellent idea, Rafe. Thank you.'

'I am good for some things besides sex, you know.'

Isabel frowned at the slightly bitter edge in his voice. What had got into him? Did he think she was happy about having to leave?

'Look, I'm sorry, Rafe. I hardly planned this. I'd rather be staying here with you than going back home to a heartbroken friend. But fate has decided otherwise. Rachel needs me and she needs me *now*. I'm not going to let her down.'

'I appreciate that. Honest I do. I admire people who are there for their friends when they're needed. I guess that's the crux of my discontent. The fact you didn't consider I'd be there for *you* during the next few undeniably difficult days. You just dismissed me like some hired gigolo whose services were no longer required. I thought we'd moved beyond that. I thought you genuinely liked me.'

'I…I do like you. But what we've had together here… We both knew it was just a fantasy trip, Rafe. It's been fantastic but it's not real life. Come on the plane with me by all means, but once we get back to Sydney I think we should go our separate ways.'

'Do you, now?' he bit out. 'Well, I don't.'

'You don't?'

'No. As far as what we've had here… Yes, it has been fantastic, but I think we can have something better once we get back to Sydney. And we can be good friends as well.'

'But…'

'But nothing. You like me. I like you. A lot. On top of that, we are very sexually compatible. Face it, Isabel, you're not the sort of woman who's ever going to live the life of a nun. You like sex far too much. So don't look a gift-horse in the mouth. Where else are you going to find a man who's prepared to be your friend as well as your lover? A man, moreover, who knows how to turn you on just like that.' And he snapped his fingers. 'You'll go a long way before you come across that combination again.'

He was right, of course. He was ideal.

Too ideal. She was sure to fall hopelessly in love with him. Sure to. But she hadn't as yet. She could still walk away.

But then she thought of what Rachel had said about being so lonely that she'd sleep with anyone, and she knew she wouldn't be able to walk away for ever. One night, when she was alone in that town house at Turramurra, she'd pick up the phone and call Rafe and ask him to come over.

Take what he's offering you now, came the voice of temptation. And if you fall in love with him?

She would cross that bridge when she came to it.

'So you want to be my day-time friend and night-time lover, is that it?'

'No. I want to be your friend *and* lover all the time. I see no reason to relegate our sex life just to night.'

An erotic quiver rippled down her spine. She didn't stand a chance of resisting this man. Why damage her pride by trying? But that same pride insisted she keep some control over the relationship. She could do that, surely.

'You're so right, Rafe,' she said, adopting what she hoped was a suitably firm woman-in-control expression. 'Things *have* worked out between us far better than I ever imagined they would. You're exactly what I need in my life. But please don't presume that my agreeing to continue with our relationship gives you any rights to tell me how to run my life. I know you don't agree with my decision to have a baby on my own, but I aim to do just that, and nothing and no one is going to stop me!'

CHAPTER TWELVE

RAFE sat silently beside Isabel on the flight to Sydney late that afternoon, planning and plotting his next move.

He'd been furious with fate at first for interrupting them. But, in the end, things hadn't worked out too badly. Isabel had at least agreed to go on seeing him. As for her declaration that nothing and no one was going to stop her from having a baby…little did she know but he was her best ally in that quest. He hoped to have her pregnant well before she got round to doing that artificial insemination rubbish.

The captain announcing that they'd begun their descent into Sydney had Isabel turning towards him for the first time in ages.

'I'll drop you off on the way home,' she said.

'Fine. What about tomorrow?'

'What about tomorrow?'

'Will you be needing me?'

She stared at him. 'I thought you said you didn't like my treating you like some gigolo,' she said agitatedly. 'That was a rather gigolo-sounding question.'

'I meant as a friend, Isabel,' he reproved, thinking to himself he had a long way to go to get her trust. That bastard Hal had a lot to answer for.

'Oh. Sorry. I'm not used to men just wanting to be my friend.'

'I thought you said you were friends with Luke first.'

'Yes, well, Luke was the exception to the rule.'

'St Luke,' he muttered.

'Not quite, as it turned out.'

'No. So what about tomorrow?'

She sighed. 'I think I should spend tomorrow with Rachel.'

Rafe had no option but to accept her decision. Which meant if she hadn't conceived this month he'd have to wait till her next cycle before trying again.

Still, he admired Isabel for the way she'd dropped everything and raced to this Rachel's side. There weren't too many people these days who would have done that. He liked to think he was a good friend, but he suspected he'd become somewhat selfish and self-centred during his post-Liz years, another result of his bruised male ego which he wasn't proud of.

'What about the next day?' he asked.

'The funeral's then.'

'I'll take you.'

'No.'

'*Yes*. I'm not going to let you hide me away like some nasty secret, Isabel. Your mother already knows you went off to Dream Island with a man. I heard you tell her on the phone. I also gather you took quite a bit of flak about it. I didn't like that. In fact, I wanted to snatch that phone right out of your hand and tell your mother the truth.'

'The…the truth?'

'Yes. You are *not* cheap or easy, which I gather was the gist of her insults. You are one classy lady and I'm one lucky guy to be having a relationship with you. You're also a terrific friend and, I'll warrant, a terrific daughter. Someone should tell your mum that some day, and that someone just might be me.'

'That's sweet of you, Rafe, but you'd be wasting your time. Mum suffers from a double generation gap. She's still living back in the fifties and simply can't come to terms with the fact I'd go away with you like that so soon after meeting you. She was not only shocked, but ashamed.'

'Sounds like she suffers from double standards as well,' Rafe pointed out irritably. 'I'll bet she wasn't shocked when she found out your precious ex-fiancé leapt into bed with his new dolly-bird less than an hour after meeting her. And I'll bet she thought that was perfectly all right!'

'No. No, I don't think she thought that at all. It's hard for her to accept modern ways, Rafe. She's seventy years old.'

'That's no excuse.'

'No, but it's a reason. She'll calm down eventually. Meanwhile, I think it's best not to throw you in her face.'

'Isabel,' he said firmly, '*you* are *thirty* years old. Way past the age of adulthood. You say you're going to live your life as you see fit. Well that should include in front of your mother.'

'That's all very well for you to say. You don't practise what you preach. You told me you lie to your mother all the time. You even pretend you're going to get married some day when you know very well that you're not.'

'That's all in the past. I'm going to be honest with her in future.' No trouble, Rafe thought. Because he *was* going to get married now. To Isabel.

'Yeah, right. Pity I won't be there to see the new-leaf Rafe.'

You will be. Don't you worry about that.

'I'm coming with you to that funeral, Isabel. And that's that!'

Isabel glared at him. The man simply couldn't be told!

'Be it on your head then,' she snapped. 'And don't say I didn't warn you.'

By five o-clock on the day of the funeral, Rafe almost wished he'd heeded her warning. The service was over and they were back at Isabel's parents' place for the wake, and he was looking for a place to hide.

Unfortunately, there weren't too many people for Rafe to hide behind. It had been a very small funeral. Isabel and Rachel, whom Rafe had warmed to on first meeting today, had been cornered by some large woman, leaving Rafe to fend for himself.

The chill coming his way from Mrs Hunt was becoming hard to take, so were the disapproving looks at his earring. Goodness knew what would have been the woman's reaction if he hadn't shaved that morning. Or put on his one and only dark and thankfully conservatively styled suit.

Rafe valiantly ignored the dagger-like glances he was getting from his hostess as he filled his plate from the buffet set out in the lounge room. After checking that Isabel and Rachel were still occupied in the corner, he headed out to the front porch, where he'd seen a seat on the way in, and where he hoped to eat his food in peace, without having to tolerate Mrs Hunt's deadly glares.

But fate was not going to be kind. He'd barely sat down when she followed him through the front door and marched over to stand in front of him. Rafe looked up from the plate he'd just balanced on his lap, keeping his face impassive despite his instantly thudding heart.

Formidable was the word which came to mind to describe Isabel's mother. Handsome, though. She would have been a fine-looking woman when she was younger. Though she did look trapped in a time warp, her grey hair permed into very tight waves and curls, and her belted floral dress with its pleated skirt reflecting a bygone era.

'Mr Saint Vincent…' she began, then hesitated, not because she didn't know what she was going to say, Rafe reckoned, but because she wanted to make him feel uncomfortable.

Her strategy worked. But be damned if he was going to let it show.

'Yes, Mrs Hunt?' he returned coolly, picking up a sandwich from the plate and taking a bite.

'Might I have a little word with you in private?'

He shrugged. 'We're perfectly alone here, so feel free to go for it.'

Her top lip curled. 'That's rather the catch cry of your generation, isn't it?' she sneered. 'Feeling free to go for whatever you want.'

'Good, isn't it? Better than being all uptight and hypocritical, like your generation.'

'How dare you?' she exclaimed, her cheeks looking as if they'd been dabbed with rouge.

'How dare *you*, Mrs Hunt? I am a guest in your home. Are you always this rude to your guests?'

'I have every right to be rude to a man who's taking wicked advantage of my daughter.'

'You think that's what I'm doing?'

'I know that's what you're doing. Isabel would never normally go off like that with some man she'd only just met. You knew she was on the rebound. But that didn't stop you, did it?'

Rafe decided to nip this in the bud once and for all. He figured he had nothing to lose, anyway. 'No,' he agreed, putting his plate down on the seat beside him and standing up, brushing his hands of crumbs as he did so. 'No, it didn't stop me, Mrs Hunt. And I'll tell you why. Because I'm in love with your daughter. I have been ever since the first moment we met. I love her and I want to marry her.'

The woman's eyes almost popped out of her head.

'Of course, I haven't told her this yet,' he went on. 'She's not ready for it. She won't be ready for it for a while, because at this moment her trust in the male sex is so low that she simply won't believe me. She, like you, thinks I'm only with her for the sex. Which is not true.'

'You mean you're…you're *not* sleeping with her?'

Rafe had to smile. 'Now, ma'am, let's not get our wires crossed here. I didn't say that. I *am* a man, not a eunuch. And your daughter is *very* beautiful. But Isabel has much more to offer a man than just sex. She's one very special lady with a special brand of pride and courage. It's a shame her own mother doesn't recognise that fact.'

'But I *do*! Why, I think she's just wonderful.'

'Funny. I get the impression you haven't told her that too often. Or at all. I gather she thinks you think she's some kind of slut.'

'I do not think anything of the kind! The very idea!'

'Well, she must have got that idea from somewhere. Get with it, Mrs Hunt, or you just might lose your daughter altogether. She's a woman of independent means now and doesn't need you to put a roof over her head. She doesn't need your constant criticisms and disapproval either.'

'But… But… Oh, dear, me and my big mouth again…'

She looked so stricken that Rafe was moved to some sympathy for her. Perhaps he'd been a bit harsh. But someone had to stand up for Isabel. None of the men in her past had, least of all St bloody Luke!

'She needs you to love her unconditionally,' he went on more gently. 'Not just when she's doing what *you* think is right. Because what you think is right, Mrs Hunt, just might be wrong. And please…don't tell her what I said about being in love with her. If you do, you'll ruin everything.'

'You really love her?'

'More than I would ever have thought possible. I'm going to marry your daughter, Mrs Hunt. It's only a question of time.'

Her joy blinded him. 'Oh. Oh, that's wonderful news. I've been so worried for her. All her life, all she's ever wanted was to get married and…and… Oh, dear…' She broke off and gnawed at her bottom lip for a few seconds, worrying the life out of Rafe. What now?

'You do know Isabel wants a baby very badly, don't you?' she finally went on. 'That won't be a problem, will it? I know a lot of men these days aren't so keen on having children.'

Rafe smiled his relief. 'Not a problem at all, Mrs Hunt. Hopefully, it's the solution.'

'The solution?' She looked mystified for a moment. But then the clouds cleared from her astute grey eyes. 'Oh,' she said, nodding and smiling. 'Oh, I see.'

'I trust Isabel will have your full approval and support if I'm successful in my plan? You won't start judging and throwing verbal stones again.'

'You can depend on me, Rafe.'

'That's great, Mrs Hunt.'

'Dot. Call me Dot.'

'Dot.' He grinned at her. 'Wish me luck, Dot.'

'You won't need too much luck, you sexy devil.'

'Dot! I'm shocked.'

'I'm not too old that I can't see what Isabel sees in you. But I'm not so sure that not telling her you love her is the right tactic.'

'Trust me, Dot. It is.'

'If you say so. Heavens, I have to confess you've surprised me. Look, I'd better go inside or Isabel might come out and catch us together, and she might start asking awkward questions. She thinks I don't like you.'

'Gee. I wonder what gave her that idea?'

Dot's fine grey eyes sparkled with a mixture of guilt and good humour. 'You are a cheeky young man too, aren't you?'

'Go lightly on the young, Dot. I'm over thirty.'

She laughed. 'That's young to me. But I take your point and I'll try to get with it, as you said.'

Dot was not long gone and Rafe had just sat down again to finish his food when Isabel burst out onto the porch. 'I've been looking for you. Mum said you were out here. What on earth did you say to her just now?'

'Nothing much.' Rafe hoped his face was a lot calmer than his insides. The more time he spent with Isabel the more hopelessly in love with her he was. And the more desperate for all his plans to succeed. 'Why?'

'Well, she actually smiled at me and told me how much she liked you. You could have knocked me over with a feather. She's been giving you killer looks all day, then suddenly she *likes* you? You must have said something.'

'I told her she had a wonderful daughter and I was going to marry you.'

Isabel blinked, stared, then burst out laughing. 'You *didn't*!'

'I did, indeed.'

'Oh, Rafe, you're wicked. First you lie to your mother about getting married, and now to mine. Still, it worked.'

Rafe almost told her then. Told her it wasn't a lie, that he was crazy about her and did want to marry her. But it simply was too premature for such declarations.

'How's Rachel coping?' he asked, deftly changing the subject.

'Not too bad, actually. Did you see that woman we were talking to?'

'The one built like a battleship?'

'That's the one. Her name's Alice McCarthy and Rachel does alterations for her. Did I tell you that's how Rachel's been making some money at home?'

'Yes, I think you did mention it.'

'She's a darned good dressmaker, too, but alterations pay better and take less time. Anyway, Alice has this son. His name's Justin.'

'Oh, no, not another match-making mother. Poor Rachel. She's deep in grief and some old battleaxe is already lining her up for her son.'

'Oh, do stop being paranoid. And Alice is not a battle-axe. She's very sweet. Anyway, this Justin doesn't want a wife. He wants a secretary. As for Rachel being in grief, she needs to get out and about as quickly as possible, otherwise she'll get even more lonely and depressed than she already is. A job is ideal. She'll have to interview, of course, but Alice is going to twist her son's arm to at least give her a go for a while.'

'That's nice of her, but can Rachel do the job? Has she ever been a secretary before?'

'Has she ever been a secretary before!' Isabel scoffed. 'I'll have you know that Rachel was a finalist in the Secretary of the Year award one year. Of course, that was a few years ago, and she has lost a bit of confidence since then, but nothing which can't be put to right with some boosting up from her friends.'

'Mmm. Tell me about this Alice's son. What does he do for a crust?'

'He's some high-flying executive in the city. One of those companies with fingers in lots of pies. Insurance. Property development. You know the kind of thing.'

'What happened to his present secretary? He must have one.'

'The story goes that she suddenly resigned last month. Flew over to England a few weeks back for her niece's wedding, realised how homesick she was for her mother country, came back just to get her things, and quit. He's been making do with a temp but he's not thrilled. Says she's far too flashy-looking and far too flirtatious. He can't concentrate on his work.'

'My heart goes out to him,' Rafe said drily. 'Still, I guess his wife might not be pleased.'

'He's divorced.'

'What's his problem, then?'

Isabel sighed. She should have known a man like Rafe

wouldn't see a problem. If he was in the same position, he'd just have the girl on his desk every lunchtime and not think twice about it.

'Office romances are never a good idea, Rafe,' she tried explaining. 'This is something you might not appreciate, since you don't work in a traditional office. *And* since you're not female. If a female employee has an affair with a male colleague, especially her boss, it's always the girl who ends up getting the rough end of the pineapple.'

He laughed. 'What a delicate way of putting it.'

Isabel rolled her eyes with utter exasperation. 'Truly. Must you always put a sexual connotation on everything?'

'Honey, I'm not the one putting a sexual connotation on this. This divorced bloke thinks his sexy temp has the hots for him and he doesn't like it. Rather makes you wonder why. Is he mentally deranged? Otherwise involved? Gay? Or just bitter and twisted?'

'Maybe he's the kind of man who doesn't like mixing business with pleasure. Unlike *some* men we know.'

'Man's a fool. He's got it made by the sound of it. Still, Rachel should suit him. She's hardly what you'd call flashy. *Or* flirtatious.' More like shy and retiring. Sweet, though. Rafe really liked her.

'No, not at the moment. But she used to be very outgoing. And drop-dead gorgeous.'

'Mmm. Hard to visualise.' The Rachel he'd met today had been a long way from drop-dead gorgeous. Okay, so there were some lingering remnants of past beauty in her thin face and gaunt body. Her eyes certainly had something.

But the hardships of minding a loved one with Alzheimer's twenty-four hours a day for over four years had clearly taken its toll. Isabel had told him Rachel was only thirty-one. But she looked forty if she was a day.

'She just needs some tender loving care,' Isabel said.

'And a serious makeover,' Rafe added. 'New hair colour. Clothes. Make-up.'

'Don't be ridiculous, Rafe. Haven't you been listening? This man doesn't want a glamour-puss for a secretary. He wants a woman who looks sensible and who doesn't turn him on.'

'Oh, yeah, I forgot. Better get her a pair of glasses then, because she has got nice eyes.'

'Yes, she does, doesn't she?'

'And get her to put on a few pounds. That anorexic look she's sporting is considered pretty desirable nowadays.'

'Are you being sarcastic?'

'Not at all. Oh, and tell her to wear black for the interview. It looks bloody awful on her. Unlike you, my darling,' he whispered in her ear, 'who looks so sexy in black that it's criminal.'

'Stop that,' Isabel choked out, shivering when he began to blow softly in her ear.

But she didn't really want him to stop. It felt like an eon since they'd been alone together, since he'd held her in his arms. She was going to go mad if she wasn't with him soon.

'Stay with me tonight,' he murmured.

'I…I can't,' she groaned. 'I'm taking Rachel home to Turramurra with me for a few days. I don't want to leave her alone just yet.'

'When, then?'

'I don't know. I'll give you a call.'

Rafe didn't want to press. But he wanted her so much. He *needed* her. And it had nothing to do with getting her pregnant.

Being in love, he decided, was hell, especially if the person you loved didn't love you back.

And she didn't. Not yet. No use pretending she did.

It was a depressing thought. The confidence which Rafe had projected to Isabel's mother suddenly seemed like so much hot air. What if she never fell in love with him? What if she never fell pregnant to him?

Then he would have nothing.

She had to fall pregnant. *Had* to. Which meant that he had to do absolutely nothing to frighten her off. He had to keep her wanting him. Had to keep her sexually intrigued.

'How about a couple of hours, then?' he suggested boldly. 'After Rachel's gone to bed. I'll pick you up and we'll go somewhere local for a nightcap, then I'll find a private place for us to park.'

Isabel was startled. '*Park*?'

'Neck, then.'

'I haven't necked in a car since I was a teenager.'

He grinned. 'Neither have I.'

'Your car has buckets seats.'

'It has a big back seat.'

She stared at him, her heart hammering inside her chest.

'Well, Isabel, what do you say?'

What did she say?

What she would always say to him.

'Make sure you bring protection with you.'

CHAPTER THIRTEEN

AS RAFE turned down Isabel's street in Turramurra he glanced at the clock on the dash. Just after seven. It had taken him over an hour to drive through the rush-hour traffic from the airport to Turramurra.

Rush-hour traffic through the city was the pits at the best of times, and he wouldn't normally venture outside his front door, let alone catch a flight which landed at Mascot, anywhere near the evening peak. Unless there was a dire emergency.

In Rafe's eyes, there had been more than a dire emergency. It had been a case of life and death.

Two weeks had passed since the funeral, and almost a week since he'd seen Isabel, work having taken him to Melbourne for some magazine shoots this past week.

He'd rung her, of course. Every evening.

She'd been very chuffed on the night after Rachel got the job with Justin McCarthy. Rafe had been subjected to an hour of girl-talk stuff. Not that he'd minded. He loved hearing Isabel happy.

The next night she'd been even more excited. The two girls had spent the day shopping for a new work wardrobe for Rachel. All non-flashy, non-flirtatious clothes, Rafe had been assured. He'd received a dollar-by-dollar description of everything they'd bought.

The night after that, she'd raved on about how she was now helping Rachel clear out and clean up Lettie's house. Rachel was going to sell it, then buy a unit closer to the city. Isabel was going to look around for one for her, since she wasn't working and wasn't going to get herself another job for a while, if ever.

The following evening, however, she had been very subdued. When Rafe had asked her what was wrong she'd been evasive, saying in the end that she was just tired. But Rafe believed he knew what was bothering her. Her period—that event she could always set her clock by—hadn't arrived as expected that day.

He'd contained his own secret elation at being successful so soon, and had rung her again today from Tullamarine Airport just before he'd caught an earlier plane than he'd been intending. His original booking had been for a later flight, but he was anxious to get back to Isabel.

She'd been even more distracted during this phone-call, and when he'd said he was coming over as soon as he'd landed she'd fobbed him off, saying she was cooking dinner for her parents that night and to give her a call on the weekend.

Rafe suspected she'd come up with another excuse not to see him then as well. Which was why he'd decided to just show up on her doorstep.

The lights on in her town house told him she'd lied about going to her parents, and that really worried him.

What on earth was going through her mind? Had she

realised she didn't want a baby so badly after all? Or was it just *his* baby she didn't want?

Rafe hoped it wasn't anything like that. He hoped she was just a little shocked, and perhaps worried over what to do where he was concerned. Perhaps she'd decided not to tell him. Naturally, she'd think the pregnancy was an accident on his part and not deliberate. Perhaps she was worried he wouldn't want the child. He stupidly hadn't thought of that. Perhaps she was going to break it off with him and have his baby on her own, as she'd always planned to do.

He didn't want to entertain that other awful worry that she might get rid of his baby. Surely Isabel wouldn't do that. Even if she was late, and thought she was pregnant, she couldn't be sure yet. Even the most regular women were sometimes late.

But she wasn't late, Rafe believed as he sat there, mulling everything over. She was pregnant with his child. That was why she was acting out of character.

The time had come for a confession.

A wave of nausea claimed his stomach as he alighted from his car. Rafe hadn't felt this nervous in years, in fact, he'd *never* felt this nervous. This was worse than having his photographs exhibited, or judged. This was *him* about to be judged. Rafe, the man.

What if Isabel found him wanting in the role as father of her child? What if she didn't think him worthy? What then?

Rafe had no idea. He'd just have to take this one step at a time.

* * *

Isabel couldn't settle to anything. She wandered out into the kitchen and started making herself a cup of coffee. Not because she really wanted one but just to do something.

She *couldn't* be pregnant, she began thinking for the umpteenth time as she waited for the water to boil. Rafe had religiously used protection.

But condoms *weren't* one hundred per cent safe, came the niggling thought. Nothing was one hundred per cent safe except abstinence. And they certainly hadn't abstained during the few days they'd spent together on Dream Island. It had been full-on sex all the time. Mind-blowing, multi-orgasm sex. The kind of sex which might cause a condom to spring a little leak.

And a little leak was all that it took. Isabel recalled seeing a documentary once where just a drop of sperm had millions of eggs in it. Millions of very active eggs with the capacity to impregnate lots of women, if the timing was right.

And the timing had been pretty right, hadn't it? Perhaps not optimum time, she conceded. That had been from the Thursday till the Saturday. But they'd had sex late on the Wednesday night and that could easily have done the trick. Sperm could live for forty-eight hours, that same documentary had proudly proclaimed. Surviving half a miserable day was a cinch.

Oh, dear…

Her front doorbell ringing had Isabel spilling coffee beans all over the grey granite-topped bench. It wasn't

Rachel calling round. Isabel had not long got off the phone to Rachel, who'd told her not to be silly, she was only a day and a half late, she probably wasn't pregnant at all. Rachel had sensibly suggested buying a home-pregnancy test in the morning and putting her mind at rest.

But Isabel already knew what the result would be. She was pregnant with Rafe's child. She just knew it.

The doorbell rang a second time with Isabel still standing there, her mind still whirling.

It wasn't her parents. Tonight was raffle night down at their club. Nothing short of her giving birth would drag her mother away from that raffle.

Which event was a little way off yet.

Unlikely to be any of her new neighbours—whose names she didn't even know—wanting a cup of sugar. People rarely did that kind of the thing in the city.

No, it was Rafe. She'd heard the puzzled note in his voice when she'd put him off from coming round. But she simply hadn't been in a fit state to face him.

The fear had first begun yesterday, within hours of her not getting her period around noon, as usual. By this afternoon she'd been in a right royal flap.

Already, she could see it all. Rafe not wanting this child. Rafe making her feel terrible about her decision to have it. Rafe perhaps trying to talk her into a termination.

No, no, she could not stand that. He was the one she had to get rid of, not the baby.

The ringing changed to a loud knocking, followed by

Rafe's voice through the door. 'I know you're in there, Isabel, so please open up. I'm not going away till I speak to you.'

Isabel valiantly pulled herself together. Now's your opportunity, she lectured herself as she marched towards the front door. He already knows you lied to him about tonight. He'll be wondering why. The timing is perfect to tell him you don't want to see him any more. That this relationship—despite the great sex—isn't working for you.

Rafe knew, the moment she opened the door, that he was in trouble. She had that look in her eyes, a combination of steel and ice. He'd seen it before, the day they'd first met at his place.

'Come in,' she said curtly. 'Please excuse my appearance. I wasn't expecting any visitors tonight.'

She was wearing a simple black tracksuit and white joggers. Her hair was down and her face was free of make-up. Rafe thought she looked even more lovely than usual.

'I was just making coffee.' She turned her back on him and headed across the cream-tiled foyer towards the archway which led into the living room. 'Would you like a cup?' she threw over her shoulder.

Rafe decided to circumvent any social niceties and go straight to the heart of the matter.

'No,' he said firmly as he shut the door behind him and followed her into the stylishly furnished living room. 'I didn't come here for coffee.'

She watched him walk over to one of the cream

leather armchairs. He had a sexy walk, did Rafe. Actually, he had a sexy way of doing most things. Once settled, he glanced back up at her, his dark eyes raking her up and down, reminding Isabel that she was braless underneath her top.

Feeling her nipples automatically harden annoyed her, self-disgust giving her the courage to do what she had to do. 'If you came for sex, Rafe,' she said as she crossed her arms, 'then you're out of luck. There won't be any more sex. In fact, there won't be any more us. Period.'

'Mmm. Was that a Freudian slip, Isabel?'

Her resolve cracked a little. 'What…what do you mean?'

'I mean that's the problem, isn't it? You haven't got your period.'

She literally gaped at him, her crossed arms unfolding to dangle in limp shock at her sides.

Rafe sucked in sharply. Bingo! He was right. She was pregnant.

Suddenly, he was no longer afraid. He felt nothing but joy and pride, and love. Isabel didn't know it yet but he was going to make a great father. And a great husband, if she'd let him.

'I understand your reaction,' he said carefully. 'But you have no reason to worry. I'm here to tell you that if you are pregnant, then I will support you and the child in every way.'

She still didn't say a word.

'You *are* late, aren't you?' he probed softly.

She blinked, then shook her head as though trying to

clear the wool from her brain. 'I don't understand any of this,' she said, her hands lifting agitatedly, first to touch her hair and then to rest over her heart. 'Why would you even *think* I was pregnant?'

'I have a confession to make. There was this one occasion on Dream Island when the condom failed.'

Isabel gasped. 'Oh, that's what I thought must have happened. But why didn't you tell me?'

'I didn't want to worry you. It was too late to do anything after the event, other than get you to a doctor for the morning-after pill. And I didn't think you'd want to do that. Was I wrong, Isabel? Would you have taken that option?'

He could see by the expression in her eyes that she wouldn't have even considered it.

'I thought as much,' he said.

She almost staggered over to perch on the cream leather sofa adjacent to him. 'When…when did this happen?'

'On the Wednesday.'

She frowned. 'That night after dinner?'

'No, earlier on in the day.'

Her frown deepened. 'So all those questions you asked about my plans to get pregnant on my honeymoon… You were trying to find out what the likelihood was of my getting pregnant that day?'

'Yes,' he admitted.

'You had to have been worried.'

'No. Actually, I wasn't.'

'But that's insane! You yourself told me you never wanted to become a father.'

'Oddly enough, once it became a distinct possibility, I found I was taken with the idea.'

'*Taken* with the idea?' she exclaimed, stunned at first, then angry. 'Oh, isn't that just like a man? *Taken* with the idea. A baby's not just a fad, Rafe. It's a reality. A forever reality. A forever responsibility.'

'You think I don't know that?' he countered, his own temper rising. 'I've had longer than you to get acquainted with the reality and the responsibility entailed in my being the father of your baby, and I still like the idea. If you must know, when it seemed like a pregnancy might only be a fifty-fifty possibility, I made a conscious decision to up the odds in favour of your conceiving.'

The words were not out of his mouth more than a split second before Rafe recognised his mistake. Isabel was having enough trouble coming to terms with her 'accidental' pregnancy without his confessing to such an action. His desire to reassure her that he really did want her child could very well rebound on him. All of a sudden what he'd always considered a rather romantic decision that Wednesday night on Dream Island began developing various shades of grey about it.

'What did you do?' she demanded to know, her eyes widening.

His guilty face must have been very revealing.

'Rafe, you *didn't*!'

'Well, I...I...'

'You *did*! You had sex with me without using anything. And you deliberately got me drunk so that I wouldn't notice.'

'Well, I…I…' He'd turned into a bumbling idiot!

'How dare you do something like that without my permission? How dare you think you had that right? What kind of man are you?' She jumped to her feet, her hands finding her hips as she glared down at him.

Her ongoing outrage finally galvanised his brain, and his tongue. 'A man who's madly in love with you!' he roared back, propelling himself to his feet also. 'And I'd do it all over again. In fact, I *intended* to do it all over again, as often as I could get away with it. I even doctored a whole lot of condoms in readiness!'

Her eyes became great blue pools.

'I couldn't bear the thought of the woman I loved artificially inseminating her body with some stranger's child, when I wanted to give her *my* child. I was prepared to do anything, break every rule and cross every line, to do just that, and I don't mind admitting it. I love you, Isabel,' he claimed, grasping her shoulders, 'and I think you love me, only you're too scared to admit it, and you're too scared to trust me.

'But you shouldn't be,' he pleaded, his hands curling even more firmly over her shoulders. 'I'm nothing like the other losers you've been involved with. A fool, maybe, up till now. But a fool no longer. Seeing Liz again on that island cured me of my foolishness by making me see I was heading for the same kind of future she's ended up with. Empty and shallow, without really loving anyone or being loved in return. I took one look at you that night and thought, *This* is what I want. This woman, as my wife and the mother of my children. I love you, Isabel. Tell me you love me, too.'

Isabel searched his face, her own a tortured maze of mixed emotions. Shock. Confusion. Anguish. Maybe a measure of desperate hope in there somewhere.

'Love is more than sex, Rafe.'

'I know that.'

'Do you? Do I? Sometimes the lines between lust and love can be very blurred. I've thought myself in love so many times before, and all I've ended up with is a broken heart. And broken dreams.'

'I can understand your fear. I used to be afraid of love, too. But life without love is no life at all. Even your stupid bloody Luke found that out. Look, just tell me if you *think* you're in love with me.'

She moaned her distress at having to admit such a thing.

'All right,' Rafe said. 'You don't have to say it. I'll say it for both of us. We love each other. We've loved each other from the start. That's the truth of it and I won't let you deny it. But I also won't ask you to marry me. Not yet, anyway. All I'm asking is that you let me be a part of your life, and our baby's life, on a permanent basis.'

Isabel could hardly think. Everything was going way too fast for her. 'I…we…we don't know if there is a baby yet. Not for sure, anyway.'

'Then let's find out. Go see a doctor. We'll find one

of those twenty-four hour-surgeries. There has to be one open somewhere around here.'

'There's no need to do that. All we need is a chemist. And they're open till nine tonight.'

'Let's go, then.'

Rafe could feel the tension in her growing during the time it took to drive to a local mall, buy a pregnancy testing kit, then return. They read the instructions together, then Isabel retired to the bathroom to do what had to be done. In a couple of minutes she would confirm what he already knew. She was expecting his child.

Rafe waited patiently for the first few minutes, but when she hadn't come back downstairs after ten he marched halfway up the stairs and called out.

'Isabel? What's taking so long?'

She eventually appeared at the top of the stairs, pale-faced.

Rafe melted with love and concern for her obvious distress. 'Oh, darling, there's no need to be upset. A baby is what you wanted most in the world after all.'

'There's no baby,' she choked out. 'The test was negative.' And she burst into tears.

CHAPTER FOURTEEN

'OH, RAFE,' she sobbed, the tears spilling over and streaming down her face.

Rafe brushed aside his own disappointment to leap up the remaining steps which separated them and pull her into his arms.

'It's all right, darling,' he murmured as he pressed her shaking body to his. 'We'll make a baby for you next month. You'll see. There, there, sweetheart, don't cry so. You know what they say. If at first you don't succeed, try, try again.'

But nothing he could say would console her. She wept on and on, as though her very soul was shattered. In the end he didn't believe her pain was just because the test was negative. He believed it was caused by the build-up of all the disappointments in her life so far, culminating in this last most distressing disappointment.

When she virtually collapsed in his arms, he picked her up and carried her to bed. He didn't bother to undress her, just pulled back the covers and tipped her gently onto the mattress. Though he did yank off her joggers before covering her up with the quilt.

'Don't leave me,' she cried as he tucked her in.

'I won't,' he promised. 'I'll just go make you a hot drink.'

'No, no, I don't want a drink. I just want you. Hold me, Rafe. I feel safe when you hold me.'

He sighed at the thought. How could he stop at just holding her? Yet, at the same time, how could he refuse her? She needed him. Not as a lover, but as a friend.

Kicking off his own shoes, he climbed in beside her with the rest of his clothes on, hoping that would help. And it did. For a while. But, in the end, neither of them was content with such a platonic embrace. Yet it was Isabel who started the touching and the undressing, Isabel who decided she needed him as women had been needing the men they loved since the Garden of Eden.

Rafe could not resist her overtures and, strangely, their lovemaking turned out totally different from anything they'd shared before. It was truly *love*making. Soft. Slow. And so sweet.

Nothing but the simplest of foreplay, just face-stroking and the most innocent of kisses. Rafe's hands were gentle on her breasts and hers caressing on his back. And when the yearning to become one overwhelmed them both they merely fused together, Rafe on top, Isabel gazing adoringly up at him. They took a long time in coming, but when they did it was with such feeling, waves of rapturous pleasure rippling through their bodies, bringing with them the most amazing peace and contentment.

'I do love you,' she murmured as she lay in his arms afterwards.

Rafe sighed and stroked her hair. 'Good.'

'And I will marry you,' she added. 'If you still want me to.'

'Even better.'

'But I don't want to wait till we're married before we try again for a baby. Can we try again next month, like you said?'

'I'm putty in your hands, Isabel.'

When she hugged him even more tightly, Rafe was startled to feel tears pricking at his eyes. But that was how much he loved her, and how much her loving him meant to him. At that moment, his cup indeed runneth over.

He lay thinking about their future for a long time after she was fast asleep.

'I want you to come to lunch with my mother tomorrow,' he told her the following morning over breakfast.

Isabel pushed her hair out of her face as she glanced up at him. 'Oh, dear. Do you think she'll like me?'

'She's going to adore you.'

'You really think so? Mothers worry me a bit. She's had you all to herself all these years. I'll bet you're the apple of her eye.'

Rafe had to laugh. His mother had always found him a very difficult child. And an even more difficult teenager. He'd been one-eyed and extremely focused, determined to be a famous photographer, and even more determined never to be poor, as they'd been for many years after his father had died. At sixteen, he'd used money he'd saved from various after-school jobs to convert their single garage into a darkroom, consigning his mother's car to the street.

She'd been thrilled when he'd finally moved out of home. He believed the only reason she was fanatical about his getting married was because she was paranoid that one day fate would step in and he'd have to come home for some reason.

'Trust me, Isabel,' he said. 'My mother is not one of those mothers. She has her own life, with her own friends, pleasures and pastimes. She just wants me settled and safely married because she doesn't want to worry about me any more. Of course, she would love a grandchild or two. I won't deny that. By the way, any sign of that missing period yet?'

'No. I can't imagine where it is. I'm never late.'

'You don't think that test could have been wrong, do you?'

Isabel's stomach fluttered. She hadn't thought of that. 'I...I'm sure I followed the instructions correctly.'

'Yes, but you're not all that late yet. How far along do you have to be for it to be a reliable test?'

'It's supposed to work from two weeks.'

'Yes, but you would have only been two weeks and a day at best yesterday, Isabel. That's borderline. Perhaps we should buy another test and try again in a couple of days' time.'

Isabel recoiled at the idea. She didn't want to build up her hopes only to have them dashed again. Her emotions had been such a mess last night after Rafe arrived and made all his most amazing confessions. She'd swung from distress to delight to despair, all in the space of an hour.

She hadn't cried like that ever in her life, not even when she'd found out Hal had been a drug-dealer. Still, crying her heart out in Rafe's arms had been a deeply cleansing experience, and their lovemaking later had filled her with such hope and joy for the future that she didn't need to be pregnant now to make her happy. She was already happy just being with Rafe and knowing that he really loved her. They'd have a baby eventually. It had been silly of her to be so disappointed. And it would be silly to torture herself with another test. Better to just calmly wait for her period to arrive, then make plans for trying again during her next cycle.

'No,' she said. 'I don't want to do that. I'm sure my period is going to arrive any minute now, provided I don't start stressing about it. I think that's the problem with it. Stress.'

'I think you could be right. From now on, you are going to be relaxed and happy.'

'Sounds wonderful. So what are we going to do today?'

'I'm going to take you shopping for an engagement ring. That way, at lunch tomorrow, Mum will know I'm deadly serious about marrying you. Though it's going to cost me a pretty penny to top that rock you're still sporting on your left hand and which I presume Luke gave you.'

Isabel frowned. 'You're not jealous of Luke, are you, Rafe?'

'Well…'

'There's no need to be. I didn't love him.'

'Maybe, but you do have a lot of reminders of him around you. That ring, for starters. And this place. I don't mind the money he gave you but do you have to live in his house?'

'This was never really Luke's house. I mean, nothing in it reflects him on a personal basis. He bought it already furnished. And he wasn't living here all that long. Still, I'm quite happy to move in with *you*, Rafe, if you like. Though a terrace is not really suitable for a family. What say we sell both places and buy another one? Together.'

'Done.' Rafe smiled his satisfaction at that idea. 'Now, let's get dressed and go into the city for some serious ring-shopping.'

'Are you sure you can afford this?' Isabel asked Rafe later that morning, after she'd selected a gorgeous but expensive-looking diamond and emerald ring.

'No trouble. I'll just go ring my bank manager for a second mortgage.'

Isabel looked at him with alarm. 'I don't mind getting something cheaper.'

Rafe smiled and kissed her. 'Don't be silly. I was only joking. I can easily afford this ring, Isabel. I might not be a multi-millionaire but I have more than enough to support a wife and family. I am a very successful photographer and an astute investor, even if I say so myself.

I'll tell your dad that when I officially ask for your hand in marriage tonight.'

'When you *what*?'

'As you once pointed out to me, Isabel, your parents come from a different generation. I want to get off on the right foot with your father as well as your mother.'

'You'll get off on the right foot with my mother by just marrying me,' Isabel said drily.

Rafe smiled. 'That's what I gathered when I told her I was going to do just that at the funeral a couple of weeks back.'

Isabel was astonished, then amused. 'So that's what you did to make her like you! You are a mischievous and manipulative devil, Rafe Saint Vincent. But I love you all the same.'

'You'd want to after costing me this much money.'

'Don't worry,' she murmured, reaching up to kiss his cheek. 'If you ever run out, I have plenty.'

'Huh. Now I'm not so sure I like Luke giving you all that money, either. A man likes to be his family's provider, you know. He likes to be needed for more than just his body.'

Isabel giggled and Rafe bristled. 'What's so funny?'

'You are, going all primal male on me. Who would have believed it from the man who let me buy his body to do with as I willed for a whole fortnight?'

'I did not!'

'Oh, yes, you did. You didn't pay for a single thing on that jaunt to Dream Island.'

'I did so, too.'

'Name one.'

'I paid for the condoms.'

'Only half.'

'The three dozen I bought should have been more than enough. How was I to know I was going way with a raving nymphomaniac?'

They both realised all of a sudden that everyone in the jewellery shop had stopped what they were doing and were listening to their highly provocative bickering.

Isabel blushed fiercely whilst Rafe laughed.

'How embarrassing!' Isabel cried once they'd paid for the ring and fled outside. 'Lord knows what they thought of us.'

'Probably that you're a rich bitch and I'm your gigolo lover.'

Rafe loved it when she looked so mortified. She was such a delightful contradiction when it came to sex. So wildly uninhibited behind closed doors, but so easily embarrassed in public. Being with her was like being with a virgin and a vamp at the same time. It was a tantalising combination and one which he aimed to enjoy for the rest of their lives.

'Let's get right away from here,' Isabel urged, grabbing his arm, 'before someone comes out of that shop.'

Rafe found himself being dragged forcibly down the street. 'That's better,' she said, stopping at last. 'Oh look, Rafe, a chemist. I think I will buy another of those tests.'

'I thought you said you didn't want to.'

'I know but I...I've changed my mind.'

'Oh. Why's that?'

'Well, just now I felt kind of funny in my breasts.'

'What do you mean? Kind of funny?'

'All tingly and tight around the nipples.'

He gave her an amused glance. 'There are other explanations for that besides pregnancy, sweetness. You were just embarrassed by what happened in that shop. You find embarrassment a turn-on.'

'I do not!' She was taken aback by such an idea, and even more embarrassed.

'Yes, you do. But let's not fight about it in public. We'll pop in and buy another test, then go home. My place this time.' Thinking about her being turned on had turned *Rafe* on. He couldn't wait to get her behind closed doors again. He had a mind to photograph her as well. Afterwards. She always looked incredible afterwards. Relaxed and dreamy. He'd been wanting to capture that look with his camera for a long time. Not a nude shot. Just her face.

But she dashed upstairs for the bathroom as soon as they arrived back at his place, taking that damned test with her. A disgruntled Rafe collected his favourite camera from the darkroom, but he already knew he was wasting his time. Her mood would change once the test came back negative again. He'd been foolish to suggest the first one might have been wrong. It had just seemed logical at the time. Now he wished he'd never opened his big mouth.

Once again, she was gone ages. Lord, he hoped she wasn't up there crying again. Eventually he trudged up the stairs, not even bothering with the camera. He knew when he was beaten.

'Isabel,' he said wearily as he knocked on the bathroom door, 'please let's not go through all this again.'

The door opened and there she stood, and, yes, she was crying again, though not noisily. The tears were just running silently down her lovely cheeks.

'I should never have let you buy that bloody thing,' he muttered, hating to see her in such distress. 'Isabel, there's no need to get all upset again.'

Her smile startled him. So did the sudden sparkle in her soggy eyes.

'You don't understand, darling,' she said. 'I'm not upset. I'm crying with happiness. The test was positive, Rafe. We're pregnant!'

Rafe was to wonder later in his life exactly what he felt at that moment. Time and distance did fog the memory. But it had to go down as one of the great moments in his life. He'd put it on a par with their wedding day, just over a month later, even if he had been forced to tolerate Les taking a zillion photographs and both mothers hugging and kissing him all the time.

Nothing, however, would ever eclipse the magic moment when his firstborn entered the world.

Rafe would never forget the look in Isabel's eyes as she cradled her son to her breast, then looked up at him and said, 'I'd like to call him Michael, Rafe. After your father.'

Oh, yes, that was the moment he would remember above all others.

Perhaps because he was weeping at the time.

FACING UP TO FATHERHOOD

MIRANDA LEE

CHAPTER ONE

TINA glanced up at the towering office block, then down at the pram, and the baby lying within.

'Here we are, darling!' she announced to the pretty pink-clad infant. 'Your daddy's workplace. Unfortunately, your daddy'll be in a meeting all afternoon, according to his secretary. Didn't have time for any appointments. Which is just too bad, isn't it? Because he's going to see us today whether he likes it or not!'

Arching a well-plucked eyebrow, she angled the pram determinedly towards the revolving glass doors, hoping for more success than her encounter with the train doors earlier on. Manoeuvring a pram, Tina had found, was as hazardous as one of those wayward shopping trolleys, the kind whose wheels had a mind of their own. Still, she'd only been doing it for a week, so she supposed there were excuses for her ineptitude.

It was a struggle, but she finally emerged unscathed into the cavernous semicircular foyer with its acre or two of black granite flooring. Tina negotiated this pram-friendly surface with thankful ease, bypassing the busy reception desk and skirting several large lumps of marble masquerading as art, finally halting beneath the huge directory which hung on the wall beside the bank of lifts.

Hunter & Associates, she swiftly noted, occupied floors nineteen and twenty. Tina also noted Hunter & Associates carried no description of what services or utilities the company provided, other than to say 'Management' was on the twentieth floor.

This might have been a modest oversight, but Tina rather imagined it reflected its owner's character. Dominic Hunter arrogantly assumed everyone knew his company was one of Sydney's most successful stockbroking and investment firms.

He had also arrogantly assumed his affair with his secretary last year would never rise up to bite him on his arrogant backside.

But he was wrong!

Sarah might have been a softie. And a push-over where men were concerned. But Tina was not!

Sarah's daughter deserved the very best. And Tina aimed to make sure she got it. She would give Dominic Hunter a second chance to be a proper father to his beautiful little daughter. If he didn't come to the party willingly, then he would be made to pay. And pay handsomely. In this day of DNA testing, simply denying fatherhood was a thing of the past.

'Just let him try it, darling,' she informed the baby girl as she wheeled the pram into the lift. 'If he does, we're going to have his guts for garters!'

CHAPTER TWO

DOMINIC raised his eyes to the ceiling as he hung up the phone.

'Women!' he muttered frustratedly, before standing up to gather his papers together for that afternoon's meeting, almost knocking over a cold, half-drunk cup of coffee in the process. Only a desperate lunge and grab prevented coffee spilling all over his desk.

He righted the mug and plonked it well to one side, his sigh carrying total exasperation. He was having a really bad day.

His colleagues might have thought it was the present economic crisis which was causing his tetchy mood. But that wasn't the case. Dominic thrived on the challenges the financial arena kept throwing at him, finding great excitement and personal satisfaction in making money, both for himself and all his clients. He'd been called a stockmarket junkie more than once, and had to admit it was true.

No, Dominic could always cope with business problems. It was the opposite sex which was irritating the death out of him.

Frankly, he just didn't understand the species, especially their obsession with marriage and babies. Couldn't they see that, in this present day and age, the world would actually be better off with less of both? There certainly wouldn't be as many divorces, or so many unhappy neglected children!

But, no! Such common sense views never seemed

to cut the mustard with women. They went on wanting marriage and babies as though they were the panacea for all the world's ills, instead of adding to them.

The same thing applied to romantic love. Crazy, really. When had this unfortunate state ever brought women—or men for that matter—any happiness?

Dominic had grown up in a household where that kind of love had caused nothing but emotional torment and misery.

He wanted none of it. Love *or* marriage *or* babies—a fact reinforced in his early twenties when a girlfriend had tried to trap him into marriage with a false pregnancy.

The thought of imminent fatherhood and marriage had horrified him. Perhaps his panic had had something to do with own father being a lousy parent—as well as a faithless husband—producing a subconscious fear he might turn out to be just as big a jerk in that department. He'd already *looked* like the man.

Whatever, Dominic's relief at discovering the pregnancy had been a lie had been very telling. It had also been his first intimate experience at just how far a female would go in pursuit of that old romantic fantasy called 'love and marriage'.

After that sobering experience, Dominic always took care of protection personally when having sex. He was never swayed by any female's assertion that she was on the pill, or that it was a 'safe' time of the month. He also always made his position quite clear to every woman he became involved with. Marriage was not on his agenda, no matter what!

His mother found his views on the subject totally unfathomable. With typical female logic, she simply dismissed them as a temporary aberration.

'You'll change your mind one day,' she would say every now and then. 'When you fall in love…'

Now *that* was another romantic illusion his mother harboured. His *falling in love*! He'd never fallen in love in his life. And he had no intention of doing so. The very word 'falling' suggested a lack—and a loss—of control which he found quite distasteful, and which could only lead to one disastrous decision after another!

Fortunately for him, his mother had been able to channel her grandmotherly hopes up till now towards his younger brother, Mark, who'd married a couple of years back. Dominic had simply assumed Mark and his wife would reproduce in time, thereby letting him permanently off the hook.

But a few months ago his one and only sibling had unexpectedly arrived home and announced he was leaving his wife to go off to Tibet to become a Buddhist monk! To prove it, he'd promptly given all his considerable worldly goods to his rapidly recovering wife and taken off, his subsequent letters revealing he was happy as a lark living on some mountain-top monastery with only a yak for companionship!

It didn't take a genius to conclude there would be no imminent hope of a grandchild from *that* quarter!

Which had brought his widowed mother's focus right back on him, her only other offspring, and now her only other hope of providing her with a grandchild!

She'd been driving him mad with her none too subtle pressure, inviting all sorts of unattached females home to dinner. All of them beautiful. All of them sexy. And all of them wanting—or pretending to want—the same thing his mother wanted. Marriage and babies.

She'd just rung to check that he wouldn't be too late home for dinner tonight, because she'd invited Joanna Parsons over.

'The poor darling has been so lonely since Damien died,' Ida had purred down the line.

Lonely? Joanna Parsons? Dear God! The woman was a sexual vampire. Even before Damien's death, in a car crash six months ago, she'd done her best to seduce him. As a merry widow, there would be no holds barred!

Dominic liked his sex, but he liked it unencumbered, thank you very much. And with women who held the same views as he did. His current lady-friend was an advertising account executive whose marriage had broken up because she'd been already married to her job. Dominic saw her two or three times a week, either at her apartment after work or in a hotel room at lunchtimes, an arrangement which suited them both admirably.

Shani was thirty-two, an attractive brunette with a trim gym-honed body. She wasn't into endless foreplay or mindless chit-chat or sentimentality, the word 'love' never entering what little conversation they had. She was also fanatical when it came to her health. If ever Dominic might have been tempted to believe a woman when she said it was safe, it would have been Shani.

But long-ingrained habits died hard, and Dominic maintained a cynical distrust of the female psyche. It would never surprise him to discover that his latest bed-partner, no matter how career-minded, had fallen victim to her infernal biological clock. In his experience, not even the most unlikely female was immune to *that* disease!

Take the case of Melinda, his invaluable PA, who'd been with him for years and always said she wanted a career, not the role of wife and mother. So what happened? She'd turned thirty and in less than twelve months had married and left to have a baby. On top of that, she'd refused to come back to work, abandoning him totally for the home front.

He'd been most put out!

Naturally he'd had to take steps to ensure such a thing wasn't going to become a regular occurrence, though at the time finding a replacement for Melinda had been a right pain in the neck. There'd been no question of keeping the girl on who'd filled in during Melinda's supposedly temporary maternity leave. As efficient and sweet as Sarah was, beautiful, young, unattached females were out—a decision reinforced by what had happened when he'd taken Sarah out for a thank-you meal on the last evening of her employ.

Dominic shuddered to think that even *he* could become a temporary victim of his hormones, if the circumstances were right. He'd been between women at the time, and had drunk far too much wine with his meal. When he'd taken Sarah home in a taxi and walked her to the door of her flat she'd unexpectedly started to cry. Her louse of a boyfriend, it seemed, had just the day before dumped her for some other woman.

Dominic had only meant to comfort her, but somehow comfort had turned to something else and they'd ended up in bed together for the night. They'd both regretted it in the morning, both agreed not to mention it again.

Sarah had gone back to her normal job as a secretary in Accounts on the floor below his, and he'd met Shani at a dinner party that very weekend.

His new secretary, Doris, had started the following Monday morning.

Thank God for Doris.

Now Doris would never cause him any worries. She was fifty-four, for starters, happily married, with a healthy, undemanding husband and grown-up children who didn't live at home. She didn't mind working late when required, and didn't object to making him coffee at all hours of the day. If his tendency to untidiness bothered her—and he suspected it did—she didn't say so to his face, just quietly cleaned up after him. A woman of great common sense and tact was Doris.

The intercom on his desk buzzed and he flicked the switch. 'Yes, Doris?'

'The others are waiting for you in the boardroom, Mr Hunter.'

That was another thing he liked about Doris.

She called him Mr Hunter, and not Dominic. It had a nice, respectful ring about it, and made him feel older than his thirty-three years.

'Yes, yes, I'm coming. Hold all calls, will you, Doris? Absolutely no interruptions. We have a lot of work to get through this afternoon.'

The lift doors opened, and Tina steered the pram, along with the now sleeping infant, onto the twentieth floor. Straight ahead was a long glass wall with floor-to-ceiling glass doors upon which was written in gold lettering 'Hunter & Associates—Management'.

Beyond was another sea of black granite, dominated by a shiny black reception desk.

Tina wondered caustically if the glossy blonde perched behind the desk had been chosen personally by Dominic Hunter himself.

Maybe he had a penchant for blondes. She recalled Sarah saying something about the big boss being present at her second interview for Hunter & Associates, after which she'd swiftly been hired.

Of course Sarah hadn't just been any old blonde. Though her long fair hair had been her crowning glory, she'd been equally striking of face and figure. Her stunning looks had been a problem all her life, and hadn't brought her any happiness. Men hadn't been able to keep their eyes, or their hands, off.

Poor, sweet Sarah had always believed the declarations of love which had poured forth from her current pursuer's mouth. After she'd become a secretary working in the city, she'd been especially susceptible to the smoothly suited variety of male, especially good-looking ones with dark hair, bedroom blue eyes and a convincing line of patter to get her into the cot and keep her there without actually offering any solid commitment.

Sarah had been a sucker for that combination every time, always believing herself *in love*. Once *in love*, Sarah had become her latest lover's doormat, thinking that was the road to the wedding ring and the family of her own she'd always craved.

Naturally it had never turned out that way, and Sarah had been dumped in the end. It had driven Tina mad to watch her friend being used and abused by one silver-tongued creep after another. Married, divorced or single, it hadn't mattered. If they'd told Sarah they loved her, she'd been putty in their hands.

Tina had tried to give solace and advice after each break-up, but her patience had worn thin over the years. She'd finally seen red when, shortly after Sarah had been promoted to the plum job of PA to Dominic Hunter, Sarah had confessed to being *in love* again. When pressed, she'd admitted the object of her affections was her new boss. A terrible argument had ensued. Tina had told Sarah that she'd sleep with any man if he said he loved her, and Sarah had retaliated that Tina had a heart of stone, was incapable of really loving anything or anyone but herself.

They were the last words the two friends had said to each other. That had been just over a year ago.

And now Sarah was dead.

Tina's chin began to wobble. She had to swallow hard to stop herself from bursting into tears.

'I won't let you down, Sarah,' she whispered as she gazed down at Sarah's beautiful little baby girl. 'Your Bonnie's going to have everything you would have wanted for her. Every possible advantage. There will be no feeling of not being loved or wanted. No hand-me-down clothes. No leaving school at fifteen. As for Welfare and foster homes! Never! Not as long as I've got breath in my body!'

Hardening herself for the fray which undoubtedly lay ahead, Tina pushed the glass door open with the pram and forged over to the desk.

'I'm here to see Dominic Hunter,' she announced firmly to the glamorous green-eyed blonde. 'And, yes, before you ask, I do have an appointment,' came the bald lie.

Faint heart never won fat turkey, Tina always believed. She'd never have gained entry to the most prestigious drama school in Australia if she hadn't been confident of her acting ability. Admittedly, she'd auditioned for three consecutive years before she'd won one of the coveted positions of entry. But that wasn't a measure of ability, she'd always told herself. It was as hard to get into AIDA as Fort Knox!

The blonde directed her towards a long polished corridor which led into another smaller reception area covered in plush dark blue carpet. The pram wheels immediately floundered in the thick pile, then came to a rebellious halt.

'Can I help you?' came the puzzled but cool query.

Tina glanced up at the severely suited woman seated behind the now familiar shiny black desk.

Dominic Hunter's secretary, Tina concluded with much surprise. For the woman wasn't blonde. Or pretty. Or young.

Tina wondered cynically if Dominic Hunter had finally learned his lesson about mixing business and pleasure.

'I'm here to see Dominic,' she returned, just as coolly.

The secretary frowned. 'Mr Hunter is in a meeting all afternoon. He specifically asked that I not disturb him for anything.'

Tina finally got the wheels straight and bulldozed the pram across the carpet. 'I doubt he meant me,' she said, stopping in front of the desk. 'Or his daughter, here.'

The woman's eyes widened as she rose to peer over her desk, down into the pram. 'His…daughter?' she repeated, startled.

'That's right,' Tina answered crisply. 'Her name is Bonnie. She's three months old. Could you please tell Dominic that she's here and would like to meet her father at long last?'

The secretary blinked, then cleared her throat. 'Er…perhaps you'd best come into Mr Hunter's office and I'll go get him.'

Tina's smile was icy. 'What a good idea.'

Dominic Hunter's office was another surprise. Although the room was huge, the carpet still plush, and the view of Sydney breathtaking, it was an office laid out for working, not impressing. There were several work stations around the walls, each with its own computer, printer, phone, fax and swivel chair. Every computer was still on, winking figures at Tina. Every surface was messy, littered with papers of various kinds. The main desk wasn't much better.

The secretary made an exasperated sound at the sight of it, shaking her head as she lifted a half-drunk coffee mug from its glossy black surface, Snatching a tissue out of a nearby box, she vigorously rubbed at the stain left behind, muttering 'truly' under her breath.

Meanwhile, Tina lowered herself into one of the two empty upright chairs facing the main desk, crossing her long legs and angling the pram closer so she could check that Bonnie was still sleeping.

'What a good little baby you are,' she crooned softly as she tucked the pink bunny rug tightly around the tiny feet. When she'd finished, and looked up, it was to find the secretary staring at her as though she'd just landed from Mars.

'I dare say Mr Hunter will be with you shortly,'

the woman said, and, shaking her head again, left the room, shutting the door behind her.

That same door burst open less than two minutes later, and Tina's head whipped round to encounter her first view of Bonnie's father.

Dominic Hunter was even more of a surprise than his secretary, or his office.

Yes, he was tall, as she'd anticipated. And dark-haired. And handsome, in a hard-boned fashion. He even had blue eyes.

But, despite all that, the man glaring at her across the room didn't fit the picture she'd formed of him in her imagination.

Sarah's lovers had usually been suave and elegant, perfectly groomed and beautifully dressed. They'd oozed a smooth charm and sophisticated sex appeal which girls of Sarah's upbringing seemed to find irresistibly attractive.

Dominic Hunter hardly fitted that description.

He marched into the room, a menacingly macho male with his big, broad-shouldered body and close-cropped haircut. The sleeves of his blue shirt were rolled up as though ready for battle, his tie was missing, and the top button around his muscular neck undone. His scowl was such that his dark straight brows momentarily met above his nose.

Frankly, he looked more like a construction site foreman about to bawl out his labourers rather than a successful stockbroker who should have been able to handle even *this* sticky situation with some aplomb.

Grinding to a halt next to the pram, he glowered, first down at Bonnie and then up at Tina again. 'I hear you're claiming this is my daughter!' he snarled.

Tina refused to be intimidated by this macho bully.

She wondered what on earth Sarah had seen in the man. She could only speculate that he came up better in bed than out of it.

'That's right,' she said.

He gave her a look which would have sent poor Sarah running for cover. Tina began to understand why her friend hadn't approached Bonnie's biological father for help and support a second time. When this man finished with a woman, he would expect her to stay finished.

But she wasn't Sarah, was she?

Tina almost smiled as she thought of what Mr Hunter was up against this time. Brother, was he in for a surprise or two of his own!

'Wait here,' he growled.

'I'm certainly not going anywhere,' she said in a calm voice, and received another of those blistering looks.

Tina didn't even blink, holding his killer gaze without the slightest waver.

He stared hard at her for several more seconds, then whirled and left the room, slamming the door shut behind him.

Tina sat there, whistling and swinging her left foot. It was to be hoped Mr Macho was out there getting a grip on himself and finding some manners. Or at least some common sense. Because she wasn't about to go away, not this side of Armageddon!

The minutes ticked steadily away.

Five…

Ten…

Her blood pressure began to rise a little, but she'd been mentally ready for this. She hadn't expected the man to come to the party willingly, not when he'd already denied paternity, given Sarah money for a termination and sent her on her way.

Frankly, Tina had expected nothing from him, and he was living up to her low opinion of men of his ilk. Obviously she had a fight on her hands to get the financial support she needed to raise Sarah's daughter in the manner Bonnie deserved.

But she enjoyed a good fight, didn't she? She was always at her best when her back was against the wall.

The sound of the door finally opening had her swivelling in her chair with an aggressive glint in her eye. How dared he keep her waiting this long?

The sight of two burly security guards entering startled her, then sent her blood pressure sky-high. So *that* was how he was going to play it, was it?

Gritting her teeth, she stood up and gave the approaching guards a haughty look of disdain. 'I gather Mr Hunter won't be returning?'

'That's right, ma'am,' the bigger and older of the two informed her. 'He said to tell you that next time he'd be calling the police.'

'Really? Well, we'll see about that, won't we? No, that's not necessary!' she snapped when the guard who'd spoken forcibly took her by the elbow. 'I'll go quietly.'

Despite her protests, the two guards still escorted her till she was outside the building.

She stood there on the pavement for several moments, glaring up at the top floors, struggling to get her temper under control. She imagined the bastard peering back down at her from his lofty position, smug and smirking with triumph.

'You'll get yours, Dominic Hunter,' she threatened

under her breath. 'I'm going to take you to the cleaners!'

Scooping in several deep breaths, Tina forcibly slowed her pounding heart and found some much-needed composure. Her brain finally began ticking over, and she started wondering *why* Bonnie's father was so sure of his ground that he would dare have her thrown out. It was a stupid move to bluff about paternity in this day and age.

No matter what else he might be, Dominic Hunter was not stupid.

It suddenly dawned on Tina that he probably believed Sarah had had that termination he'd paid for, which meant he might not have realised Bonnie was the baby Sarah had come to see him about, despite her being the right age. He possibly thought Bonnie was another baby entirely, and she, Tina, was the mother. When he'd stared so hard at her it could have been because he was trying to recall if he'd ever slept with her or not. Since he hadn't, naturally he'd assumed she was trying to pull off some kind of false paternity suit.

That had to be it!

Tina could have kicked herself. She should have said straight up that she wasn't the biological mother.

'Your new mummy's an idiot,' she told the now wide-awake infant as she wheeled the pram towards the taxi rank on the corner. 'But don't worry, I have a contingency plan. Since I've temporarily blotted my copybook with your father, we'll go see your grandmother and gain entry that way. Yes, I know you're getting hungry and wet. I'll feed and change you in the taxi. I've brought everything with me. Bottles. Nappies. Spare clothes. Aren't you impressed?'

Several passersby glanced over their shoulders at the tall, striking brunette wheeling the brand-new navy pram along the pavement, oblivious of everything but the baby to whom she was talking fifteen to the dozen.

'Just wait till your nanna sees how beautiful you are. And how good. She won't be able to resist you. I couldn't, could I? And look at me? A hard-nosed piece if ever there was one. Or so your real mummy used to say. And she was probably right. But she wasn't right about my not being able to love anything or anybody. No, my darling, she was quite wrong about that...'

CHAPTER THREE

THE nerve of the woman! The darned nerve!

Dominic fumed as he glared down at the pavement below and watched her pushing the pram down the street. What on earth did she think she was playing at? How did she think she was going to get away with such an outrageous claim? Even if he was one of the unlucky few whose condom had failed, did she honestly imagine that he wouldn't remember sleeping with someone like her?

She wasn't the sort of female he would forget in a hurry. For one thing, she was exactly his type. Dominic had always been attracted to tall, slim brunettes with interesting faces and dark, glittering eyes who made it obvious from their first meeting that men were not their favourite species. He liked the challenge of getting them into bed, then watching them abandon their feminist aggression for the short time his sexual know-how—and their own basic needs—overcame their natural antagonism. He'd had several rather lengthy involvements with such women, and prided himself on keeping them as friends afterwards.

Oh, yes, he would have remembered having sex with…damn it all, he didn't even know her name! She'd only supplied Doris with the name of her baby.

Bonnie.

As if that would mean anything to him!

He watched till she disappeared under a street awning, certain that that would be the last he'd see of her.

Perversely, he almost regretted having had her thrown out so hastily. He should have questioned her further, listened to her tall tale, found out what it was she wanted from him.

Money, he supposed, as he turned from the window and strode across his office towards the door. What else could she possibly have wanted?

He ground to a halt with his hand reaching for the doorknob, his forehead creasing into a frown.

But why had *he* been the target of her attempted con? It wasn't as though he had a reputation for indiscriminate and promiscuous behaviour. He certainly wasn't the sort of man who could be convinced he'd slept with some stranger whilst drunk or under the influence of drugs. He never drank to *that* much excess and he never took drugs!

Maybe she'd mixed him up with someone else, he speculated. Maybe *she* was the one who'd forgotten who it was she'd slept with. Maybe the father of her baby was someone else working at Hunter & Associates. Or a stockbroker from another firm. Someone who looked like him, perhaps.

Yes, that had to be it, he decided firmly. It was a case of mistaken identity.

Now, forget her and get back to work, he ordered himself. You've wasted enough time for one day!

Mrs Hunter's address was in Clifton Gardens, an old but exclusive Northshore suburb which hugged Sydney Harbour and where even the simplest house had an asking price of a million.

Mrs Hunter's house, however, wasn't simple. It turned out to be a stately sandstone residence, two-storeyed, with a wide wooden verandah. The block was huge, and the gardens, a visual delight, immaculately kept.

Tina frowned at the sight, and the conclusions such a property evoked. Dominic Hunter's family possessed old money, the kind which inevitably produced people who thought they were a cut above ordinary folk. Arrogance was as natural to them as breathing.

If Mrs Hunter proved to be such a snob, maybe she wouldn't welcome an illegitimate grandchild into her life, regardless of how adorable Bonnie was. Maybe she would be as sceptical—and as rude—as her son. Maybe she would swiftly show Tina and Bonnie the door, as he had done.

Tina's resolve wavered only momentarily, her confidence regained by a glance at the beautiful baby in her arms.

No woman in the world could resist Bonnie, she reasoned. Not if she had any kind of heart at all!

Tina was climbing out of the taxi before a second dampening thought occurred to her. What if Dominic Hunter's mother wasn't at home?

She'd set about discovering the woman's existence and her address that morning, *after* she'd been told by Dominic Hunter's secretary that she couldn't see the great man himself that day.

Severely irritated at the time, Tina had swiftly rung Dominic Hunter's secretary back, putting on an English accent and pretending to be an embarrassed florist who was supposed to deliver flowers to Mr Hunter's mother that day but had lost her particulars.

At the time, she hadn't even known if his mother was still of this world. Presuming he did *have* a mother. It would never surprise Tina to find out that the Dominic Hunters of this world were spawned in a test-tube. Or cloned from some other selfish macho creep with a megalomania complex.

A couple of minutes later she had hung up, with everything she needed to know. Mrs Hunter *was* still alive and well. And Tina knew where she lived.

She'd been going to go straight to the grandmother, but an indignant anger had sent her to Bonnie's father first. An impulsive decision.

Turning up on Mrs Hunter's doorstep without even ringing first wasn't much better.

Tina sighed. 'Would you mind waiting a few moments till I check to see if anyone's at home?' she asked the taxi driver as he paid him. 'I just realised the lady of the house might be out.'

'No sweat,' the driver said, and walked over to open the front gate for her.

Giving him an appreciative smile, Tina popped Bonnie back in the pram and set off up the paved front path, feeling too nervous now to admire the bloom-filled rose-beds which dotted the spacious front yard. It had been one thing to confront Bonnie's father. She'd known he was going to be difficult from the start.

His mother was proving a different kettle of fish entirely.

Although Tina tried to feel confident of the woman's reaction, she really could only hope.

But, oh, how she hoped! She desperately wanted Bonnie to have a grandmother who would lavish love upon her in the way only a grandmother could.

Not that Tina had any personal experience of a grandmother's love. But she gathered they specialised in the sort of unconditional affection and outrageous spoiling which both she and Sarah had only dreamt about during their growing-up years.

She also wanted Mrs Hunter to talk her son into recognising his daughter and agreeing to help support Bonnie financially, *without* Tina having to resort to legal pressures.

Pulling the pram to a halt at the base of the four stone steps which led up onto the wide wooden verandah, Tina put on the brake, then left the pram there while she hurried up the steps and rang the front doorbell.

For a nerve-racking twenty seconds, it looked as if no one was home, but then the door opened and there stood a woman of about sixty. Casually dressed in navy slacks and a floral blouse, she was tall and slim, with a handsome face and short, naturally grey hair. Best of all, there was a reassuring softness in her intelligent blue eyes.

'Yes?' she said with an enquiring smile.

'Are you Mrs Hunter?' Tina asked.

'Yes, I am, dear. How can I help you?'

The dear did it. And the sweet offer of help. Tina had studied human psychology during the course of her acting career, and had become a pretty good judge in assessing character, especially when it came to women.

Mrs Hunter was no snob, for starters. Most important of all, she was kind.

Smiling with relief, Tina turned and waved to the taxi driver. 'It's okay,' she called. 'You can go now.'

'Righto.'

She turned back, just as the woman spotted the pram at the bottom of the steps. It was facing the house so that she could see Bonnie's sweet little face quite clearly.

'Oh, what a beautiful-looking baby!' she exclaimed, and moved down the steps for a closer look. 'A girl, I presume?' she said, glancing up at Tina over her shoulder.

'Yes.'

'May I hold her? She's wide awake.'

'Please do.'

A warm, squishy feeling settled in Tina's stomach as she watched the woman carefully scoop her grandchild up and start rocking her. Even after the seven short days Tina had cared for Bonnie she knew nothing enchanted the child more than being held and rocked in just that way. She would never cry while someone was doing that. She would just lie there and gaze up at the person rocking her, a look of total bliss on her lovely little face.

'What's her name?' her unwitting grandmother asked.

'Bonnie.'

'And yours, dear?'

'Tina. Tina Highsmith.'

'So, what are you selling, Tina?' Mrs Hunter asked while she smiled down at Bonnie. 'If you're an Avon lady, then I'm sorry, but I don't wear make-up any more other than a bit of lipstick. If you're with that other mob, then I also already have everything that opens and shuts in the houseware department. My son has no imagination when it comes to presents and always gives me something for the house. He's into practicality, is Dominic,' she added ruefully.

'Actually, Mrs Hunter, I'm not selling anything.

And it's your son, Dominic, I've come to see you about.'

This got her attention, startled blue eyes blinking up to stare at Tina. 'Dominic? Really? What about?'

'About Bonnie, there,' she said, nodding towards the baby. Tina swallowed, steeling herself for any possible negative reaction to her next announcement. She could only hope the woman was as nice as she seemed. 'She…she's Dominic's daughter.'

Tina was amazed at the speed and intensity of the various emotions which raced across Mrs Hunter's face. Shock gave way to a moment's uninhibited joy, swiftly followed by a deeply troubled concern.

She walked slowly up the steps to stand close to Tina, her expression still troubled. 'Does Dominic know?' she asked warily.

'I tried to tell him today, but I made a stupid mistake in the telling and he had Security throw me out of the building.'

Concern gave way to outrage. 'He *what*?'

'It was my fault, Mrs Hunter,' Tina explained hurriedly. 'I see that now. When I told him that Bonnie was his daughter I forgot to add that I am *not* the mother. I think he took one look at me, knew I was a stranger to him, and jumped to the conclusion I was trying to operate some kind of scam.'

Outrage changed to puzzlement. 'If you're not the mother…then, who is? Your sister?'

'No. My best friend.' Tina swallowed as that awful lump filled her throat, the one which always came when she thought of Sarah's dying. 'Sarah worked at Hunter & Associates all last year. She was Dominic's secretary from late July till the 25th November. Bonnie was born on August 19th. Sarah was critically injured when she was knocked down by a bus last month. She…she lived a few days, but didn't make it. Before she died, she made me Bonnie's legal guardian. Her birth certificate actually says 'father unknown', but I know Bonnie's father is your son.'

'You're sure?'

'*Very* sure, Mrs Hunter.'

Mrs Hunter was frowning. 'Did your friend actually tell you Dominic was the father of her baby?'

Tina hesitated. She didn't want to lie to the woman. It was just that the truth was so complicated, and possibly confusing to anyone who hadn't known Sarah well. The actual evidence Tina had concerning the identity of Bonnie's father was largely circumstantial, and partly second-hand. Mrs Hunter might think Tina was jumping to conclusions, but she knew better.

'Sarah and I told each other everything,' she said firmly at last, happy that this had been the truth—at least till they'd parted company. 'We were more like sisters than friends. Your son is Bonnie's father all right, Mrs Hunter. A DNA test should remove any doubt, however, if he continues to deny paternity.'

'What…what do you mean…*continues*?'

'Sarah went to see him when she found out she was pregnant. Dominic refused to believe the baby was his, though he did give her some money for a termination.'

'Which she obviously didn't have…'

'No. Sarah didn't believe in abortion.'

'Thank God,' the woman sighed, and smiled down at the baby in her arms before glancing up at Tina, tears in her eyes. 'I've always wanted a grandchild. You've no idea. I honestly thought I would never have one. Dominic was so adamant about not wanting marriage and children. And then his brother, Mark…well—'

She broke off and frowned at Tina. 'You said you were made the baby's legal guardian. Why is that, Tina? I know you said you were like a sister to this Sarah, but what about the child's maternal grandparents? Or aunts and uncles?'

'Sarah's mother died in a house fire when she was nine. Sarah never knew her father, or her grandparents. Her mum was a bit of a black sheep, you see. Ran away from her home in the country to the city when she was a teenager. She wasn't married when she had Sarah. I gather the father abandoned them before she was born. So, no, there are no close relatives interested in Bonnie. I'm all she's got at the moment.'

'I see. And what is *your* situation, dear? Are you married?'

'No, I'm not.'

Mrs Hunter's expression was thoughtful. 'I see. Er…are going to raise little Bonnie all by yourself, then?'

'I will if I have to, Mrs Hunter. But I'd prefer to have some help. I haven't any family, either, you see. My mother died in the same house fire Sarah's did. She was an unmarried mother too, you see. And a runaway as well.'

Not to mention a woman of the night. *Both* women had been. But Tina thought it best not to bring up too much of their unsavoury backgrounds lest Mrs Hunter be the sort of person who thought such things were hereditary and not environmental.

'When Welfare could find no relatives who wanted us,' she went on matter-of-factly, 'Sarah and I spent the rest of our growing-up years in a state institution.' When they hadn't been fostered out to people, that was.

'Goodness. You poor things!'

'We survived, Mrs Hunter. But you can understand how we became so close. Sarah has entrusted me with the care and upbringing of her daughter and I aim to make sure she has the very best. I have no intention of Bonnie ever ending up like we did, with no money, and no adult to love and care for her.'

'You won't have to worry about that, dear. I'll be here for her, and for you. And so will Dominic, once I have a word or two with him. You can depend on that! Look, I think you'd best come inside and tell me absolutely everything. Then I think you'd best stay till Dominic gets home this evening and we can have a family pow-wow over all this.'

Tina was taken aback. 'Your son lives with you?'

'Well, yes…he does.'

'Oh, dear!'

'He's not a Mummy's boy, if that's what you're thinking. His decision to live with me was a practical decision, not a sentimental one.'

'Believe me,' Tina said drily, 'I don't think your son is a Mummy's boy. It's just that he's not going to be pleased to find me here when he comes home. Maybe you could ring him at the office and forewarn him.'

'Absolutely not! No! He doesn't deserve forewarning,' she said brusquely. 'Besides, Fridays are never a good day to ring Dominic at the office. I've already rung him once today and received a very poor reception. Which reminds me. I'd best ring Joanna and cancel her dinner invitation for tonight.'

'Not because of me, I hope,' Tina said, while wondering who Joanna was. A friend of Mrs Hunter's? Or Dominic's?

Mrs Hunter smiled a strange little smile. 'Not at all, dear. She's just a widow friend of mine. She can come another night. I'm a widow too, so little Bonnie won't be having a grandfather, I'm afraid. But you'll have me, won't you, darling?' she crooned down at the baby. 'Now, come along, dear, you bring the pram and I'll carry Bonnie. We'll have a cup of tea and a nice long chat. Then, afterwards, we might fill in the rest of the afternoon down at the shopping mall, buying a few little things for Bonnie here. Would you mind?'

'Oh, er…not at all.'

Off the woman went, making baby talk at Bonnie as she went, leaving Tina to do as ordered, trailing after her with the pram in rather a daze. There she'd been, thinking Mrs Hunter was such a sweet, gentle soul.

Which she *was*. But she was also a whirlwind of energy and decisiveness. Tina supposed it was unlikely that a too soft or susceptible personality could have produced a son like Dominic Hunter.

Dominic Hunter…

A lesser girl might have quailed to think of his reaction when he first spied her in his home this evening. She could just imagine it. Those hard blue eyes of his would narrow dangerously. The thick straight brows above them would beetle together again while smoke would waft from his flared nostrils. His broad shoulders would broaden while that huge chest of his would fill with outraged air. He would be ready to explode in seconds!

Tina smiled to herself.

She could hardly wait.

CHAPTER FOUR

DOMINIC considered being deliberately late home. He even contemplated ringing his mother at the last moment and claiming a fictitious business dinner in town.

But cowardice wasn't really his bag and he climbed into his blue BMW just before six and headed for the bridge. He would endure the dinner but had no intention of making any effort with that woman.

With a bit of luck Damien's merry widow—and his matchmaking mother—would finally see he was a lost cause where she was concerned. Lord, nothing turned him off quicker than gold-digging females who gushed all over him.

Blondes weren't really his thing, either. Nor double D cup breasts which jiggled like unset bowls of jelly.

Give him a tall, slender brunette, with long legs, a tight butt and firm boobs, and he was instantly interested. Make her a challenge and the combination was irresistible.

Joanna Parsons was neither.

An image of the brunette who'd been in his office today popped into his mind.

Again.

She'd been doing that all afternoon, even distracting him from work on several occasions.

Still, she'd been deliciously sexy in those tight white pedal-pusher pants and chest-hugging white ribbed top. Her hair was sexy too. Long and dark and kind of wild-looking, just like its owner.

Pity she was a con-artist. Or a fool.

Dominic was wondering which she might be when he turned into the driveway and parked the car outside the double garage. He still hadn't made up his mind by the time he slipped in the back door.

He was halfway up the stairs, heading for the sanctuary of his bedroom and private *en suite* bathroom when the sound of a baby crying stopped him in his tracks.

Frowning, Dominic turned and listened. It seemed to be coming from the front living room.

The television?

Not the television, he decided when the cries came again. Too loud. And too…real.

An appalling possibility popped into his mind.

Surely not, he thought. She wouldn't *dare*!

But then the baby cried again and he knew she had.

Whirling, he flew back down the stairs and over to the doorway of the room in question, disbelief and fury sending his blood pressure sky-high.

And there she was, large as life, wheeling a pram up and down on the polished wooden floor, singing very softly as she did so.

Dominic had opened his mouth to let her have it when she abruptly stopped the singing, and the wheeling. When she bent over to inspect the suddenly silent contents of the pram, the sight of those already tight white pants pulling even tighter across her extremely attractive derrière made him almost forget how angry he was for a moment.

But only for a moment.

'Hey, you there!' he boomed out.

She spun round, her dark hair flying out in a shining halo before settling more sedately on her slender shoulders. Her dark eyes flashed with extreme irritation as she hurried over, her fingers pressed to her lips.

'Hush up, for pity's sake,' she hissed. 'I've had the devil of a time getting her off to sleep. I think it's the strange house. Normally she goes off like clockwork after her bottle.'

Before he could say another word, she put a firm hand on his chest and pushed him backwards into the hallway, after which she carefully closed the door behind them, as though this whole scenario was perfectly normal and reasonable.

Dominic could only shake his head in amazement. Not a con-woman, he decided in total exasperation. A fool! A deliciously attractive fool, but a fool nevertheless!

'I don't know what you've told my mother,' he muttered, 'but you've got the wrong man. I am *not* the father of your baby.'

'Keep your shirt on, Mr Hunter. I never said you were.'

Instant bewilderment scrambled his brains. 'Huh?' was all he could manage.

'You can't be the father of *my* baby because I don't have one,' she explained, as though he were an idiot. 'I should have told you in your office but I simply didn't think. Bonnie belongs to Sarah.'

'Sarah?' he repeated blankly.

The brunette gave him a very droll look. 'I hope you're not going to tell me you don't know Sarah, either. Sarah Palmer,' she repeated coldly. 'In case you've forgotten, she was your secretary for several months last year, Mr Hunter, during which time you had an affair with her.'

Shock held Dominic speechless for a split second. But then anger swept back in. If Sarah thought she was going to pin the paternity of a baby on him on the strength of that one night, then she could think again!

'Sarah was my secretary, I admit,' he ground out. 'But we did *not* have an affair!'

The brunette folded her arms and practically rolled her eyes at him. 'Oh, come now, Mr Hunter. I didn't come down in the last shower. I know exactly what happened between you and Sarah. How you can stand there and deny having slept with her is beyond me!'

'I don't deny having slept with her,' he bit out. 'But it was only the once and I used protection. I repeat, I am not the father of that baby, or any other baby. As I said to you before, honey, you've got the wrong man.'

She actually smiled at him, an icy smile which set his teeth on edge. 'You are Dominic Hunter, the head of Hunter & Associates, aren't you?'

'You know damned well I am.'

'Then I've got the right man. But if you insist on a DNA test, I won't object.'

'A DNA test!' he exploded. 'I'm not having any damned DNA test!'

'Oh, yes, you are, Dominic.'

Dominic spun round to find his mother eyeing him with one of those stern looks which spelt her complete unwillingness to be persuaded otherwise. He knew because he'd seen that look many times during his lifetime. He groaned, then sighed his resignation to the inevitable. If he didn't succumb to a DNA test his life was going to be hell!

Still, once he'd calmed down a little, Dominic realised it was probably a good idea to have the test done. What better way to back his denial of paternity than with irretrievable scientific proof?

'Very well,' he agreed, with a return to composure, and both women looked surprised, even the dark-eyed brunette.

Who in hell *was* she? he began wondering. And what was she to Sarah? Her sister, perhaps?

He stared at her, thinking she looked nothing like Sarah at all. 'So tell me, Miss Know-it-all, why didn't Sarah come and see me in person about this baby of hers? Why send someone else in her place? Don't tell me it's because she's afraid of me because I won't believe that.'

Dominic was taken aback when those coal-black eyes, which till now had held such cynicism and contempt for him, suddenly shimmered with tears. When his mother walked over and put a comforting arm around the girl's shoulders, the penny dropped.

Sarah was dead.

That beautiful, sweet, lovely girl was dead.

His heart squeezed tight, and he wondered how she'd died. In childbirth, perhaps? But surely that kind of thing didn't happen these days.

'Sarah was killed in a road accident a couple of weeks ago,' his mother explained before he could ask, her own eyes reproachful towards him. 'She stepped out in front of a bus and was critically injured. Witnesses said she seemed to be daydreaming. Sarah didn't have any close relatives so she made Tina

Bonnie's legal guardian. They were best friends. Tina's come here today to see if we'll help raise the child.'

'That's all very sad,' Dominic said. 'And I'd be glad to give Tina some money, if that will help out. But, Mum, I am *not* Sarah's baby's father.'

His mother nodded. 'I appreciate you probably believe that, son. It explains your otherwise appalling behaviour. But Tina says Sarah told her you were the father for certain. She also said Sarah came to you and told you about her pregnancy when she was just a few weeks along. You denied you were the father back then, but gave her some money for a termination.'

'But that's just not true!' Dominic denied, truly shocked. 'If Sarah told you this, then she lied,' he directed forcibly at the brunette, who seemed to have swiftly recovered from the threat of tears to look at him coldly once more, her mouth pursed with scorn. 'I swear to you, I knew nothing of Sarah's pregnancy. Neither did she come and see me about it.'

The brunette's already disapproving lips curled over in even more derision. 'Sarah didn't tell lies.'

'Oh, for pity's sake, everyone tells lies!' he snapped.

'Do they indeed?'

Her sarcasm stung, as did her ongoing scepticism. She didn't believe a word he'd said. Dominic wasn't used to having his credibility doubted, and he didn't like it one bit.

He glared into those hard black eyes of hers, but they held his easily, and scornfully. Suddenly, he was overwhelmed by the most amazingly strong feeling, a mad compulsion to *make* her believe him, to take her in his arms and kiss that contemptuous mouth of hers till she melted against him, till she was all soft and compliant, till she was incapable of disbelieving, or denying him anything.

His head whirled with the dark intensity of his desires, his hands actually twitching with the urge to grab her right then and there. If his mother hadn't been standing guard he might actually have done so.

The realisation stunned him. For he wasn't that kind of man. Not normally.

Shaken at such an uncharacteristic loss of control, he curled his wayward fingers into fists and jammed them into his trouser pockets, only to discover to his horror that he was partially aroused.

He could not believe it. Never in his life had a woman got under his skin like this. He was torn between a black fury and an even blacker frustration. The more he tried to will his flesh into subsidence, the harder it became. Finally, he whipped his hands out of his pockets and did up the buttons on his suit jacket, at the same time drawing himself up tall in an outer display of dignity.

The irony of his actions was not lost on him, but be damned if he was going to risk being humiliated in front of this female.

'You actually believe all this rubbish?' he demanded of his mother, looking for distraction in argument.

'Tina showed me a photograph of Sarah,' she replied coolly. 'She's one of the most beautiful girls I've ever seen.'

'Meaning I wouldn't have been able to resist her, is that it?'

'Most men couldn't, Mr Hunter,' the object of his torment piped up. 'Especially when Sarah imagined herself in love with them. She confessed to me she was in love with you last October, not long before Bonnie must have been conceived. When Sarah was in love with a man, there wasn't anything she wouldn't do for them.'

Not like you, Dominic thought as he glared at her scorn-filled face. You would never be any man's slave.

Which only made him want her all the more.

The discovery of where this over-the-top and stunningly uncontrollable desire was coming from was little comfort to Dominic. His flesh remained stubbornly resistant to reasoning.

Okay, so he'd always liked a sexual challenge in a woman, but this was ridiculous. This woman despised him. It was extremely perverse to desire someone who was making it blatantly obvious he would be the last man on earth she'd go to bed with.

'I repeat,' he stated forcibly. 'I only slept with Sarah the once. And I used protection. It was the last night of her employ as my secretary. Her boyfriend had just gone off with some other woman and Sarah was very upset.'

'So you *comforted* her,' Tina said, the most blistering sarcasm in her tone.

His eyes clashed with her coldly cynical gaze, and again, something happened within him. Something deep and dark and even more dangerous. For this time he could not even control his thoughts.

One day, madam, he vowed hotly, I'll make you look at me differently to that. One day you'll give me fire, not ice. *One* day!

The moment of mental madness was over as quickly as it had come. But it still rattled Dominic, for it betrayed a lack of control previously unknown to his character.

He really had to get a grip on this situation.

And his body.

Or was it his mind playing havoc with him?

No, no, not his mind. This woman.

'Something like that,' he grated out.

'Condoms have been known to fail, you know,' she challenged tartly.

'Not the ones I buy.'

Her eyebrows lifted. Wickedly mocking, taunting eyebrows. 'I know of no such infallible brand.'

Neither did Dominic. But he was not going to give an inch where this woman was concerned.

'When and where can I take this test?' he asked, determined to have done with this appalling scenario as quickly as possible.

'I've rung the doctor,' his mother informed him. 'He said if you and Bonnie come in first thing on Monday morning, he'll take the required blood tests and have them sent off straight away. But, given it's not an urgent criminal case, the results might take anything up to a couple of weeks.'

'Surely they can do it quicker than that!'

'You can ask, I suppose. But I doubt it will make any difference. Apparently there's a bit of a backlog, due to increased demand for DNA tests, and they only give priority to real emergencies. Police work and such. Meanwhile, I've asked Tina and Bonnie to stay here with us. She's been working and living in Melbourne this past year and doesn't have anywhere decent to stay in Sydney other than the little bedsit Sarah was renting.'

'I don't think that's a very good idea, Mum,'

Dominic said firmly, gratified that he didn't sound as panic-stricken as he felt at this development.

'Why not?'

'For one thing, you'll grow attached to that baby in two weeks. How do you think you're going to feel when you find out she's not your granddaughter?'

She gave him a disturbingly smug look, as though she had some secret knowledge he wasn't privy to. 'I'll cope, *if* and when that happens. What other objections do you have?'

'I don't like to be pedantic, but you really know nothing about this woman, here, except what she's told you. For all you know, that baby in there could be anyone!'

Actually, this thought hadn't occurred to him before, but now that it had, he ran with it.

'And so could *she*!' he said, jabbing a finger towards the brunette. 'To invite a stranger into our home without checking her story with independent sources is not only naive, but downright stupid!'

CHAPTER FIVE

TINA'S eyes narrowed to dark slits at this last insult. Right, she thought savagely. This was war!

She'd put up with his looking at her as though he wanted to strangle her with his bare hands. She'd endured his huffing and puffing in pretend outrage. She'd even listened to his heated denials and unimaginative lies without actually laughing.

But this attack on *her* character and honesty was beyond the pale. First he'd called *Sarah* a liar, and now…now he was accusing *her* of the same. Worse! He was virtually calling her a shyster! She might have twisted the truth a little here today, but only because the truth was…well…complicated. Nothing changed the fact that this man *was* Bonnie's father. And now he was trying to worm his way out of accepting his responsibilities a second time!

'I had hoped to avoid bringing lawyers into this,' Tina flung at him in clipped tones, black eyes blazing. 'I'd hoped we could come to some amicable arrangement where Bonnie was concerned. But I see that was optimistic of me. I'm sorry, Mrs Hunter,' she said, turning to Bonnie's grandmother. 'I would have dearly liked to stay here with you. I can see you're not of your son's ilk. You're a good woman. But this is not going to work.'

'Oh, yes it will,' Mrs Hunter refuted strongly, and Tina blinked her astonishment. 'This is *my* house and I will have you here to stay if I want to. If you don't like it, Dominic, then you can be the one to go. Perhaps it's time you found a place of your own, anyway. The mortgages have long been paid off. And just think. If you lived on your own, you wouldn't have to worry about my matchmaking.'

Mortgages? Matchmaking?

Tina's eyebrows lifted. It seemed life in the Hunter household wasn't always smooth sailing.

'Fine,' the man himself snapped, and was actually whirling away when common sense returned to Tina. This was not what she wanted. Not at all!

'No, *wait*!' she said swiftly, and he stopped in mid-turn. 'Mrs Hunter, please,' she said pleadingly. 'I...I don't want to cause any trouble between you and your son.'

And she didn't. There was no advantage in it for her. Or for Bonnie. As much as she might like to tear strips off the man, it wasn't going to get her anywhere.

As for threatening to get a lawyer...she really didn't want to take that road, either. Court cases took time. And money.

Money she couldn't spare. Sarah's superannuation pay-out on her death had been a tidy little sum, but Tina had put that away in a special savings account for Bonnie's education. Her own savings were negligible. Acting wasn't the most steady or reliable of professions. Besides, she'd only been out of AIDA a year.

Common sense told Tina that conciliation was the way to go, not confrontation. She already had his mother on her side. Time to play a more clever and subtle hand.

It would almost kill her to back down, or make

compromising noises, but if Bonnie would eventually benefit, then she would do it.

Steeling herself, she harnessed her acting ability once more.

'Your son does have a point, Mrs Hunter,' Tina said with a convincing display of concession. 'I could be anyone. I do have my driver's licence and other ID with me, but I suppose that's not really enough. I dare say con-artists have such things all at the ready. Still, I can give you several phone numbers you can call to check out my identity. Friends. Employers. The legal aid lawyer who handled Sarah's will. I'm quite happy for you to have me checked out, Mr Hunter.'

She forced herself not to scowl at the man.

'As for Bonnie, I can certainly prove who *she* is. I brought her birth certificate with me. I also have the keys to Sarah's place, where there's a copy of her will and other personal papers which should help prove what I've told you and your mother today. I could get them and show them to you, if you like.'

He didn't exactly jump at her offer. In fact, he still looked decidedly reluctant. And remained grimly silent.

Tina sighed. So much for her humiliating herself. So much for compromise.

'Fair's fair, Dominic,' his mother intervened. 'Tina can't do much more than that, can she? Look, why don't you drive her over to Sarah's place tonight after dinner? That way you could start satisfying your doubts straight away and bring back anything Tina might need for herself and Bonnie at the same time.'

Tina saw the muscles along Dominic's strong jawline tighten appreciably. Clearly he didn't want to drive her anywhere. He didn't want to have anything to do with her.

Or with Bonnie.

Well, that was just too bad, she thought savagely.

Tina tried not to look as livid as she felt, but something must have shown in her face for his whole body seemed to stiffen, not just his jaw muscles.

It was probably her eyes. People often told her that her eyes gave her away every time. She'd tried to learn to control them, tried to make them project whatever emotion she wanted rather than what she was feeling at the time. An actress should be able to do that. But when she was this angry, when she disliked someone *this* much, she invariably failed.

'I'm not going to have any say in all this, am I?' the object of her intense dislike directed towards his mother, a black frustration in every word. 'Just don't blame me if things don't work out the way you hope they will.' He sucked in a deep breath which expanded his already large chest, then let it out slowly. 'I take it Joanna won't be coming for dinner tonight?'

'No,' his mother returned crisply. 'I postponed that till another night.'

'Well, thank heavens for small mercies,' he mocked. 'Who would have thought I'd be grateful to this fiasco for anything?'

Tina reacted poorly to the word 'fiasco'. But she bit her tongue. She had a feeling she was going to have to bite her tongue a lot around this man. He'd pressed the wrong buttons in her before she'd even met him. Dealing with him in the flesh stirred additional negative responses, not all of them strictly rational.

The truth was she'd never liked big men. Their size

sometimes unnerved her, making her feel small and defensive and vulnerable. Silly, really, when she was five foot nine inches tall and quite strong for her slender frame. But she'd often been grateful that most male actors were of the shorter, slighter variety.

Dominic Hunter was a big man. He looked extra big in this confined space, as opposed to his huge, airy office. Her gaze travelled up and down him as she assessed his actual height and weight. At least six foot four and a hundred kilos. Not fat, judging by his flat stomach, but with massive shoulders and long, strong arms. Large hands. Large fingers.

No doubt the rest of him was just as large.

Tina shuddered at the thought and he shot her a sharp glance. His hard blue eyes locked with hers, before dropping to her mouth, and then to her breasts.

Tina was flustered to find that her heart was racing madly.

Not that he was leering. He was simply subjecting her to the same cold appraisal she'd just given him. Tit for tat.

Immediately her chin shot up, her stomach clenching down hard in defiance of her unwanted and highly annoying inner turmoil. Be damned if she was going to start trembling in front of him like some nervous nelly!

But she was rattled all the same.

'I need to shower and change,' he said brusquely, and wrenched his gaze away from her breasts to land on his mother, who was watching her son with interest. 'Dinner still at the same time?' he rapped out.

'A little earlier, I think, since you're going out afterwards. June prepared everything this morning—thinking, of course, that I'd be having Joanna to dinner tonight. But Tina can eat Joanna's share. I just have to set the table and heat some things up. Say...seven-thirty?'

'Fine,' he muttered, and was gone, striding over to the stairs and swiftly disappearing from view. A door banged shut shortly afterwards and Tina let out a ragged sigh before she could think better of it.

Mrs Hunter reached over and patted her on the back of her hand. 'His bark's worse than his bite,' she said. 'Actually, I thought you handled the situation very well, standing up to him like that. Mentioning a lawyer was a very good idea. If there's one thing which will bring Dominic to heel it's the thought he might have to waste time fighting a paternity suit in court. He's a workaholic, you see, and workaholics never have time for anything else but work. It rather explains why he had an affair with your friend. The only woman he ever sees regularly is his secretary.'

'I don't think he's having an affair with his present secretary,' Tina said drily, and Mrs Hunter laughed.

'I'd have to agree with you there. I find it odd, though, that Dominic's so vehement in his denials over this affair. Why claim he only slept with Sarah the once if that wasn't so?'

Tina didn't like to call Dominic an out-and-out liar to his mother's face, but she had solid evidence he'd slept with Sarah more than once. 'Er...I'm not sure why he said that.'

'Could there have been another man?'

'Oh, no! Now that I *do* know. Sarah fell in love a lot, but only with one man at a time. She was in love with your son in late October, and even Dominic is admitting he slept with her towards the end of November. Believe me when I tell you there would have been no other man in the meantime. When Sarah loved, she loved exclusively and obsessively.'

'Fair enough. But why would Dominic say Sarah hadn't come to see him about the pregnancy if she had? My son is no saint, but he's usually honest.'

Clearly the woman couldn't embrace the fact her son could lie with the best of them.

'Um…I honestly can't say,' she murmured. 'Maybe he didn't want to look badly in your eyes. Look, I don't know what's going on in your son's mind, Mrs Hunter. But I know he's Bonnie's father and the DNA test will show that.'

'Oh, yes, I agree with you there. In fact, I have no doubts whatsoever!'

'You haven't?' Tina had begun to worry that Dominic's denials might have brought some doubt. She herself didn't have any, but she wasn't Dominic's mother.

'Heavens, no,' the woman said, smiling. 'Bonnie's the spitting image of Dominic when he was a baby. I noticed that straight away. Such a pretty child, he was. And a pretty lad too, till puberty turned him into the big lug he is today.'

Tina found it difficult to see any resemblance. She thought Bonnie looked like Sarah. Still, she hadn't known Dominic when he was a baby.

'Er…what do you think Dominic will do when the DNA test comes back and he can no longer deny he's the father?' Tina asked.

The woman sighed. 'I have to admit he won't be pleased. Hopefully, he'll come round.'

'I wonder if he will…'

Tina was gnawing at her bottom lip when she became aware of Mrs Hunter looking her over with an assessing gaze.

'Do you have a boyfriend, Tina?' she asked with seeming innocence, and Tina almost laughed. If Dominic Hunter's mother was thinking what Tina imagined she was thinking, then she'd better think again. Hell would freeze over before she fell for *that* man. Or any man, for that matter, she thought caustically.

Still, it was hardly the right moment to reveal what Sarah had always castigated her over: her inability to love or trust the opposite sex. Given both their backgrounds, Tina thought her negative attitude to the male species was justifiable. It amazed her that Sarah had always been so willing to be taken in by them.

Tina couldn't help being hard and cynical in her dealings with men, and sex. Not that she was a virgin. She'd slept with a couple of the species, though never for love. Simply to know how to act in sex scenes. She'd also wanted to see what all the hoo-ha was all about.

She still had no idea.

'No,' she denied. 'No boyfriend at the moment.'

The answer pleased Bonnie's grandmother.

'And is there any reason you *have* to return to Melbourne to live? You did say the part you were playing in that soap opera was over.'

'For the time being. But if the viewing public miss me, they might write me back in.'

'Can't you get an acting job here in Sydney?'

'Unfortunately there are more production companies in Melbourne.'

'Oh…'

'Please don't concern yourself, Mrs Hunter. Bonnie

is my number one priority at the moment, not my career. If you want me to stay in Sydney, I will.' Actually, Tina was disillusioned with her choice of career at the moment. It wasn't bringing her the pleasure and satisfaction she'd once thought it would. She was more than happy to put acting aside for a while and look after Bonnie.

Mrs Hunter beamed, and Tina thought how lucky Bonnie was to have a grandmother like this.

'You know, you really must stop calling me Mrs Hunter. My name is Ida.'

'Ida,' Tina repeated, smiling.

'Wonderful. Now I suppose I'd better go get dinner ready before grumpy-bumps comes downstairs.'

Tina tried not to laugh, but 'grumpy-bumps' described Dominic Hunter to a T. Men like him didn't like women making waves in their lives. Clearly he was most put out by all this.

Tough, she thought.

'Can I be of any help?' she offered.

'Oh, no, dear, I'll be fine. Why don't you pop along to the powder room and freshen up for dinner?'

'Fine,' she said. 'I'll do just that.'

CHAPTER SIX

DOMINIC stepped under a deliberately cold shower, all the breath rushing from his lungs as the icy spray hit his seriously overheated flesh. Swearing, he gritted his teeth and stood there staunchly while the freezing water achieved what his will-power could not.

Finally, he turned the taps onto a warmer setting and reached for the shower gel, squirting several dollops into his hands, then lathering it all over his body, finding some satisfaction in having his hormones under control once again.

But for how long, with that female living under his roof?

Hell! He hadn't been the victim of such a wayward and unwanted burst of lust since he was fourteen!

Don't even *think* about her, he warned himself, when his flesh prickled once more.

But he *had* to think about her, *and* the situation.

Okay, so maybe it wasn't a scam, and maybe Tina wasn't a con-artist, but she was seriously deluded.

She had to be if she believed he was that baby's father.

Because it was impossible!

Well…not a hundred per cent impossible, he conceded reluctantly. Tina was right. Condoms had been known to fail. But the likelihood was extremely low. Besides, if Sarah had believed even for a moment he could be Bonnie's father, she *would* have come to see him.

But she hadn't!

No, Bonnie wasn't his child. Sarah had known that.

Yet Tina believed he was.

Which meant Sarah had lied to her best friend.

Why did people lie? he speculated. Because of shame? To protect someone?

Perhaps the baby's father was a married man, someone who worked at Hunter & Associates…

Dominic frowned as he tipped his head back into the shower to let the soap wash free. He needed to find out the real father's identity—and quickly—before his own mother had time to get too attached to the child. And before he went stark raving mad!

My God, the thought of having that female under his roof for the next two weeks or more was too awful to contemplate. Those fantastic eyes of hers. That sulky, pouting mouth. Those small, high, firm breasts.

Dominic groaned. It seemed he only had to *think* about her now and he was in trouble. Reaching up, he snapped off the hot water tap and braced himself for more torture.

This time, the cold water didn't work nearly as quickly.

Twenty minutes later, dressed in too tight jeans and a navy golf shirt, a still agitated Dominic clomped downstairs. He hadn't bothered to shave, and a five o'clock shadow was beginning to sprout. His hair was still wet from his elongated shower and his tan loafers covered feet which looked like prunes, they'd been wet for so long.

At least dinner shouldn't be too bad, he conceded grudgingly as he strode along the hallway. He'd be sitting down, hidden from view. But he didn't fancy driving Tina anywhere afterwards. He didn't fancy being anywhere within touching distance of that woman!

He also didn't fancy having to keep defending himself to her when he was innocent. Damn it all, what had he done to deserve any of this? He'd been a good guy all his life, hadn't he? He'd been a good son. A good brother. A good friend. He didn't take drugs; didn't drink to excess; didn't cheat on his clients.

He worked hard and he gave money to charity.

Most important of all, he didn't indulge in heartless seductions and he *hadn't* impregnated any of his secretaries!

Hearing female voices coming from the kitchen on the right, Dominic turned left into the dining room, where he marched over to the sideboard and proceeded to pour himself a stiff shot of Scotch. There were times when only a drink would do!

'Don't drink that, Dominic.'

The glass froze just short of his mouth. He glared over at his mother as she walked in carrying a steaming soup tureen. 'Why?' he demanded to know.

'You have to drive after dinner, remember? And there's a bottle of your favourite red to have with the meal. You can't have both and be under the limit.'

'Then I'll only have one glass of wine,' he grated out, and took a deep swallow.

The alcohol hadn't had time to hit when Tina entered the room.

She'd put her hair up while he'd been upstairs, he noted. And glossed her mouth a tantalising pink. She looked as deliciously inviting to him as fairy-floss to a sugar-addicted child.

Her dark eyes glittered in his direction as she made her way to her seat at the table, their expression just short of scathing. Perversely, that seemed to be just what his body was waiting for.

Despairingly, Dominic jerked his eyes away from her and downed the rest of the whisky.

Tina watched him quaff back the drink as if he really needed it, but felt not the slightest twinge of sympathy for him. If ever there was a man who was acting guilty, it was Dominic Hunter.

His eyes were getting a hunted look to them, his body language betraying extreme annoyance which was way beyond the justified anger of the innocent. He was acting like some wild beast backed into a corner, practically quivering with the effort of controlling his frustration and suppressing his simmering fury.

Whenever he looked at her, Tina had the feeling he'd like nothing better than to grab hold of her and shake her till her teeth rattled. His appearance tonight didn't lessen his threatening air, either.

Out of his business suit he looked more like a construction foreman than ever. When he'd lifted that glass to his lips just now, his muscular bicep had bulged underneath the short sleeve. In fact, in that chest-hugging navy top and in those tight blue jeans, his whole body seemed to be bulging with menacing muscle.

The thought of being alone with him later was not a pleasant one.

Not that Tina seriously thought he would lay a finger on her. It was her own disquieting reaction to his macho size which was bothering her. Again.

Why couldn't he have been more like Sarah's usual boyfriends? came the irritable thought.

Perhaps because he *hadn't been* her boyfriend, shot back the highly disturbing answer.

Tina's eyes snapped up from the table to stare at Dominic as he settled himself opposite her. An unhappy frown creased her forehead as her mind grappled with this unexpected and unwanted thought.

What if he was telling the truth? What if he *had* only slept with Sarah the once? What if he *had* practised safe sex and Bonnie's father was really the mystery boyfriend Dominic claimed had dumped Sarah that week?

It was possible, Tina supposed. But, if so, then she was sitting at the wrong table, in the wrong home, with the wrong family.

No, I'm not, she refuted sternly in her mind, pushing away the split second of nausea. Sarah had told her personally that her boss, Dominic Hunter, was the man she was in love with, *and* sleeping with. There was also what Sarah had told her neighbour, as well as those cards from florists amongst Sarah's things, with all those intimate little messages, all signed 'D'. What were the odds on Sarah having two lovers working at Hunter & Associates with the initial D?

No, it had to be Dominic. Just because he wasn't Sarah's usual physical type that didn't let him off the hook. He was Bonnie's father all right.

Tina sighed her relief, dropped her eyes and started on with her soup.

Grumpy-bumps did the same, the meal progressing mostly in silence. Ida tried to make conversation, but Dominic refused to be drawn in. Tina didn't help much, she supposed, but, frankly, it was less stressful saying nothing and just eating.

Soup gave way to a veal dish done in a creamy sauce, followed by a thankfully fat-free fruit salad.

Tina had to watch what she ate. She was naturally slim, but television put ten pounds on you, and television was where the parts were at at the moment. She wasn't so foolish as to count her chickens before they hatched. As much as she might like to devote herself full-time to raising Bonnie, life just might not work out that way.

Tina was just finishing her fruit salad when a high-pitched cry infiltrated the dining room.

Tina immediately jumped up from the table. 'The baby!' she exclaimed, and dashed from the room.

Dominic rolled his eyes, which brought a sharp glance from his mother as she too rose from her seat.

'I'd get used to that sound, if I were you.'

'How many times do I have to tell you, Mum?' he said with a weary sigh. 'That baby is *not* mine.'

She laughed. She actually laughed. She was still laughing when she left the room.

Dominic shook his head after her. *Women,* he thought once again, with a wealth of frustration. They never gave up. There he'd been, actually worrying about his mother getting upset when she found out the baby *wasn't* her grandchild.

But she simply refused to be warned, refused to listen to reason—*and* her own son. She'd rather listen to the tissue of lies being fed to her by that perhaps well-meaning but seriously deluded creature.

The seriously deluded creature came back into the room, carrying a now silent pink bundle over her shoulder, patting what he supposed was the baby's back and making motherly noises.

'There, there, darling, yes, I know you're hungry and you're wet. I just need to…oh,' she cried on glancing around and seeing he was alone in the room. 'Where's Ida?'

'I have no idea,' he told her drily. 'I thought she'd gone to be with you and the baby.'

'I need to know where she put the disposable nappies she bought. Here! Why don't you hold your daughter while I go find her?'

Dominic's immediately horrified look brought an answering look of disgust. 'She won't bite, you know,' Tina snapped as she walked over and shoved the bundle into Dominic's startled arms. 'If she cries, just walk around the room and rock her backwards and forwards. She's a sucker for that.'

'But…but…'

But Tina was gone.

Dominic pressed his lips together and glared down at the baby lying in his stiffly outstretched arms. Two big blue eyes looked back up at him, two undeniably lovely and very engaging blue eyes. They showed no signs of any recent crying, which suggested a case of crocodile tears, undoubtedly the come-and-get-me-I'm-bored kind of crying.

'A little con-artist already, eh, kid?' he muttered. 'Just like your adopted mother. If she thinks this is going to work, then she can darned well think again!'

Startled by his deep male voice, that cute little baby face screwed up into a less cute expression and let rip.

Dominic's eyebrows hit the ceiling. How could so much noise come from such a sweet little bow-shaped mouth?

He was on his feet in a flash, pacing around the

room and rocking away like mad. He even resorted to some hopefully soothing small talk of his own.

'There, there, don't cry now. I didn't mean to make you cry. I'm not angry at you. It's this crazy situation I'm angry at. I guess you're not used to loud voices. Or men. I'll talk softly in future. I promise…'

All the pacing, rocking and promises didn't work. The cries got louder, if that were possible. Bunched little fists escaped the bunny rug she was wrapped in and starting flailing around like mad, hitting him once on the chin.

'I see you're not a natural-born father,' his mother said drily as she came in and took the baby from him. 'Let me show you.'

Lying the messy bundle down on the empty end of the dining table, she swiftly hooked those lethal weapons underneath the turned-in edges of the bunny rug, then wound the rug around very tight.

'Babies liked to be wrapped up tightly,' his mother lectured as she hoisted the papoose-like bundle up and over her shoulder. 'That way they feel safe and secure.'

All crying immediately ceased, two instantly dry blue eyes eyeing Dominic sanguinely from the safety of distance.

'See?' Ida said smugly.

'Yeah, I see,' came his dry reply. 'All females use tears to get what they want, right from the cradle. I'm going upstairs to make a phone call. Tell our guest to be ready to go in five minutes. I don't want to be all night doing this. It's already nine and I'm going out later.'

'Where to?'

He gave his mother a baleful look. 'Mum, I'm

thirty-three years old. I won't be grilled like some schoolboy. But, if you must know, I'm going to see my girlfriend.'

'Your *girlfriend*!'

'That's right.'

'But you've never mentioned having a girlfriend. At least…not lately.'

'I wonder why?' he said testily.

'I hate to think,' she retorted.

Dominic decided it was time to lay down the law. Unequivocally this time. He'd been a bit weak, letting his mother try to matchmake him with women like Joanna Parsons. He supposed he'd gone along with it in a fashion because he hadn't wanted to crush *all* her hopes at once. Mark decamping to a monastery had upset her a lot.

But enough was enough!

'Mum,' he stated firmly. 'You know my feelings about marriage and children. They're not for me. Look, I know you think I'm going to change my mind about that one day, but I won't. I know you think I'm going to fall in love one day, but I won't.'

'Does this girlfriend of yours know that?' she asked archly.

'She certainly does.'

'Strange girlfriend.'

'Shani understands me. We have an…arrangement.'

'Meaning you just use each other for sex.'

Dominic winced. 'I wouldn't put it quite that crudely.'

'Then how would you put it?'

'We're…lovers.'

'No, you're not. Love has nothing whatsoever to do with what you do with each other.'

His mother's scorn stung. Dominic also resented being made to feel ashamed of what was really a very practical and sensible relationship. He wasn't hurting anyone, least of all Shani.

'That's a very old-fashioned viewpoint,' he snapped, and swung round to leave the room, only to find Tina standing in the doorway, a bottle in one hand and a nappy in the other.

How much had she overheard? he wondered.

If the shock in her eyes was any judge, then everything about his relationship with Shani.

'If you'll excuse me,' he ground out as he approached the doorway.

She stepped aside with a speed and a flash of panic in her eyes which was downright insulting. What did she think? That physical contact with him would contaminate her?

Dominic almost laughed. She'd have a right to be scared if she knew what he'd been thinking and feeling about her all through dinner.

Fortunately, those feelings seemed to have taken a temporary back seat. Perhaps because he'd decided to take positive action to rid himself of them, once and for all!

He strode on down the hallway, then mounted the stairs two at a time.

Five minutes later he walked more sedately back downstairs, his equilibrium restored, his temper well under control. Shani would be waiting for him, regardless of when he arrived.

Sensible, sexy Shani.

If only there were more women like her!

CHAPTER SEVEN

TINA sat stiffly and silently in the passenger seat of Dominic Hunter's plush and new-smelling car, trying desperately to ignore the undermining and somewhat confusing feelings flooding through her.

She'd known it would not be a pleasant experience being alone with this man in the confines of a car.

But it wasn't his broad shoulders bothering her at that moment. It was something which had happened when she'd overheard his tiff with Ida in the dining room.

As she'd listened to Dominic Hunter admitting to a strictly sexual relationship with some secret girlfriend, she'd experienced the strangest reaction.

Not contempt, as one might have imagined.

But a weird kind of excitement.

Excitement, for pity's sake!

Tina had been so shocked that she'd stood rooted to the spot, her mouth half open, her heart racing with a dark rush of adrenaline. Her mind had instantly flooded with the most appalling erotic pictures, involving not him and this Shani woman, but herself!

When he'd started striding towards where she was standing in the doorway, she hadn't been able to get out of his way quickly enough.

Fifteen minutes later, she was still in shock, even more so because those disturbing feelings hadn't abated. If anything, they'd grown worse. She was pricklingly aware of her own body as she sat in the car so close to him. And awesomely aware of his!

Tina could not understand what was happening to her. She didn't like big men, for starters. And she didn't like sex at all!

'Tell me about your friendship with Sarah,' he said abruptly into the tortured silence.

'Why?' she burst out, angry with him for doing this to her. 'What's the point?'

'No point,' he grumped. 'Just something to talk about. It'll take us at least half an hour to get over the bridge and out to Sarah's place. You did say Lewisham, didn't you?'

'Yes,' she muttered.

Lewisham was an inner western suburb which straddled the railway line and was full of old blocks of flats, plus old houses cut up into small apartments and bedsits. Sarah had rented one of the latter. It was cramped, but clean, and possibly all she'd been able to afford on her single mother's allowance.

'Well?' he prompted impatiently.

Tina shrugged. Why not tell him? He would have to know in the end. Sarah was the mother of his child, after all. And it was better than sitting there thinking thoughts she'd much rather not think.

So she told him. And she didn't bother to water anything down. She told him the whole unvarnished, unsavoury truth.

It was blessedly distracting, watching his initial shock to her sordid tale, then trying to guess his thoughts and reactions.

There was no doubting he could hold a superb poker face when he wanted to. She had no idea what he was really thinking.

To give him credit, he didn't pass any superficial judgements, or express any false sympathies. When she'd finished the first part of her story, his questions weren't cruel, just inquisitive.

'So when the terrace house burnt down that night, killing both your mothers and several…er…guests, where were you and Sarah?'

'Out.'

'*Out?* In the middle of the night up at the Cross?'

Tina shrugged. 'Better than staying at home. A ship was in port and our mums had brought home quite a party. They'd all had a lot to drink, and when that happened I knew to keep Sarah out of harm's way. Even at nine, Sarah was attracting male attention.'

'Good God. At *nine*?'

He fell silent, as though having difficulty absorbing such an unimaginable lifestyle. Tina had no such difficulty. She'd lived it. And she'd lived the difficult years after their mothers had died, when she'd still had to protect Sarah from the opposite sex.

It had been hard when Sarah herself had been such a willing victim, right from her early teenage years. As much as she regretted it now, Tina understood why she'd walked out of Sarah's life. She simply hadn't been able to stand by and watch Sarah being used any more. She'd had enough!

'So where did you and Sarah go after the fire?' came the next question.

'We became wards of the state.'

'What about your grandparents?'

'Never knew them. After our mothers died, the welfare people must have searched. Maybe they found them, but obviously, at the time, they didn't want anything to do with the offspring of their black sheep daughters. You see, both our birth certificates said 'fathers unknown'. By the time *we* were old enough to search, Sarah's grandparents were dead and she had no aunts and uncles. I discovered a grandfather and three uncles living in England. I wrote several times. One of my uncles eventually wrote back to tell me that my letters had upset my grandfather very much, that my mother had been a bad seed, who'd brought the family nothing but shame and misery, and they would appreciate it if I didn't write or contact them ever again.'

'That must have been tough.'

'Life isn't meant to be easy, I'm told,' she said caustically, happy to be back to her old, cynical, hard-hearted self.

Thinking about her past was always a sobering experience. It didn't leave much room for any other feelings besides bitterness. How she could have even momentarily succumbed to such a crazy thing as sexual desire for the man sitting next to her was beyond her! She knew better than anyone what men were like, especially where sex was concerned.

'Anyway, back to Sarah and me,' she went on, quite coldly. 'Neither of us could be legally adopted because there were no parents to sign the papers. We were both fostered out once, but that didn't work too well. The darling man of the house couldn't keep his hands off Sarah. I complained to the authorities and, after another equally disastrous placement, they just kept us in a home they had for wards of the state. We went to the local school during the day, but neither of us excelled. Not that we were dumb, but Sarah was too busy chatting up the boys and I was off in a world of my own. As soon as we were fifteen, we left school and got jobs serving in shops. Sarah did a secretarial course at night, and worked her way up to better and better positions, while I did any old job and furthered my education. We flatted together till last year, when I went to Melbourne to find work.'

No way was she going to tell him about their argument and estrangement.

'What kind of work?'

'Didn't your mother tell you?'

'Tell me what?'

'I'm an aspiring actor.'

'No, she didn't tell me. So are you a good actor?'

'I graduated from AIDA.'

'Mmm. I hear that's a very difficult course to get in to.'

'It is. I auditioned every year for three years before I won a place.'

'Driving ambition or just plain stubborn?'

'I would have once said driving ambition. Now I lean towards just plain stubborn.'

'I can believe that,' he said drily. 'And did you find yourself a good acting job in Melbourne?'

'That depends on how you look at it. I got regular work on a soap playing a *femme fatale* who unfortunately was written out at the end of the season. Some people look down on doing soaps, but they're a good showcase if you have talent. And it's something to put in my rather thin resumé.'

'So what's going to happen to your acting career now you have Bonnie to look after?'

'It'll just have to take a back seat for a while.'

'How old are you, by the way?'

'Twenty-six. Why?'

'What's your money situation like?' he asked, ignoring her 'why'.

'Is this just curiosity or are you planning on making a charitable donation?' she flung at him caustically.

'Stop being stroppy and just answer the question.'

Stroppy, was she? She hadn't *begun* to be stroppy! 'My financial status is my own private and personal business. You don't honestly think I'd give such information to a man I might have to sue, do you?'

'Meaning you're not exactly flush, otherwise you'd throw it in my face.'

'Meaning you and I are enemies, Mr Hunter. I won't be supplying you with any knowledge which might give you an advantage over me. Sarah was the sweetest, softest person in the entire world and she's entrusted me with her daughter. Believe me when I tell you I aim to do anything and everything in my power to force you to accept her as such, and to provide for her, for *life*, in the manner she deserves.'

'So money's the bottom line, is that it?'

'God, but I pity you. *Love's* the bottom line, you fool. I love Bonnie, but I'm not her blood. You and your mother are. Ida can give Bonnie the kind of love I can't give her, and which a child always craves. Believe me, I know. I don't delude myself *you'll* ever give your daughter love. From what I've heard and seen of you, you're impervious to the emotion. But money can provide a child with the illusion of love. And who knows? In time, you might grow to care for Bonnie. If she's anything like her mother in nature—and I suspect she is—it will be hard not to.'

'Don't you think this lecture would be best left till the DNA test comes back?'

'You wanted me to talk about Sarah,' she retorted.

'I can't talk about Sarah without bringing up Bonnie. Not to mention Bonnie's defunct father!'

'Since you feel so strongly—and so angrily—about my supposed part in all this, why didn't you come and see me sooner? When Sarah told you that I denied being Bonnie's father and gave her money for an abortion, why didn't you come flying into my office like an avenging angel back then? The woman who barged into my life today would not have shrunk from such an action. Why wait till now?'

Tina hadn't been anticipating this question and it flustered her for a moment. 'Well, I…I…I was in Melbourne, remember?'

'Surely you came back to see Sarah when Bonnie was born?'

Tina coloured guiltily as she felt him staring at her. 'Actually, no…I…I didn't,' she confessed, a lump forming in her throat.

There was a short, sharp silence.

'Are you going to tell me why?' he asked, sounding puzzled and almost angry. 'Or are you going to leave me to think you're the strangest kind of best friend God ever put breath into?'

'I…we…we'd argued,' Tina choked out, and looked away from him and out through the passenger window. They were approaching the Harbour Bridge at the time, but Tina saw nothing of the spectacular view. She was busy battling for control.

'What about?' he demanded to know.

She could not speak. She just shook her head at him as tears flooded her eyes.

He sighed. 'There are tissues in the glove-box.'

She'd just retrieved a handful when her long-held

grief and guilt broke free and she burst into deep, gut-wrenching sobs.

Dominic was grateful he was driving across the bridge at the time. For he could not stop, or pull over to the side. Thank the Lord he could not do anything really stupid like take her into his arms.

He did have to eventually slow down for the toll gates. But his stop was only minimal. Even so, the man collecting the money glowered at him as if he was some heartless bastard for making his woman cry like that.

The sound of her weeping moved him more than he liked, as had her story of her wretched upbringing. It explained a lot about her, and her determination to give Sarah's child the best. It also sparked a weird guilt in him which he couldn't fathom, or reason with. Perhaps it came with her accusation that he was incapable of loving or caring for a person.

Finally her sobs quietened, and she straightened in the seat, the no doubt sodden tissues still clenched tightly in her lap.

'Better now?' he asked gently.

She nodded.

'Would you like to talk about it? Your argument with Sarah?'

'Not really,' she said tautly.

'Fair enough. I presume you were still in Melbourne when she was killed?'

Again, she nodded, her hands twisting in her lap.

'You hadn't made up after your argument?' he probed.

She looked pained at this question. 'I…I tried to call her several times. But she'd left her job and moved out of our old flat. Her name wasn't in the directory. She didn't have a phone, you see. I knew she knew where *I* was, so I thought…I thought she didn't want to have anything further to do with me…'

'Did you think she'd had an abortion?'

Her eyes flashed round, still luminous from her tears, but filled with outrage. 'Sarah would *never* have had an abortion!'

'Fair enough. Don't overreact, now. I'm just trying to figure this out. I thought you might have argued over her not having an abortion. I mean…I would imagine a girl of your unhappy background might not agree with bringing an unwanted child into the world.'

'Then it just shows you know nothing whatsoever about girls like me. Or girls at all, for that matter. If you must know, we argued about *you*!'

'Me?' He could not have been more shocked.

'That's right. Look, you have to understand Sarah's life-long behaviour with men to know why I reacted as badly as I did. She was forever falling in love, often with men she worked with, and never with men who loved her back. I'd grown so tired of picking up the pieces after her latest affair had blown up in her face. I was also sick and tired of her having to change jobs because she'd become involved yet again in some sordid affair with a married man.'

'She had affairs with married men?'

'Sometimes. Look, she wasn't a slut or anything like that. She just couldn't resist being loved. If a man told her he loved her then she simply could not resist him. It wasn't sex she wanted, but love. When she went to work for Hunter & Associates she promised me it would be different. But I soon began to see the signs that she was in love again. The hours she took getting ready for work. The new clothes. The sexy perfume. So I tackled her on who the new man was. Initially she denied being involved with anyone at work, but I knew she was. I wouldn't let it drop. When she finally confessed to me she was in love with you, her new boss, I just saw red.'

'Sarah was in love with me?' Dominic repeated, stunned.

'Please don't pretend you didn't know that,' came her scathing remark.

'But I didn't! I swear to you.'

'Maybe she hid the depth of her feelings from you because she knew the sort of man you were,' she suggested scornfully. 'Who knows now? Anyway, I tore strips off her, called her a fool and, yes, I called her a slut. All the usual insults between friends. She defended her love for you with such passion, said it was deeper than anything she'd ever felt before. She even called *me* the fool because I didn't know what love was.'

Tina's sigh sounded so sad, and full of regret. 'Things were said that shouldn't have been said, I guess. I was already packed to go to Melbourne for a while. Sarah told me to get out and that she didn't want to see or hear from me ever again.'

'I see,' Dominic murmured, while his mind raced, this more in-depth perspective on Sarah disturbing his till now confident stance over his being Bonnie's father.

That night he'd slept with her…had she lied about the mystery boyfriend? Had she contrived a situation where he'd feel sorry for her and take her into his arms? Had she skilfully engineered a seduction scene, undermining his will-power with wine before going in for the kill with the oldest trick in the book? Tears!

If she had, then for what purpose?

There really was only one possible answer.

To entrap him with a pregnancy…

His mind searched that night for exactly what had happened, but in all honesty he was a bit fuzzy about the details. It was so long ago, and he'd had quite a bit to drink that night.

Still, he was absolutely sure they'd used protection both times.

Both times?

His stomach crunched down hard at this sudden added memory. Sarah had snuggled up to him during the night and aroused him again with a very seductive and experienced hand. It had been *she* who'd put the condom on him that second time, now that he came to think of it. Had she done something to it? Had she hoped in her one-sided and silly love that she might conceive and that he would subsequently marry her?

From what Tina had told him, the girl had been a hopeless romantic, a needy, neglected soul who'd craved affection and sought it in all the wrong places.

She certainly didn't find it in *you*, then, came the brutal and uncomfortable thought.

The next morning, he'd made it quite clear that the night before had been a mistake and a oncer. He'd taken her distressed silence for embarrassment and agreement, whereas maybe it had been the futility of her feelings sinking in. Maybe, when she'd found out she was pregnant, she'd been loath to come to him and admit her trickery.

Which brought him right back to one of Tina's original accusations: that Sarah had come to him with news of her pregnancy and that he'd denied paternity and given her money for a termination.

Some more pennies dropped, and he shot Tina a bewildered look. 'You didn't even know she was pregnant, did you?'

'No,' she muttered.

Dominic's temper shot up. 'In that case, how could she have told you she'd come to me after she found out about the baby? Hell on earth, you lied about that, didn't you?'

He watched her shoulders straighten, her eyes once again hard and cold. 'Only in so many words. The fact still remains she did just that. She told her new neighbour all about it, and that woman related the whole sorry episode to me only yesterday. She said Sarah cried and cried for days afterwards.'

Dominic could not believe what he was hearing. 'You condemned me on second-hand hearsay?'

She flashed him a look of utter scorn. 'No. I have *other* damning evidence against you.'

'What other evidence?'

'Never you mind.'

'But I *do* mind,' he bit out. 'I mind very much indeed.'

'And I mind your letting Sarah down,' she lashed out. 'Whether you loved her or not, you could at least have supported her, both emotionally and financially. It breaks my heart to think of her having that baby all alone, and her dying all alone.'

'What breaks your heart, madam,' he countered savagely, 'is that *you* let her down. You weren't there when she needed you. You called her a silly slut and left her to fend for herself when you knew she wasn't nearly as strong as you were.'

Her face went dead white in the dim light of the car, and Dominic wished with all his heart that he could take the nasty words back again.

'Don't you dare cry again!' he ground out when her chin started quivering. They were far too close to the address she'd given him. Far too close to his stopping the car and having no excuse not to extend her some physical sympathy.

Immediately her chin stopped trembling, and she blazed black fury at him.

Hell, but she was something to behold when she was in a rage. Her face flushed. Her eyes flashed. And those lovely full lips of hers alternately pressed and pouted.

'I'll never cry in front of you again, you unconscionable bastard!' she pronounced.

Thank heaven for more small mercies, he thought ruefully as he turned off Parramatta Road and headed for the bridge which crossed the railway line and led to their destination.

CHAPTER EIGHT

THE house looked just as shabby at night as it did in daylight, Tina thought as she led Dominic down the side path to the door which led into Sarah's bedsit. Tina still cringed at the sight of it.

It had probably been a grand old residence once, many years before someone had bought it and divided it into several flats and bedsits. Time and neglect now saw the roof and guttering badly in need of repair. The paint was peeling from the old wooden window-frames. Some of panes were cracked. The garden was overgrown; the paths were full of weeds.

Tina unlocked the door and snapped on the light, once again feeling overwhelmed with sadness at Sarah being forced to live in a place like this with her baby. Maybe it would do Dominic Hunter good to see what the mother of his child had been reduced to.

He didn't say a word as he glanced around the wretched room which had been Sarah and Bonnie's home. Tina glanced around again as well, looking past the surface cleaniless to the harsh reality beyond.

The paint on the wall was cracked and peeling. The rug on the floor was threadbare. A cheap plastic light fitting covered the bare bulb in the ceiling. All the furniture was shabby and second-hand, except for the quilt on the bed and the things Sarah had bought for the baby. Now *they* were all brand, spanking new, and quite expensive.

How like Sarah, Tina had thought when she'd first

walked in here just over a week ago. Only the best for her baby.

At the time, she'd wondered how Sarah had afforded to buy the imported cradle and pram and Bouncinette, not to mention the expensive baby outfits. Sarah had never been one to save. She'd spent everything she'd earned every week on her appearance, spending a fortune on clothes and accessories, not to mention make-up and visits to the hairdresser.

Tina had discovered the answer to that particular riddle when she'd looked in the battered wardrobe and discovered all Sarah's own lovely clothes had gone, replaced by a few cheap outfits. The dressing table drawers had revealed a similar dearth of personal possessions. All her jewellery had gone, along with her collection of leather handbags and designer scarves.

The dressing table top was bare of any feminine frippery, only one small photo of Sarah and Bonnie propped against the mirror.

The old lady in the adjoining bedsit—the one who'd supplied the information about Sarah's disastrous visit to Dominic—had confirmed that Sarah had sold everything she could to outfit her precious baby girl. It seemed Sarah had known the sex of the baby from the time of her ultrasound at four months, a couple of months after she'd come here to live. Apparently she'd left Hunter & Associates early in her pregnancy because she'd been too sick to work.

This last piece of information had upset Tina as well. If only she'd known, she'd have been on the first plane back to Sydney.

'You've been staying here?' Dominic asked at last, his expression almost disbelieving.

'Yes,' she replied defensively. Where else? 'They're my two suitcases against the wall.' Still with her things in them. She hadn't wanted to unpack. She hadn't planned on staying too long.

'Then don't go trying to bluff me about having money,' he snapped. 'Come on, collect what you need so we can get the hell out of here. I've seen some depressing places in my life but this wins hands down. Believe me when I tell you if Sarah *had* come to me and told me she was pregnant, she and her baby wouldn't have had to live like this!'

Tina stared at him as the most bewildering confusion claimed her. For he sounded so sincere. And genuinely upset.

'She really didn't come to see you?' she found herself asking.

'No,' he said, and looked her straight in the eye without wavering. 'The morning after she stopped working for me was the last time I saw Sarah. I never even ran into her in the lift after that. To be brutally honest, I didn't even realise she'd left the company.'

'But *why* would she say she'd been to see you if she hadn't?'

'I have no idea. Who was it who told you that?'

'The old lady who lives in the next bedsit.'

'What's her name?'

'What? Oh…er…Betty. I don't know her second name.'

'I see. Well, maybe Sarah told her she was coming to see me, but then changed her mind. Maybe when this Betty asked her what happened, she made up a little white lie out of embarrassment. I don't think we'll ever know what really happened, or what was going through her mind at the time.'

'I guess not,' Tina said wearily, and sat down on the edge of the bed. The mattress sagged, as did her shoulders. 'What does it matter now, anyway?'

'It matters to me when people call me a liar,' Dominic ground out. 'I'm no saint, Tina, but I'm not an unconscionable bastard, either.'

She winced at her words, well aware the insult had been flung more out of shame than genuine belief in his total wickedness. It was *she* who'd felt wicked at the time. Wicked and way, way out of control.

She glanced up at him, and tried to be fair.

Because let's face it, Tina, her conscience demanded, you haven't been fair to him all day. Before you even met the man you were right and ready to accuse. And not to listen. You played the avenging angel role to a T, and gave Sarah saintly qualities which she didn't have.

The truth was Sarah had used to lie quite a bit, whenever she'd thought the truth might get her into trouble, or into an argument. Sarah had hated to confront, or be confronted. She'd always taken the line of least resistance.

'I...I'm sorry I said that,' she muttered.

'And I'm sorry I said you let Sarah down,' he returned, more gently than she deserved. 'From what I've seen, she couldn't have asked for a better friend. Or a better mother for her baby.'

'Oh,' Tina choked out, her chin wobbling while tears filled her eyes.

'You vowed you'd never cry in front of me again!' he warned sharply.

'I...I can't help it,' she sobbed, her hands flying up to cover her face as the tears spilled over.

* * *

Dominic stared at her in horror.

Why me? he agonised.

He grimaced at the sight of her shaking shoulders, then groaned at the sounds of her heartfelt sobs, torn by his natural male urge to offer comfort to a weeping woman, yet worried sick over what might overtake him once he touched her.

Look what had happened the last time he'd gathered a crying female in his arms! And Sarah hadn't even been his type!

Tina, however, was very definitely his type.

And *how*!

He was standing there at a safe distance when the thought occurred to him that he was worrying for nothing, because *he* wasn't *Tina's* type!

There really was little danger of anything untoward happening when the woman in your arms couldn't stand a bar of you.

That apology of hers just now had been nothing but a grudging concession. She still believed he was a liar and a heartless seducer.

Reassured, Dominic walked over and sat down on the narrow bed beside her, sending the ancient mattress into a dangerous dip which instantly propelled Tina hard against his side.

'Oh!' she gasped, her hands flying away from her face in panic.

'It's all right,' he said gruffly, and curved an arm around her shoulders.

But it wasn't all right. Everything was all wrong.

The way she was looking at him for starters, her eyes wide and lustrous. The way her face remained upturned, with her lips invitingly parted. The way her hands fluttered against his chest then remained there, faintly trembling.

Dominic gave her a chance. He really did. She could have wrenched away from him, could have stopped him at any point during the time it took for his free hand to lift and capture that quivering chin with his fingers.

But she didn't struggle, or stop him. She just stared up into his eyes, her lips gasping even further apart when his mouth began to descend.

Tina knew he was going to kiss her. She *knew*, but she did nothing, said nothing.

She let his lips cover hers without protest. Let his tongue slide deep into her mouth. Let his hand slide down her neck and over one of her treacherously throbbing breasts.

This is madness, was her last coherent thought, before a wild explosion of desire blew her brain apart, skittering all common sense and evoking in its place the most urgent need. Her arms slid up around his neck and she was pulling him down, down onto the bed with her.

Dominic had little time to feel shock at her wild response. If his mind momentarily questioned her unexpected passion, his body didn't. His own arousal soared, tipping him over that edge on which he'd balanced precariously all evening.

Tina moaned when he stopped kissing her to lift her up onto the pillow. She moaned again when he pushed her legs apart and fell upon her once more, his mouth crashing back down on hers, his hard, heavy body pressing her deep into the mattress.

She felt as if she was drowning, with no air for her lungs. Her head was spinning wildly. But she didn't care. What a delicious death, she thought, and wrapped her arms even tighter around his neck.

He twisted slightly to one side, but this time he didn't stop the kissing. She felt his hand on her body, as hot and hungry as his mouth as it stroked roughly down her chest before scooping up underneath her top to where her braless breasts were waiting for him, aching and tense. Everything inside her contracted when his hands grazed over her exquisitely erect nipples, a moan of raw pleasure echoing deep in her throat.

Men had touched her breasts before, but never like this, never with such a wild, uncontrollable ardour. There was no finesse in his questing fingers, just naked animal passion as he squeezed the sensitive peaks over and over and left them aching for more.

When his mouth wrenched away and his hand slid down from her breasts, she cried out with dismay. No, don't stop, don't stop, came the almost despairing but silent plea.

But he wasn't stopping.

She watched, eyes wide and lungs heaving, as he pushed up her top and slid down to put his mouth where his hands had been.

His tongue and teeth were as merciless as his fingers, laving and nipping at her nipples till they felt like pokers hot from a fire. She couldn't get enough, arching her back and pressing them up into his face for more. She even liked it when he rubbed his stubbly chin over their burning peaks, gasping as spears of the most delicious sensation darted all through her body.

Her eyes squeezed shut, perhaps in denial of the dizzying pleasure of it all. But Tina found no safe haven in the darkness. If anything, being unable to see what he was doing enhanced the experience, sharpening her awareness of her body and its responses. Her breasts had never felt so swollen, or so exquisitely sensitive. Her body had never felt so restless, so craving.

His abrupt abandonment of her needy, greedy flesh sent her eyes flying open.

He was kneeling back on his haunches between her outstretched legs, his dark head bent over, his hands reaching for the button at her waistband. Somewhat dazedly, she stared down at the sight she made lying there, semi-naked, her top bunched up around her neck, her breasts bare, her nipples still wet and tingling.

Dominic started peeling the tight stretch pants down from her hips, taking her G-string with them, bending to kiss her quivering stomach as he did so.

Groaning, she twisted her head to one side, and might have closed her eyes again, ready to wallow in whatever he did to her, when her dilated gaze encountered the small photograph of Sarah and Bonnie on the dressing table.

The erotic haze which had been enslaving Tina so totally immediately lifted. If someone had thrown a bucket of iced water on her, the effect could not have been more dramatic.

Instant coldness where a moment before there had been the most blistering heat. A crippling dismay in place of that incredible desire.

'Oh, God…*no*!' she cried out, and sat bolt-upright, pushing him back off the bed with an adrenaline-induced burst of strength. He staggered to his feet, then just stood there, staring at her while she frantically pulled down her top, then started yanking up the tight white pants. It was difficult, but she managed. Finally, she swung her feet over the side of the bed and might have bolted for the door, but she started shaking. So she just sat there, hugging herself as great tremors raced all through her.

When Dominic went to sit down beside her, she froze him with her eyes.

'Don't you d…dare come near me,' she warned, her teeth still chattering. 'Or t…t…touch me ever again.'

'Tina, for pity's sake! Be fair. You wanted me to. You know you did.'

She shook her head violently. 'No, I d…d…didn't. I didn't *want* you to. You're the last man on earth I'd want making love to me. I hate and d…despise you.'

'But why? I thought you believed me about Sarah now.'

Tina gritted her teeth, using every ounce of will she possessed to stop shaking and face this man. 'You still used and abused her,' she bit out. 'You didn't love her but you made love to her anyway. Then, when she stopped working for you, you just moved on to that…that Shani person. I wonder if *she* knows the sort of man she's tangled up with. A cold-blooded sex machine, that's what you are. Oh, you know the right moves all right. And you certainly know when to strike: when a girl is at her lowest emotionally, tired and vulnerable and sick at heart. That's when you move in for the kill, isn't it? You...you...callous, unfeeling pig!'

Her tirade over, Tina buried her face in her hands and dissolved into distressed tears.

Dominic had never felt worse in his whole life.

Physically and emotionally.

The fiercest frustration raged, along with remorse and guilt and, yes, confusion.

In one way he was glad she'd stopped him. Because he would not have been able to stop himself. He would have continued on. Without any thought of the consequences. Without a condom.

Such a reality was as alien to him as it was bewildering. What was it about this woman which made him lose all control and common sense? Was it just a matter of a unique chemistry, or could something else be at work here, that age-old emotional trap which made fools of men and which Dominic had sworn never to fall victim to?

He shook his head in denial of this last possibility. Surely falling in love took longer than this!

Still, as he stared at the wretched figure hunched on the bed a huge wave of tenderness flooded through him. He just had to go to her. Had to make things right. Had to.

He knelt down at her knees and took her hands in his, holding them tight even while she tried to wrench them away.

'No, you must listen to me,' he said firmly. 'You've had your say. Now let me have mine.'

She glared at him with daggers in her tear-filled eyes.

'I didn't mean for that to happen. I didn't really

want it, either, or plan it. But the truth is I've been attracted to you since I first set eyes on you in my office.

'Yes, it's true,' he insisted when he saw the disbelief in her eyes. 'I couldn't get you out of my mind. I've always been attracted to slender, dark-eyed brunettes. Then, when I came home and found you there, my brain and body started a war which has been going on ever since. I was as angry with you as you were with me. Because I *hadn't* done what you accused me of. But at the same time I kept wanting to pull you in my arms and make mad, passionate love to you. To be brutally honest, I had an erection all through dinner.'

Her dark eyes rounded and her lips fell tantalisingly apart. It took all of his will-power not to close the relatively short distance between their mouths once more.

He suspected he could seduce her even now, if he were ruthless enough. But Dominic didn't want that. He wanted more from this woman than just her body. He wanted her respect as well.

And she didn't respect him at the moment. Not one iota.

'I think you're attracted to me too,' he added, and waited for her to deny it.

She didn't, and his heart began to beat faster, his mind already racing to the time when he would have her again under him on a bed. He would not let her stop him the next time. He would use every erotic skill he'd ever learned to keep her there till they were both satisfied. Not once, but over and over!

It's just lust, he realised abruptly with a great whoosh of relief. Hell, for a moment there…

'There's nothing wrong with us being friends, is there?' he suggested reasonably. 'If it turns out I'm Bonnie's father, then surely it would be best all round if we got on well.'

'You're…you're admitting you could be Bonnie's father?'

'It's possible, I suppose,' he said, though privately Dominic brushed aside this slim possibility as not worth worrying about, certainly not till the test results came back. He saw little point in facing a problem till it really existed. Still, if admitting he might be Bonnie's father would get him into Tina's good books…

'What about the mystery boyfriend?' she said, wariness in her voice. 'Or are you admitting he doesn't exist?'

'He exists all right. I intend to find him myself.'

'Best look in the mirror, then.' She extricated her hands from his and gave him a cold look. 'As for our being…*friends*,' she scoffed. 'I can't see that happening. Now that I know what I'm dealing with I'll be on guard, believe me.'

Dominic stood up and did his best to keep reasonably calm in the face of her ongoing scorn. It was one step forward and three steps backwards with this woman. 'What do you mean…what you're dealing with?'

'You know exactly what I mean,' she snapped. 'You're a predator, Dominic. A taker. You think you can have any woman you want. I'm sure there are countless scores on your gun. But don't mark a notch for me, because I'm not like Sarah or Shani or any of the other poor creatures you've used and discarded. I might have seemed like one tonight, but everyone's entitled to one error in judgement. I underestimated you, and I overestimated myself. I didn't realise I could be got at that way. Now I know differently.'

'I don't believe this!' He spun away and began to pace agitatedly around the room. She was doing it to him again, making him feel a heel when he'd bent over backwards to be reasonable. Hell, anyone would think that wanting to make love with a woman was a capital offence!

Her glance was scathing as she stood up. 'I'm sure after you've visited your Shani later tonight you'll feel much better. After all, one slender, dark-eyed brunette is pretty much like another to a man like you!'

Her sarcasm stung him to the quick, bringing an angry flush to his face. 'I'll have you know that Shani is a very intelligent woman, with a mind of her own. I do not use her, any more than she uses me.'

'How nice. Then you're well suited, aren't you?'

'Too right.'

'Then leave me alone in future.'

'Don't worry. I will!'

CHAPTER NINE

IT WAS just on eleven when Shani let a still fuming Dominic into her apartment. Normally Dominic wouldn't have got past the small foyer before the sex started. This time he stalked past Shani and went straight for the cabinet in the living room where she kept her hard liquor and clean glasses.

'Bad day, darling?' she drawled as he slopped some Scotch into a glass.

He grunted, then quaffed back the lot.

She came up behind him and slid her hands over his already tense shoulders in a seductive fashion. His fingers stiffened around the glass as her hands slid down his arms then snaked around his waist before travelling lower.

'Mmm,' she said with salacious pleasure.

Confusion crashed through him as his conscience screamed at him not to do this. *This is all wrong! It's Tina you're wanting. Not Shani.*

But Tina despises you, the devil tempted. *You'll never have her in your bed. Never! You can't walk around like this for ever. You'll go insane. And it's not as though Shani minds.*

With a tortured groan he whirled, scooped her up into his arms and carried her into the bedroom. Five minutes later, a stunned Shani was pulling the sheet up over her unsated nakedness and staring at the brooding figure standing at her bedroom window.

'What's on earth's wrong, Dominic?' she asked. 'You wanted me. I know you did.'

He turned to stare at her, at her still avid eyes, and thought of other dark eyes, eyes which flashed scornfully when they clashed with his, eyes which he would give anything to have look at him as Shani's were at that moment.

'It wasn't you I was wanting,' he admitted at last on a ragged sigh.

'Ahh,' she said knowingly, nodding and reaching for the packet of cigarettes she kept by the bed.

Smoking after sex was Shani's only vice, health-wise. She often joked that she liked to keep her two vices together, lest they both get out of control.

Control was as important to Shani as it was to Dominic.

He watched as the sheet fell down to her waist, exposing her bare breasts. She didn't bother to cover herself again as she pulled herself up against the head-board. She just sat there smoking, without a conscious thought of her nakedness.

The memory of Tina agitatedly pulling her top down over *her* bared breasts popped into his mind. How she'd hated having exposed herself to him that way! Her disgust that she'd let him almost seduce her had been incredibly intense.

Dominic wondered if it was just him she despised, or all men. That appalling childhood of hers must have jaundiced her view of the male sex. Sarah's obvious vulnerability to men and sex had certainly galled her.

Still, she wasn't immune to the pleasures of the flesh. Obviously she *liked* lovemaking. So it was probably just him she didn't like.

'Who is she?' Shani asked between puffs.

Dominic snapped out of his see-sawing thoughts. 'Someone I met today.'

'At work?'

'In the office, yes.'

'Client or colleague?'

'Neither.'

'What, then?'

'An angel,' he said.

'An *angel*!' Shani laughed. 'Oh, dear, dear, dear, you *have* got it bad.'

'Not that kind of angel,' he returned ruefully. 'An avenging angel. Straight out of hell. And I'm *not* in love with her.'

'Is that so? Well, if you haven't fallen for her, then why aren't you over here, doing what comes naturally? It's not as though your equipment isn't working.'

Dominic had to confess she was right. He wasn't impotent. Not physically, anyway.

'I simply can't get her out of my mind,' he confessed. 'But it's not love.'

'Love has a way of creeping up on you when you're not looking,' she said, and he frowned at the odd note in her voice.

'My God!' he exclaimed, alarmed. 'Shani… You're not…with me, are you?'

'No, I'm not. Thank heavens. But I was beginning to grow very fond of you, darling. *Too* fond. So it's best we come to an end, I think.'

Dominic didn't know what to say. The thought that Shani was becoming emotionally involved with him was a real shock. Who next?

He made up his mind then and there. He had to

keep away from Tina. Well away. Love was not on his agenda. Not now. Not ever. He wanted his old life back. And his old self. He didn't like being out of control. He didn't like anything that had happened to him today one little bit!

He shot a look at Shani, sitting there, smoking. 'Will you be all right, Shani?' he asked gently.

Her mouth curved into a smile, one of her brassy, confident smiles. 'Perfectly all right, but thank you for asking. Fact is I met this incredibly sexy man the other day whom I fancy something rotten. He fancies me too. Gave me his card. He's a lawyer. Not a tender bone in his body. Unlike you, darling. You really are a big softie at heart, you know that?'

'Me?

You have to be kidding!'

'Actually, no, I'm not.'

He laughed. 'And I thought advertising people were supposed to be good judges of character!'

'Oh, but we are,' Shani said with a perfectly straight face. 'We are.'

CHAPTER TEN

TINA was sitting at the dressing table in her bedroom, vigorously brushing her hair. The radio clock on the bedside table showed eight-thirteen. It was Sunday night, forty-eight hours since all Tina's misconceptions about sex and herself had been totally blown apart.

She sighed and stopped the brushing. What an endless weekend it had been!

Initially, she'd been glad when Dominic had stormed out of the house on their return from Sarah's, having informed his mother curtly not to expect him back that weekend.

Any relief, however, had been short-lived. That night she'd lain awake for hours, thinking of what Dominic was doing with his girlfriend, tormented with erotic images and her own insane jealousy.

She'd kept thinking about what he'd said to her, how he'd been attracted to her from the first moment he'd seen her, how he'd been aroused all through dinner. She'd felt tortured by the thought it could have been *her* in his arms that night, not Shani.

No wonder she hadn't slept a wink Friday night!

Tina now knew what Sarah had meant when she'd tried to explain how she'd felt sometimes when she'd been with a lover. The mindless madness of it all. The flights of fantasy which took you out of reality into a world where nothing existed but your yearning, burning body with its dark desires and wicked needs.

Tina groaned at the memory of how she'd felt on that bed with Dominic. She'd been shameless. Even now her face burned with mortification that she'd fallen victim to his practised expertise so easily.

Still, if nothing else, she now understood the driving power of sex. She saw why people transgressed normal moral boundaries when in the grip of lust. It explained so much about life which had previously confused her.

But all this new knowledge didn't make her own situation any easier to bear. She still lusted after Dominic Hunter like mad—a man she despised. Which, of course, was the main crux of her problem.

If it had been any other man, she could have indulged her feelings without fear of losing too much respect for herself. But how could she succumb to the man who'd seduced Sarah, who'd produced and abandoned Bonnie?

It was an impossible situation, made even more impossible by the fact her normally tough, hard-nosed brain seemed to no longer have any control over her body. Common sense and sheer decency demanded she put aside such a potentially disastrous desire, but she simply couldn't. It obsessed her mind all the time.

During the daytime, she'd managed to get a marginal grip, having things to distract her. Yesterday she'd done the washing in the morning—there was always washing with a baby—and in the afternoon Ida had taken her shopping again.

The dear woman was obviously making up for lost grandmother time by buying Bonnie toys and clothes. Tina hadn't had the heart to tell her not to, that Bonnie already had everything she needed for a while. She already understood full well how a baby like Bonnie, with her unfortunate start in life, could tug at the heartstrings. You just wanted to lavish so much love and attention on her to make up for her losing her mother and not having a father who wanted her.

Today, she and Ida had gone down to the park in the morning, with Bonnie in her pram, then stopped at a local café for a leisurely lunch.

It had been a beautiful spring day, still and sunny without being too hot. After they'd come home, and Bonnie had been bathed, fed and settled for a sleep, Tina had joined Ida picking some roses in the garden. They'd spent a couple of hours arranging them in various vases around the house, during which Tina had kept up a happy face.

But inside she'd still been fretting over her feelings for Dominic Hunter. Every time Ida had brought her son into the conversation—which had been often—Tina had found herself tensing. Of course she hadn't shown it, but it had been a strain, acting all the while.

She'd been rather relieved when Ida had had to go out after dinner. A woman from her bridge club had called, explaining that one of her regular Sunday night players was unwell and they desperately needed a fourth. Could Ida possibly come? She hadn't wanted to at first, but Tina had insisted, thinking it would be good to be alone for a while. Now, she regretted that insistence. Being alone with her thoughts and feelings was *not* such a good idea at all.

Putting the hairbrush down, Tina stood up and walked across the plush cream carpet to the window, which looked down onto the front yard. The driveway was deserted. Tina hoped it would remain that way. The last thing she wanted was Dominic coming home with his mother out. He'd said he wouldn't be home all weekend, which meant that, with a bit of luck, he didn't intend showing up till very late tonight or, even better, Monday morning.

Turning, Tina walked over and into the attached bathroom, which had another door leading into a smaller bedroom where Bonnie was sleeping.

Ida had confessed to Tina when she'd assigned her and Bonnie these rooms that she'd decorated this part of the house, and had this extra door put in, in anticipation of her younger son, Mark, and his wife having children.

Tina had then heard all about Mark, who sounded like an irresponsible dreamer, especially where money was concerned, and nothing like his older brother whom, Ida had explained, had been her financial and emotional rock when her husband had died. A stroke had claimed Dominic's father unexpectedly, seven years earlier. If that hadn't been shock enough for the family, he'd died leaving his business affairs in a right old mess. Overdrawn accounts and second mortgages everywhere!

Dominic had come to the rescue, working crippling hours to get everything back into the black, which was one of the reasons he'd returned to live at home. Firstly because there weren't enough hours in the day for him to look after himself. And secondly because it had saved money on renting elsewhere, his weekly contribution enabling the mortgages on the house to be cleared more quickly.

Of course, everything was fine now, Ida had hastened to explain, perhaps thinking Tina might be worried they weren't in a financial position to help Bonnie. Ida claimed Dominic was as brilliant a financial investor and advisor as his grandfather, who'd apparently made millions in the post-war years, most of which his less skilled son—Dominic's father—had lost, in several speculative and high-risk investments.

Actually, there was no need for Dominic to continue to live at home, Ida had added. She suspected he did it because he thought she'd be lonely without his company.

Tina suspected he did it because he'd discovered it was much easier to have someone else—a woman, naturally—do all the mundane things in life, leaving him free to do the really important things, like make money and seduce women!

Her heart hardening at this thought, Tina tiptoed from the bathroom into the room where Bonnie was sleeping.

Her heart melted as she peered down at the lovely little face. What an incredibly beautiful child she was. Sarah all over again, with perfect skin, long curling eyelashes and the loveliest of mouths. Sweetly shaped, with full lips.

Already you could see she would be a beauty when she grew up. She would need protecting. She would need a father as well as a mother.

'And a father you shall have, my love,' she vowed staunchly.

Making sure Bonnie was firmly tucked in, Tina crept out of the room, leaving the door into the bathroom slightly ajar so that she could hear when Bonnie woke during the night. She was sure to, at least once, having not yet learned to sleep through the night. Ida had said she probably wouldn't till she was on solids, which started around four months. This was confirmed by one of the three books on child-raising Tina had bought that afternoon while Ida had been looking at baby clothes.

Once back in her bedroom, a still restless Tina contemplated going downstairs to watch television, but quickly discarded that idea. She'd already showered and was wearing her night things.

The prospect of Dominic arriving home and finding her downstairs attired in skimpy nightwear was foolish in the extreme.

'If you don't want to get burnt,' she warned herself aloud, 'then stay away from potential fires.'

Being alone with Dominic Hunter would be a highly flammable situation. Being alone with Dominic Hunter with nothing covering her sexually charged body but two thin layers of blue silk would be inevitable spontaneous combustion.

She didn't have to look down to see that her nipples were already erect, as they were every time she even *thought* of that man in connection with anything remotely sexual.

No, there was nothing for it but bed. Thankfully, she had a novel which she'd taken from one of Ida's bookshelves and brought up with her earlier. A thriller which promised to be unputdownable.

She had a feeling she would still be reading it when Ida arrived home. Around eleven-thirty, she'd said.

Tina had just slipped off her wrap when the sound of a door slamming downstairs had her scrambling back into it.

Ida would not have slammed the door that way. Only a man would do that with a sleeping baby in the house.

Dominic, it seemed, had finally deigned to come home.

She heard him call for his mother and receive no reply; heard him hurry up the stairs; heard him prowl along the hallway to his room, then come back again.

Her heart stopped when he halted outside her door, then jumped when he knocked.

'Tina? Are you in there?'

She clasped the brass doorknob with both hands to stop him from turning it. If there'd been a bolt she would have thrown it, but there was no bolt and no key in the lock.

'Yes,' she choked out through the door. 'Why?'

'I can't seem to find Mum.'

He sounded angry. And impatient.

'Your...your mother's out. Playing bridge.'

'But it's not her bridge night!'

'She's standing in for someone.'

'For pity's sake, open the damned door and talk to me properly,' he snapped. 'I can hardly hear you.'

'I can't. I...I'm not dressed.'

'At *this* hour of the night? Since when do grown women go to bed before eight-thirty?'

'Since they started getting up in the middle of the night to look after babies!' she snapped back. 'Now go away and leave me alone.'

He hesitated, then went, the wooden floorboards protesting as he clomped his way down the upstairs hallway back in the direction of his rooms. A door banged shut, shortly after which the water pipes registered the whooshing sound of someone having a shower.

When Tina finally let go of the doorknob her knees went to jelly. So close, she thought shakily, and stumbled over to the bed. Once there, she fell in, then just lay there, a tremor claiming her every now and then.

She felt weak as a kitten, and strangely bereft. Tears filled her eyes. Angry with herself, she blinked them away and pulled the bedclothes over her.

'I will not cry over that man,' she resolved, and determinedly picked up the novel.

Tina was still on page one several minutes later when the water pipes fell silent. Once again she found herself tensing and listening for him. She was just about to relax and return to reading when the sound of a door opening and shutting put her nerve-endings on red alert once more.

He was walking along the hallway back towards her door again, moving closer and closer. The fact that he had to pass her room to go downstairs did come to mind, but was instantly dismissed. He wasn't going to go past. She just knew it.

And she was right. His footsteps stopped outside her room. She could almost hear him breathing, which was crazy since the door was one of the old-fashioned kind. Solid wood and thick. Not the sort of door you could hear things through easily. Certainly not mere breathing.

The abrupt knocking tightened her nerves further.

'Tina?' he called through the door, his voice a low growl.

She didn't answer, her breath frozen in her lungs. At the same time her heart was hammering behind her ribs and some simply dreadful part of her wanted him to walk right in without asking.

'Your light's still on,' he ground out.

'I…I'm reading,' she croaked.

'We have to talk, Tina.'

'No, we don't,' she countered, panic in her voice and in her heart.

'I have things I have to say to you.'

'Tell me in the morning.'

'No. I need to say them now, or I won't sleep.'

When Tina saw the doorknob turn, she squawked and dived out of the bed, colliding forcibly with Dominic's big broad chest as he came in. Her hands flew up in a defenceless gesture, only to encounter a deep V of bare chest, along with a surprisingly soft triangle of black curls.

'Oh!' she cried, her flustered eyes finally focusing on this provocative expanse of naked flesh before flicking agitatedly down, then up again.

He was wearing long black silk pyjama bottoms, with a matching dressing-gown sashed inadequately around his impressive body. His feet were bare, the skin under her hands cool and faintly damp.

Tina tried not to stare, or to feel, but that was all she seemed to be able to do at that moment.

Stare…and feel.

Her eyes would not obey her mental commands. As for her hands…they were frozen flat on his flesh, but her sensitive fingertips were registering—and revelling in—the feel of all that macho maleness beneath them.

Her head fairly spun with desire.

Suddenly, his size didn't intimidate her at all. She found it tantalising. And irresistible. She ached to touch him all over, to discover all that made him the man he was.

It was like being possessed, she realised dazedly as her eyes lifted inexorably to his. Someone else was inhabiting her body, some reckless and very foolish female who was about to ignore the fact that this was the last man on earth she should let seduce her.

Her brain screamed at her that it wasn't too late to stop.

But her brain was powerless against the commands of her suddenly awakened sexuality, with all its urgent desires and needy, greedy demands.

CHAPTER ELEVEN

DOMINIC only wanted to tell Tina he'd found out who Bonnie's real father was. Damn it all, he'd spent all weekend finding out!

He'd raced home, anxious to tell both his mother and Tina the truth, and put an end to this farce. He'd even planned to generously offer a sum of money to Tina for the child, so his stupid conscience wouldn't bother him afterwards.

He'd arrived home, desperate to have done with it all before he went to bed and tried to get a decent night's sleep for the first time since Friday. And what had happened? His mother was out and Tina wouldn't talk to him.

Who could blame him for insisting? A man could only take so much.

And now look where his impatience had got him! In a bedroom with a scantily clad Tina. Hell, a near *naked* Tina, who was looking up at him in a way he'd thought she'd *never* look at him. Worse, she was actually touching him, her palms hot against the treacherous flesh he'd so desperately tried to calm and control under a long cold shower.

For a few seconds he tried to struggle out from under the white-hot haze of desire which had instantly clouded his mind. But it was hard when she was so darned desirable-looking. That glorious black hair tumbled wildly over her bare shoulders. The hardened nipples outlined in pale blue silk. The wide, sensual mouth already parted in the most provocative way.

What was he to do? Stop and try to work out what was going on here? Complain that she was the most contradictory, infuriating woman in the world? Refuse to touch her till she listened and agreed he wasn't the rat she thought he was?

With any other woman Dominic might have managed any of those courses of action. Easily. With *this* woman, however, he could not wait, or think straight. He had to touch her back right then and there, had to make love to her. *Had* to.

These compulsive feelings were not accepted happily by Dominic. He still didn't like his lack of control where Tina was concerned. Or the confusion she evoked in him. Even as he surrendered to the inevitable, he felt angry with himself.

And her.

Tina saw his eyes darken, then narrow. She knew what he was going to do. She didn't need to be told.

The knowledge electrified her.

Yes, kiss me, she willed with a wild, wanton recklessness. *Kiss me. Touch me. Do anything you want with me.*

Kicking the door shut behind him, he grasped her wrists in a less than gentle grip and wound them around behind her back, pulling downwards till her back arched almost painfully. She gasped, then watched, open-mouthed, as his head bent, not to her lips but to one of her silk-encased breasts.

His lips parted and closed over the already erect peak, sucking on it, drawing it in deep before abruptly letting it go. By then the silk was soaked and the nipple throbbing. When he began licking and nibbling at it, Tina made mewing little sounds of pleasure.

His head jerked up and he glowered down at her, a wild man with wild eyes. He let her wrists go and yanked the straps of the nightie off her shoulders, tugging it downwards till it pooled at her feet.

She straightened and just stood there, naked, dazed.

He stared at her for a long moment, before stripping himself just as quickly, Tina only having a brief glimpse of his impressive body before he scooped her up and carried her over to the bed, falling with her into its cool, downy depths.

And then they were kissing and clawing at each other, tongues tangling, limbs entwining, hands frantically exploring. He groaned when her fingers brushed over the tip of his penis, then moaned when she returned to stroke the full length of him.

He growled some kind of protest and took her wrists once more, locking them up above her head within a single iron grip. His other hand spread her legs, then zeroed in on what lay between them.

Tina had never known anything as exciting, or as electric. Her head whipped from side to side between her captured arms, her heart racing like an express train. Sensation built upon sensation as those merciless fingers explored and probed, tantalised and tormented.

'Please, oh, please,' she whimpered, her body desperately wanting more, wanting *him*, not his hands. Her legs moved wider apart in the most wanton invitation.

And then he was there, thrusting into her emptiness, satisfying her need to be filled, and fulfilled.

Tina gasped at the force and power of his possession, then groaned when he began to move. Inspired by sheer instinct, she moved with him, meeting each forward surge with an upward lift of her hips. Heat built up in her body and she was panting as if she'd run up a thousand steps. A pressure was forming within her, a tightness gripping her chest. Her head was spinning and the air became thick and heavy.

Tina was just thinking she might have a heart attack when suddenly something seemed to shatter inside her. Great grasping spasms came in waves, bringing with them flashes of blinding pleasure.

Groaning, she clutched at a pillow and squeezed her eyes tightly shut. But his tortured cry sent them flying open again and she watched, her own chest heaving, while Dominic came, his back arching, his mouth grimacing in a mixture of agony and ecstasy. She felt his flesh pumping deep within her, felt the flood of heat, felt a satisfaction so deep that she feared nothing would stop her from wanting to experience this again and again and again.

It was a very sobering thought.

This was what had turned Sarah into a fool, she realised with a bitter dismay. This was what would turn *her* into a fool, she conceded.

If she let it.

If she let him.

Dominic collapsed across her, exhausted. For a few moments he could not help but wallow in the sheer pleasure of it all, because nothing in his sexual experience could match what he and Tina had just shared.

The moment he'd surged into her for the first time would live in his mind for ever. The mad mixture of erotic rapture and dark triumph. The glorious feel of his naked flesh fusing with hers. And then the actual climax itself, releasing him finally from the physical and emotional tension which had been building up in him since Friday.

But any wallowing swiftly came to an end as reality intervened. Because, of course, he hadn't used a condom. He'd thought of it briefly at one stage, but had swiftly pushed the impulse aside. He'd been too desperate to make love, too much out of control to stop.

Dear God. What a mess he'd made of his vow to avoid Tina at all costs!

Slowly, he levered himself up onto his elbows and looked down at her. When she looked back up at him with coldly contemptuous eyes he shuddered inside.

'Glad to see you always use protection,' she bit out.

Dominic sighed, realising his credibility had just been shattered. Whatever he had to say about Sarah's mystery boyfriend would be water off a duck's back now. Even worse was the possibility that, this time, he *might* have conceived an unwanted child.

His life since he'd met Tina, he realised wearily, was becoming very complicated indeed.

'Is that going to be a big problem?' he forced himself to ask in a reasonably calm voice.

'Fortunately…no.'

He could not disguise his relief. 'Thank God. You're on the pill, I presume?'

She gave him another long, cold look. 'That's right,' she snapped, then added tartly, 'Unlike poor Sarah.'

Dominic eyed her sharply, about to say something in his defence, then decided, Why bother? That particular problem would sort itself out when the DNA test came back. Then and only then would he tell her the truth as he saw it. Any earlier and he would just be wasting his breath.

Meanwhile, what was he going to do about what had just happened?

'We really do need to talk now, Tina,' he said in all seriousness.

'No, we don't,' she retorted, and rolled out from under him, ejecting him from her body so abruptly that he gasped in pain. He watched, stunned, while she snatched up a blue satin robe from the end of the bed and slid into it, wrapping it tightly around her naked body before looking at him again.

'What's to talk about?' she threw at him defiantly while her dark eyes glittered and flashed. 'So we had sex? Big deal. You wanted it. I wanted it. We had it. End of story.'

Dominic was shocked how much her attitude hurt. If Shani had said the same thing, he would not have felt offended. He would have laughed.

Instead, a fierce resentment fired his blood.

How dared she reduce what they had just shared to nothing but sex? It might not have been love, but it had been more than two animals mindlessly mating. There was something emotional at work here, something complex and very, very human.

'Don't talk such rubbish!' he snapped. 'If that was your attitude then you would have let me have sex with you on Sarah's bed last Friday night. Because you wanted it then, all right, as well. Instead, you stopped me. And rightly so. That would have been in very poor taste.'

'And you think it's not very poor taste for you to

sleep with me after spending the weekend in another woman's bed?' she countered savagely.

'I did no such thing,' he grated out. 'I went to Shani's flat on Friday night but I left without sleeping with her. In fact, Shani and I have agreed to call it quits. I spent the weekend at a hotel. I found I couldn't go to bed with another woman when it was you I wanted. Only you, Tina.'

For a split second he saw something wonderful in her eyes. They lit up with amazement and pleasure and…

But then the light died, replaced by an implacable coldness. 'I'm sorry, Dominic,' she said in chilling tones, 'but I don't believe you. Just as I don't believe you used a condom with Sarah. I can only hope and pray you don't make a habit of unsafe sex. Now I'm going to the bathroom, if you don't mind.'

He lay there on the rumpled bed, broodily waiting for her return, furious with her ongoing poor opinion of him. As the minutes ticked away he was seriously tempted to reveal the facts he'd learned over the weekend, even though he had no proof of what he'd been told. It was only hearsay.

Still, if he could convince Tina he *might* not be Bonnie's father, and that Sarah *hadn't* come to him asking for help, then maybe…well, maybe…

Well, maybe *what*, you jerk? the voice of male reason demanded testily. Surely you don't want to go anywhere with this, do you?

Serious self-irritation was beginning to set him.

When Dominic heard the shower running at full bore, a different irritation surfaced to scrape over his already raw ego. She just couldn't wait to wash him from her body, could she? As if he'd made her dirty or something.

There'd been nothing dirty done here tonight in his opinion. It had been one darned special experience for both of them, and the sooner she recognised that the better! The sooner she recognised he wasn't the womanising rat she thought he was the better too!

She was ages in the bathroom, even after the shower had been turned off—so long, in fact, that he almost jumped up and banged on the door.

He was about to do so when the door opened and she came in looking upset, the baby in her arms.

'I woke her up with the shower,' she explained, her face flushed. 'I didn't think. I'll have to go and get her a bottle now. Do you think you could mind her for a minute while I run downstairs?'

Recalling the last time she'd handed him the baby, Dominic experienced a brief moment of panic, but hid it well, hoping to redeem himself a little in Tina's eyes.

'Sure,' he said breezily, and hauled himself up into a sitting position in the bed, popping a couple of pillows behind his back. 'Bring her over here.'

'Could you put some clothes on first, please?' she said, glaring at him.

He doubted a three-month-old baby would have minded his nudity, but thought it best not to point that out.

Diving out of the bed, he retrieved his pyjama bottoms from the floor and dragged them on. Her sense of modesty hopefully satisfied, Dominic returned to his position on the bed before looking her way.

'Ready,' he said.

She glowered at the amount of bare chest still

showing, but didn't say anything, merely sighed, walked over and handed him the baby. 'I'll try not to be too long,' she said. 'If she cries, then rock her, or walk her up and down and sing to her.'

'Right,' he said softly, remembering how the last time his deep voice had frightened the child. With a bit of luck, none of those things would be required, especially the singing bit. He was so tone deaf that he'd been offered bribes by his classmates *not* to sing at school concerts.

As luck would have it, no sooner had Tina departed than the baby took one look at the big male face peering down at her and began to bawl. Dominic was not only walking in a flash, but rocking at the same time. That worked for a few seconds, till the little pink terror realised *who* it was doing the walking and rocking and let rip again.

'No way I'm going to sing too,' he told the crying but tearless infant. 'I'm not much good at telling fairy stories either. They always say to talk about what you know, so here goes…' And he launched into a description of his job.

Dominic paused to draw breath a couple of minutes later, only then realising that the baby's pretty pink mouth had stopped squawking. In fact her baby blue eyes were fixed on his in rapt attention, almost as though she'd been listening to every word he said, and was holding her breath waiting for more.

'Well, blow me down,' he whispered under his breath. 'She likes hearing about business. Oh, what a smart girl you are,' he crooned, relieved at having found a way to stop that nerve-scraping noise.

'Now, the stockmarket is like a big international sports arena,' he explained as he settled them both back on the bed, 'where this very complex game is being played twenty-four hours a day, with thousands of different rules and pitfalls. But, oh, what fun once you master those rules and avoid those pitfalls. There's nothing else like it in the world! Still, you have a lot to learn if you're going to grow up and play *that* particular game, my girl. Now…where shall I begin?'

CHAPTER TWELVE

TINA heard Bonnie start to cry just as she reached the bottom of the stairs, but she kept on going, her need to be away from that man far greater than any worry about the baby.

A little crying wasn't going to kill Bonnie. But staying in the same room as Dominic Hunter might just result in Tina killing *him*!

Oh, the smugness of the man! The arrogance! And the insensitivity!

Couldn't he appreciate how she must feel, having gone to bed with *him*, of all men? Couldn't he understand how this had to be affecting her pride, and her self-respect?

Of course not, she realised angrily. Men like him didn't think about a woman's pride or self-respect. Women were just sex-objects to be toyed with, lied to, then discarded.

What gall he had to claim he hadn't been to bed with his girlfriend that weekend, that he'd broken up with this Shani because of *her*.

Yeah, right! And the tooth fairy got engaged to Santa Claus this weekend as well!

And then there was the matter of his not using protection, something he'd claimed he never, ever did. Okay, so maybe he *did* use a condom most of the time. He struck Tina as a normally intelligent and pragmatic individual who wouldn't make a habit of sexual stupidity. But tonight proved his flesh could be as weak as the next man's.

Tina wondered what would have happened if she'd told him she *wasn't* on the pill at all. Which she wasn't. It might have almost been worth it just to see the look on his face!

Actually, she hadn't lied about that for *his* benefit but for her own. She hadn't wanted to explain that you could set a clock by her cycle, that she knew her body like the back of her hand and that she was positive she'd ovulated over a week ago. If she were a betting person, she'd put a billion dollars on her period arriving around midday the following Saturday.

No, there would be no baby from what had transpired up in that bedroom tonight. Thank God. Still, Tina found the thought appalling that if she'd met Dominic a week ago, right around the wrong time, she would still have gone to bed with him. She wouldn't have given conception a moment's thought, till *after* the event.

Which brought her to the other reason she'd lied to him about being on the pill. She wanted him to think she was sexually active. No way did she want him finding out it had been a couple of years since her last sexual encounter, or that she'd only ever had two very brief and unsuccessful affairs in her whole life. She wanted him to believe her claim that it had just been sex between them, and that he wasn't anything special to her.

Because he darned well wasn't!

He was just an…an…aberration. A perverse infatuation. For some weird and wonderful reason unbeknown to her, he turned her on in a big, big way. Now more than ever. She'd hardly been able to look at him in that bedroom a minute ago without wanting to touch him again. If only he'd put on the black silk dressing-gown as well, instead of just the pyjama bottoms. He'd left far too much exposed flesh for her needy, greedy gaze. She'd ached to run her hands over that magnificent chest again.

Tina groaned as desire contracted her own stomach once more. Oh, why had she brought the baby in to him like that? Why?

She'd thought she was using Bonnie as some kind of protection, to guard her from these dark desires. Instead, she now knew to her shame that nothing was going to protect her from this ungovernable lust. She would just have to endure it as best she could. *Hide* it as best she could.

Men like him enjoyed having power over women. They probably revelled in being adored, and fawned over, and *loved*. In hindsight, she recalled a triumphant glint in his eyes when he'd had her spreadeagled before him. He'd liked it when she'd begged, then become annoyed when she'd left the bed so abruptly afterwards.

Well, she wouldn't beg the next time.

Tina sucked in a sharp breath. The next time. She was already thinking of the *next* time. Dear Lord, what was happening to her?

With a shaking hand she picked the bottle out of the simmering water and tested the temperature on her wrist. Warm enough, she decided. Time to go upstairs, sweep Bonnie out of Dominic's too tempting arms and escape into the sanctuary of the baby's room.

With the bottle in hand, she was hurrying up the stairs when the surprise of silence upstairs slowed her step. Frowning, she listened, but there was no baby crying at all.

Once she reached the top landing, however, she could hear voices coming through the slightly ajar doorway. No, not voices, she soon realised. One voice. Dominic's, talking with expression, as though he were reading Bonnie a story.

She drew closer and listened, her eyes widening as she heard the content of that story. Not *The Three Bears*. Or *Red Riding-Hood*. Or *Jack and the Beanstalk*. He was telling Bonnie all about stocks and shares!

Amazed, Tina peeped in through the gap in the doorway and blinked at the scene before her eyes. Dominic was sitting back against the bedhead with his knees bent and Bonnie lying against his silk-encased thighs. He was holding both her hands out wide and regaling her with what signs to look for in a bull market, as opposed to a bear market.

Bonnie was staring up at him as though he were one of the gods on Mount Olympus.

Exasperation battled with the sudden awful temptation to be charmed by the scene.

Exasperation won. How like Sarah's daughter to be so easily captivated by a man!

Letting out an irritable sigh, Tina pushed open the door and stalked in, halting by the bed to glare down at him. Dominic simply ignored her while he finished educating his daughter about the various stockmarket crashes over the years.

Fury sent an impatient hand to her hip and a combative glint to her eyes.

'The smarties always read the signs and get out before the rot sets in,' Dominic was advising. 'I'd tell you all those signs in detail, but your mummy's here with your bottle. We'll have to leave the rest of this till later, sweetie.'

Dominic's calling her 'mummy' and Bonnie 'sweetie' like that caused Tina's stomach to curl over and her heart to go to mush. As did the sight of him very gently scooping Bonnie up from his thighs and placing her so carefully in the crook of his left arm. 'I'll feed her if you like,' he offered, and held out his right hand for the bottle. 'Give you a break.'

Tina swallowed, then rather reluctantly gave it to him. As much as it was her dream for Dominic to accept and bond with his child, how could she continue to hate him when face to face with such tenderness?

She watched him angle the bottle into the baby's eager mouth, noting the startled pleasure in his face when Bonnie's tiny hand came up to cover his, as was her habit with anyone who fed her. Tina remembered how she'd felt the first time Bonnie had done it to her, the innocently trusting gesture tugging at her till then hard heart, sparking the beginning of her new and amazing maternal feelings. Was her father feeling something similar? Had the first seed of love just been sown?

Dominic looked up suddenly, his expression pained. 'You know, Tina, I would never deny being Bonnie's father if I thought I really *was* her father. You must believe me on this.'

For the first time real doubt seeped in, and Tina felt sick.

Dominic looked back down at Bonnie but kept on speaking, his voice low and reasoned. 'I think I know who her father is. I spent a great deal of time over the weekend finding out.'

'You did?' she echoed faintly.

He glanced up again. 'Yes. I told you. I wasn't with Shani. Good Lord, what does it take to have you believe me for once? Think, woman! What motive could I possibly have to lie? I've agreed to have the DNA test tomorrow, but I already know what the result will be. I know you think tonight proves I'm sexually irresponsible, but I swear to you, Tina, that tonight was the first time in twelve years that I've had unsafe sex. I'm fanatical about it, usually.'

Tina was inclined to believe him. About the condom, anyway.

'Tonight was a first for me too,' she confessed. 'For unsafe sex, that is.'

'I think tonight was a first for both of us in lots of ways, don't you?' he said softly.

'What…what do you mean?'

'I mean it was something very special, Tina. Something unique. I don't know about you but I know I've never felt for another woman what I've been feeling since I met you. To be honest, it's rattled the hell out of me. I like to live an ordered life. I like to be in control. Falling madly in love is not on my agenda. But I'm not one to—'

'It's not love,' she broke in firmly, frightened over where this was going. 'It's just lust.'

'You sound pretty sure of that.'

'I'm very sure. I've been there, done that. Lots of times.'

He looked taken aback. 'You're saying tonight wasn't anything special for you? That you've felt this kind of passion before?'

'It's always pretty exciting the first time.'

He just stared at her, and she felt worse than she'd ever felt in her life. Chilled, and ashamed.

He swung his feet over the side of the bed, stood up, and handed Bonnie back to her. 'You can finish this. I'm wasting my time here, with both of you.'

'But aren't you going to tell me what you found out?' she asked.

His eyes stabbed disgust at her. 'What's the point? I have no real proof of my findings, only hearsay. You already have much more hearsay evidence against me. Not to mention that other mysterious evidence you won't show me. I only hope that by the time the DNA test comes back my mother isn't too attached to that sweet little child, because Mum doesn't deserve to be hurt. She's endured enough emotional pain in her life. Maybe you should give that some thought when you're lying in your bed tonight, all alone with your prejudices and your hypocrisies. Oh, and I sure hope you enjoyed your first time with me, honey, because it was your first and last!'

Scooping up his robe from the floor, he stormed out of the room, banging the door shut behind him so loudly that Bonnie spat out the bottle and started crying.

CHAPTER THIRTEEN

DOMINIC muttered into his beard as he clomped down the hallway and into his bedroom, slamming that door for good measure as well. He'd never been a door-slammer till he'd met Miss Tina Ballbreaker Highsmith, but he rather imagined he would get very good at it by the time she left his abode.

"It's always pretty exciting the first time," he mimicked aloud in that dismissive fashion she specialised in, and which set his teeth on edge at the best of times. This time, however, she'd cut him to the quick.

Okay, so she'd probably had great sex hundreds of times. Well, so had he! But this hadn't been just great sex. It had been a great *experience*. A combination of the emotional and the physical. Or it had been for him.

Clearly she didn't have enough sensitivity to know the damned difference!

He paced angrily around the large room, calling her all sorts of uncomplimentary names, working his way through the alphabet. When he came to witch and whore, he couldn't think of any more and sank down wearily onto the side of the bed.

No point in trying to sleep, he knew.

Dominic rose and walked over to turn on the computer he kept at home.

'Might as well work,' he muttered, and sat down.

But his mind kept wandering, first back to Tina,

then to the bed behind him, then idly around the room.

It had once been the master bedroom, but after his father had died and he'd come back home to live his mother had insisted he have it. After much argument, he'd agreed.

Admittedly, it was the only bedroom in the house which had enough space for a small home office, along with other normal bedroom-type furniture. But the thought of sleeping in his parents' bed had made him cringe at first. He'd overheard far too many arguments over what had transpired there, or *not* transpired there. He knew personally of one young lady in his father's employ—a cleaner—whom the master of the house had regularly bonked on the marital mattress.

Lord knows how many others there had been!

So, with his mother's permission, Dominic had donated her old bedroom suite to charity and bought himself a nice large new bed, after which he'd brought in the carpenters.

Now, one wall carried built-in storage for his clothes and personal effects while another housed a compact home office, the PC linked to the computers at work. His own television and video remained hidden behind a cupboard, the wall of which slid back at the touch of a switch.

Not that he used them much. But they were there, when needed.

His mother's bedroom was now downstairs, in what had once been his father's study. She rarely had to trudge up and down the stairs these days, which was a lot easier on her varicose veins. Dominic paid for a cleaner to come in every Monday and Friday to do all the heavy housework, along with the laundry. He also paid for the cook, June, who came in most afternoons for a few hours. Money well spent, in his opinion. His mother was the most appalling cook. Other than that, he had a chap pop round once a fortnight to mow the lawns and trim the edges, as well as occasionally dig up a garden bed. His mother did most of the gardening. It was her pride and joy, as well as her hobby.

Thinking about his mother turned his mind back to what he'd found out this past weekend. Sheer stubbornness now prevented his telling Tina, but he really had to tell his mother. So he went downstairs, poured himself a hefty glass of port and settled in front of the television to await her arrival home.

He heard her key in the door just as the Sunday night movie's credits went up, shortly after eleven.

He stayed where he was, knowing full well she would pop her head in to see who was still up.

'Oh, it's you,' she said shortly afterwards, in the sort of tone he might have expected from Tina.

Clearly he was still not the flavour of the month.

'Yes, it's me,' he returned drily from where he remained seated in his favourite armchair. 'Your loving son.'

'Where's Tina? I suppose you've bullied her into her room with your presence?'

'Yep, that's me as well,' he drawled. 'Bully-boy. Not to mention callous seducer and abandoner of pregnant women. So, yes, Tina has retired, but only after I'd dragged her up there by the hair on her head and had my wicked way with her.'

His mother sighed. 'You've argued again.'

He half smiled. If only she knew. 'You could say that,' he murmured.

'What about *this* time?'

'Let's just say Tina and I couldn't agree if our lives depended on it.'

'Bonnie's asleep?'

'I imagine so. Everything's certainly quiet on the upstairs front.'

'I think I'll go to bed too, then. I'm tired.'

'Before you do, Mum, there's something I have to tell you.'

She hesitated in the doorway, her glance rueful. 'It's a little late to confess all, don't you think? I already know you're Bonnie's father.'

'That's just it, Mum. I'm not. Damien Parsons is. I did some investigating over the weekend and Sarah had been having an affair with him.'

'Oh, Dominic, Dominic,' Ida said sadly, shaking her head at him. 'Putting the blame on a dead man is such a shoddy thing to do.'

Dominic could not believe his ears. What was wrong with these women? 'But, Mum, Sarah *slept* with him! I know it for a fact.'

'And she slept with you too, didn't she? Bonnie is *your* child, son. Believe me on this.'

'But she doesn't even *look* like me.'

'Don't be ridiculous!' she countered impatiently. 'Of course she does. It's just that she's a girl and you're blind to the resemblances.'

Dominic rolled his eyes. This was hopeless. He rose from the chair and walked over to his mother, placing a caring hand on her shoulder.

'Mum,' he said softly, 'I just don't want you to get hurt.'

Her expression was genuinely bewildered. 'But how can I get hurt? Tina's a lovely, generous-hearted girl. She *wants* me to be a part of Bonnie's life. She wants *you* to be a part of Bonnie's life too.'

'Mum, for pity's sake, will you *listen* to me?'

He looked at her imploringly, but could see by her eyes that she'd already clicked off to that subject. 'You know,' she said, shaking her head, 'when I first saw Tina I thought to myself she was just your type of girl. You always did go for feisty females. And most women seem to go for you, though to be honest I'm not sure why. Oh, you're good-looking enough, I suppose. And you've been blessed with a great body. But you don't go to any trouble to attract them. I guess it was hoping for too much to think you two might hit it off and get married.'

'Married!' he exclaimed. 'Good God, has everyone in this house gone insane?'

'Everyone? Who else are you talking about?'

'Me, Mum,' he muttered, and brushed past her to march back upstairs. *'Me!'*

CHAPTER FOURTEEN

'AREN'T you feeling well, Tina?' Ida asked as they came out of the doctor's surgery. Dominic had just stalked off in the direction of the car park, Tina sighing with relief at his departure.

Breakfast had been a nightmare. And so had sitting in the waiting room together till they'd been called in to the surgery.

Dominic hadn't said a word all morning, not even during the process of the nurse taking his blood, or Bonnie's, only afterwards brusquely asking the doctor to see if he could hurry up the pathologist with the results, to which the doctor had said he'd do his best, but he doubted they'd get them in under two weeks. Tina had seen Dominic's mouth thin at this, and knew he was having as hard a time as she was.

'No, I'm fine,' she lied to Ida. 'I'm just a little tense this morning. I was worried Bonnie might get upset at the needle.'

'That's understandable. But she only cried for a minute. Look,' she said, nodding down at the pram, 'she's gone back to sleep already.'

'Yes. She's such a good little baby. Such a good little sleeper.'

'You look like *you* could do with a sleep.'

'Yes,' she admitted wearily. 'I didn't get much last night.'

'And I know why!' Ida pronounced. 'Dominic told me.'

Tina froze, then stared at Dominic's mother. 'He told you…what?' she managed to get out.

'That you'd argued again last night.'

'Oh. Oh, yes. Yes, I'm afraid we did.'

'I can understand how annoyed you must be over that Damien Parsons business.'

'Damien Parsons?' she echoed blankly.

'The man Dominic is claiming Sarah had an affair with. He was the head accountant for Hunter & Associates. Married, of course. Not that that stopped Damien from sleeping around. He was always a one for the ladies. An extremely good-looking man. And as suave as they come.'

Tina frowned. He sounded just like the type Sarah would have fallen for. Now *why* did that name Parsons ring a bell?

'Poor Joanna,' Ida murmured, and the penny dropped for Tina. Damien Parsons must be married to Joanna Parsons, the woman Ida had put off coming to dinner the other night. Tina gnawed at her bottom lip while she bounced possibilities back and forth in her mind. This Damien's being a married man could explain Sarah not wanting to reveal his identity and perhaps using Dominic as the perfect patsy when Tina had mercilessly grilled her friend over her new lover.

Tina frowned, then frowned some more when another thought hit. 'You said Joanna was a widow, didn't you?' she asked Ida.

'Yes, Damien was killed in a car accident earlier this year. His own fault. He'd been drinking and driving. Lost control on a wet road and skidded into a telegraph pole.'

Tina was mulling all this information over in her

head when she suddenly realised something else. Damien's name began with a D.

All the blood drained from Tina's face. Oh, dear God…what have I done?

'But none of this matters, you know,' Ida was rattling on. 'I told Dominic straight. Little Bonnie is *your* child, I said. It's useless pointing the finger elsewhere. Face up to fatherhood like a man.'

A clamminess claimed Tina which wasn't the humidity. 'I…I think I'd better sit down,' she said, and sank onto a low cement wall which ran along the side of the pavement.

'Oh, dearie me,' Ida fussed. 'You've gone as white as a sheet. Look, I think we should get you over to my car and into some air-conditioning. It's rather hot out here. Here, lean on the pram. Then, after we get home, I think you should have a lie-down. I'll mind Bonnie. We can bring her bassinette downstairs for the day while you get a good sleep. That way, if she cries, she won't wake you.'

'You're very kind,' Tina said weakly, tears awfully close. What was it Dominic had said to her? He didn't want his mother hurt. She'd been through enough in her life.

Tina supposed he'd been referring to his mother losing her husband as a relatively young woman, then that married son of hers deserting his wife to become a monk. And now *she'd* come along and foolishly raised the poor woman's hopes over the grandchild she'd always wanted.

Tina felt awful. Simply awful!

Dominic paced up and down his office.

He felt awful. Simply awful!

What a pig he'd been this morning: giving everyone the cold shoulder; acting like a sulky child; clomping out of the surgery without a word even to his mother. No wonder she'd looked at him with such disappointment in her eyes.

As for Tina. She'd seemed to have had the stuffing knocked out of her this morning. There hadn't been a hint of the girl who'd bulldozed herself into his life last week, spitting fire and vengeance at him. She'd looked pale and fragile, with dark circles under her eyes and a depressed slump in her normally assertive shoulders.

It had come to him during the slow drive across the bridge and into the city that maybe she'd been protecting herself last night by adopting that good-time-girl attitude. Maybe she'd been acting a part. She was an actress after all.

Given her antagonism towards him, their out-of-control, out-of-this-world lovemaking must have come as a shock. The blushing girl who'd agitatedly pulled down her top last Friday night could not possibly be the hard-nosed promiscuous piece she'd portrayed herself as afterwards.

Maybe she'd bolted out of that bed because she'd been afraid to stay with him. Afraid of what she might say and feel and do.

It hadn't just been sex for her, Dominic had finally concluded, just as he was reaching the toll gates on the bridge. It had been anything but!

He'd almost driven right through the gate without paying at that point, braking savagely at the last second. The collector had given him a narrow-eyed glare, and Dominic had wondered if he'd recognised him from his crossing the other night when Tina had been sitting in the passenger seat, weeping.

This thought had swiftly wiped away any ecstatic joy Dominic had been feeling, an agonised guilt taking over. By the time he'd closed his office door behind him he'd been sweating with the reality he would never be able to make it right with Tina.

She had every reason to hate him, he accepted now as he paced up and down. He'd been brutal to her from the start. First he'd had her forcibly thrown out of this building. Then he'd accused her of being a con-artist. He'd been rude and hostile and downright difficult.

To top it all off, when he'd been besieged with what he'd seen as nothing more than an inconvenient lust, he'd taken advantage of her when she'd been vulnerable and upset. Then, last night, once he'd realised the chemistry was mutual, he'd really gone for the jugular, making love to her like a man possessed, without even protecting her.

No wonder she'd been desperate to protect herself afterwards, to keep him at a safe distance. She had to have been shell-shocked.

And now she was lost to him. Hell, in two weeks' time, she would be irretrievably lost to him. The DNA test would come back and she would be gone from his life. For ever.

Unless…

Dominic sat down at his desk and put his mind to coming up with a plan of action.

Once he did, the ruthless daring of his idea took his breath away. But he only had two weeks at best, and he couldn't let her go, could he? Not now that he'd found the woman his mother had always said he'd one day meet, not now he'd actually fallen in love!

Tina tossed and turned on top of the bed. She could not sleep. It was useless. Her mind went round and round. As tired as she was, she simply could not lie there and do nothing. She had to go to Dominic; to talk to him; apologise; explain.

She knew he must hate her now, but she wasn't thinking of herself so much but his mother, and Bonnie.

A sob caught in her throat. Poor little Bonnie. No father to love her. And probably no grandparents, either. Even if this Damien's parents were alive, would they accept the child of their dead son's bit on the side? Tina doubted it. Besides, what right had she to upset them further in their grief, spoiling their son's reputation and their memory of him?

And what of Ida's friend, Joanna, Damien's widow? Did she deserve to have someone come along and claim her husband had an illegitimate child?

Tina could not imagine any woman wanting to know about her dead husband's baby by another woman.

No, Tina decided. She could not do it, could not barge into another family's life and cause the havoc she'd caused here. She no longer had the stomach for it. Or the will.

Which meant she would have to raise Bonnie all by herself, with no financial or emotional help.

Tina swung her legs over the side of the bed and stood up, squaring her shoulders. She could do it. She could do anything.

But first she had to go and see Dominic and try to put things right.

Dominic was making a list of how he could get around the problem of the DNA results when the telephone rang. He lifted the receiver and said, 'Yes, Doris,' just as he printed, *'IF ALL ELSE FAILS, BRIBE THE PATHOLOGIST'* against tactic number three.

Number one was to win Tina's love and trust so he could happily ring the doctor and cancel the test altogether. Number two was to instruct the doctor to send the results to him first, where he would feed the page—or pages—into his computer, change the results and print out a new report.

'I have a young lady here who wants to see you, Mr Hunter,' Doris whispered in a conspiratorial voice. 'It's *her*.'

'Her?'

'The same one as last Friday. The one with the baby. Only this time the baby's not with her. Do you want me to call Security to throw her out again?'

Dominic dropped his pen. 'Good grief, no, Doris. Don't do that!'

'But, Mr Hunter, on Friday you said I was to call Security if she so much as walked past the door!'

He shook his head. Was it only Friday when that had happened? Only three days ago?

It felt like a lifetime!

'I made a mistake, Doris. She's not who I thought she was. And that gorgeous baby *is* mine, as it turns out. I'll be right out.'

* * *

Tina watched the secretary's eyes grow round, then stare up at her.

Tina groaned. 'He's not going to have me thrown out again, is he?' The woman had cupped the phone so that Tina couldn't hear what had been said, though the word 'security' had filtered through.

Dominic's secretary was still sitting there, her mouth open, the phone clutched in her hand, when the man himself reefed open the door leading into his office and just stood there, staring at her as well.

She stared back, perhaps really seeing him for the first time, without those bitter blinkers she'd been wearing. Once again, she was forcibly struck by how different he was from any man Sarah had ever been involved with.

This time, however, Tina saw more than his macho physique. She saw the strength of character in his face, and the capacity for softness in his eyes.

He wasn't the stuff suave, cold-blooded seducers were made of.

In addition to having no capacity for softness, suave, cold-blooded seducers always paid attention to their appearance. Vanity was one of their many flaws.

Tina liked the fact that the navy single-breasted suit Dominic was wearing that morning was obviously off the peg; that his blue shirt wasn't lawn, or silk, or hand-made; that his tie was so out of date that any other man would have long donated it to charity.

She also liked it that he was passionate about his work, and caring of his mother, and careful now with his choice of secretary.

She liked more about Dominic Hunter's personality than she'd ever realised. And she liked Dominic Hunter, the sexy virile man, even more.

'I...I had to see you,' she blurted out, and brushed past him into his office.

She made it to his desk, where she leant on her handbag, quivering inside. She heard him quietly shut the door, then make a slow, thoughtful progress across the thick blue carpet. When he came into view, she noted he was still staring at her, his intense gaze betraying a degree of curiosity in her appearance.

She'd put her hair up and changed clothes since their appointment at the surgery, the escalating heat demanding something cooler than jeans and T-shirt. So she'd showered and put on a shift dress, light and flowery, with no sleeves, a deep round neck and a hem just above the knees. Although she'd left her legs bare, it wasn't really a provocative outfit, but it was feminine and fresh.

With Dominic's eyes on her in it, Tina felt *very* feminine, and totally flustered.

Hard to concentrate on abject apologies when every nerve-ending you owned was on instant sexual alert, when every female part in your body began tingling with an exquisitely sharp awareness.

He sat down in the big black chair behind the desk, still staring up at her.

Start saying something, she urged herself, *before you make a total mess of this.*

'I...I came to apologise,' she began, not wanting to keep looking at him but compelled by the way he was looking at her. As if he was mesmerised.

He leant forward at her opening words, his blue eyes glittering with a mixture of surprise and anticipation.

'I've been so wrong,' she blathered on. 'About you. I...I can see that now. After you left to go to work this morning, your mother told me about Damien Parsons, about the man he is…or *was*, I mean. I saw straight away he was just the kind of creep Sarah was always getting tangled up with. You're not Sarah's type at all. But…but the crunch really came when I realised his name began with a D.'

Dominic leant back in his chair, startled and puzzled. 'A D?'

'Yes.' Hurriedly she opened the bag she'd been leaning on and pulled out a pile of florist's cards. 'I found these amongst Sarah's bits and pieces. They all say the same sort of thing. Love notes. They were all signed 'D'.'

'Which you thought stood for Dominic,' he said, glancing at a couple of them. 'So you believed I sent these, along with flowers?'

'Yes…' Her voice was small. Shaky.

He looked up and their eyes met. Tears filled her.

'I'm so sorry, Dominic,' she cried. 'I jumped to conclusions which I shouldn't have. And I refused to listen to a word you said. You were right when you said Sarah must have lied about you. And you were right when you called me prejudiced. I was. I accept now that you're not Bonnie's father. Damien Parsons is. But the damage has been done, hasn't it? I've hurt you, and now I've hurt your mother. Your dear, *dear* mother.'

More tears flooded her eyes, and she was having the devil of a time blinking them away. But she was determined not to burst into hysterical weeping. What good would that do?

'I can't tell you how dreadful I feel, Dominic. I hate myself more than you do, believe me, but I…I don't know what to do for the best. I don't want to hurt any more people, least of all that man's widow and family. Do…do you happen to know if this Damien's parents are still alive?'

'No, they're not,' he said.

Tina sighed. 'I'm relieved. It would have been difficult not to give Bonnie the chance to know them, but I didn't want to upset them. I was also afraid they wouldn't want to know *her*. And I wouldn't have liked that.'

Dominic smiled a wry smile. 'No. I can imagine.'

'What about his widow? I suppose she wouldn't want to know Bonnie, either.'

'I doubt it,' he said drily. 'Look, Tina, I can't have you go on any further under these misconceptions of yours.'

She blinked her bewilderment. 'Misconceptions? What misconceptions?'

'Firstly, I do not hate you. Far from it.'

'Oh,' she said, and quivered helplessly.

'Secondly, and perhaps more important, is your misconception that Damien Parsons is Bonnie's father.'

'But…but…you said. I mean…'

'He and Sarah had an affair all right. That part's correct. Sarah probably thought he *was* the father. I'm convinced she went to him and told him of her pregnancy. I know for a fact she never mentioned my name personally to that neighbour of hers. I went back to that house in Lewisham yesterday and checked with that old lady. Betty. Sarah only said she'd been to see the father of her baby, her ex-boss. She didn't name names.'

Tina was none the wiser so far. Dominic seemed

to have proved even more conclusively that Damien *was* the father. 'So?' she probed, still puzzled.

'I believe when Damien denied being responsible and gave Sarah that money for a termination, he might not have explained the real reason why he couldn't be Bonnie's father. Maybe he simply let Sarah think he thought she was a slut and slept around. Maybe he wanted to keep the truth a secret.'

'The truth?'

'Damien had a vasectomy some years earlier because he didn't want children. He couldn't father any child, Tina, not even his own.'

Tina could not have been more shocked. 'When…when did you find this out?'

'Only this morning.'

'Who from?'

'I…can't tell you that. This is all very confidential information, Tina.'

'His poor wife. Did she know, do you think?'

'Don't waste any sympathy on Joanna Parsons,' he said sharply. 'She slept around as much as Damien. They had one of those…modern…marriages.'

Tina could not help grimacing with distaste.

'Quite,' Dominic drawled.

Tina noted his disgusted tone. Dominic really was extremely old-fashioned in some ways. One partner after another was fine by him when single, but marriage meant loyalty and commitment to one person only. Perhaps he'd always shied away from getting married because he didn't feel up to loving only the one woman for the rest of his life.

Which at least was honest.

Better he stay single than end up in a divorce court. Divorce was so hard on children, and…

'Oh!' she cried, her eyes flying to his. 'I just realised. If Damien's not Bonnie's father, then that just leaves…'

'Yes,' he finished for her, an odd smile curving his mouth. 'That just leaves yours truly.'

'But…but…why are you smiling like that? Aren't you upset? I know you don't want Bonnie.'

'Who says so?'

He actually sounded indignant!

'Why…*you* did!' Tina told him.

'That was just anger and shock talking,' he pronounced, waving his hand dismissively. 'I resented being accused of something I hadn't done, namely seducing Sarah then abandoning her, pregnant and practically destitute. I would *never* do something like that, Tina. *Never!*' he repeated forcibly.

'I know that now,' she said in chastened tones whilst inside her heart was singing. Dominic *was* Bonnie's father. Everything was going to be all right. Ida would not be devastated. Bonnie would have a good father. And she…well, she would survive, as long as she could see him sometimes. Who knew? Maybe she'd stop panting after him one day. Maybe they would end up good friends.

He stood up and began to pace up and down in front of the large window behind the desk, his hands linked behind his back, his expression serious. 'I'm not a man afraid to face up to his responsibilities,' he pronounced while he paced. 'Now that I've got used to the idea of having a child, I find I rather like it. Bonnie's a beautiful baby. And smart too. Anyone can see that. I have two good women eager to help me bring my daughter up,' he said, stopping to flash her a grateful smile. 'What more could a man want?'

'This…this is just too good to be true!' Tina exclaimed, and Dominic actually looked a little embarrassed for a moment. But only for a moment.

His eyes took on a different look altogether as he walked towards her. They narrowed and glinted with an intensity which sent another quiver all through her.

'And then, of course,' he said softly as he curved his large strong hands over her slight, slender shoulders, 'there is the added bonus of my daughter's guardian sending me into a sexual spin the like of which I have never known.' His fingers tightened and he drew her against him. 'She's doing it to me now,' he rasped. 'Looking at me with those big, dark, sexy eyes of hers, telling me of what she wants me to do, forcing me to obey their silent commands…' And his mouth began to descend.

Tina's lips parted, about to protest her innocence of such desires. But no protest came, unless one counted the small moan which escaped when their mouths met.

It was a kiss of the most passionate persuasion, his hands capturing her face and allowing her no room for anything but to return his passion, to drown in it, then go with it, riding the rapids of desire, racing on and on down the raging river of desire till its unstoppable force spilled into the ocean, its power finally spent and becalmed.

And so it was with Dominic and Tina that day.

Less than five minutes later, Tina came through the storm to find herself sitting on the edge of Dominic's desk, her legs still entwined round his hips, her mouth slowly disengaging from his, her breathing raw and ragged.

Dazed, she let her arms slip away from where

they'd been snaked around his neck, falling limply onto the shiny black surface on either side of her. She might have collapsed backwards if she hadn't grabbed at the edge of the desk. At the same time her leaden legs slipped downwards. When he withdrew, she let out a shuddering sigh, which sounded more like a groan.

His eyes searched hers while he attended to his clothes. Tina winced slightly at the sound of the zipper.

'You all right?' he asked with some concern in his voice.

'I...I don't know,' she returned shakily.

But she knew what he meant. Dominic had been less than gentle when he'd hoisted her up onto the desk, ripping off her pants before plunging into her, swift and savage in his passion.

Not that she blamed him for losing it. She'd been the one to free him from his trousers whilst he'd kissed her. She'd been the one to be utterly shameless, touching him like that.

Tina could only shake her head at herself in utter amazement, her eyes dropping in part embarrassment, part confusion. Was this the same girl who'd thought sex was boring and overrated, who'd previously felt nothing but disgust for females who were easy and fast?

No one could have been easier and faster than she had just been!

Tina would have liked to call what they'd just done lovemaking, but somehow she didn't think love ever came into the equation where Dominic and sex were concerned.

Still...she couldn't deny it had been incredibly exciting. Her eyelashes fluttered as she looked up at him, an ambivalent heat claiming her cheeks. Was she feeling shame, or more excitement?

Surely she couldn't possibly want more.

'Come on,' Dominic murmured, and gently lifted her down off the desk. 'The washroom's over there,' he directed, nodding towards a side door as he took a large lock of errant hair and tucked it behind her ear. 'I'll call you a taxi while you…um…repair any damage. Time you went home. You look like you could do with a sleep. We'll get back to this later tonight, when good little babies are fast asleep.'

Tina sucked in a startled gasp and he smiled the slowest, sexiest smile. 'You didn't think I was going to let it go at that, did you, Tina? We've had two quickies so far, both of which were fantastic but which really only whet the appetite for more. I want an opportunity to make love properly for once, at our leisure. You want that too, don't you?'

She swallowed convulsively. Dear heaven, what did he *mean* by properly? Surely he didn't mean all those shockingly intimate activities she'd read about, the ones which she couldn't believe *any* woman really enjoyed.

Yes, of course he did, came back the cool voice of reason. He was a man of the world. And after the way she'd acted last night—and today—he believed her to be a *woman* of the world.

The thought had her nervously licking her lips.

'I can see you do,' he misinterpreted, and bent to brush his lips over her trembling ones. 'It's going to be so hard trying to work for the rest of the day,' he murmured. 'Thinking of tonight… Thinking of you… Thinking of this…'

And he kissed her again.

CHAPTER FIFTEEN

THE taxi delivered Tina to the door, Ida coming down to the front gate to meet her, Bonnie hoisted happily over her shoulder.

'So how did it go?' she asked, her intuitive blue eyes giving a still stunned Tina a curious once-over. 'You don't look all that happy. Did you sort out whatever it was you had to sort out with Dominic?'

The question put Tina's distracted mind back on track. Any personal problems she had with Dominic were irrelevant in the face of the big picture, which was that Bonnie's future, and Ida's happiness, were assured.

'Yes, I did,' she said, smiling at Ida as she took Bonnie into her arms. 'Once we really talked, your son agreed it was very likely he was Bonnie's father, and that Damien Parsons wasn't. The timing was all wrong for it to be Damien's,' Tina invented, since she didn't have permission to mention the vasectomy.

'Timing, schiming,' Ida tossed back impatiently. 'You only have to look at little Bonnie there to see she's Dominic's. She has the Hunter genes stamped all over her.'

Privately, Tina still thought Bonnie was *nothing* like Dominic. She was dainty and fair and ultra-feminine, just like Sarah. But who was she to spoil a grandmother's pleasure in her granddaughter?

'If he'd listened to reason, I could have pointed out all the evidence for his own blind eyes,' Ida swept on, 'but he was being so pig-headed that I thought it would do him good to stew in his own juice till the tests came back, and then he'd have egg all over his face. I'm almost sorry he's now facing up his responsibility. I was rather looking forward to him looking a little foolish for once.'

'I can't imagine Dominic ever looking foolish,' Tina murmured as they walked towards the house.

'He certainly did last Friday,' Ida said drily. 'You rattled his sabre, I can tell you.'

Tina thought that was a very apt turn of phrase. She certainly *had*. But he'd soon found a scabbard for that rattling sabre, hadn't he? Hers truly.

'Dominic has this ingrained determination to control everything in his life,' Ida raved on. 'No doubt this change of heart is him still trying to do that. Today at the surgery made him face that soon he wouldn't be able to pretend he *wasn't* Bonnie's father. That the test would prove differently. I'll bet he decided to embrace the truth first, so that he feels in control again. Dominic has to be the boss of everything, you know. When he's being his most nice and reasonable, he's at his most dangerous and devious. Was he nice and reasonable to you when you got in there to see him?'

'Well…um…yes, I suppose he was. In a way…'

'Then watch yourself. He's probably planning how to get you to do exactly what he wants.'

Tina's mouth went dry at the thought of what Dominic wanted tonight.

Ida opened the front door for her without drawing breath. 'No doubt he's trying to organise his life so that Bonnie will make the least amount of change to his routine. He's sure to ask you to move in here permanently now, so that he has two women on tap to do all the baby-minding. Dominic will be a responsible father, but not in a full-time hands-on way. That would interfere with his work!'

Tina dragged her mind back from the abyss to listen to what Ida was saying.

'*Nothing* is allowed to interfere with my son's work, not even his extra-curricular activities. Why do you think I didn't know about that Shani woman? Because he slots sex into his life like his dental appointments—well after office hours or during his lunchbreak. Yes, you can look shocked, but I've seen his bank card statement. How else can you explain bills for city hotel rooms when I know full well he came home those nights and was working in his office all those days, except lunchtime?'

They were by then standing in the blessedly cool hallway, at the bottom of the stairs. Tina's eyes were wide on Ida, and her heart was racing. If what Dominic's mother was saying was true, then *she* was about to be slotted into Dominic's life even more conveniently than Shani. He wouldn't even have to leave the house to have sex with *her*!

'*Has* he asked you to move in here?' Ida asked.

'No.'

Ida nodded wryly. 'He will, dear. He will. And when he does, what will your answer be?'

Tina could tell that, despite Ida's critical attitude towards her son, she was eager for her to say yes. And, really, it was the perfect solution all round. If she and Dominic hadn't become lovers, she would not have had second thoughts.

But they *had* become lovers, and nothing would change that.

Tina was beginning to appreciate how weak a woman could become when in the grip of a sexual infatuation.

She refused to call it love. Sarah had always called her infatuations 'love', but time had always proved her wrong.

Still, Tina could certainly understand why a girl like Sarah had been out of her depth if she'd felt like this all the time. It was difficult to stay strong, and independent-minded; difficult to ignore the yearnings Dominic had set up within her body.

'What will I say?' she said, and sighed in recognition of her own weak flesh. 'I'll say yes, I suppose.'

Ida beamed. 'That's what I'd hoped you say. Here now, give me Bonnie back and you go upstairs and have a nap. You look awfully tired, dear.'

'I am, Ida. I am.'

Dominic felt some alarm when he came home that night. Tina was acting strangely with him, tensing up whenever he came within three feet of her. She seemed to deliberately avoid being alone with him, using the baby or his mother to keep him from having the opportunity to speak to her privately, or to even steal a simple kiss.

And he wanted to kiss her. He wanted to kiss her very badly.

The three of them sat down to dinner at seven-thirty, with the pram pulled up beside him, Bonnie inside.

Dominic had insisted, hoping to impress Tina with this sudden burst of fatherly attention. She hadn't seemed impressed, however. She remained distracted and tense all through the meal. Even his coochiecooing the baby occasionally hadn't raised much more than a tight little smile.

'Did you manage to get some sleep this afternoon?' he asked when his mother left the table to get the coffee pot.

Immediately her shoulders stiffened and her eyes skittered away from his. 'A little…'

'Tina, what *is* it?' he asked, but she didn't answer. 'Is it something I've done, or not done?'

She shook her head.

'Is this your way of telling me you don't want to come to my room later?'

Her head whipped back, her eyes shocked yet glittering. '*Your* room?' she said huskily.

Any fear he'd had that she no longer wanted him was firmly routed. He understood where she was coming from now. Underneath, she was as excited as he was. But she wasn't as sure of herself sexually as their raw encounter in the office earlier in the day might have suggested.

Dominic suspected that Tina was essentially a shy girl, with few lovers in the past and a deep distrust of the opposite sex. He would have to be careful tonight, and not frighten her with demands beyond her limited experience.

Not that he was looking for just sex. He wanted so much more than that.

'It's further away from the stairs,' he explained softly. 'And it has a lock on the door.'

'But I won't be able to hear Bonnie from there if she cries.'

Incredible, he thought. She was practically quivering with desire, but she still thought of the baby. What power this little child had!

Of course, Bonnie *was* a sweet little thing. Very pretty and very engaging. Anyone could easily become entranced by her winning little smiles.

'I've asked Mum to keep Bonnie downstairs with her tonight,' he told a startled Tina. 'She said she was going to suggest it herself. She said you needed a good night's sleep, and naturally I agreed.'

Tina trembled at the wickedness of the man. He had it all thought out, didn't he? All planned, as Ida had said. Nothing was to be allowed to interrupt his pleasure.

Or hers, came the added corrupting thought.

Devious and dangerous, his mother had called him. She was right there. He wanted what he wanted, when he wanted it.

The trouble was, she was a willing victim of what he wanted at the moment. But what would happen when he tired of her? When the sex grew boring and some new and more exciting woman walked into his life?

She'd swiftly supplanted Shani, after all.

One day someone would supplant her.

Who next? she wondered. Joanna Parsons, perhaps? Or had he already tasted that particular pie?

No, no, he would not seduce another man's wife. That was not Dominic's way. He had his own moral code when it came to sex and it didn't include adultery.

'What on earth are you thinking about?' he asked a tad irritably, just as his mother came back into the room, carrying the coffee pot.

Tina decided to take back some control over her life, at least superficially. 'I was thinking it might be a good idea if I moved in here on a semi-permanent basis,' she said, before Dominic had a chance to ask. Or coerce. 'What do you think, Ida? After all, it's *your* house.'

Ida threw her an admiring glance. 'I think that's a splendid idea. That way we can share the babysitting. All three of us.'

Tina watched Dominic as his mother's words sank in. 'All *three* of us?' he repeated, frowning.

'Yes, of course,' Ida returned sweetly as she poured the coffee. 'You're Bonnie's father, after all. You have to do your share.'

'Mmm. I don't have much time for babysitting, you know. I work very long hours.'

Ida exchanged knowing looks with Tina. 'Really? Well, maybe you'll have to work less long hours in future.'

His smile was as sudden as it was unexpected. 'You're absolutely right. I will. But not tonight, I'm afraid. Tonight I've brought some important work home with me which needs my urgent attention. Tomorrow night, however, I'm all yours. Night-night, sweetie.' He blew Bonnie a kiss before scraping his chair back and rising to his feet. 'I'll be in my room if I'm desperately needed.'

Tina's stomach contracted at his choice of words, and she steadfastly avoided his eyes as he left the room, his coffee in hand.

She busied herself spooning some sugar into her own coffee, then adding cream. 'Seems you were wrong, Ida,' she said casually whilst her insides were in knots. 'He's going to do his bit.'

'You think so? Remember what I said, Tina. When Dominic is being nice and co-operative, he's up to something. Some secret agenda of his own. Don't ever...*ever* underestimate him.'

Tina didn't. But she thought Ida was being a little harsh. Dominic had been very good since finding out he was Bonnie's father.

Well, not good exactly. A *good* man wouldn't have had her on his desk in twenty seconds flat today. A *good* man would not manipulate his mother to mind his baby so that he could have his wicked way with his baby's guardian half the night long.

Tina's spoon rattled in the cup as she stirred in the sugar. How long could she delay, she wondered agitatedly, before Dominic came to her room tonight and dragged her down to his?

CHAPTER SIXTEEN

THE bedside clock said eleven-thirteen. Tina had stayed downstairs watching television with Ida till ten-thirty, at which point Ida had announced she'd best get to bed. Bonnie had had a bottle at nine-thirty and would wake again around two or three. When Tina had promised to be downstairs for the morning feed, Ida had told her not to be so silly.

'I'm not so old that I can't remember how it feels to be sleep-deprived. You sleep in as late as you like for once. If I get desperate by morning, I'll go get Bonnie's father up bright and early to help. I'm sure he'll be thrilled,' she'd cackled.

Tina hadn't dared say anything to this. But she vowed not to be tricked into spending the whole night in Dominic's bed.

If she ever *reached* his bed. At that moment she was sitting on the side of her own bed, body showered and legs smooth, skin powdered and erogenous zones perfumed.

She'd felt hopelessly turned on during all these erotic preparations, her hands shaking so much while she'd shaved her legs that she was lucky not to have nicks all over her.

Now, she just felt sick.

Time ticked by towards midnight, which seemed to her the deadline for staying in her room. Dominic would surely come to see where she was after midnight. And, when he did, the humiliation would be greater than any endured by going to his room first.

Swallowing, Tina rose and walked towards the door.

Dominic tried not to clock-watch. After his second cold shower of the night, he sat at his computer, pretending to work, when all the while he was listening for Tina. It was nearly midnight, damn it! Surely she was going to come. Surely.

And then he heard something: the soft squeaks of a door being opened and closed. He strained his ears and thought he heard the soft fall of her footsteps coming down the hall, at which point he could not stay sitting a moment longer. Leaping up, he swept open his door and found himself looking down into her upturned eyes, her wide, dark, fear-filled eyes.

With a groan, he reached out to cup her frightened face, drawing her towards him and upwards till she was on tiptoe and their mouths were almost touching.

'There's nothing to be afraid of,' he whispered. 'Nothing at all…'

Tina had to give him credit. He knew all the right moves and said all the right things.

At his soft touch and equally soft words her fears were scattered, and all she wanted was to sink against his hard male body and surrender to its power.

Which was exactly what she did. And oh…how wonderful he felt. And how wonderful he smelt, his skin freshly washed, with just a splash of expensive cologne.

His first kiss was hungry and long, their mouths staying glued while he angled her inside and locked the door behind them. His second kiss was softer, yet just as seductive, his hands expertly divesting her of her wrap and nightie without missing a beat.

Once she was naked, a long tremor ran down Tina's spine, and Dominic drew back to look at her.

'Don't tell me you don't like showing off this perfect body of yours,' he murmured.

Tina had never thought her body perfect. It was a far cry from the hourglass shape and voluptuous breasts men seemed to favour, and which Sarah had been blessed with. Though perhaps Sarah's figure had been more of a curse than a blessing.

'You like my body?' came her surprised reply.

'I adore it,' he growled, and scooped her up into his large strong arms. 'I love your small breasts and your slender hips. I love your flat stomach and your tight little butt. I especially love your long legs and your slender ankles. Hell, I love everything about you, woman. I thought you knew that.'

He carried her quickly to the bed, where he lowered her onto the crisp clean sheets and snowy pillows. He tossed aside his black silk robe as if it was a rag and would have joined her on the bed still wearing his pyjama bottoms, if Tina hadn't protested.

'No, no,' she said with a boldness which shocked and excited her at the same time. 'I want you naked too.'

His eyebrows arched, but he didn't seem to mind complying.

And why would he? she thought breathlessly as her eyes roved hotly over him, this time without skittering nervously away. The man was magnificent.

'Do…do you work out a lot?' she asked, once he'd lain down beside her. Tina had automatically rolled onto her side, and Dominic did likewise, propping himself up on one elbow.

'Some,' he said. 'It relieves stress. There's a convenient gym in my building.'

'And the all-over tan?'

'Sunbed.'

He smiled and she frowned. 'What's so funny?'

'I don't usually like to talk when I'm in bed with a woman.'

'Oh.' Suddenly she felt foolish. And shy. If she could have fled, she would have.

'But I like talking to you, my darling Tina,' he went on, reaching out to stroke a soft hand down her arm and over her hip onto her thigh. She could not believe what a turn-on she found such a simple gesture.

'I like it so much,' he murmured, 'that I could just talk to you and touch you all night.' His hand kept moving, trailing up and down her body. 'Would you like that, my love?' he crooned in a voice almost as mesmerising as his hand, which at that moment was trickling over her breasts, teasing their expectant nipples. 'You wouldn't have to do a thing. Just lie back, close your eyes and enjoy…'

And somehow, in no time, that was exactly what she was doing, lying on her back and enjoying, with his hand finding increasingly intimate places and his voice in her ear promising her the most incredible pleasures if only she'd trust him. With his erotic whispers and caresses, she felt every vestige of control slip away, every fear, every inhibition. When his hand stopped and his mouth took over, protesting never entered Tina's mind.

And so it was for the next few hours.

Dominic made love to her several times, surprising Tina with his gentleness, but also with his stamina. He could not seem to get enough of her body. Touching it. Tasting it. Taking it. Over and over. Her fears about what he might demand of her never eventuated. He didn't make any demands she couldn't meet. In fact, he didn't make any demands on her at all except to surrender to what he wanted to do to *her* body, which, though stunningly intimate, never crossed the line into anything which made her uncomfortable.

Between times, they talked, telling each other the silliest little things, sharing childhood experiences, exchanging compliments. Lovers' talk, Tina supposed. But it was nice. So very nice. She could almost imagine Dominic genuinely cared about her, that he wanted to spend time with her even when they weren't making love.

When he finally fell asleep, Tina lay there for quite some time, trying to come to terms with all that had just happened.

Was it still just sex? she pondered.

Not for her, came back the honest answer.

But it probably was for him. Why else would he be going about it like this, in the dead of night? No, he wasn't in love with her. She was just his latest sex partner, being slotted into his life with the least amount of time or trouble.

Sighing, she slipped from between the sheets, dressed, then snuck quietly back to her room where, surprisingly, she fell asleep as soon as her head hit the pillow. When she finally made it downstairs around noon, Tina was amazed to learn that Dominic had been up at seven as usual.

'He was in such a good mood,' Ida informed her

over brunch. 'He even took time to give Bonnie her bottle, then asked me to show him how to change her nappy. Did it like a champion on his first go and was ever so pleased with himself. If I didn't know better, I'd think he might actually get to *like* being a father.'

Tina could only shake her head. Dominic was an enigma all right. She didn't know what to make of him.

'And another thing,' Ida went on. 'You know the doctor said we had to bring Bonnie back this week for her three-month vaccinations.'

'Yes.'

'Well, I made an appointment for first thing Thursday morning, and guess what?'

'What?'

'Dominic wants to take you and Bonnie himself.'

Tina frowned. 'But he'll be late for work.'

'That's what I said. But he said that didn't matter. He said you might need him. He said he saw how upset you got when they took Bonnie's blood yesterday.'

Tina had to admit she did feel anxious about taking Bonnie for another needle. She would rather have fifty injections herself than watch her little charge have one. Still, she was surprised by Dominic's having been this observant of her feelings.

'That's very...thoughtful...of him,' she said, wondering if she had misjudged the man.

'Yes, it is,' Ida said, then pursed her lips. 'I wish I could work out what he's up to.'

'Maybe he's not up to anything,' Tina defended. 'Maybe he really cares about Bonnie now that he knows she is.'

'Yes. Yes, that's possible, I suppose. I always believed he had the makings of a good father in him somewhere.'

Tina hoped she was right.

Dominic felt Bonnie's shock and pain the moment the needle started to go into her thigh.

And why not? The darned thing was *huge*! He wouldn't have liked to have it himself. His heart twisted when she flinched in his arms, then started to cry.

Dear God, he felt like a monster, an inhuman, cruel monster, holding her there to be tortured. It was an illogical reaction, he knew. Vaccinations were essential for any child's well-being. Without them, she might succumb to any of a number of childhood diseases.

But logic didn't seem to play a part in how he was feeling as he tried to hold a struggling Bonnie still. Afterwards, he walked her around the room and did his best to soothe her loud sobbing.

'There, there, darling. Don't cry. Daddy's here.'

Dominic pulled himself up with a jolt.

Daddy?

My God, had he really said that?

Daddy, he mused as he rubbed Bonnie's back.

The word stirred something in him. Made him feel all soft, yet strong at the same time.

'Sorry about that,' the doctor excused once Bonnie's sobs had subsided to hiccups. 'But it's all for the best.'

'Easy to say when you're on the other end of the needle,' Dominic grumped.

'I guess so.' The doctor gave Dominic a sharp look.

'Am I to presume you're no longer questioning the child's parentage?'

Dominic was about to tell him he could cancel the test when Tina burst into the room, her eyes agitated and shimmering. 'I couldn't stand listening to her cry like that. Is she all right?'

'She's fine,' the doctor said. 'Her daddy here has things firmly in hand.'

Dominic wasn't too sure of that. He'd just missed his chance to tell the doctor to cancel the test, and now he had a teary Tina looking at him with distress and scepticism in her eyes. Admittedly, Bonnie *had* begun to cry again.

'Give her to me,' Tina demanded, and swept the child from his arms.

Dominic watched, somewhat disgruntled, when the baby quietened immediately. It seemed he still had some way to go before he won the award for Father of the Year.

'Bonnie might run a little temperature during the next twenty-four hours,' the doctor warned. 'If she does, then give her some infant's paracetamol. Other than that, everything should be fine.'

'Fine, my foot,' Dominic muttered as he trailed after Tina, who was already hurrying through the waiting room full of coughing, wheezing people.

He'd thought she trusted him now, thought she might even be falling in love with him.

Now he wasn't so sure…

Bonnie went to sleep as soon as the car moved off, bringing about an awkward silence between its two adult occupants.

Tina didn't say a word.

Dominic could not understand her mood. She'd seemed fine the night before.

'Is there anything wrong, Tina?' he finally asked.

'No. What could possibly be wrong?'

He frowned. 'Is that sarcasm I hear?'

She sighed and turned her head away.

When he jerked the car over to the kerb and cut the engine, her head whipped round to glower at him. 'What do you think you're doing? You'll be even later for work now!'

'Work can wait.'

'Well, that's a new one, according to your mother.'

'Oh? And what *else* has my darling mother had to say behind my back?'

'Nothing I didn't already know.'

'Such as?'

'Such as your attitude to women and sex.'

'Which is what?'

'You know very well what your attitude to women and sex is, Dominic. I overheard you voice it the very first night I met you. Perhaps your past women have gone in for cold-blooded, sex-only affairs, but I find I don't like it one bit. In fact, I'm very angry with myself for letting you use me in that way.' Once again, she turned her head away from him.

'But I'm not using you,' he denied, panic-stricken at the way this conversation was going.

'Yeah, right,' she snapped.

'Look at me, Tina,' he pleaded. 'And try to listen to what I'm saying.'

She actually gave him one of those contemptuous looks which had first turned him on. Now, it churned his stomach.

'I'm listening,' she said coldly.

Dominic hesitated, not sure where to start. It was too early to tell her he loved her. She wouldn't believe him. He knew it. But he wanted her to know she was special to him, not just a convenient lay.

Hell, he'd handled this all very badly. In hindsight, he could see slipping into her bed after lights out the last two nights didn't make him look good, especially as he'd left her bed after the lovemaking was over. No wonder she thought all he wanted from her was sex.

But he'd mistakenly believed that was what *she* wanted at this point in their relationship.

He wasn't used to being with a woman who wanted more. He wasn't used to *himself* wanting for. Frankly, he just didn't know how to conduct a normal relationship with a woman.

But he had to learn. And quickly.

Unclipping his seat belt, he reached over to take her hands in his, steadfastly ignoring the instant wariness on her face. 'What I feel for you, Tina,' he said with genuine feeling, 'is so much more than just sex. I told you once before I thought what we had was special. You think so too, *don't* you? I can tell you're not the sort of woman who jumps into bed with just anyone, no matter what you said last Monday night.'

She looked oddly discomfited by his words. 'Is it that obvious?'

'Is what that obvious?'

'That I'm pretty hopeless in bed.'

'What on earth are you talking about? You're not hopeless in bed. You're a darling in bed. So warm and responsive. You make me feel like a king.'

'But I…I haven't done any of those things men

really like. I mean…oh, you know what I mean, Dominic.'

'But I haven't *wanted* you to,' he insisted in all honesty. 'It's given me such pleasure to give *you* pleasure. Oh, my darling, darling Tina,' he murmured, lifting her fingers to kiss them. 'You have no idea what just being with you does to me. I have no need of fancy positions or kinky foreplay. All I need is your lovely mouth on mine and I'm in heaven.'

Her big dark eyes searched his face with a desperation he found infinitely reassuring. 'Then why am I a secret, Dominic? Why do we have to sneak into each other's beds. Make me understand that and I'll believe you.'

'I can only apologise for that. I have to confess to some terrible habits when it comes to the women in my life so far. I've been appallingly selfish. My only excuse is that I didn't want to turn out like my father.'

'Your father?'

'Yes. He was an incorrigible philanderer, then tried to justify everything by claiming he'd *fallen in love* with all his other women. He claimed he couldn't help himself. God, I despised him, especially for what he did to Mum. How she kept loving him, and forgiving him, I'll never know.'

'You know…that's how I used to feel about Sarah. I couldn't understand why she let the men in her life treat her so badly…all in the name of *love*.'

'So you vowed not to be like her,' Dominic muttered, thinking he could well understand that. *He'd* vowed never to be like his father, whom he'd thought a fool of the first order, not only in his personal life but in business. A stockbroker too, he'd taken such stupid risks, both with his own money and his clients'. When he'd died, the family firm, as well as the family finances, had been in a damned awful mess.

But that was all in the past, Dominic realised, brushing aside any bitter thoughts. He had the here and now to worry about.

'Let's start again, shall we?' he suggested.

A startled Tina stared at him. 'In what way?'

'We'll go out, like a normal couple.'

Her eyes lit up. 'Date, you mean?'

'Yes. Starting tomorrow night. You get all dressed up and I'll take you to a fancy restaurant for dinner. That way Mum will know we're getting on well, and it won't come as a shock once she eventually realises we're more than just good friends.'

'But...but what about the bedroom arrangements? I mean...'

'We'll cross that bridge when we come to it.'

'Knowing you,' she said a little drily, 'we'll come to it later tonight.'

'Ahh no, I don't think so,' he said, smiling.

'You're too tired?' she returned, looking deliciously disappointed.

'No. It's Mum's bridge night tonight. She'll be gone from the house by seven-thirty.'

He watched the instant excitement leap into her eyes and thought perhaps it was time Tina's sexual experience was extended. He couldn't really have her thinking she was hopeless in bed. Or out of it!

CHAPTER SEVENTEEN

'I STILL don't believe it!' Ida exclaimed excitedly. 'Dominic asked you out and you actually said yes! I mean, I knew you'd mellowed a bit towards him this past week, and I *always* knew you were his type, but I never hoped...never expected...' She sank down onto the side of Tina's bed, holding a hand over her heart. 'It's too much.'

Tina turned from where she'd been titivating herself in the dressing table mirror for ages.

'Now don't get your hopes up too high, Ida,' she warned gently. 'Dominic is still Dominic.'

'But you like him, don't you? You really, really like him.'

'I really, really like him.'

'More than like, I'll warrant,' Ida said with sly glint in her eyes. 'He's a sexy beast, is my son.'

'That he is,' Tina agreed, a shiver running down her spine. 'Beast' was the exact word to describe him last night. Ida had barely left the house when he'd pounced. Thank the Lord Bonnie had been upstairs asleep at the time.

'Not in bed,' he'd growled as he'd grabbed her from behind, his mouth clamping down into her throat.

Bed had certainly not figured in their lovemaking that evening. The change of scene had brought a change in Dominic's needs. Suddenly he'd wanted more from her. Surprisingly, so had she wanted to give more.

Tina was still stunned at how willingly she'd done what she'd thought she would never do with a man. Yet doing it had seemed to liberate her to want so much more, finding the wildest excitement in Dominic's making love to her in all sorts of exotic positions and places. She'd been utterly shameless. And quite demanding in her own right.

Even now, although the memories still slightly shocked her, she felt no shame. For she loved Dominic. How could anything be wrong when you loved someone?

But did he love her in return?

He hadn't said so. Even if he had, would she have believed him? Men often said they loved a woman when they didn't. It was sex they wanted in the main, not love. Sarah's many one-sided love affairs had taught Tina that.

But she could not deny she had her hopes. Just as Ida did. Best she heed her own warnings, however, and not let those hopes get too high.

'So how do you think I look?' she asked Ida.

'Beautiful,' Ida praised. 'Just beautiful!'

Actually, Tina thought she looked pretty good too. She didn't have a lot of dressy clothes—she lived in jeans and pants most of the time—but what she had was of the best quality.

The dress she was wearing was a simple black number in an uncrushable material which looked like a cross between velvet and suede. The style was an elegant sheath of simple lines, cut in at the shoulders, with a high, round neckline. It was short without being too short. Tight without being too tight. When combined with black strappy high heels and dangling rhinestone earrings, the dress looked a million dollars.

'Dominic's going to drool when he sees you,' Ida said. 'I hope you know what you're doing.'

'What do you mean?'

'My dear, my son is not one to play the gentleman with a beautiful woman for too long, especially if she dolls herself up for him.'

'Ida,' Tina told her firmly. 'I'm twenty-six years old. I've been around. I know exactly what I'm doing.'

Ida's eyebrows arched. 'Well, well, well. Still, do be careful, love. I wouldn't like to see you get hurt. Men can be so selfish sometimes, telling a girl they love them when in fact all they really want to do is get them into bed.'

Tina sighed. Too true, Ida. Too true.

'Your mother thinks you're an incorrigible rake.'

Dominic's teeth clenched down hard in his jaw. Slowly, he put down his wine glass and surveyed the woman he loved. She looked so beautiful tonight, and so desirable. When he'd first seen her on coming home he'd been quite overcome by the trouble she'd taken with her appearance. Surely this was what a woman did for the man she loved.

This belief came from the fact he himself had raced out at lunchtime and bought some new clothes. Knowing his limitations in matters of fashion, he'd asked the elegantly dressed salesman to direct him to what would suit him and be stylish at the same time. He'd never been interested in how he looked before. But he wanted to look good for Tina. Hell, he wanted to take her breath away.

And he had. But along with her admiration for his new look had come a return to wariness, betraying a lack of trust in him. So different from the way she'd acted the previous night. She'd been so incredible, so passionate and uninhibited and, yes, trusting. He'd hoped her responses and behaviour meant he'd won more than her desire. He'd hoped love would surely follow.

Now it seemed he was back to square one. And all because of his mother, the one woman who should have been fostering their relationship, not sabotaging it. He would have to have a few words with her when he got home tonight, before any more damage was done.

'She probably thinks that because of Dad,' he said carefully. 'But she's wrong. I'm no rake. Just a fool who's finally woken up to himself.'

'Meaning?'

He looked at her hard and decided to take his destiny into his hands, with courage and no more games. 'I was going to wait a bit longer before telling you this, Tina, but the truth is I've fallen in love with you. Hard.'

She looked as if she might faint. Her hand trembled so much that some wine spilt from her glass, splashing over the white linen tablecloth.

'You…you don't mean that,' she said, her face pale, her voice shaking.

'I do. I've known it since last Monday, when you came into my office, but I thought it was too premature to say anything back then. If I've made a mistake making love to you as much as I've been doing, then I sincerely apologise. I was trying to get you to fall in love with me in return. Clearly, by the look on your face, I've failed.'

'Oh, no,' she cried, and his heart leapt into his mouth. 'You haven't failed. I...I *do* love you. I've known since last Monday as well. I just didn't dare believe...or hope...that you loved me back. But are you sure, Dominic? I mean...'

Dominic reached out to take her hand across the table, crushing it in both of his. 'I'm *very* sure. I'd do anything for you. And I mean anything,' he muttered, thinking of the lies he'd told and the way he'd pretended with the baby.

No not entirely pretended, he amended swiftly. He *did* feel something for the child.

A tap on his shoulder had him withdrawing his hands from Tina's and lifting irritable eyes. A waiter was hovering with a mobile phone in his hands.

'Sorry to interrupt your meal, Mr Hunter,' the young man said apologetically. 'But there's a phone-call for you. An emergency, the lady says.'

An emergency? Dominic took the phone, thinking that the only person who knew where he was tonight was his mother.

'Dominic Hunter,' he said somewhat testily down the line.

'Oh, Dominic, I'm so glad I reached you. I was terrified you might have gone on somewhere else.'

Dominic's stomach tightened at the near panic in his mother's voice. 'What is it, Mum?' he asked, and immediately heard Tina's sharp intake of breath.

Their eyes met across the table while he listened to his mother's distressed explanation with escalating alarm.

Apparently Bonnie had woken around nine with

what looked like the beginnings of a cold. She'd been coughing and her temperature had been up slightly. Ida given her some paracetamol. But by ten she'd started having difficulty breathing. Worried that it might be an allergic reaction to the vaccination, Ida had called the doctor, who'd said it didn't sound like that and suggested she take the baby straight to Casualty at the nearest large hospital. Apparently they'd taken one look at Bonnie and whisked her straight into Intensive Care.

'What hospital?' Dominic asked, a jolt of fear-filled adrenaline putting urgency in his voice. Dear God, if anything happened to Bonnie, Tina would just die!

'Royal North Shore.'

'We'll be there as quickly as we can,' he said, simultaneously rising to his feet.

Tina was already up, her purse in hand. Dominic took her elbow and began steering her between the busy tables.

'Have to go,' he told the waiter on the way by. 'Family emergency. Get the boss to send me a bill. He knows I'm good for it.'

'It's Bonnie, isn't it?' Tina choked out as they hurried outside the restaurant into the balmy night air. 'She's sick.'

'Yes.'

'What is it?'

'I don't know. She's coughing and having trouble breathing. Maybe it's asthma, or something like that.'

'Oh, dear God…'

Dominic took a moment to turn Tina his way, placing solid and hopefully calming hands on her shoulders. 'Now don't panic, Tina. Mum's taken her to a very good hospital. She'll be all right.'

'How can you *say* that? She might not be. She might die!'

'She can't die,' he muttered and, gripping Tina's elbow, ushered her towards the car.

It was a nightmare drive to the hospital, with a silent and ashen-faced Tina beside him and his thoughts all a-jumble. Because his worries weren't just for the woman he loved but the child herself. She was so little and so precious, to *all* of them. Surely God wouldn't take her. Surely not…

As they drew closer to the hospital Dominic began to really pray for the first time in his life. He was even driven to try to bargain with the Almighty.

Spare this innocent child, God, and I'll…I'll…

What? he thought with self-disgust. Be a good boy in future? Go to church every Sunday? Tell Tina the truth…that Damien Parsons hadn't had a vasectomy? That he'd lied about that, then used his assured position as Bonnie's father to look good in her eyes?

What would be the point in such a confession?

Tina would stop loving him, and he couldn't bear that.

But a relationship shouldn't be built on lies and deceit, came back the alternative argument.

Oh, hell, he thought!

His mother was waiting for them at the main door, looking older than he'd ever seen her look. Her eyes were haunted as she looked at Tina.

'I feel so guilty,' she blurted out. 'I think she might have been awake for some time before I heard her. I was talking on the telephone for quite a while, and it's some way from where Bonnie was sleeping.'

'Don't go blaming yourself for anything, Ida,' Tina said gently. 'We don't.'

'Where is she?' Dominic demanded.

'I'll take you to her,' she said, and off they went, a wretched little threesome if ever there was one.

Ida led them down various corridors, which echoed to their anxious steps, and finally into a room where little Bonnie lay in what looked like an oxygen tent, such a tiny thing amongst a lot of medical paraphernalia.

Tina promptly burst into tears and Dominic put his arms around her, his heart almost breaking as he gathered her close.

The nurse, who'd been standing beside the bed, ushered them out of the room. 'Are you the parents?' she asked.

'This is Bonnie's guardian,' Dominic volunteered whilst Tina sobbed against his chest. 'Her mother's dead. But I'm the father,' he added, thinking this wasn't the time for any confessions. The Lord would just have to do his best for Bonnie without any bribes.

'And I'm the grandmother,' Ida piped up. 'I brought her in.'

'And thank goodness you did,' the nurse said. 'She's a pretty sick little girl. Some new strain of bronchiolitis. Strikes very quickly. She's not doing too badly now that she can breathe more easily, but it's going to be long night. The doctor should be back shortly to check on her again. Meanwhile, try not to worry. It's good that she's not allergic to penicillin. Not that it'll kill the virus, but it's the best antibiotic for any secondary infections. Pneumonia can be a problem in these cases, we find, especially with a tot as young as this.'

'How did you know she wasn't allergic to penicillin?' Dominic asked.

The nurse looked momentarily confused. 'It's on her chart. Someone must have supplied that information when she was brought in.'

They all looked at Ida, who immediately became defensive. 'I didn't say she wasn't for sure. I just said her father wasn't allergic to it, and that it didn't run in the family.'

'For pity's sake, Mum!' Dominic exploded. 'What if I'm *not* Bonnie's father? We're not one hundred per cent sure yet, you know.'

Tina lifted her tearstained face to his. 'But, Dominic, you *must* be. Who else is there?'

'Not to worry,' the nurse hastily intervened. 'She hasn't been given any antibiotics yet. We're waiting on some blood tests. Look, I'll strike that information from the chart, but I suggest you tell the doctor when you see him what the situation is regarding her known medical history. Now, I'm sorry, but I must get back to my patient.'

She bustled back into the room, leaving Dominic with the two women staring up at him. 'I just meant we couldn't be absolutely sure,' he muttered. 'Not till the test results come back.'

'But you *can*, Dominic,' Ida insisted. 'I have a piece of news for you which puts Bonnie's parenthood beyond any doubt whatsoever. That phone call I felt guilty about tonight. It was to Joanna. I wanted to explain about Bonnie, and why I hadn't invited her to dinner again after cancelling last Friday night. Anyway, she started telling me how she would have liked to have had a baby, but that Damien despised children and had had one of those operations to make sure he didn't. A vis…ves…vis…'

'A vasectomy,' Dominic said, hoping he didn't sound as stunned as he felt.

'Yes, that's it. So you see, Dominic? Damien couldn't possibly be Bonnie's father.'

Dominic must have looked strange, because Tina asked if he was all right.

He blinked, then just stared down at her, his mind a mess.

'It's just hit you for real, hasn't it?' she said softly, her lovely eyes lustrous with tears. 'That it's really *your* baby daughter lying in there.'

Oh, God, he thought. If only she knew!

'Yes,' he managed, and his mind turned to the tiny scrap of humanity lying in that room.

He'd thought he cared about her before, but the knowledge that she *was* his child evoked feelings he'd never have imagined. His level of anguish and worry went up a thousandfold. An ache claimed his heart and squeezed and squeezed, till he wanted to cry out with the pain.

Dear God, he would do *anything* to make her well, to have her come home with them, safe and sound. He would even tell Tina the truth, if it would make any difference to the powers that be.

And who knew? Maybe it would!

'I…I need to talk to you, Tina,' he said, his voice strained, his throat thick. 'Mum, do you think you could give me a few minutes alone with Tina?'

'I'll go sit with Bonnie,' she offered.

'What is it, Dominic?' Tina asked as soon as they were alone.

'I have something to tell you. Something important.'

'What?'

'I lied to you.'

Her hand fluttered up to her throat. 'Lied? You…you mean…you…you *don't* love me?'

'No, no. Of course I love you. I love you so much that that's why I lied. About the vasectomy.'

'But Dominic… That doesn't make sense. I'm very confused.'

'When I told you Damien had had a vasectomy it was because I believed he *was* the father. I'd just realised how much I loved you and I ruthlessly decided to use every means at my disposal to win your love. I invented that story about the vasectomy and claimed Bonnie was my own because I thought being Bonnie's father would help win you. You could have knocked me over with a feather when Mum said what she said just now.'

'So you really just found out she's yours?'

'Yes.'

'So all that good father stuff was just an act?'

'Yes. No. Well…in a way.' He sighed. 'Oh, I could water my guilt down and say I truly did grow fond of the child. Which is true. I did. But it was still wrong of me.'

'Dangerous and devious,' she mumbled, shaking her head and looking down at the floor.

But then her head snapped up, and she was frowning at him as though trying to work out something. 'Why are you telling me this now? You didn't *have* to.'

He shrugged, feeling both helpless and hopeless. 'I had this crazy idea that maybe God is punishing me, that maybe I could make Bonnie well if I told you the truth. Then there's another voice in my head which keeps telling me a real relationship isn't built on lies and deceit. I don't want to ever hurt you like my father hurt my mother. I want you to trust me and respect me, Tina. And I want us to stay together. Not just for a while, but for the rest of our lives.'

She looked at him for what felt like an eternity. And then she did something so wonderful and warm that he almost broke down. She folded him into her arms and told him not to worry, that Bonnie would be all right, that she *did* trust and respect him, and that, yes, she wanted them to stay together too. For the rest of their lives.

CHAPTER EIGHTEEN

TINA sat in the small waiting room, her hands cradled around a polystyrene mug of coffee. Dominic sat across from her, his elbows on his knees, his head buried in his hands. Ida had long been sent home to get some rest.

'We don't want you getting sick too, Mum,' Dominic had told Ida after the three of them had sat up with Bonnie all night. Now it was approaching noon, and Dominic and Tina had finally abandoned Bonnie's room to get something to drink.

'Dominic, stop torturing yourself,' Tina said, though she understood what he was going through.

Or maybe she didn't. She loved Bonnie, but she wasn't the baby's real mother.

Dominic straightened, and Tina was shocked by his appearance. 'I think you should go home too, Dominic,' she said. 'You need some sleep.'

'Good God, no, I couldn't sleep. Not till I know Bonnie's out of the woods.'

Tina was still amazed by the depth and intensity of Dominic's feelings. No one could doubt he loved Bonnie now. No one.

Tina didn't doubt he loved *her*, too. She still could hardly believe what he'd done to win her.

How ironic that the lie he'd told had turned out to be true! Life could be so perverse. After all, who would have believed that *she'd* end up falling in love with the father of Sarah's baby, the man she'd thought she despised.

Though maybe it *wasn't* perverse. Maybe it was written…

Tina was deep in thought when Bonnie's nurse popped a smiling face into the room and said, 'Good news. Bonnie's lungs are much better. Her temperature's down and she's awake, complaining her head off. Would one of you like to come and give her her bottle?'

It was a rush to see who made it to the room first, but Dominic won in a photo finish. Not that Tina minded. It gave her such pleasure to see this big macho man being so emotional and tender with his little daughter. Her heart tripped over when he surreptitiously wiped away some tears from his eyes before cuddling Bonnie to him as though she was the most precious thing in the whole wide world.

He looked up at her and their eyes met. She smiled at him. 'I'll go give your mother a call, will I?' she suggested.

'Would you?'

'Of course.' And while she was at it a trip to the ladies' room was in order by the way she was feeling. Tina shook her head wryly as she walked along the corridor. If there was one thing she could rely on in life, it was the regularity of her cycle.

Which was just as well, she realised. As much as Dominic had finally embraced fatherhood with a passion, Tina didn't think he could handle a further little addition to his life at the moment.

They were driving home from the hospital that evening when Dominic put paid to *that* little theory. He put paid to another belief she'd had about him as well.

'I think we should get married, Tina,' he said out of the blue, and then, without giving her time to blink, he added, 'And I think we should try for a brother or sister for Bonnie straight away.'

Tina sat there, absolutely speechless.

'I realise now what I missed out on where Bonnie is concerned,' he went on in all seriousness. 'I want to experience everything, Tina. I want to be there from the start. I want to be there when my son or daughter is born. I want to help choose the name. I want to be a part of everything next time. And the next. And the next.'

Tina gulped. 'Er…run those 'nexts' by me again? How many were there?'

He smiled over at her. 'Don't go telling me you're afraid. Not my Tina. Why, you're the bravest, strongest, most courageous woman I've ever met. I'll never forget the way you looked at me in the office that first time, and then when I got home that night. I didn't intimidate you one bit, did I?'

Tina smiled. If only he knew…

'Do I have any say in any of this?' she asked, her eyes sparkling at him.

'How about yes, yes and yes?'

'You're rushing me, as usual. First into bed, and now into marriage and babies.'

'It's only called rushing when you're not sure. When you are, it's called decisiveness. So what's it to be, my darling?'

'I can't think straight when you talk dirty to me.'

He grinned. 'Then you agree? Marriage and babies?'

'I might as well. Lord knows what devious methods you'll use to get me to agree if I say no.'

'And you'll throw away that pill you've been taking?'

Tina didn't think it was the right moment to say *What pill?* 'Er...don't you think we should wait till we're married?'

'Hell, no. Knowing my mother, that'll take ages. She'll want all that white dress and church and stuff. I want a baby with you, Tina. And I want it as soon as possible.'

A man of decision, her Dominic.

'Okay,' she agreed, and he grinned.

'That's my girl.'

'I am that, Dominic. And you're my man.'

'For the rest of your life, my darling.'

Her heart filled at the certainty in his voice and the love in his eyes.

'Whatever is your mother going to say?'

'She's going to be so happy she'll be obnoxious.'

'I don't believe it!' Ida exclaimed when she heard the news. 'I mean...you two couldn't stand each other last week. Oh, I see, you're just doing this for Bonnie, is that it?'

Dominic put his arm around Tina. 'Mum,' he said sternly. 'Do you honestly think I would marry for anything other than true love?'

'Well...er...I wouldn't put it past you!' she said defensively.

'I *love* Tina. I've loved her for some time. Tina loves me too, don't you darling?'

'Truly, madly, deeply,' she returned.

Ida was still not looking as happy as they'd thought she would. 'But...where are you going to live?' she asked a little plaintively.

Tina didn't give Dominic a chance to say a word,

jumping in first. 'Right here, Ida,' she said. 'If you'll be kind enough to have us, that is.'

'I think I could just about stand it,' she said, trying to hide her pleasure.

'Yes, but will I?' Dominic muttered under his breath.

Dominic went to work extra early Tuesday morning, because he was taking the afternoon off. Bonnie was being allowed home from hospital and he wanted to be there. He found it hard to put his mind to the present state of the economy, along with the fall in commodity prices, but forced himself. After all, he had added responsibilities now. And more to come. He couldn't wait till Tina's period finished and he could get on with making another baby.

And to think if it hadn't been for a failed condom, he would never have known the wonder of fatherhood. Not to mention love. How he had lasted thirty-three years without love, he had no idea!

Tina was a fantastic girl. Fancy her putting aside her acting career just like that to have a family. Without any coercion on his part, she'd made the decision to become a full-time mother to Bonnie and whatever other children they had.

Not that he'd hold her to it. If she ever wanted to return to the stage, or television, or whatever, he would support her wholeheartedly. A girl as smart and spirited as Tina might need creative outlets outside the home at some time in the future.

Still, he would cross that bridge when they came to it!

Doris interrupted his happy thoughts by bringing in the morning mail. 'A parcel for you, Mr Hunter,' she said, and popped it on his desk. 'It was marked for your attention only.'

'Thank you, Doris.'

He frowned at the small book-sized package.

Shrugging, Dominic ripped it open and tipped the contents out onto the desk.

It wasn't a book. It was a diary. Flowers on the cover. And fairly new-looking. A letter accompanied it.

Dear Mr Hunter

You told me to let you know if I remembered anything else Sarah might have told me. I haven't, but I recently moved into the bedsit Sarah occupied and found this under the mattress. I think you'll find it tells you all you need to know about the baby and its real father.

Yours, Betty Longford

Dominic stared at the diary as though it were a deadly spider.

Burn it! came the instant thought.

But he knew he couldn't. He had to read it. Had to find out.

His hands shook as he picked it up and opened the contents.

Half an hour later, he closed it and just sat there, numb. Slowly he rose and walked over to the window, staring blankly down at the street below.

He wasn't Bonnie's father.

Dominic dragged in a deep breath, then exhaled. He couldn't put a name on what he felt. 'Dismay' didn't describe it. Neither did 'disappointment'. 'Shock' was more like it.

Till fury took over. What in heaven's name had possessed Sarah to pick up some sleazebag at a pub whose name she didn't even know? And then to do it with him in a car without using a condom. The girl must have been mad!

It had happened a week after the night she'd spent with him. She hadn't religiously written in her diary every day, and what she'd written sometimes didn't give the full picture. But there was enough detail to put two and two together.

The diary contained answers to other questions as well.

When she'd found out she was pregnant, Sarah had initially thought Damien was the father, because he'd had sex with her without using a condom sometimes, and the date of her last period had seemed to indicate he was the father. But when she'd gone to him with the news he'd scoffed at her, revealing his sterility and giving her money for an abortion.

At this point Sarah's diary clearly indicated she'd believed the father was this stranger she had picked up. Dominic had been dismissed as the potential father because he'd used protection, although Sarah did say she'd wished he *was* the father. She'd wished she could have fallen in love with someone decent, like him, instead of a creep like Damien.

With no way of tracing the real father, Sarah had set about having her baby alone, too ashamed to contact Tina and tell her the truth. After Bonnie had been born, she'd become depressed and started thinking of Damien again. It did seem she'd really loved the man.

She'd rung Hunter & Associates, only to be told Damien was dead. That was the last entry in the diary.

Dominic did his best to find some good news within that wretched journal, finding some solace in the fact that at least the real father would never come and claim Bonnie.

He would still marry Tina, after which he would adopt Bonnie. She might not be his biological daughter, but she could be his daughter in every other way.

Dominic's depressed mood rallied at this last thought. Yes, that was what he would do!

But what about the diary? Did he show it to Tina, or destroy it? Would knowing he *wasn't* Bonnie's real father affect her feelings for him?

He worried that maybe Tina's love for him was somehow bound up in her deathbed promise to look after her best friend's baby.

Dominic hoped not, but his pragmatic side insisted it was possible. Tina's love for Bonnie *was* incredibly strong. She might do anything to make the child happy, even convince herself she loved the baby's father. Or the man she *believed* was the father…

Tina sensed something was wrong the moment Dominic came home to take her to the hospital, but she waited till she was alone with him before she said anything.

He didn't deny there was a problem, then somewhat reluctantly handed her a small diary, his handsome face looking almost as worried as when Bonnie had been ill.

'It's Sarah's,' he explained while she frowned down at it.

'But Sarah never *kept* a diary!' Tina protested.

'It seems she started one this last year.'

'How…how did you come by it?'

'Remember that weekend when I tried to find Bonnie's real father?'

She nodded, unable to take her eyes off the diary, equally unable to open it, Dominic's tension sparking a crippling tension of her own.

'I went back to Lewisham on the Saturday and questioned that Betty woman, then left my business card with her in case she remembered anything. Anyway, she sent me this in the mail. She found it under Sarah's mattress. Apparently she's since moved in there.'

Tina swallowed. 'Will I…not like what's in here?'

'That depends.'

'On what?'

'On your point of view.'

'What do you mean by that?'

'Just read it, Tina. Then we'll talk.'

So she read it. Alternately, she felt angry with Sarah, then just so terribly, terribly sad.

'Oh, Dominic,' she said at last, her voice cracking. 'You must feel terrible.'

His smile was rueful. 'At least you sound as though you care about what I feel.'

'But of course I care about what you feel. Why on earth would you think I wouldn't?'

'I guess I was worried you might not love me any more once you found out I wasn't Bonnie's father.'

'But Dominic, that's crazy! My love for you happened almost *despite* Bonnie, not *because* of her. I could say the same to you, you know. Maybe your so-called love for me was bound up in your love for Bonnie. Maybe now that you know she's not your daughter, you don't love her any more. Or me, either, for that matter.'

'But that's not true. God, don't say things like that!'

'Then don't *you*! It's demeaning to my love for you.'

'You're right. I'm sorry. I've been going crazy ever since that damned thing came in the mail. Hell, I've never been so devastated, or so disappointed. Not that I don't still love the child. I do! And I've been thinking. This needn't change any of our plans. Not really. I can still be her father, in every way that counts. And I could adopt her after we're married. Is that all right with you?'

Tina's heart flooded with emotion. 'Of course it's all right with me,' she said in choked tones. 'You'll be a wonderful father.'

'I'll certainly do my best.'

'Dominic…have you thought about what you're going to tell your mother?'

'Yes. And it'll have to be the truth. Look what happened this last weekend at the hospital about the penicillin. No…unfortunately, she has to know.'

'She'll still love her too, you know.'

'Yes. But she'll be disappointed. It's only natural.' He sighed. 'Poor Mum. She was so sure.'

'Yes, she was.'

'Oh, well…life stinks sometimes.'

Neither of them said a word for the rest of the trip. Seeing Bonnie so well improved their spirits, and by the time they arrived home Tina was glad to see Dominic had shaken off the worst of his underlying depression. But his eyes were still a little flat.

If only she could think of some way to cheer him up.

She watched the careful way he extracted the baby capsule out of the car and thought to herself that life just wasn't fair. He *deserved* to be Bonnie's father, not some drunken idiot.

When Ida came outside to meet them, all smiles and relief, Dominic darted Tina a meaningful glance, as if to say, Not now. She nodded her agreement, thankful that she'd left Sarah's diary in the glove-box of the car.

Ida scooped the baby capsule out of Dominic's hands, her happy eyes peering down at Bonnie's bright little face before lifting to her son.

'While you were away the doctor rang,' she said, still beaming. 'It seems he contacted the pathology clinic on Monday and gave them a come-hurry, because of Bonnie's sickness. He told them it was a medical emergency and he needed to know if you were the father post-haste. Anyway, the results came back this afternoon.'

'I'll go get them after we've settled Bonnie,' Dominic said tautly, and Tina's heart went out to him. 'But first, Mum, perhaps...'

'You don't have to go get them, silly. The doctor told me over the phone. Can't you tell?' She began shaking her head at her son. 'I do wish I was a betting person, because I could have made a fortune on this if I'd put some bets on earlier!'

Tina forgot to breathe while Dominic simply looked shell-shocked.

Ida began to look exasperated. 'For pity's sake, why are you both standing there like stunned mullets? It's not as if we weren't ninety-nine per cent sure of the result, especially after what Joanna told me. Of course, if you hadn't been so pig-headed, Dominic, I could have shown you on that very first day how many of your genes Bonnie had inherited. She even has the Hunter birthmark! But you men always think you know everything.'

Dominic didn't know whether to kill his mother, or kiss her.

'What birthmark?'

'The one behind her ear? Both you and Mark have one. Your father did too.'

'We do?'

'Yes. Haven't you ever noticed?

'I can't see behind my ears. And I didn't make a practice of inspecting Mark's.'

'Well, it's there. Trust me. Mothers wash behind little boys' ears a lot.'

Dominic couldn't help it. He started to laugh. His eyes met Tina's, but she wasn't laughing. She was crying. With undisguised happiness.

Ida looked from one to the other in bewilderment. 'Come on, Bonnie dear,' she said, shaking her head at them both. 'Best get you inside out of the sun. Your parents have temporarily gone mad. Anyone would think they'd just been told they'd won the lottery.'

'Better than the lottery, isn't it, my darling?' Dominic said, putting an arm around Tina's shoulders.

'It's a miracle,' she sniffed.

'Yes,' Dominic agreed. 'Yes, it surely is. Which reminds me…'

'What?'

'I was thinking of going to church tomorrow morning. Care to accompany me?'

EPILOGUE

TINA knelt down and arranged the red roses in the built-in vase, thinking how well they always looked against the grey marble grave and headstone.

'Hello, Sarah,' she said as she worked. 'Here I am again to tell you all the news. All good, so not to worry. Bonnie started going to kindergarten a while back. Just two days a week. She didn't want to go at first. Didn't want to leave her precious baby brothers. She's just like you, you know. A born little mother. I was in such a quandary that first morning. When Bonnie started crying, I almost relented and told her she didn't have to go, but Dominic insisted, and of course he was right. Now she loves it.'

The flowers fixed, Tina settled herself more comfortably on the soft grass verge next to Sarah's grave, stretching out and lying on her side.

'I have some special news for you, my friend,' she murmured. 'I'm pregnant again. Just on four months. Dominic's thrilled to pieces. Not too many men would be, what with Stevie not even out of nappies yet, but he just loves being a dad. Lord knows how it happened, though. The pregnancy, that is. I thought breastfeeding was supposed to stop such things. But, as we both know, Dominic could probably get a girl pregnant wearing lead piping.'

Tina laughed softly. 'Not the girl. Dominic, I mean. Actually, that man continues to amaze me in more ways than one. Do you know, we all trot off to church every Sunday? I mean…can you imagine me in church, Sarah?'

Tina rolled her eyes to the heavens, then smiled. 'To be honest, I think it's rather nice. And it's good for the kids. Bonnie loves it, although I'm not sure if it's church she loves or getting dressed up. Chip off the old block there, dear heart. She's going to be a beauty too, just like her mummy. Dominic will have his work cut out for him, keeping the boys away. His mother teases him about it all the time. But he's up to task, believe me. I've never known a man so loving and protective of his daughter. Yet he doesn't spoil her. He's quite firm. But she loves him to death.

'I love him too, Sarah. More than I would ever have thought possible. Certainly more than *you* thought possible. But it's so good to have a partner who knows where he's going in life. We grew up without security, Sarah, and if ever there was a man who exudes security, it's Dominic.

'He exudes a few other wonderful qualities as well,' she whispered, spying her handsome husband walking slowly towards her, looking sexier than ever. No wonder she'd spent most of the last few years pregnant!

Fatherhood certainly suited him. He looked perfectly relaxed and content with ten-month-old Stevie propped on one hip and two-year-old Beau holding his spare hand whilst his three-year-old daughter skipped by his other side. He'd taken them all for a walk so Tina had a chance to talk privately to Sarah, something she liked to do.

'Anyway, my dearest friend,' Tina said, her heart catching. 'I hope you think I'm doing a good job raising Bonnie. I also hope you've finally forgiven me for letting you down the way I did before she was born. You know, I used to wish you'd told me you were pregnant. But now I think maybe there was some higher purpose to everything that happened. Maybe it was written.'

Tina stood up, throwing a warm smile in the direction of her approaching family. 'They're a good-looking bunch, aren't they?' she whispered, her gaze full of pride and love as it roved over the four of them. 'Oh, and one last thing. The ultrasound showed my baby's a girl this time. When I told Dominic he suggested we call her Sarah. I thought it was a lovely idea. I hope you don't mind.'

Tina didn't think she would.

'All those girlie secrets shared yet?' Dominic asked with a teasing smile.

'Pretty well.'

'In that case, it's time to go home. Stevie needs a nappy change and a feed, and Beau has just announced he wants a gog. So I thought after lunch we'd go gog-hunting.'

'Oh, no, not a gog,' Tina groaned.

'Yes, a gog, Mummy!' Beau insisted. 'A *big* gog!'

'Not a *big* one,' she protested.

'Yes, a big one,' Bonnie chimed in.

'And are *you* going to look after it, missie?' Tina asked her.

'Yes,' she pronounced solemnly. 'I promise.'

And so a dog joined the Hunter household, a big black dog named Bill. He wasn't as good-looking as the rest of the inmates, but he was well loved. And well looked after.

Dominic saw to that.

NOT A MARRYING MAN

MIRANDA LEE

PROLOGUE

Excerpts from Amber Roberts's diary during September of her twenty-fifth year.

Tuesday

What a tiresome day! Arrived at work to find that the hotel had been sold and the new owner would be visiting the premises mid-morning. He's a British businessman called Warwick Kincaid. According to Jill, he's a rather infamous entrepreneur with fingers in lots of pies and a reputation for not holding on to anything for long—his girlfriends as well as his many and varied commercial ventures. How she knew all that I have no idea. But then I'm not addicted to gossip mags the way Jill is. Naturally, everyone went into a flap, wondering if their jobs were safe. Not me so much since I'm not all that wrapped in mine. Though I don't want to lose it just at the moment. Hard to save up a deposit on a house without a salary. Anyway, Warwick Kincaid never showed up in the end. Too busy, we were eventually told. Not sure if that's good news or bad news. He's supposed to reschedule for tomorrow.

Wednesday
Well, he showed up this time. Seriously wish he hadn't. What can I say? He's as up himself as I imagined. But younger. Late thirties, maybe forty. He's also the best-looking man I've ever met. I couldn't stop staring at him. He noticed of course. And he stared right back. I've never blushed so much in all my life. He didn't stay all that long but he's coming back tomorrow to talk to all the staff, one at a time, on a mission to find out why a stylish boutique hotel situated in one of the best areas of Sydney isn't turning over a profit. His words, not mine. Jill said afterwards that he fancied me and that I should watch myself. I laughed and told her not to be so silly, that I was in love with Cory and no man, no matter how tall, dark and handsome—or rich—would get to even first base with me. But you know what? When Cory picked me up tonight, I looked at him and didn't feel anything like the buzz I felt today when I looked at Warwick Kincaid. Later, I was relieved when Cory said he wanted an early night. It sounds crazy, but meeting Warwick Kincaid has made me wonder if I'm really in love with Cory. Maybe I'm just in love with the idea of getting married and having the house and family of my own that I've always wanted. It's a worry all right. So's the way I've been fussing over what I'll wear tomorrow. I have a feeling I'm not going to sleep too well tonight. But I have to if I want to look beautiful in the morning. Oh, goodness, did I just think that? Maybe it would be better if I didn't sleep. Must go now. Have to do my nails and put a treatment in my hair.

Thursday
I'm almost afraid to write down what happened today. Because if I do, it will become more real, more powerful, and even more disturbing. Not that anything really happened. I mean, he didn't make a pass at me or anything like that. He just talked to me about the hotel, the same way he talked to everyone else. Seemed happy with my suggestion that the hotel needed some more in-house facilities like a gym and a restaurant. At least a lounge bar where guests could relax and have a drink. On the surface our conversation was strictly business, but all the while those piercing blue eyes of his never left mine. Not for a second. And it wasn't just the way he stared at me. There was something else. I know it wasn't just me. It wasn't my imagination. Something was there, zapping back and forth across the desk that separated us. An electric charge that was both exciting and enervating. When our discussion was over and I had to stand up, I found that my legs had almost gone to jelly. Somehow I made it out of the office and back to the front desk where I slumped down into my chair. I felt faint. I still feel faint thinking about it. And all I've done this evening is think about it. My whole world has been tilted on its axis. How can I get engaged to Cory now when I know that I don't love him? I mean, how could I love him but want to sleep with another man? And I do. I want to have sex with Warwick Kincaid. I can't believe I just admitted that, but what's the point of keeping a diary if you lie to it? So, yes, I want to sleep with Warwick Kincaid. But that isn't love, is it? That's just lust. Can you be in love with

one man and in lust with another? Maybe you can. What do I know? I've never felt anything like this before. What I need is to talk to someone about it. Not with my girlfriends, though. They're all silly as wet hens when it comes to the opposite sex. Not Mum, either. She'd be dead shocked. She thinks I'm a good girl. Which I thought I was too, till today. Maybe Aunt Kate. She's seen a lot of life. I'll ring Aunt Kate tomorrow and ask her. She'll tell me how it is, warts and all. Yes, that's what I'll do.

Friday
Well, Warwick Kincaid came back again first thing this morning and totally ignored me, which I found to my disgust upset me terribly. I should have been grateful. Anyway, I was so annoyed with myself that by lunchtime I made the decision to resign. I knew I couldn't work for that man a minute longer. I waited till he was heading for home at the end of the day before I handed him the letter of resignation that I'd typed up during my lunch hour. He read it straight away, then gave me the longest, most intense look. Of course I blushed again. Then he said fine, he accepted my resignation, after which he shocked me rigid by asking me out to dinner tonight. I know I should have said no. I know he's the kind of man who wants pretty young girls like me for one thing, and one thing only. But I didn't say no. I said yes. Because the shocking truth is that I want him for the same thing. I'm not in love with him. Heavens, I'm not sure I even like him. But I'm going to end up in bed with him tonight. I'd be a fool to think

he's going to feed me then bring me straight home. On top of that, I have an awful feeling that going to bed with Warwick Kincaid is going to change my life in ways that I can't as yet imagine. There's no point in ringing Aunt Kate now. She can't help me. No one can. I feel like crying. This is not what I want but I can't seem to help myself. Mum thinks I'm going out with Cory tonight so she won't be worried if I don't come home. I always stay at Cory's place on a Friday night. At least I did the right thing by ringing Cory and breaking up with him. I told him that I'd met someone else and that I was sorry. He took the news rather well, I thought, which was of some comfort. But there's no going back now. I've made my bed, so speak, and I'll just have to lie in it…

CHAPTER ONE

July, ten months later...

AMBER'S teeth clenched hard in her jaw as she checked her phone for messages again. Still nothing from Warwick. She punched in his mobile number and was told for the umpteenth time that his phone was not available. She didn't leave a message. There was no point. She'd already left three, each one sounding more frustrated than the last.

When she'd suggested a romantic dinner for two tonight rather than a restaurant meal, Warwick had promised to be home by seven-thirty. But then he'd messaged her shortly before six saying he'd been delayed and that he might be back a bit late, maybe by eight o'clock.

It was now almost nine and still there was no sign of him. No more messages, either.

'Surely you have time to call me,' Amber muttered under her breath as she returned to the kitchen, threw her cell phone onto the black granite counter-top, then switched off the oven in which the already overdone beef stroganoff had been keeping warm.

At least she hadn't started cooking the rice. Maybe the meal was still salvageable. Though her own appetite had long gone.

Opening the oversized stainless-steel fridge, which never held all that much food—not much point when they rarely ate at home—Amber reached for the bottle of New Zealand Sauvignon Blanc, which had become her favourite, and poured herself a glass. Carrying it with her and sipping at the same time, she made her way back through the dining room, grimacing as she passed the beautifully set table before heading for the balcony and the hopefully soothing effect of the water view.

Using her free hand, she slid open one of the glass doors that led out onto the huge curving balcony and that fronted the entire apartment, providing a spectacular view of Sydney Harbour. Unfortunately, it was freezing out there, the stiff breeze that came off the water quickly making a mess of Amber's long hair. Grimacing, she turned and hurried back into the temperature-controlled interior, shutting the glass door behind her. She'd forgotten for a moment that it was winter, Warwick always keeping the apartment pleasantly warm.

Putting her wine glass down on one of the glass-topped side tables that flanked the white leather sofa, Amber made her way across the plushly furnished living room and into the vast expanse of the master bedroom. Her chest tightened as she took in the turned-down bed, the cream satin sheets and the scented candles she'd placed on the bedside tables, in anticipation of the evening ahead.

'Bastard,' she muttered, and marched on into the cream marble en suite bathroom where she took a brush out of the drawer on her side of the twin vanities and began attacking her ruffled hair with angry strokes.

It didn't take her long to put order into her hair which

was easily managed, being long and straight with a blunt-cut fringe.

Her ruffled emotions, however, were not so easily controlled.

Amber could still remember the first time she'd stood on this very spot, looking into this mirror, her blue eyes wide with excitement. It had been the night she'd gone to dinner with Warwick, the night her life had changed for ever…

He'd taken her to a five-star restaurant first, where he'd impressed her with the very best of food and wine, along with his highly entertaining conversation. It'd been impossible for a twenty-five-year-old girl who'd only left Australia for family holidays in Bali and Fiji not to be impressed with this man who'd been everywhere and done everything. Impossible not to be flattered by the fact that someone of his intelligence and status would choose to be with her: Amber Roberts, receptionist.

Afterwards, he'd brought her back here, without bothering to make any excuses, his intentions perfectly clear to Amber as they had been from the moment he'd asked her out.

She'd tried not to appear too blown away, either by his Italian sports car, or his multimillion-dollar Point Piper apartment, which he'd bought two weeks earlier, fully furnished. But she was an ordinary working-class girl who'd been brought up in the western suburbs of Sydney. She wasn't used to this kind of luxury living. She certainly wasn't used to this kind of man.

He hadn't just swept her off her feet and into his bed that night. He'd taken possession of her with a power and a passion that had left her, not only reeling, but ready to say yes to anything he wanted.

But what he'd wanted had been slightly surprising.

She'd feared, when she'd woken in his king-sized bed the following morning, that that might be that. She was sure it would be a case of *hasta la vista, baby.*

Instead, he'd pulled her to him, told her he was crazy about her and asked her to become his girlfriend. Not just in a casual relationship, either. He wanted her to move in with him, travel with him, *be* with him all the time. She wouldn't be able to work, of course. She had to be ready to accompany him at a moment's notice. He travelled quite a lot, both for business and pleasure.

She'd been about to blindly say yes when he'd qualified the terms of the relationship he was proposing.

'Just so you don't get the wrong idea,' he'd added. 'I don't do marriage and children. And I don't do for ever. I have a notoriously low boredom threshold. Twelve months is usually my limit when it comes to any woman. Though with you, my sweet lovely Amber, I just might make an exception. To be honest, you're already one big exception. Up till now, I've never asked a woman to live with me. I dare say it's going to cost me dearly in the end, but there's something about you which I find totally irresistible. So what do you say, beautiful? Do you want to get aboard the Kincaid roller-coaster ride, or not?'

She should still have said no, despite the seductive flattery he'd included in what was really a totally appalling and extremely selfish proposition. But how did a girl say no to more of what she'd experienced the night before? Amber had never known such excitement, or such pleasure. There were things Warwick knew about lovemaking that had quite blown her away. He'd been able to turn her on and keep her that way for hours, reducing her to total mush.

So of course she'd said yes, and now here she was ten

months later, still his live-in girlfriend. Or his mistress, as Aunt Kate had once caustically called her.

But for how much longer?

This was the third time lately, Amber conceded as she stared blankly into the vanity mirror, that Warwick had let her down. A couple of weeks ago, he'd cancelled a weekend getaway to the Hunter Valley that she'd been looking forward to, instead jetting off by himself to New Zealand with two of his business associates to go heli-skiing, a high-risk, thrill-seeking, extremely dangerous sport that had recently cost other lives and that had left her worried sick all weekend. But his worst transgression, in her opinion, had been when he'd refused to accompany her to Aunt Kate's funeral last week, claiming he'd had important business to attend to that day, then adding insult to injury by saying that the old duck hadn't liked him and he hadn't liked her, either!

Which was totally beside the point. Amber had been very fond of her aunt Kate and terribly upset by her aunt's rather sudden death of a stroke. She'd only been seventy-two, hardly ancient.

It had been horrible, sitting in that church all by herself, then having to defend Warwick's absence afterwards. Her relationship with him had already alienated her from her family to a degree. He'd only accompanied her to two family gatherings during the time they'd been together, Christmas Day at her parents' house in Carlingford, and then last Easter, to a family barbecue at her aunt Kate's place up at Wamberal Beach on the Central Coast.

And whilst he'd been quite polite to everyone, he'd somehow made it obvious—to her at least—that he'd been bored rigid. On both occasions they'd been the first to leave.

Amber's two older brothers hadn't pulled any punches last week when it had come to making forthright remarks about her wealthy lover not bothering to attend Aunt Kate's funeral. Even Warwick's lending to her of his flashy red Ferrari for the drive up to Wamberal hadn't softened their disapproval over his absence.

And they'd been quite right. He should have gone with her. His claiming that he'd had important business to attend to that day had just been an excuse. If he'd cared about her at all, he would have made other arrangements and driven her to the funeral himself.

By the time Amber had arrived back home after the wake, she hadn't been able to contain her emotions, telling Warwick exactly what she thought of his lack of sensitivity and support, before flouncing off to sleep in one of the two guest bedrooms.

She'd been half expecting him to come to the room and persuade her back into the master bedroom. But he hadn't. In fact he hadn't made love to her since, which was unusual. When Warwick wanted sex, he could be quite ruthless.

Clearly, he hadn't wanted sex this past week. But she'd wanted him to want it. Wanted him to want *her*.

If she'd been a bolder type of girl, she would have attempted a seduction of her own. But playing the femme fatale was not Amber's style. Although not exactly shy, she never made the first move—although she'd never needed to where Warwick was concerned: he had more than enough moves for both of them.

By now, an increasingly desperate Amber knew she would have to do something to allay her growing fears that he was definitely growing bored with her. Her suggestion this morning over breakfast of a candlelit dinner at home seemed to have gone down well, with Warwick giving her a long lingering kiss at the door before going off to attend to his latest property development.

Not a hotel this time. Warwick wasn't interested in buying another Sydney hotel, despite his earlier acquisition now making a nice profit after he'd put in a gym and a lounge bar, as she'd suggested. This time he'd chosen a night club up at the Cross, a rather run-down, seedy establishment that had definitely seen better days. But Warwick had seen potential in its position and was currently making the place over into the kind of high-class club that would attract the rich and famous with its luxurious ambience, wonderful food and top entertainment. He'd consulted Amber quite a lot about the refurbishing, complimenting her often over her various suggestions. In truth, she was as excited by the project as he was and often accompanied him to the site.

Not this past week, however. He hadn't offered to take her and she hadn't asked. Even if he'd asked her today, she probably would have said no. She'd had other plans.

Amber had known it would take many hours to prepare for the evening ahead. She'd gone to the hairdresser first, after which she'd bought herself a new dress, something extra pretty and feminine. Then she'd had to shop for food, set the table, prepare the bedroom, and, finally, herself.

Oh, yes, Amber thought ruefully as her eyes cleared to rake over her reflection. She'd spent hours on herself, making sure that she looked exactly as Warwick liked her to look.

On the surface, her appearance hadn't changed much since the first day they'd met. Her hairstyle was exactly the same, though she'd given in to Warwick's request to have her honey colour lightened to a cool, creamy blonde. And it did look classier somehow. Her eyebrows were more finely plucked these days, and the make-up she now wore was extremely expensive, not from the supermarket ranges that she used to buy. Although she couldn't see all that much difference, despite the time it took to apply everything. Maybe the lipsticks stayed on a little longer and the mascara was definitely waterproof.

Her figure was still basically the same, longer work-outs in the gym ensuring that all the restaurant food she'd devoured over the past ten months hadn't settled on her thighs or her stomach. Slightly taller than average, Amber had been blessed with a naturally slim body, yet enough curves to attract male attention.

Of course, her wardrobe had changed dramatically, Warwick insisting that she allow him to dress her the way a woman of her 'exquisite beauty' should be dressed. He always called her a woman, never a girl. She'd been powerless to resist his compliments—as she'd been powerless to resist him—and now had a walk-in robe full of designer clothes; something for every possible occasion.

Nothing too sexy, though. Warwick said that true sexiness was what was hidden, not what was displayed.

A shiver trickled down Amber's spine when she thought about what was hidden under the softly feminine Orsini original she was wearing.

The long-awaited sound of her cell phone ringing had her throwing her hairbrush down and racing back out into the living room, where she thought she'd left it. But the sound wasn't coming from there. Had she left the handset out on the balcony? She didn't think she had.

And then she remembered.

'The kitchen!'

Amber prayed for it to keep on ringing as she bolted for the kitchen, wishing that the rooms in this place weren't quite so big.

At last she snatched the phone up into her hands, sweeping it up to her ear and saying, 'Thank heavens you didn't hang up,' rather breathlessly at the same time.

'Er...it's Mum, Amber. Not...who you thought it was.'

Amber suppressed a groan of dismay. Thank goodness she had a call waiting facility or she'd go stark raving bonkers, having to talk to her mother when Warwick might be trying to contact her.

'Hi, Mum,' she said much more calmly than she was feeling. 'What's up?'

Her mother rarely rang her these days, their relationship having become strained since the day she'd announced that she'd quit her job, broken off with Cory and moved in with her billionaire boss.

Amber could well understand why her family didn't approve of her actions and she'd finally given up trying to justify what she'd done. Because there *was* no justification. She couldn't even use love as an excuse. There'd been no love back then, just lust. Though she preferred to think of it as passion—the kind of passion that was as powerful as it was impossible to describe, especially to your mother.

It had been quite a few months before Amber realised she'd actually fallen in love with Warwick. Up till then she'd been so blinded by her desire for the man that she'd been unaware of the deepening of her emotional attachment. The illumination of her true feelings had happened with all the suddenness and force of a bolt of lightning. They'd been staying at a resort in far North Queensland one weekend late last summer, when Warwick had decided to go bungee-jumping. She'd refused to participate herself but had gone along to watch, knowing it was better on her nerves to accompany Warwick on his thrill-seeking activities rather than stay behind and worry. Something had gone wrong with the length of the rope and his head had almost hit the rocks below. Amber had been absolutely horrified, both by his near miss and the realisation of her love.

Up till then, she'd convinced herself—perhaps as a form of self-protection—that she wouldn't be heartbroken when her time with Warwick was up. After all, broken hearts were for people who truly loved each other. She'd told herself repeatedly that going back to the real world would be difficult, but she would survive.

Suddenly, with Warwick's near-death experience, Amber saw what her life would be like without him. The wool was violently pulled from her eyes and she saw with painful clarity that she'd been fooling herself, big time.

She did love him. Not just truly, but madly and very very deeply.

But she certainly didn't say as much to Warwick, who'd made it clear right from the start that love was no more on his agenda than marriage and children. Quietly, however, like any typical female, Amber had begun to harbour the hope that she might be the exception to that rule as well; that one day he'd discover that he'd fallen madly in love with her too and wanted to keep her for ever. But that hope was rapidly fading.

'Something strange has happened regarding Kate's will,' her mother announced, cutting into her thoughts.

'Oh? What? She left everything to Dad, didn't she?'

Who else? Aunt Kate had been a spinster and Amber's father's only sibling.

'She did in her old will. But it seemed she made a new will, witnessed by those two friends of hers. Max and Tara Richmond. You know who I mean, don't you?'

'Yes, of course.' Amber had first met the Richmonds on Christmas day two years ago, when Christmas dinner had been held at Aunt Kate's place.

Max Richmond was the owner of the Royale chain of international hotels, including the Regency Royale in Sydney, but had semi-retired to the Central Coast after his marriage. He and his wife were good friends of her Aunt Kate. They were a very glamorous-looking couple, with two amazingly well-behaved children: a darling little boy named Stevie and a very pretty blonde baby named Jasmine, who just sat in her stroller and smiled at everyone.

Amber recalled thinking on more than one occasion that they seemed the perfect family.

'You may or may not have noticed,' her mother said, 'but the Richmonds weren't at Kate's funeral last week.'

'No, I didn't notice.' She'd been too upset to notice anything much.

'They were overseas at the time of Kate's death and didn't learn about it till they returned home yesterday. Anyway, to cut a long story short, they immediately got in touch with us to let us know that they were in possession of a new will, made just after Easter this year. In it, Kate has left her superannuation policy to your father, but her home and all its contents go to you.'

'What? But that's not right. I don't deserve it!'

'Whether you deserve it or not is not the point,' her mother said archly. 'Kate's bed and breakfast is now legally yours.'

Amber blinked with shock. Her aunt's B & B was

situated a stone's throw from Wamberal Beach, a much-sought-after location during the warmer months of the year. Any seaside town within a couple of hours' drive from Sydney was never lacking for guests, especially during the school holidays. Aunt Kate had made a good living for herself over the years, though she'd wound the business down a lot lately, because of her age. She didn't even have a website, relying on past customers and word of mouth for guests, plus the sign that stood at the entrance to her driveway. Even if it wasn't a going concern as a B & B any more, the house would still be worth close to a million dollars.

'How does Dad feel about this?' Amber asked worriedly. 'Is he upset?'

'He was at first. Not because he wanted the place himself. As you know, we've done very well with our fencing business over the last few years and we're not wanting for money. But we both thought Tom and Tim should have been included in Kate's will. Yet when your father spoke to them, they said they didn't mind at all. They actually seemed very pleased for you. They pointed out that they weren't close to Kate the way you were. They didn't visit her or love her the way you did. Of course, both my boys have very good jobs,' her mother said proudly. 'They don't need a helping hand. Unlike you.'

'What do you mean by that?' Amber snapped, hurt by the pride that her mother always voiced in Tom and Tim. Doreen Roberts was one of those women who doted on her sons and largely ignored her only daughter. Amber's father was just the same. It was no wonder her sole ambition in life had been to leave home and make a family of her own, one where the love was shared around equally.

'We're all worried about you, Amber, living with that heartless man. Kate was especially worried. I have a suspicion she knew she didn't have long to live, and changed her will in your favour to throw you a lifeline, so to speak. At least you'll have a home and a job when that man's finished with you. Which, if he runs true to form, will be any day now.'

'You don't know that,' Amber threw at her mother before she could think better of it.

'That's where you're wrong, dear. I know quite a lot about Warwick Kincaid and none of it's very complimentary. He might be successful in his business dealings, but his personal life is another matter. It's a case of like father, like son.'

'Meaning?'

'His father was a notorious womaniser who hung himself after losing millions at a casino, according to the inquest.'

Amber was truly shocked. Warwick had told her that his father had died unexpectedly at fifty-one, but she'd just assumed it was from a heart attack or a stroke. He'd said nothing about suicide.

'His wife divorced him soon after their only child was born,' her mother rattled on, 'the price of her freedom being that she had to give up custody of her son. At the time, James Kincaid was one of the richest bankers in England with lots of power and influence. It's all there to read on the Internet if you ever want to look it up.'

'I don't have to, Mum. I know all about Warwick's family background.' Which was an exaggeration of the highest order. Warwick was a man who lived in the here and now. He rarely talked about his past life. Neither did he ask her about hers. He'd told her a few brief details just before Christmas last year when she'd enquired about his family. She did know about the divorce and that his mother—from whom Warwick remained estranged—was an actress of sorts. She knew his mother had never remarried, so he didn't have any half-brothers or -sisters. She knew nothing of his father's womanising, or his suicide.

'Then you must know that your boyfriend's a womaniser as well,' her mother swept on waspishly. 'With a mistress left behind in every country he's lived in. It's a different country each year: France, Spain, Italy, Turkey, Egypt, India, China, Vietnam… And now Australia. Next year he'll probably hop over to New Zealand, then on to the Americas. He's an adventurer, Amber. And a gambler, just like his father. Maybe not at cards or roulette, but with his life. He does dangerous things.'

'Yes, I do know that, Mum,' Amber said ruefully. Bungee-jumping and heli-skiing weren't her lover's only thrill-seeking activities. Warwick liked to drive fast cars and boats. He liked everything that smacked of speed and risk. 'Please, can we stop this conversation right now? You're not telling me anything I don't already know.' Okay, so she hadn't known the detailed itinerary of his past love life, but she'd been warned about his womanising reputation right from the start, both by Jill and Warwick himself.

'And still, you stay with him,' her mother said with incredulity in her voice.

'I love him, Mum.'

It was the first time Amber had said the words out loud to anyone other than herself.

'I very much doubt it,' her mother snapped. 'You're just infatuated with his looks and his lifestyle.'

'You're wrong, Mum. I *do* love him,' Amber insisted hotly. 'And I won't leave him. Not unless he asks me to.'

Her mother sighed. 'There's nothing more to be said on that subject, then. So what are you going to do about Kate's place? You can't just leave it empty indefinitely. You'll have to do something with it.'

'Could I rent it out, do you think? I mean…as a holiday house?' She didn't want to sell it. Not straight away.

'I suppose so. But you'll have to find yourself a reliable agent. And soon. Your father went up there last weekend and mowed the lawns and watered the garden but you can't expect him to keep on doing that. The place is your responsibility now.'

Amber's heart jumped when she heard the familiar sound of the front door being opened. Warwick was home at last. Thank heavens! She was beginning to worry that he might have had an accident.

'Mum, I'm sorry, but I have to go now. I'll come over tomorrow and pick up the keys. Will you be home?'

'Yes. But only till twelve. I have a hairdressing appointment at twelve-thirty.'

'I'll be there before then. Bye.'

Amber tossed the phone back down on the granite counter-top and hurried out of the kitchen, her heart thudding behind her ribs in a maddening mixture of excitement and annoyance.

Just the sight of him tipped her emotions more towards excitement. Warwick was still the most handsome man she'd ever seen, with a strongly masculine face, a well-shaped head, sexy blue eyes, and an even sexier mouth. Combine that with a body to die for and an English accent that could cut glass and you had a man who'd give James Bond a run for his money. In fact, he would make an excellent James Bond in Amber's opinion, his suave man-about-town façade hiding a ruthless inner core. He wasn't totally heartless, as her mother had said. But he was extremely formidable.

It took courage to confront Warwick with anything, even his tardiness. Normally, Amber forgave his tendency to be late for things.

But not this time.

'Where on earth have you been?' she demanded to know. 'You knew I was cooking a special dinner for us tonight. Why didn't you call me? I left enough messages on that damned phone of yours!'

CHAPTER TWO

WARWICK closed the front door behind him, slipping the security chain into place before turning his attention back to his understandably upset girlfriend.

How exquisitely beautiful she looked in that glorious pink dress! Beautiful and desirable. Not that it was a sexy garment, by any means. There was no provocative décolletage on display. The neckline was modestly scooped, and the simple flowing style skimmed rather than clung to her curves, the handkerchief hemline reaching down past her knees.

But never before had a girl turned Warwick on the way Amber could—so damned effortlessly. She didn't have to flirt, or do any of the boldly seductive things his previous women had done. She only had to be in the same room and his hormones jumped to attention.

Suddenly, Warwick wasn't sure if he could continue with the plan he'd started putting into action recently, the one where he showed himself to be the ruthless man he actually was. Much easier to give up on that idea—however perversely noble it was—apologise profusely for being late and do what his body was urging him to do: ravish her all night long.

The temptation was powerful. But so—as Warwick kept discovering to his surprise—was his conscience.

For some time now it had troubled him deeply. Thanks to that wretched aunt of Amber's.

Of course, he himself had known right from the start that it had been wrong to take a girl like Amber to his bed. She'd been too young, too sweet and too sensitive.

But he just hadn't been able to resist her. The chemistry between them had been electric, right from the first moment they'd set eyes on each other.

Just one night, he'd told himself at the time. To see how it would feel to make love to someone wholesome. Someone who blushed when you looked deep into her eyes; someone whose attraction for him shocked her enough to make her resign.

Well, he'd found out what it was like and, come the next morning, he hadn't been able to let her go.

But now the time had come for him to do so.

Time to be cruel to be kind.

'Please don't start sounding like a wife, Amber,' he said coldly as he strode into the room, loosening his tie and undoing the top button of his shirt as he headed for the built-in bar in the corner. 'I texted you that I'd be late,' he threw at her after selecting a glass and reaching for the whisky decanter. 'For pity's sake, woman, don't nag.'

'I...I don't think it's nagging to demand politeness,' she returned in a small, almost crushed voice.

He should not have glanced up at her, not then. Not when her soft blue eyes looked so wounded.

Hell on earth, he couldn't do this. Not tonight. That would be just too cruel.

'You're right,' he said more gently. 'Sorry, sweetheart. I'm a bit wound up. Had to sort out a few problems with one of the building contractors. That's who I was with all this time,' he lied. He'd actually been sitting in a bar in town all by himself, nursing a whisky for two long hours till he was rudely late. 'What say I go shower and change into something more comfortable whilst you rustle up dinner?' he suggested. 'It's not spoiled, is it?'

'No.' Immediately, her dulled eyes glowed with happiness, sending a dagger of guilt plunging into his own wretchedly dark heart.

Oh, Warwick, Warwick, he thought almost despairingly. How are you going to get yourself out of this mess? The girl loves you. Can't you see that?

Yes, of course I can see it, came a frustrated voice from within.

It wasn't the first time this realisation had jumped into Warwick's head. That day he'd gone bunjee-jumping, for instance, when the damned rope had gone awry and he hadn't been killed. More was the pity. Amber's feelings had been written all over her face. She'd been trembling with shock and relief when he was brought back up, unharmed.

Unfortunately, being loved the way Amber loved him—with such sweet sincerity—was as powerful as the most addictive drug. Giving up the way she made him feel was going to take a massive act of will, one that Warwick didn't think he was capable of this evening. Knowing she wanted him to make love to her after dinner was weakening his resolve to end their relationship.

Maybe it was time to tell her the truth about himself, to force Amber to face the fact that there was no future with him.

Could he do that? *Should* he?

Unfortunately, revealing his genetic flaw and all its

appalling inevitabilities might not bring about the desired result. If Warwick had learned one thing about Amber's character during the last ten months, it was that she was as compassionate as she was passionate. She would become visibly upset whenever she saw those ads about poor starving children, and could only be soothed when he promised to make regular donations to whatever charity was canvassing for help. Stories about neglected animals inevitably brought similar distress, as did reports on the news about more bombs killing innocent women and children in war-torn countries. Warwick had taken to putting a box of tissues at the ready by the sofa to mop up her tears.

Finding out what awaited her lover in the future might send her running, not in the other direction, but right into his arms.

It was a risk Warwick decided he could not take. He would have to find some other way to end their relationship.

'Is that your glass of wine over there?' He nodded towards the nearly full glass that was sitting on the side table next to the box of tissues.

'Oh, yes, it is. I was having a drink earlier when I was waiting for you to come home.'

Another stab of guilt. Still, he was here now.

'Bet I can guess what it is,' he said. 'A Sauvignon Blanc from the Marlborough region.'

She smiled as she walked over to pick up the glass. 'You know me too well.'

Yes, he thought as he dropped a few cubes of ice in his glass then slurped in some whisky. I do. And you deserve better than me. You deserve a man who'll marry you, give you children and grow old with you.

I can't do any of those things.

Warwick scowled as he lifted the glass to his lips, irritated suddenly by his maudlin thoughts. What good did they do? He'd always been a realist, and the reality of his life was that he couldn't offer Amber any more than he'd originally offered her.

But damn it all, surely the time she'd spent living with him hadn't been totally wasted. She'd travelled a lot and learned a lot. She'd socialised with some of the world's most successful people, been dressed by the world's most fashionable designers, stayed in the world's most luxurious resorts.

Some women would kill for what Amber had experienced during these past ten months.

Unfortunately, Amber wasn't one of those women. Warwick knew she didn't give a fig about any of those things. All she wanted was his love and his ring on her finger.

Not that *she'd* told him so. Not once.

Her aunt Kate had told him, last Easter at a family barbecue at her home that Amber had dragged him along to.

What an old tartar she'd been. But she'd obviously loved her niece and wanted to see her happy.

'You do realise,' Kate had snapped at him when Amber had left them to go to the bathroom, 'that Amber was practically engaged when she met you. To a perfectly nice boy who would have given her the only things she's wanted since she was knee high to a grasshopper: a loving husband and a family of her own. Two things you'll never give her, Warwick Kincaid.'

The old dragon probably could have said a lot more but didn't get the opportunity.

'Shame on you,' she'd hissed under her breath as Amber had walked back towards them.

That had been three months ago. Warwick hadn't told Amber what her aunt had said. Hadn't asked her about the man she'd been on the verge of marrying. He certainly hadn't embraced the undeniable shame the woman's forceful words had momentarily evoked. Instead, he'd gone on wallowing in Amber's warmth and passion, telling himself that he hadn't forced her to choose him over that other fellow. He'd never forced her to do a single thing. She had free will, didn't she? She *wanted* to be with him.

But gradually, the shame had resurfaced. So had his conscience, something that he'd kept buried for a long time. In hindsight, his plan to stop acting like a besotted bridegroom and start showing his true colours had not been well thought out. He hadn't anticipated the hurt that his abrupt change in behaviour would bring her. Hadn't anticipated his own level of self-disgust.

Far better that the break be clean and swift.

When the time came, that was.

Her walking over and bending forward to pick up her glass of wine showed him that that time definitely wasn't tonight, his flesh stirring as he imagined how she would look doing that *without* that dress on.

'Dinner won't be ready for at least fifteen minutes,' she said as she straightened. 'I haven't cooked the rice yet.'

'What are we having?'

'Beef stroganoff.' Her free hand lifted to push her long hair back from where it had fallen over one of her shoulders. 'I wanted something plain for a change.'

Warwick's flesh stiffened as he noted the telling outline of erect nipples under the pink silk. She was as frustrated as he was, by the look of things. Understandable considering there'd been no sex this past week, the longest time he'd abstained from touching her since their first night together. It had been damned difficult. But at the time he'd been on a mission to make her hate him; to make her give him the flick, instead of the other way around.

Now that that idea had been tossed out of the window, Warwick had no weapons against the desires that were, at this very moment, taking dark possession of him. Various erotic scenarios filled his mind, none of which involved waiting till after dinner to satisfy his already clamouring flesh. His hunger had nothing to do with food. It was primal and sexual and urgent.

'I've changed my mind,' he said abruptly.

'About what?'

'About eating.'

She looked confused. 'You don't want any dinner?'

'Not yet.'

'Then what do you want?'

'I want you to take your dress off.'

Amber's eyes flung wide. 'What?'

Warwick appreciated that he'd never ordered her to take her clothes off for him. Not even in the bedroom. Why now? he wondered, even as he banished any qualms and surrendered to the temptation to exercise his sexual power over her.

'You heard me,' he said in a voice that was as hard as his erection.

'But...but people might see me,' she stammered. 'From out on the water.'

'Not up close,' he countered. 'Come now, Amber, you've nothing to be shy about. You have a glorious body. Do you need a little help, is that it?'

CHAPTER THREE

AMBER just stared at him.

What I need, she suddenly felt like screaming, is a little respect.

But no words came from her mouth—her rapidly drying mouth.

She stood there, rooted to the spot, as he started walking towards her, bringing his drink with him, lifting it to his lips and sipping it slowly. Their eyes met over the rim of the glass, his shocking her with their coldness. Or was that desire glittering in their ice-blue depths?

She couldn't be sure. He'd run hot and cold ever since he'd come home, leaving her hopelessly bewildered.

Amber told herself to move. To do something, say something.

Anything!

But her tongue was as useless as her legs.

She remained frozen as he moved around behind her, a soft gasp breaking from her lips when he pushed aside her long curtain of hair, draping it over her left shoulder before bending his mouth to her exposed right ear.

But it wasn't his lips that made her shiver. It was the fear of what she was about to allow…and enjoy.

'Don't,' she heard herself whisper just as his tongue tip dipped into the shell of her ear.

'Don't what?' he whispered a few seconds later.

'Don't do this to me...'

'But you want me to,' he murmured, and nibbled at her ear lobe. 'This is what tonight was all about. Not food.'

'No,' she choked out. 'Not...entirely.'

His laugh was low and sexy. 'Yes. Entirely.'

She stiffened when he ran the zipper down past her waist, a shudder following when he stroked the cold glass he was holding down her spine.

'You want this as much as I do,' he said thickly as he pushed the sides of her dress off her shoulders.

It pooled around her feet in a silky pink puddle, leaving her wearing nothing but her pink high heels.

This wasn't the first time she'd left off her underwear. But it was the first time she'd felt ashamed of having done so.

I'm exactly what Aunt Kate said I am, Amber accepted despairingly as she stood there, naked, before her wealthy lover's gaze. Not a proper girlfriend or a much loved partner, but a mistress, a kept woman. Kept for nothing but her master's sexual pleasure.

Her stomach contracted when he moved around to look at her from the front, her feelings of shame at war with those other wickedly powerful emotions he could so easily evoke. Not just desire but need—the need to be caressed, and kissed, and filled.

She closed her eyes, blotting out the way his glittering blue eyes were gobbling her up. Perversely, her not being able to see him only increased her awareness of her own appalling excitement. Every muscle in her body tensed up, waiting for his touch. Yearning for it. *Dying* for it.

His breath on the nape of her neck told her that he'd moved behind her again. He must have put his drink down too, both his hands free to slide up and down her arms, which immediately broke into goose bumps.

'Do you have any idea what *you* do to *me*?' he murmured as he pressed himself against her naked back, his mouth hovering just above her right ear.

'No,' came her shaky reply. She only knew what he did to her, and what he'd done. Reduced to this…this pitiful state where shame and pride were no match for the pleasure of his lovemaking.

Though this wasn't lovemaking tonight. This was just sex—raw, unadulterated sex.

'If I were a prince in the Middle Ages,' he whispered as he took her hands and lifted them high above her head, 'I would keep you…just like this…locked in a dungeon…with nothing to do but wait for me to come to you.'

She shuddered at the image he'd created.

Why it excited her so much she could not fathom. She should have been repulsed. Instead, she was shaking with excitement.

'Would you like that?' he demanded to know, his breathing growing heavier as he pressed himself even harder against her bare buttocks.

'Yes,' she choked out.

His naked groan betrayed a level of need possibly even greater than her own.

'What on earth am I going to do with you?' he growled.

Amber moaned, having reached that point where pride and shame had become totally irrelevant. She needed Warwick inside her, right then and there, regardless of the fact that she was standing in the middle of a well-lit, glass-walled living room, less than a hundred metres away from where boats full of tourists were enjoying evening dinner cruises on Sydney Harbour.

'Please,' she heard herself practically beg as she moved her legs wantonly apart.

Warwick heard the wild desperation in her voice, felt the uncontrollable excitement that had taken possession of her. He should have felt triumphant. Clever old Warwick, knowing exactly what buttons to press and words to say to seduce her into a state of total surrender.

Why, then, did he suddenly feel bitterly ashamed of himself?

The answer was obvious.

Because she loves you, you bastard. She's not some cheap whore who doesn't care what you do to her.

But even as he told himself all this Warwick was unzipping his trousers. His conscience kept screaming at him not to, but Amber wasn't the only one who'd reached the point of no return.

He groaned as he slid into her, wallowing in the feel of her flesh enclosing his like a tightening fist. She made some sound, a moan perhaps, though not of pain, but of pleasure. It was impossible to stop now. With his right hand splayed firmly over her stomach, and his left cupping her right breast, he began to move his hips.

Not so fast, Warwick, he warned himself as his body immediately surged towards a decidedly premature release. His hips, however, refused to obey him. They jerked back and forth with an urgency that would not be denied, his outspread fingers pressing upwards on her belly, lifting her buttocks up higher against his abdomen, the angle affording him a deeper penetration.

Warwick grimaced as he felt the hot blood rushing along his veins. He was going to come! Hell on earth, he hadn't come this fast in decades!

Amber's suddenly shattering apart in his arms was a huge relief to his pride, allowing him to abandon what little control he had left.

He cried out, holding her tight against him as he ejaculated with the ferocity of an erupting volcano.

She shuddered with him, the contractions of her orgasm more intense, he thought, than ever before. The fantasy he'd painted about keeping her imprisoned in a dungeon had really turned her on. So much so that she'd forgotten who might be watching what they were up to.

You should do this more often, Warwick. Play erotic games with her.

Up till now he'd hardly touched the sides of what he'd learned over many years of hedonistic behaviour. There was so much more he could show her, and do with her.

The only question was…should he?

As much as Warwick was tempted by the thought of becoming Amber's tutor in the erotic arts, he knew that the more imaginative and adventurous practices—whilst wildly exciting—carried a degree of danger; the danger of corruption.

The last thing he wanted to do was corrupt Amber. Pleasure her…yes. Satisfy her…yes. Corrupt her? No.

He would not destroy her basic innocence, he decided as he gently withdrew, then scooped her up into his arms. Such innocence was too precious. *She* was too precious.

He was going to miss her terribly, he thought as he carried her into the bedroom. But not tonight. For now she was still his.

He wouldn't think about the future. Tonight was for nothing but pleasure.

Hers.

His.

But mostly hers.

CHAPTER FOUR

WHEN Amber woke the next morning, all her fears that her relationship with Warwick was coming to an end in the near future had been firmly pushed aside. She smiled as she glanced over at his naked body spreadeagled across the satin sheets, his arms and legs flung wide, his chest rising and falling in the slow, deep rhythm of the truly spent.

Amber could well understand his exhaustion. He'd been insatiable with her last night, showing her with his tireless lovemaking that he was in no way bored with her. It still amazed Amber how well he knew a woman's body and how to uncover a woman's secret desires. There'd been a time—pre Warwick—when she hadn't been that fussed about sex. But, from the first night she'd spent with Warwick, she'd become a virtual slave to the cravings he evoked and satisfied, oh, so well. Amber could not imagine living without the pleasure of his lovemaking…could not imagine living without him!

But you might have to one day, whispered the voice of reason as she slipped out of the rumpled bed and headed for the bathroom.

It was a disturbing thought. What *would* she do when and if that happened?

Amber grimaced, clinging to the hope that maybe it wouldn't. Maybe her dream of Warwick falling in love with her and asking her to marry him was still a possibility. There were times, like last night, when she was confident that he had. There *was* love in his lovemaking: a tenderness and consideration that didn't equate with the cold-blooded womaniser that her mother had more or less described him as last night.

'Oh, my goodness!' Amber exclaimed, bolting back to the bedroom and checking the time on the digital bedside clock.

'Twenty to eleven!' she gasped aloud.

She immediately raced over to shake Warwick on the shoulder.

'Warwick! Wake up! Wake up! I need you.'

He lifted one heavy eyelid, giving her a droll if bleary look. 'You have to be joking, Amber,' he drawled in that cultured voice of his. 'I would have thought you'd had enough for at least twenty-four hours.'

'Not for that, silly!' she said. 'I need you to drive me over to Mum's place before midday, then up to Wamberal. To Aunt Kate's place.'

His second eyelid opened much more quickly, his sleepy expression replaced by bewilderment. 'Run that by me again, would you? I mean…I'm absolutely sure that your aunt Kate is no longer in residence. So why are we driving up to her place?'

'She left it to me,' Amber announced rather baldly. 'In her will. A new one which she'd made recently and which has only just come to light. Mum rang me about it last night but I forgot to tell you. No, don't start asking me endless questions right now,' she raced on when he sat up abruptly with his mouth already opening. 'We haven't the time. We have to be out of here in about fifteen minutes flat if we're going to get to Carlingford before midday. I promised to pick up the keys to Aunt Kate's before Mum leaves to go to the hairdresser's.'

Amber took it as testimony to Warwick's caring that he didn't argue, or tell her that he had more important things to do that day. He just got up and got on with what she'd asked. Just after eleven they were zooming through the harbour tunnel, though Amber was still a little tense that they might not make it in time.

'I'll give Mum a ring once we're out of the tunnel,' she said, and fished her mobile out of her handbag. 'Let her know my estimated time of arrival.'

'So tell me,' Warwick asked with a brief glance her way. 'In your aunt's new will—are you the only beneficiary?'

'No. She left her superannuation policy to Dad. But her house and contents go to me alone.'

'Hmm. I'll bet your mother's somewhat peeved at you being left your aunt's place, rather than her precious boys.'

Amber's head swung round at this quite intuitive remark.

'Did you think I didn't notice the way she favoured your brothers over you?' he swept on before she could say a single word. 'Your father, too. I didn't have to be in their home for more than five minutes to see the lie of the land. Why do you think I couldn't wait to get you out of there on Christmas Day? I'm not good at keeping my mouth shut when I'm bearing witness to such an injustice, especially against someone I care about.'

Amber didn't know what to say. This was the closest

Warwick had ever come to saying that he loved her. She was so touched, a huge lump formed in her throat.

'I…I didn't realise you noticed,' she mumbled at last.

'I noticed all right. The only reason I didn't say something was because it was Christmas, plus I didn't want to give your parents more reason to put you down. They'd already made it patently obvious that they didn't approve of your relationship with me. Not that they said so to my face. I would have thought more of them if they had. Your aunt Kate was a bit of dragon, but at least she loved you enough to give me a piece of her mind.'

'She did?'

'Indeed she did,' he said drily.

Kate had had a reputation for speaking her mind. And a reputation for being a bit of a man hater. Though she hadn't hated all men. She'd liked Max Richmond and had always sung his praises. But then it *was* highly unusual, Amber supposed, for a billionaire to give up his jet-setting lifestyle to get married and raise a family away from the spotlight of wealth and fame.

'What did she say?' Amber asked, though she feared she already knew the answer.

Warwick shrugged his shoulders. 'The usual. I was a selfish you-know-what who should be hung, drawn and quartered for taking a sweet young thing like you as my mistress.'

'Oh,' Amber choked out.

Warwick's head snapped round. 'You're not crying, are you?'

'No,' she denied, but shakily.

'You are,' he said with a sigh. 'I can't stand it when you cry.'

'I don't cry all that often,' Amber said defensively.

'You have to be kidding, sweetheart. You cry at the news, and at ads, and during all those soppy movies you like to watch. I put a box of tissues by the sofa to mop up your tears.'

'They're not real tears. I'm talking about real tears.' She'd only wept a few times since moving in with Warwick. Once, when her mother was highly critical of her relationship. And then, when she'd heard that her aunt Kate had died. Oh, and yes, after her argument with Warwick last week.

But he hadn't been witness to that, had he? He hadn't even been in the same room.

'Tears don't solve anything, you know,' he growled.

'They're not meant to solve anything,' she shot back, dabbing the moisture from her eyes. 'They just happen.'

'I don't like the way women use tears to get what they want.'

'*I* don't.'

'No,' he said, if a little reluctantly. 'You don't.'

'Let's not argue, Warwick,' she said, worried that the happiness she'd felt this morning was beginning to disintegrate.

'Only if you promise not to cry.'

She smiled over at him. 'See? I've already stopped.'

'What about later when you get to your aunt's place?'

'I'll do my best not to.' But she rather suspected she would shed a few tears then. She hadn't been there since her aunt died, the wake having been held at a local club.

'Mmm. I think I should have given you the car for the day. Let you drive yourself up to Wamberal.'

'But I want you with me. I need your advice on what I

should do with Aunt Kate's place. Besides, I don't much like driving your car.'

'What? You don't like driving a Ferrari? Are you insane?'

'I don't like speed the way you do. Promise me you won't go fast when we get on the expressway. There's no reason to. We have all the time in the world.'

Warwick almost laughed. All the time in the world was something he certainly did not have. Which meant he didn't want to spend what precious time he did have with her at Wamberal where she was sure to get weepy over her aunt all over again. Next thing he knew, she'd want to keep the damned place. Maybe even go up there on weekends.

She wanted his advice? Warwick already knew what that advice would be. Put the property in the hands of a good real estate agent to sell, then come back to Sydney with him. He'd already decided he couldn't be without her just yet. Last night had shown him that. He hadn't been able to get enough of her. But maybe soon he'd find the strength to end things. Until then, however, he aimed to keep things exactly as they were, with her by his side, and in his bed.

'I'll wait for you in the car,' he said when they finally arrived at her parents' home in Carlingford just before midday. 'Got a few things to attend to.' And he picked up his BlackBerry.

Amber didn't argue with him. Quite frankly, the last thing she wanted was him by her side when her mother answered the door. She climbed out of the car and hurried up the steep front path to the equally steep front steps. Running up them, she reached the front porch and was about to ring the bell when the door was wrenched open and her mother stood there, looking very annoyed.

'I'd almost given up on you coming,' she said sourly.

'But I rang you from the car to say I'd be here.'

'I don't know why you had to leave it to the last minute,' her mother snapped. 'It's not as though you work.'

Amber could think of nothing to say to that. It was true, after all.

'I'm sorry, Mum,' she heard herself apologising the way she'd been doing all her life. 'We had a late night and we…er…slept in. If you'll just give me the keys I'll be on my way.'

Doreen sniffed her distaste as she swung away and picked up two sets of keys from the nearby hall table. 'Here they are,' she said, and handed them over. 'The second set belongs to Kate's car. That's yours too, it seems.'

'Really?' Amber could not help feeling pleased at this news. She'd only ever owned one car, a rust-bucket she'd bought when she'd been eighteen and had taken a second job as a waitress and needed wheels to get to and from work at night. Naturally, her parents had refused to let her use either of their vehicles. Neither had they offered to subsidise the purchase of one for her as they had with the boys.

It had taken all of her savings—frugally put together when she'd started working at a fast-food restaurant at sixteen—to buy the ancient car, which had broken down within weeks of her purchasing it. After that Amber had decided to do without it and had managed by only ever applying for jobs where public transport was available.

She'd occasionally thought about buying herself another car, but had decided that if she couldn't afford a good one, then she'd rather not have one.

Now, she had her aunt Kate's, which was a very good one, if she recalled rightly, a relatively new white hatchback.

'So what does Lover Boy think of your becoming an heiress?' her mother asked in acid tones.

'Don't call him that, Mum. His name is Warwick and he's very happy for me.'

'I doubt that, dear. Men like that enjoy pulling the strings. The last thing he'll want is for you to have independent means.'

'I don't know why you keep saying such dreadful things about him. What's he ever done to you?'

'It's what he's done to you that I object to.'

'And what's he done to me that's so dreadful? Tim lived with his wife before they got married. And Tom was a real tomcat before he met Viv. It seems to me that you have one set of standards for my brothers and a different one for me. But then, you love them a lot more than you love me, don't you?'

Her mother looked shocked. 'That's not true!'

'Oh, yes, it is, Mum. It's always been true. I'm not sure why. I've tried to be a good daughter. But nothing I've ever done has been good enough. Not that I could ever match it with either of the boys. I wasn't brilliant at school, or at sport the way they were.'

All she'd ever had going for her was her looks, which her mother had rarely complimented her on.

Yet she looked very much like her mother. Or as Doreen had been when she was younger.

It came to Amber suddenly that maybe her mother was jealous of her youthful beauty. Although Doreen

Roberts had aged quite gracefully, she could never compete with a girl thirty years younger.

'I'm sorry you feel that way, Amber,' her mother said stiffly. 'But you're wrong. All I want is for you to be happy.'

'Then you have a strange way of showing it,' Amber said sharply. 'You'd better get going to your hairdresser. I wouldn't want to make you late for anything so important. Bye.'

Amber battled to keep the tears at bay as she whirled and hurried back down the steps, clutching the keys in her hand so tightly that they dug painfully into her palm. Warwick was still on his phone when she climbed into the car, talking no doubt to one of his many contacts. He did most of his business on his BlackBerry.

'Sounds good,' he was saying. 'We'll be there by then. Thanks, Jim.'

'We'll be where by when?' Amber asked as Warwick put his phone away.

'Your aunt's place around two. I've organised for one of the area's top real estate agents to meet us there.'

Amber could not help feeling mildly irritated. Which was crazy. She didn't really want to keep the place, did she? That would be a rather silly decision. An emotional one.

'Did I do something wrong?' Warwick asked.

'No,' Amber replied with a sigh.

'I thought you'd want to sell.'

'I do. It's just...'

'Just what?'

'I don't know, Warwick. Honestly.'

'Your mother said something to upset you.'

Amber laughed. 'My mother always says something to upset me.'

'What was it this time? Something about your relationship with me, I presume.'

'Amongst other things. Look, I really don't want to talk right now. Could you just drive, please?'

'Fair enough. I'll put some music on.'

They didn't exchange a word till the Ferrari hit the freeway north, by which time Amber's distress had calmed somewhat and she turned her mind to the problem of her aunt's place.

'I'm not sure Aunt Kate left me her place for me to sell it,' she said. 'I think she might have envisaged my actually living there and running the B & B.'

Warwick shot her a startled glance. 'Why would she think you would do that?'

'Why not? I've worked in the hospitality industry all my life. I could run a B & B, no trouble.'

'I'm sure you could. But it would be a very lonely existence. After all, now that your aunt has passed away, you have no family up here, or friends that I know of.'

'That's not strictly true. I do know the Richmonds. They live in Wamberal.'

'Who are the Richmonds? You've never mentioned them before.'

'They were close friends of Aunt Kate's. In fact they witnessed her new will. Tara and Max Richmond.'

'Good Lord, you don't mean Max Richmond, the hotel magnate!'

'Yes. Do you know him?'

'I know *of* him. I had heard on the grapevine that he'd sold off most of his international hotels and retired somewhere. I just didn't know where. I rather imagined the Riviera or Monte Carlo, not Wamberal Beach. Did he marry a local girl, is that it?'

'No. I'm sure Tara was a Sydney girl. Aunt Kate

told me a little about their romance. Apparently, she and Max had been dating for some time when Tara fell pregnant quite accidentally. But she was afraid Max wouldn't believe her and ran away, to Aunt Kate's B & B. It seems seriously rich men are paranoid about gold-diggers trying to trap them into marriage with a baby. Is that true?' she asked Warwick, such a thought having never occurred to her before. She religiously took her pill every evening, not believing in having children unless you were happily married. Nowadays she always carried a spare packet of pills with her in her handbag in case Warwick swept her off on one of his impulsive overnight getaways without her having a chance to go home and pack properly.

'Perfectly true,' Warwick replied drily.

'I would never do something like that,' she said firmly.

'I know you wouldn't. Obviously, Max Richmond came to the conclusion that his girl wouldn't, either.'

'Oh, yes, I was telling you about them, wasn't I?'

'I presume they got married and lived happily ever after.'

'As far as anyone can tell. They always look the perfect family. They have two children now, a little girl as well as their son.'

'If they were such good friends of your aunt, why weren't they at her place last Easter? I'm sure I would have remembered them if they were.'

'They were overseas. They travel quite a bit. They were actually away when Aunt Kate died.'

'So Richmond hasn't given up the hotel industry entirely?'

'Not quite. He still owns hotels in Asia and the Regency Royale in Sydney. He has a penthouse apartment there which Aunt Kate stayed in once. She said it was gorgeous.'

'How old would Richmond be? Forty?'

'Mid forties, I'd say.'

'And his wife?'

'I'm not sure. Thirty something. And drop-dead gorgeous.'

'Not surprising. Seriously rich men don't marry plain girls.'

Some don't marry at all, Amber almost shot back, just biting her tongue in time.

'I'm not surprised Richmond hasn't totally retired,' Warwick went on. 'He'd be bored if he stayed home every day, twiddling his thumbs. You'd be bored too, Amber, running a B & B. Bored and lonely.'

'But I'd meet people.'

'For one night only. Come the next morning they'd be up and gone. Running a B & B is a job for a couple. Or an old maid like your aunt was. It wouldn't suit you at all. Surely you're not seriously considering doing it.'

'That depends…'

'On what?'

Amber hesitated to answer for a long moment. When she'd woken this morning, she'd been very quick to put aside her worries over Warwick's very selfish behaviour of late. Listening to her mother's low opinion of her lover's character, however, had revived all her doubts about the depth, plus the lasting nature, of their relationship.

The temptation to keep putting her head in the sand was acute. She loved Warwick and didn't want what they had to end, however short-lived that might be. But a little voice in her head kept nagging at her to stop being naïve and so disgustingly weak.

Nausea swirled in her stomach at the prospect of

finding out she was skating on thin ice where he was concerned. But it had to be done sooner or later.

'It depends on how long our relationship lasts,' she said at last.

'I see,' he bit out.

Amber tried to gauge what he meant by that. But it was hardly a forthcoming statement, which was so typical of Warwick.

'I know you don't like talking about the future,' Amber went on, suddenly determined to have things out with him. 'I've done my best to live in the moment the way you do. But I'm not really like that, Warwick. I've always been a practical person, a planner. This past ten months with you have been marvellous and I'll never regret them. But I need to know if I have any chance of a future with you. I gave up everything to live with you: my job, a boyfriend I was going to become engaged to, my friends. Even my family, to a degree. When and if we break up, I'll have nothing.'

CHAPTER FIVE

WARWICK wished later that he'd thought before he'd opened his mouth. But, at the time, it annoyed him that Amber thought he would dump her with nothing.

'If and when we do break up, Amber,' he snapped, 'you will be well looked after. I have every intention of giving you the Point Piper apartment. *And* this car.'

Even if he hadn't glanced over and seen her face go a ghastly shade of grey, the sound of her shocked gasp warned him that his offer of a generous parting settlement did not please her.

Which he should have realised. For goodness' sake, the girl was obviously in love with him. It was perfectly understandable that Amber wouldn't want to be treated like some gold-digging mistress who was only with him for what she could get out of it, when all she actually wanted was love and marriage. And his children, no doubt.

Her aunt Kate had spelled out the truth for him. Why did he keep forgetting?

Once again Warwick was tempted to reveal everything. But the thought of seeing pity in Amber's eyes repulsed him. He'd rather see dislike, or even outright hatred.

'I gather that suggestion doesn't find favour with

you?' he said in a tone of voice that she could only interpret as indifferent.

Amber struggled for composure. She'd thought he could not hurt her any more than he had with his disgustingly materialistic offer. But, suddenly, she felt not just cheap but almost worthless.

'Did you expect that it would?' she threw at him.

He shrugged his shoulders. 'I have learned to expect the unexpected when it comes to women.'

Amber stared over at him. Was this the same man who'd made love to her so tenderly the night before?

Her family had been right. He was heartless. And she… she was a fool!

But no longer. Her own heart hardened towards him as she pushed aside her distress for the moment and considered her options.

Her decision surprised her.

'In that case,' she said boldly, 'you will be delighted to hear that I will quite happily accept your apartment as my fee for services rendered. But I do not want this car,' she swept on. 'I have Aunt Kate's now, if you recall.'

'I doubt it's a Ferrari,' he retorted.

'No. But, quite frankly, I'm not overly fond of Ferraris. If you don't mind, I'd like you to slow down. You're breaking the speed limit. And whilst I don't give a damn if you lose your driving licence, I do not want to lose my life.'

He did ease off on the accelerator a little but the Ferrari still zoomed across the Hawkesbury River bridge doing a hundred and twenty kilometres an hour, ten kilometres over the speed limit.

'On top of that,' she continued, her heart pounding inside her chest, 'once we reach Aunt Kate's place, we're finished! The thought of living with a man like you for another single day makes me feel sick.'

'For heaven's sake, don't be such a drama queen! You knew the score when you moved in with me. Don't pretend you didn't.'

'I won't. But I thought things had changed. I thought you cared about me, the same way I…I care about you.' She bit her trembling bottom lip, determined not to cry, or to blurt out that she loved him.

'I do care about you,' he insisted. 'If I didn't, I wouldn't be prepared to give you a five-million-dollar apartment. Which, I might add, you haven't refused. Not that I would have admired you if you had. I would have thought you a naïve little fool.'

'Which is what I was all this time. But not any more. I've finally had my rose-coloured glasses taken off where you're concerned.'

'Good,' he ground out. 'It's about time.'

She stared over at him. 'You've been planning to break up with me for a while, haven't you?'

He stayed silent for a few seconds, a frown drawing his dark brows together.

'I admit I've become concerned that you were getting emotionally involved with me,' he said at last.

'And that would be dreadful, wouldn't it?' she threw at him.

'Yes,' he said. 'It would.'

'But why?' she demanded to know, frustration and exasperation fuelling her tongue. 'What is it about commitment which terrifies you so much?'

'The fact that I wouldn't be able to sustain it and then I'd feel guilty. It's a case of like father, like son, Amber. My father was, to put it bluntly, a notorious womaniser.'

'That's a cop-out. Just because your father was a notorious womaniser doesn't mean you have to be one.'

'There is a saying, Amber, "The apple doesn't fall far from the tree." I am the spitting image of my father, in every way. Trust me on this. Look, I never planned to hurt you. But I've realised that I will, if you stay with me much longer. You're a truly nice girl and you deserve someone better than me, someone who will love you and give you what you really want. Which isn't being a rich man's mistress.'

Amber blinked her surprise.

'Are you saying you're being cruel to be kind?'

'I am rarely kind, Amber. But with you, it's hard not to be. So, yes, I probably am being just that.'

Amber's head whirled with a thousand conflicting thoughts. She couldn't work out what it was he felt for her.

'I don't understand you, Warwick,' she said at last.

'Don't even try, sweetheart.'

'Don't call me that,' she snapped. 'I hate it when you call me that.'

'What's wrong with it?'

'It makes me feel cheap.'

'Don't be bloody ridiculous!'

A taut silence fell between them, neither speaking a word till the Ferrari turned off the expressway and made its way down the hill towards Gosford, which was the doorway to the central coast with all its lovely beaches. Not a beach town itself, Gosford surrounded a large expanse of inland water, which on that day was very still and blue.

'It's a pretty place,' Warwick commented as he drove over an arched bridge that had the water on his right and a palm-lined sports stadium on his left.

'What?' Amber's mind was not on her surroundings.

'Gosford. It's a pretty town.'

'I suppose so.'

'Do you want to stop somewhere for lunch?' he asked.

Amber glanced at her wristwatch. It was just after one. But she didn't feel at all hungry. Distress always destroyed her appetite. Given her present circumstances, she doubted she'd ever eat again.

'I'd rather go straight to Aunt Kate's place if you don't mind. Do you remember the way?'

'I follow the coastal road till we get to a roundabout at Wamberal where I turn right, after which I turn left onto the road which runs beside the lake. Your aunt's place is just along there on the right.'

'You have a good memory for someone who's only been there the once.'

'I have a photographic memory.'

The remark surprised Amber. Warwick rarely talked of himself in that way. Although obviously very clever, he wasn't a braggart.

'Did your father have a photographic memory?' she asked, recalling his earlier insistence that he was the spitting image of his father, in every way.

'Actually, no,' came his surprising reply. 'I got that from my mother. She was an actress. Apparently, she only had to read a script through once to remember it word for word. Or so my father told me. I had no reason to doubt him, since I've inherited a similar talent. It made studying for exams a lot easier, I can tell you.'

'I suppose you were brilliant at school,' Amber said, thinking to herself how odd it was that they were talking like this. During the ten months they'd lived together, they'd never had a conversation of this vein. Warwick had always cleverly sidestepped any questions about his family, or his past life.

'Yes,' he admitted. 'I was head boy of my school.'

She wasn't surprised.

'I wasn't very good at school,' Amber said with a sigh. 'That's why I left when I was sixteen.'

'Being good at school is not all it's cracked up to be. I've seen lots of people who were brilliant academically but had no street sense. And very little common sense, either. You are an extremely capable and clever girl who, I'm sure, could turn her hand to anything. And you have social skills which are invaluable. People like you. You're quite right when you said you could run your aunt's B & B. You could do it standing on your head.'

But I don't *want* to run my aunt's B & B, Amber felt like wailing. I want to stay with you. I *love* you.

But there was no point. It was over, all her futile hopes of Warwick falling in love with her dashed to the ground. And whilst she didn't feel as angry with him as she had a little while before, there was no point in pretending that she'd ever meant anything more to him than a very pretty girlfriend who'd provided him with an accommodating social companion, an agreeable hostess when required and lots of sex.

Of course, it had been the lots of sex part that had turned her head and confused her heart. It had been oh-so-easy to imagine that his lust for her might one day turn to love. Hers had for him, after all. But super-rich men like Warwick, Amber realised, were of a different ilk. He wasn't looking for love, or commitment, just entertainment.

It was a depressing reality, made all the worse because in her mind she could hear her parents and her brothers saying, 'I told you so!'

Still, maybe they'd shut up when she gave them a whole heap of money from the sale of the Point Piper apartment. She didn't doubt that Warwick would give her the property. In a perverse way, he did have honour. And honesty. Also, she could not deny he had told her the score right from the beginning. He'd warned her that he didn't do for ever. She'd been stupid to ignore his warnings. Now, she would have to nurse a broken heart for a long time.

That breaking heart squeezed tight at this last thought, bringing home the harsh reality of life without the man she loved. The future ahead looked bleak, and empty, and infinitely depressing.

Maybe it would be a good idea for her to stay up here and run her aunt's B & B. Alternatively, she could put the B & B on the market, then take a flat somewhere in Sydney and look for a job. She had a wide range of experience in the hospitality industry, from waitressing to bar work to fronting reception desks in hotels and clubs. It shouldn't take her too long to find employment. Even if it took a while, she still had the apartment and her savings, which she hadn't touched since meeting Warwick.

But she didn't have the heart—or the courage—to put herself out there like that. Not right now. She really needed to be by herself for a while to grieve the death of all her secret hopes and dreams. What better place than her aunt's home, which would be very peaceful and quiet at this time of the year? She didn't have to try to run the B & B straight away. She could just potter around the house for a month or so. Go for long walks on the beach. Read some of the many wonderful books her aunt had collected over the years.

Maybe she'd even start keeping a diary again…

She'd given that up when she'd moved in with Warwick. Which, she should have realised, was a telling thing to do. Subconsciously, she must have known that her time with him was just a fantasy, and not of the real world.

Amber was glad that she hadn't kept a record of her stupidity. It would have hurt too much to read it over, which she no doubt would have now.

'We don't have to break up just yet,' Warwick said suddenly, startling her out of her musings.

Amber stared over at him. First at his handsome profile. Then at his long strong fingers, which were curled over the steering wheel; those same fingers that last night had given her such pleasure.

The temptation to stay with him for as long as possible was overwhelmingly strong. But how could she without sacrificing what little pride she had left?

It wouldn't be the same anyway, she argued to herself. I'd know I was on borrowed time. I'd end up hating him. And myself. Better a clean break now. Better to say goodbye with some dignity.

'No, Warwick,' she said, her voice surprisingly firm. 'I think it's better that we call it quits today. You can drop me off at Aunt Kate's and go straight back to Sydney.' The sooner he was out of her sight, the better. Not that out of sight would be out of mind.

'Just like that?' he returned, sounding not at all pleased. 'What if I don't want to break up today? And what if I don't want to go straight back to Sydney? You might at least have the decency to offer me a cup of coffee and a trip to the loo. We've been on the road for some time.'

Amber sighed. He was right. Now that she thought about it, she too wanted to go to the bathroom. But he could forget the coffee. She wasn't going to give him a single opportunity to try to change her mind. There were plenty of places along the highway where he could get himself some refreshment. Once he was finished in the bathroom, she would insist that he go.

Suddenly, she realised he'd missed the turn.

'You've just gone through the roundabout!' she exclaimed frustratedly. 'You didn't turn right…'

CHAPTER SIX

WARWICK swore. He hated feeling a fool, and he felt like one at that moment. What in hell was wrong with him, finding all sorts of excuses to prolong things? Far better that he just drop her off and leave. He could easily use the restroom at the garage they'd just passed. Nothing would be gained by accompanying Amber into Aunt Kate's property.

Nothing admirable, anyway, he realised, his thoughts turning dark.

Damn it all but he wanted her. Maybe more since she'd declared her intention to have done with him. How perverse was that? He should have been relieved that it was over, without any big scenes. He'd been half afraid that when the dreaded moment came Amber would dissolve into tears, or become hysterical and declare that she loved him and couldn't live without him.

Instead, she'd been amazingly strong and decisive. Warwick had been somewhat surprised that she'd agreed to accept the apartment. Though frankly if she'd knocked it back that would have shown her to be a romantic idealist with no common sense at all.

Instead, she'd given him a glimpse of an Amber he'd never encountered before. The girl sitting beside him at this moment—the one who dared to call it quits with *him*—wasn't the sweet, soft, amenable creature he'd been living with this past ten months. This girl was far more formidable. And, he was finding, even more attractive to him.

When he glanced over at her flushed cheeks and defiantly upturned chin he experienced a surge of desire even more intense than he had the night before. The thought that he would never make love to her again was simply not on. So was the idea that he would be leaving her up here and driving back to Sydney alone.

'There's a set of lights coming up,' Amber said. 'Turn right there and I'll direct you to Aunt Kate's the back way. It won't take much longer.'

'No sweat,' he replied. 'I'm not in any hurry.' And he glanced over at her again.

When Amber's head turned and her eyes met his, her heart jolted in her chest. She knew that look, knew what it meant.

Over my dead body, she thought angrily, even as that same body instinctively responded, as Warwick had programmed it to this past year. Her heartbeat quickened, her belly tightening, as did her nipples.

She could not let him go inside Aunt Kate's with her, she accepted immediately. That would be the kiss goodbye to her resolve to have done with him today. He was way too good at seduction—and she was way too weak once in his arms—for her to risk being alone with him in a house with bedrooms.

Amber steeled herself as she issued brusque directions to her aunt's place.

She should have foreseen that he wouldn't like her being the one to break up with him. It would have piqued his ego. Which was the reason behind that sexually charged look. His massive male ego insisted that *he* had to be the one to do the breaking up in his relationships. *He* made the rules and *he* made all the decisions.

Well not this time, buster, Amber vowed. I might have been a pushover once, but not any more. I've always despised girls who go back to boyfriends who've treated them badly, trotting out the excuse that they love them. If loving someone means you let them treat you without respect, then I don't want any part of that kind of love.

Not that she deserved his respect, came the sudden shaming realisation. In his eyes she was obviously no better than all his previous—mistresses. Worse, really. Hadn't she moved in with him without a single promise of anything but fun and games? He'd warned her right from the start that their relationship was temporary. Yet she'd still agreed. And now…now here she was, prepared to accept payment for services rendered.

How cheap could you get?

Not that her own behaviour exonerated Warwick's. His admitting that he was a callous womaniser didn't make it right.

Still, as long as silly girls like herself allowed him to use them shamelessly, then pay them off, he would continue going from woman to woman as powerful men had been doing since time began.

'I know the way from here,' Warwick said when they turned into Ocean View Drive.

Thirty seconds later they were driving down her aunt's street, which ran alongside the lagoon.

The sight of the sign announcing Kate's B & B brought a lump to Amber's throat. How strange it would be not to have Aunt Kate open the door with her wonderfully welcoming smile.

Warwick turned the Ferrari into the driveway, which led into the large back yard where there was plenty of room for guests and visitors to park. Because of the way the house was located on the block, the back door had always been used as the front door. Warwick drove right up close to the back porch whilst Amber glanced around the yard.

Despite her father having mown the lawn recently, some of the flowerbeds were looking unloved. Aunt Kate had been an avid gardener and would never normally have let her roses go unpruned during the winter months. She must have felt unwell for quite some time to neglect her garden this way.

Sadness overwhelmed Amber as she looked up at the back of the two-storeyed house with its drawn curtains and general air of emptiness. A sigh—almost a sob—escaped her lips.

'I knew it,' Warwick said rather impatiently after he cut the engine. 'You're going to cry.'

It infuriated her, his lack of compassion where her aunt's death was concerned.

Her head whipped round, her blue eyes now blazing with fury.

'Not in front of you, I won't be,' she snapped, snatching her handbag up from the floor and opening the passenger door. 'Don't bother getting out,' she swept on, when his hand went towards the handle on the driver's door. 'You're not coming inside. I don't want to see you ever again.'

His eyes narrowed as he glared over at her. 'Is that so? What about the apartment? I'll have to see you again, if you want that.'

'Actually, I've been thinking about your most generous offer,' she lied on a surge of anger. 'I've decided I don't want it. I don't want anything from you, Warwick Kincaid, except your absence from my life.'

'You don't really mean that. You're just angry with me at the moment.'

'Too right I am.'

'You don't have any right to be. I haven't treated you badly.'

'You used me and you know it.'

'I told you what kind of man I was up front. I warned you that I didn't do love and marriage, or for ever. You seemed happy enough to still come along for the ride.'

Amber shook her head in a kind of despair. 'Yes, I did. And I feel deeply ashamed of myself for doing so. All I can say in my defence is that I didn't really believe you could be that cold-blooded.'

'I'm not cold-blooded, as you very well know.' And he gave her that desire-filled look again.

Amber clenched her jaw hard. 'I don't want to have this conversation any more, Warwick,' she ground out. 'It's over. We're over. Just go.'

'I don't want to leave you like this,' he said, scowling.

'I'll well aware of that! I know what you want, Warwick Kincaid. But you're not getting it. Ever again.' She climbed out of the car and slammed the door. 'If you don't go, I'll call the police.' And she fished her mobile out of her bag.

'I'll ring you,' he said.

'Please don't.'

'You can't stop me ringing you.'

'I'll buy a new phone.'

'How will you afford that?'

'I have money, Warwick,' she enjoyed telling him. 'You think my life began the moment you walked into it? I have almost twenty thousand dollars in my savings account. I'll survive very well without your wretched apartment!'

'What about your clothes? And your jewellery?'

'I don't want them, either. Maybe you can recycle some of it for your next mistress.'

He glowered up at her before starting the engine. 'This isn't the end of us, Amber Roberts,' he threatened in an ominously low voice. 'I'll be back once you've calmed down.'

Amber gripped her handbag defensively in front of her as she watched him do a rather savage U-turn, chewing up some of the grass as he accelerated out onto the road and sped off.

For almost a minute, she just stood there, listening to the slowly decreasing noise of his angry departure, till finally the only sound she heard was the low hum of distant traffic.

It was then that she started to cry, deep wrenching sobs, which she feared the neighbours might hear. There were houses on either side.

Not wanting contact with anyone at that moment, Amber dropped her phone back into her bag and snatched up the keys to the house. Naturally, the key to the back door was the last one she tried. By the time she locked the door behind her, her weeping had subsided somewhat.

But not her distress. Amber dropped her handbag onto the hall table before burying her face in her hands.

'Oh, Warwick…Warwick,' she cried heartbrokenly.

He had vowed to come back. But she doubted that he would. That had just been his ego talking again. Once he thought about it more rationally, he'd see that there was no point in trying to keep their relationship going. Not when it was obviously on borrowed time. As soon as Warwick realised he'd disposed of his Australian mistress very cheaply indeed, he would be a fool not to cut and run.

And Warwick was no man's fool.

Despite knowing that their break-up was all for the best, such thinking depressed Amber. She'd honestly believed that he'd come to care for her; that she meant more to him than just a temporary plaything, to be bought off when he tired of her, or when she committed the unforgivable sin of becoming 'emotionally involved'.

Amber noted, however, that even then Warwick couldn't bring himself to say the world *love*. It was some comfort to her own pride that she'd never told him she'd fallen in love with him. Now, she never would.

She sighed as she lifted her head from her hands.

'Maybe I should have accepted the apartment,' she muttered dispiritedly. 'People will think *me* a fool for ending up with nothing.'

But if she had taken it, then she would have become what everyone had probably been calling her behind her back. A rich man's whore. At least she did have her pride, which, she supposed, was something.

Or was it?

What was that saying about pride being a lonely bedfellow?

Her mobile phone suddenly ringing was a telling moment. For in that split second Amber became brutally aware that pride was not as powerful as love. The truth was she *wanted* it to be Warwick calling her. She wanted him to come back.

Unable to stop herself, she hurriedly retrieved her phone from her handbag and flipped it open, her heart thudding loudly behind her ribcage.

'Yes?' she choked out.

'It's me, Amber. Your mother.'

'Oh…' Impossible to keep the disappointment from her voice, or the dismay from her heart.

'Are you at Aunt Kate's yet?' her mother asked abruptly.

Amber sighed. 'Yes.'

'Look, I forgot to tell you that Max Richmond wants you to give him a call. Kate used his solicitor, it seems, to make her new will and there are papers you will need to sign to transfer the house and car, et cetera, into your name.'

'Fine,' she said wearily. 'Do you have his number?'

Amber put the number into her menu.

'Is that all, Mum?'

'Yes. No. I…er…can you talk for a moment?'

'What about?'

'Well…I've been thinking about the things you said to me today and I feel really terrible. I do love you, Amber. Yet I can see why you might think I favour the boys. Please…I'd like to try to explain how it was when you came along.'

Did her mother honestly think she didn't know how it had been? She was well aware that her father had wanted to stop having children after the two boys were born. He'd only ever wanted sons, according to a conversation she'd once overheard. She'd been an accident, then had compounded things by turning out to be a girl, an unsporty, non-academic girl who just couldn't compete with her overachieving, highly competitive brothers.

'Mum…please…I don't want to have this conversation right now.'

'You know, Amber,' her mother said, back to her usual stroppy tone. 'Ever since you got mixed up with that man, you never have time to talk to me.'

Amber momentarily considered telling her mother that she'd broken up with Warwick, but fortunately stopped herself in time. No way could she stand the third degree over what happened. Or all the inevitable recriminations.

'We've only just arrived, Mum, and I haven't even had time to go to the toilet. I'll give you a call later.'

'Promise?'

'Yes,' Amber said, her chin beginning to wobble dangerously. 'Bye for now.' She choked back a strangled sob and hung up, after which she turned her mobile off.

For a long time she just stood there, clutching the phone and staring into space. The tears didn't come, thank heaven. But she felt awful over the way she'd reacted to the phone ringing. How could she possibly want Warwick back? He was a bastard. An arrogant, selfish bastard!

And yet she'd fallen in love with him. Why? What had he ever done to deserve her love?

Okay, so he was a good lover. No, a *great* lover, she had to admit.

Amber shook her head from side to side. Was her so-called love for Warwick based on nothing more substantial than sexual pleasure? If so, then she was a terribly shallow person.

Her mind searched for other qualities Warwick possessed that deserved loving.

He was honest. She had to give him that. He'd never lied to her. At least, she didn't think he had. He was also very generous, dispensing great chunks of money to this and that charity every other week.

But then, he could afford to, couldn't he? came a cynical voice in her head. Easy to be generous when you were filthy rich.

What kind of man would he have been if he'd been born poor?

Amber decided it would be an interesting experiment to somehow put Warwick in a position where his life wasn't so damned cushy. How would he handle adversity? Would it bring out the worst, or the best in him?

Amber shrugged her shoulders. She would never find out, would she? He was gone. Gone from her life, though not from her heart. She *did* love him, unfortunately. Love, it seemed, wasn't always subject to reason, or reasons. It just was.

At last she dropped her phone back into her bag and made her way slowly along the hall to the tiny downstairs toilet, which was tucked under the staircase.

As she washed her hands afterwards the small mirror above the equally small hand basin showed nothing of the sadness she was feeling. She actually looked good, her bout of tears not having lasted long enough to bring on puffiness or dark circles. Finger-combing her windblown hair into place, she made her way back along the hall into her aunt's roomy country-style kitchen to make herself a cuppa. There she took off her leather jacket and draped it over the back of a wooden kitchen chair before filling the kettle with water. She was just getting a mug down from the pine cupboard above the counter when the doorbell on the back door rang.

Once again, that shocking vulnerability hit home. She practically ran to the door, despising herself even as she flicked open the lock and wrenched the door wide.

It wasn't Warwick. The tall, good-looking man standing on the back porch was a perfect stranger.

CHAPTER SEVEN

'YES?' Amber said, unable to keep the dismay from her voice.

'Hi there,' he said, and flashed his business card. 'I'm Jim Hansen, from Seachange Properties. I have an appointment to meet Mr Warwick Kincaid here at two p.m.'

Amber suppressed a groan. She'd forgotten about Warwick's organising this meeting.

'Hello,' she said, using the practised smile that she'd perfected during her various jobs in the hospitality industry where you smiled no matter how lousy you felt. 'I'm Amber Roberts, the new owner here, actually, not Mr Kincaid. I inherited it from my aunt who died recently.'

'Ah. I didn't realise. Sorry,' he said.

'I dare say Warwick didn't enlighten you.'

'No, he didn't,' the agent returned. 'I thought he was the owner. So will your boyfriend be handling the sale for you, Ms Roberts?' he asked.

'Absolutely not,' she returned somewhat brusquely. 'And Warwick's not my boyfriend. He's just a friend who drove me up here today. He's already gone back to Sydney.'

The agent smiled the kind of smile men often smiled

at Amber. 'In that case this is for you, Ms Roberts,' he said, handing her the business card. 'Or can I call you Amber?'

'Amber will be fine.'

'Great. I gathered from my conversation with Mr Kincaid that you want to sell—is that right?'

'Well, to be honest, Mr Hansen—'

'Jim,' he interrupted smoothly.

'All right. *Jim*,' she said, irritated slightly at the agent's confidence. She was rather tired of confident men. 'To be honest,' she went on, 'I'm not sure yet what I'm going to do with my aunt's place. I only found out last night that I'd inherited it. I'm afraid Warwick just presumed I would want to sell straight away and took it upon himself to contact you without my say-so. I'm sorry that you've wasted your time coming out here today.'

'There's absolutely no need for you to rush such an important decision,' Jim said affably. 'But since I'm already here, why don't you give me a quick tour around the place? That way, I could give you an up-to-date valuation. Then you'll know what to expect, if and when you do decide to sell.'

Amber almost said no, which was crazy. It was a sensible move to get a valuation. On top of that, if she sent him away she would be alone again. Alone and sad. Better to do something constructive and distracting.

'That sounds like a good idea,' she said. 'Look, I was just about to have a cup of coffee. Care to join me?'

'Love to.'

'This way,' Amber said and led him into the kitchen.

'Nice-sized room,' the agent said as he pulled out a kitchen chair and sat down.

Ten minutes later, Amber was almost regretting

asking the man to stay. He wasn't exactly chatting her up. But he was exhibiting the kind of super-slick charm that successful salesmen invariably possessed.

Amber was in no mood to be charmed, or flattered.

'If you've finished your coffee, Jim,' she said, standing up abruptly, 'I'll give you that quick tour of the house and you can tell me what you think it's worth.'

'Okay,' he agreed readily, and stood up also.

'Well, as you can see, this is the kitchen,' she started in a businesslike fashion. 'I guess you'd describe it as country-style. Now, if you follow me I'll show you all the downstairs rooms first.'

The downstairs consisted of a dining room and lounge room at the true front of the house, which faced north-east, towards the beach. At the back of the house was the kitchen-cum-breakfast room, across from which was a very large room, which had once been a games room, but which Aunt Kate had had converted several years ago into her own bedroom, complete with sitting area and her own private bathroom.

Upstairs had also been renovated around the same time, Aunt Kate having decided to change her establishment from a modestly priced guest house into a more upmarket B & B. The original five-bedroom, two-bathroom layout had been changed into three large bedrooms, each with its own en suite bathroom, along with a very nice sitting room where one wall was totally devoted to bookshelves and books. Two of the bedrooms overlooked the back yard, but the largest—*plus* the sitting area—opened out onto a balcony that had a lovely view of the ocean.

Amber had always thought her aunt's house to be very nice, but as she showed the agent around she noticed for the first time that the décor was rather dated, and some of the furniture a little shabby. The lace curtains in the bedrooms looked old-fashioned, and, whilst the polished wooden floors were okay, the patterned rugs that covered them were not.

Perhaps she'd become used to living in Warwick's super-modern, super-stylish apartment, with its wall-to-wall cream carpet, slick new furniture, recessed lighting and shiny surfaces. Whatever, she suddenly saw that her aunt's place could do with some modernising. As she showed Jim around Amber began making mental notes on what she would do to the property, if she stayed on. The multicoloured walls would all be painted cream. Out would go the myriad lace curtains and in would come cream plantation shutters. The floral bedding needed replacing with something more modern, as did the overly patterned rugs. The bathrooms, fortunately, were fine, being all white. But there were far too many knick-knacks cluttering every available surface. Most of these could go to a charity shop.

Even the comfy country kitchen required some attention. The pine cupboards were okay but some granite bench tops would give the room a real lift, as would a tiled floor. There really was way too much wood.

Her head was buzzing with plans by the time the tour was over.

'I probably will sell eventually,' Amber told Jim as she escorted him out onto the back porch. 'But not just yet. I don't think I'd get the best price, the way the house is presented at the moment.' She also wanted a project that would keep her mind occupied for the next few weeks, something to distract her from the depression that was sure to descend, now that all her secret hopes and dreams for the future with Warwick were dashed.

'You're quite right,' Jim agreed. 'You would achieve

a better price with some changes. The décor spells out old lady, whereas the buyer prepared to pay top dollar for this place would be a young professional couple with a family looking for a holiday home which they could let out as well.

'Though to be honest, Amber,' he went on without drawing breath, 'there are always buyers for homes in this location, regardless of their condition and presentation. I could get you a million for this place tomorrow without your having to spend a cent. Let me warn you that changing things takes time. Time and money.'

'True. But the real-estate market is picking up at the moment from what I've heard.' She hadn't gone to countless dinners with all those wheeler-dealer contacts of Warwick's without learning something. 'And any beachside property sells for more during the spring and summer months. It would be far more sensible of me to fix this place up a bit, then put it on the market in a couple of months time.'

'Wow,' Jim said. 'Not only beautiful but brainy as well.'

Amber just smiled.

'I have your card,' she said politely. 'I'll contact you if and when I'm ready to sell.'

'You mean you might not sell at all?'

'I don't believe in making rash decisions.' She'd only done that once, and look where it had got her?

'Sensible girl. Look, I hope you won't think I'm being pushy, but would you like to go out to dinner tonight?'

Amber blinked her surprise. She'd forgotten how aggressive some men could be in their pursuit of the fairer sex. In the ten months she'd lived with Warwick, none of his male acquaintances had ever hit on her. But that was because they wouldn't have dared.

Now, however, she was single again, and living alone, with no one to protect her from unwanted advances.

'I noticed when you were making me coffee earlier that there wasn't much in the way of food in the kitchen cupboards,' Jim went on before she could open her mouth. 'There's several great restaurants in Terrigal. We could do French, or Mexican, or seafood. Whatever you fancy.'

Amber knew full well that it wasn't concern for her lack of food that had inspired that invitation, but the predatorial gleam in his eyes that she'd glimpsed every now and then. The last thing she wanted at the moment was to fend off some testosterone-laden thirty-year-old who thought he was God's gift to women.

Which Jim Hansen obviously did.

No doubt Jim was a great success in his job. Warwick would not have rung that particular agent without having found out through one of his many business contacts who on the Central Coast had sold the most houses last year. Given Jim's natural good looks and confident manner, he was also no doubt a great success with the opposite sex.

But he was fighting a losing battle with her. Amber wanted nothing to do with men for a long, long time.

'Thank you for the offer, Jim,' she said. 'It's very kind of you. But I am dining with some friends tonight who live not far from here.' Of course it was a lie, but only a little white one. Amber had never been the sort of girl to issue brutal rejections.

He did look disappointed. And perhaps a little surprised. Clearly, he was no more used to rejection than Warwick.

Damn it, she'd been trying not to think about *him*.

Jim recovered quickly. 'I'll ask again, you know.'

This time, Amber gave him a firm look. 'Please don't. You'll be wasting your time.'

'You already have a boyfriend, is that it?'

'I did. Till recently. And I don't want another right now.'

'Understood,' he replied, but with a smug little smile hovering around his lips. 'Call me if you need anything. Anything at all.'

'I will,' she lied again. No way would she be calling Jim Hansen, even if she decided to sell tomorrow. She'd find a female agent who wouldn't give her any hassles. 'Thank you for calling,' she finished up coolly, hoping that he would finally get the message.

She stood there and watched him stride over to his car, a shiny black sporty number with HANSEN spelt out on the black and white number plate. Not a Ferrari, but it looked expensive just the same. He gave her a wave and another smile as he climbed in.

Amber returned the wave but not the smile.

Just go, she thought irritably.

He did. Eventually. Though he took his time.

Amber sighed her relief once the black car disappeared up the street. And to think she'd *wanted* his company earlier.

The sun suddenly going behind a cloud sent a shiver running down her spine. Crossing her arms, Amber had just turned to go back inside when she heard a decidedly familiar sound. The noise a Ferrari made when throttling down was unlike any other sound.

She spun back round, her mouth falling open as Warwick swung his car into the driveway in much the same way as he'd left earlier. After accelerating into the back yard at a ridiculous speed, he did a U-turn across the lawn and screeched to a halt in the same space Jim Hansen's car had occupied a few seconds earlier.

This time, Amber's immediate and only reaction to Warwick's return was shock. Down deep, she'd been absolutely certain that he would not come back. He was out of the car in a flash, his face darkly frustrated as he marched around the front and over to her.

'I was beginning to think I'd have to come inside and throw that idiot out,' he ground out. 'What in hell were you doing with Hansen that took so long? Or shouldn't I ask?'

Amber's mouth finally snapped shut, her shock giving way to outrage.

'No! You *shouldn't* ask. What I do with Jim Hansen, or any other man, is none of your business. We're finished. *Remember?*'

'We're finished when I say we're finished, madam. And that's certainly not today. Now, do you want to argue out here where all the neighbours can hear? Or shall we go inside where we can talk like reasonable adults?'

He didn't wait for her to answer, cupping her right elbow with steel-like fingers and steering her firmly back inside through the open door. Once in the hallway, he kicked the door shut, then took hold of both her shoulders, forcing her to look up into his angry blue eyes.

'I'm going to ask you one more time, Amber. What took you so bloody long with that oily-looking person?'

'I don't know what you're so upset about. You're the one who arranged for Jim to call.'

'So it's Jim already, is it?'

'And why not? We don't stand on ceremony here in Australia. We get on a first-name basis pretty quickly. I would have thought a man as smart as yourself would have noticed our easy-going Aussie culture by now.'

'Very funny. Have you asked Hansen to sell the house?'

'Not as yet. I've decided to live here for a while.'

'Really. If that's the case, then I wonder why our esteemed estate agent left here with that Cheshire Cat grin on his face. Still, it doesn't take a genius to work out the reason behind his smugness. Given the amount of time you spent with him, he probably thought he was on to a sure thing.'

'Oh, for pity's sake!' Amber wrenched herself out of Warwick's almost painful grip and marched into the nearby kitchen where she was able to put the table between herself and Warwick. Not to protect herself from him, but because she wanted to hit him more than she'd wanted to hit anyone in her life.

He followed her, his body language that of a man struggling with some suppressed violence of his own.

'Hansen asked you out, didn't he?' he bit out as he gripped the back of one of the wooden chairs with whitened knuckles.

Why, oh, why did she have to look guilty?

'What's it to you if he did?' she threw at him in desperate defiance. 'You don't want me. Not really. You were going to break up with me. The only reason you're here now creating a fuss is because your precious ego's been bruised.'

His hands curled into furious fists as they dropped to his side. 'I'm warning you, Amber.'

She drew herself up to her full height, her chin lifting. 'I'm not afraid of you, Warwick Kincaid.'

'You should be. As for my not wanting you, you're very wrong about that. I do want you, Amber, more than ever. Now tell me that you haven't agreed to go out with Hansen.'

Amber stared at him. Goodness, he was jealous! Blackly, insanely jealous! That was why he wanted her more than ever. Not because he'd realised he was in love with her, but because some other man was showing interest in her.

'*Tell* me,' he repeated in ominous tones.

Her temper rose to a level previously unknown to her. 'Don't you dare try to bully me, Warwick Kincaid. I don't have to tell you anything of the kind. You don't own me!'

'Don't I? We'll just see about that!'

He was around the table in a split second, coming at her with burning eyes. Amber did the only thing she could think of to do. She shoved a chair into his shins and ran. Unfortunately, not out the back door, which would have been the more sensible escape. But up the stairs where the only barriers to being caught were the less-than-adequate locks on the bedroom doors.

Behind her she heard him coming. Fast. Her heart hammered hard in her chest as total panic set in. What was he going to do? Warwick could be a ruthless seducer when he wanted to be. But he'd never forced her to do anything she didn't ultimately want to do, even when she hadn't initially wanted to do it, like last night.

Was that his plan now? To show her that she had no power against him once she was in his arms?

But if he succeeded in seducing her, she would be left with nothing, not even her pride…

Suddenly, Amber's rushing feet clipped the edge of the slightly higher top step, sending her sprawling onto the thin strip of patterned carpet that ran along the upstairs hallway. Before she had time to get up, he'd reached her.

'Are you all right?' he asked as he lifted her, his voice as perversely gentle as the hands encircling her waist.

'You keep away from me!' she screamed, wrenching out of his arms and pushing him away quite violently.

He crashed back against the wall, grunting with pain. For a split second Amber just stood there, staring at him. But as soon as he levered himself away from the wall, she came to her senses and made a second dash for it, this time down the stairs, thinking if she could only make it outside she'd be safe.

She almost made it. Speed, however, was her undoing once more, not helped by the shiny soles of her nice new boots. Halfway down the stairs, her left foot shot out from under her, her right leg buckling when she tried to take all her weight on her right foot. It was then that she tipped forward, and the hallway floor rushed up to meet her…

CHAPTER EIGHT

'OH, MY God!' Warwick cried out.

He couldn't save her. It all happened too fast.

Warwick would never forget the horrible sound Amber's head made when it hit the floor at the bottom of the stairs, or the way she lay, in a crumpled heap. Not moving, maybe not breathing.

She's dead, came the horrifying thought as he raced down the stairs, his own heart almost stopping as he knelt beside her still body and tried to find her pulse.

'Please don't let her be dead,' he prayed for the first time in his life.

When her eyelashes fluttered and a soft moan escaped her lips, his heart lurched back to life, his relief almost as great as his guilt.

Because her falling was all his fault. What had he thought he was doing, threatening her like that, then chasing her up the stairs? No wonder she'd panicked. He'd obviously scared her.

So much for his earlier plan to return and play the role of the penitent lover, all apologies and kisses. Instead, as he'd sat outside in the street, waiting for Hansen to leave, he'd fairly seethed with uncontrollable jealousy. Because once he'd seen that black sports car with the personalised number plate, he'd known what kind of man

Jim Hansen would be. He knew the type well. When he'd spotted the handsome devil driving out with that smug smile on his face, he'd come roaring back inside like some Neanderthal caveman, his primal emotions bypassing his brain as he'd tried to get his way through sheer brute force.

Aside from the fact that he deplored that kind of macho behaviour, such tactics simply didn't work with the modern woman. You couldn't hit her on the head with a club, then drag her off to your cave and ravish her for hours.

Not without ending up in jail.

He deserved to be in jail. Or in hell.

Damn it all, he *was* in hell!

'I'm so sorry,' he groaned as he tried to work out what to do first. 'So terribly terribly sorry.'

When he started sliding his arms underneath her body, her eyelids shot up. 'Don't you touch me!' she cried out, eyes and voice alarmed.

'Don't be silly. You can't stay here on the floor. We have to get you onto a bed. Now where's the closest?'

'No!'

'For pity's sake, I'm not going to hurt you, Amber. What kind of man do you think I am?'

'I don't know,' she choked out. 'I don't know any more.' And she turned her face away from him. But not before he glimpsed tears filling her eyes.

Never in his life had Warwick felt so low, or so remorseful.

'I give you my word,' he said sincerely as he lifted her up into his arms, 'that I won't do anything more to upset you.'

Her eyes turned back to his then, haunted, unhappy eyes.

'What more could you possibly do, Warwick?'

How right she was. He'd reached new depths of reprehensible behaviour today, having had no consideration for Amber's feelings, having thought of no one but himself.

Of course he'd been treating women badly for years, using them to satisfy his own base needs, then discarding them when he'd grown bored with their wanting more from him than just sex. He'd justified his behaviour by selecting the sort of good-looking, gold-digging female who hadn't been too broken-hearted when he'd sent them off into the sunset loaded with jewellery and cars and the odd apartment or two.

He could never, however, justify what he'd done to Amber. She was just not like that.

He had to let her go. But first he had to make things right here. He couldn't just leave when she might have concussion and who knew what other injuries, all of which were his fault. The thought that she might have really hurt herself in that fall still appalled him.

'Amber, I—'

'No,' she interrupted, stiffening in his arms. 'I don't want to listen to anything more you've got to say. Just put me down and go.'

Warwick might have admired her spirit at any other time. But he could hardly do what she wanted and still live with himself.

'Please understand, Amber, that I can't do that,' he said firmly. 'Firstly you might have concussion after a bad fall like that. Secondly, I think you could have broken something.'

'I haven't done any such thing. Here. Put me down and I'll show you.'

He sighed when she began to struggle. Silly stubborn girl! In the end, it was easier to lower her to the floor—very gingerly—and let her try to stand up.

Her gasp of pain, plus the awful shade of grey to which her face turned, showed him that he was right. She'd broken something all right.

'I...I think...my ankle,' she said weakly as she tried to balance on her left leg, at the same time clutching at his arm. 'I think I will have to lie down. Aunt Kate's bedroom is just over there,' she said, biting her bottom lip as she nodded towards a doorway across the hall. 'Oh...I...I...'

He caught her this time before she hit the floor, scooping her limp body up into his arms and hurrying into the bedroom she'd indicated.

It was a truly ghastly bedroom, in Warwick's opinion, all dark wooden furniture with lace everywhere and the most hideous crocheted bedspread he'd ever seen.

He lowered Amber onto said bedspread, trying not to worry too much. She'd just fainted, that was all. No one died from fainting. He wondered if he should cover her with a blanket. It was quite chilly inside the house. Whatever heating there was clearly wasn't on. Not wanting to move her, he reefed the bedspread out from the foot of the bed and turned it back up over her legs. By the time he glanced back up at her face, her eyes were open.

'I fainted,' she said, as though it were a crime.

'Yes,' he agreed.

'I've never fainted before.'

His smile was gentle as he sat beside her on the bed. 'Possibly because you've never broken an ankle before. I have and it's not a very pleasant experience.'

'You have? When?'

'A few years back. An abseiling accident.'

'Abseiling,' she repeated drily, and shook her head at him. 'What haven't you done, Warwick?'

'I haven't tried base jumping,' he said, pleased to see the colour coming back into her face. 'Now first things first. Are you in a lot of pain?'

'Not so much now that I'm lying down. My ankle's throbbing a bit and I have a headache. Nothing I can't stand.'

'But why should you stand it? Your aunt must have kept some painkillers. Where did she store her medicines? Over there, in that bathroom?'

'No. In the kitchen. In the cupboard above the fridge.'

'I'll go and check. Now don't go trying to get up, madam,' he warned as he stood up. 'I don't want to come back here and find you on the floor.' Warwick grimaced when he glanced down at the ancient, dusty rug by the bed. 'Certainly not this floor. The mites in that rug just might have you for lunch!'

Amber did try to move once he'd left the room. But the pain was too awful to continue. There was nothing she could do but lie back and let Warwick minister to her. Which was the last thing she wanted.

Possibly it was the last thing he wanted as well. Warwick was not the sort of man who would enjoy playing Florence Nightingale. He was used to being waited on, not the other way around.

If only he hadn't come back. If only she'd never met him in the first place!

Life was cruel all right.

He returned quite quickly with a glass of water and two white tablets.

'I found some strong painkillers,' he said and popped

the tablets into her hand. 'You're not allergic to codeine, are you?'

'No,' she said, and swallowed the tablets, drinking most of the water with them.

'Right. I've been thinking. We'll have to find a doctor who'll call here at the house. No way can I get you into the Ferrari with a broken ankle. So who shall we call? What about your aunt Kate's doctor? She must have had a GP, having lived up here for so long.'

'I have some bad news for you, Warwick. Doctors don't make house calls on the coast.'

'What? Not even family doctors?'

'No, not even family doctors.'

He looked decidedly sceptical. 'Why not?'

'Because there aren't enough of them to go around as it is. I think you'll find the situation is pretty much the same all over Australia. We have a major shortage of medical staff in this country. You've been lucky not to have been sick since you came here, or to have fallen off any of those stupid mountains you climb and ski down.'

'So what do you do if you have an accident?'

'You either drive yourself to the emergency section of the local hospital, where, because of the lack of doctors and nurses, it sometimes takes hours to be seen. Or you call an ambulance in the hope that when you arrive at that same place, you'll hopefully be seen a little more quickly. Though I wouldn't bank on it. Given I can't even walk, I think an ambulance is the best course of action.'

Warwick couldn't imagine anything worse than sitting for hours with Amber in an inadequately staffed emergency room, waiting to be treated.

There had to be some other solution.

And then it came to him: Max Richmond! He might never have met the hotel magnate, but he knew Max was both rich and successful, the kind of man who'd have connections.

'What about Max Richmond?' he asked Amber. 'Didn't you say he lived not far from here? You told me that he and his wife were close friends of your aunt Kate.'

'Well, yes, but I don't think that—'

'Do you have his phone number?' Warwick interrupted.

'Yes, but—'

'But nothing, Amber. I'm not having you sit around in some hospital waiting room for hours. Max Richmond is sure to know a local doctor who'd be willing to make a house call, for a price. After that we can organise to have you taken to a private hospital. What's his number?' he asked as he pulled his phone out of his trouser pocket.

He was doing it again, Amber realised wearily. Taking over. It was what he did best, of course. But the days of his taking her over were over. She'd found the courage to leave him today, and, despite it breaking her heart, she knew she could not let him seduce her back into his life in any way, shape or form. She had to stand on her own two feet, even if she had a broken ankle.

'Warwick,' she said, after counting to ten.

'What is it?'

'I don't know Max Richmond's number off by heart and I wouldn't give it to you, even if I did. Now please… ring an ambulance for me.'

He didn't say or do anything for several seconds, but just frowned. But then he nodded with what she hoped was acceptance.

'If that's what you really want me to do.'

'It's what I really want you to do,' she repeated. 'And make it sound like an emergency, otherwise they'll take ages to come. You can do that for me, can't you?'

'Lie, you mean?'

'Just exaggerate a bit.'

'Sure.' And he did, quite brilliantly.

'They'll be here shortly,' he said after he'd completed the call.

'Good,' she said. 'Then, after they've taken me to hospital, I want you to drive back to Sydney and never contact me again.'

She saw the flash of anger in his eyes. Or was it distress? No, no, it had to be anger.

'I won't be leaving you, Amber,' he said. 'Not till I know you're going to be all right. Don't ask that of me.'

She sighed her exasperation, not just at him but herself, for feeling some pleasure at his refusing to go.

'What's the point of your staying?' she said frustratedly. 'We're finished. You know that as well as I do. It was cruel of you to come back today at all. Why did you, for pity's sake? Why couldn't you have let things be?'

He sighed. 'I wish I had. Now.'

He did, indeed, look regretful.

'It was a mistake,' he added.

She could not trust herself to answer that, knowing that she was close to crying. And she didn't want to cry. Not after he'd virtually called her a cry baby. No more tears, she lectured herself, no more weak, silly, soppy tears!

'I'm really sorry, Amber,' he said. 'I never meant to hurt you.'

This time, it wasn't tears that filled her eyes but fury.

'No kidding!' she snapped. 'What did you mean to do today, then?'

He just stared at her for a long time with bleak eyes.

Suddenly, she realised she didn't want their relationship to end without telling him the truth.

'I was never going to say this to you, Warwick, but the time has come.'

'Say what?'

'That I love you.'

'Amber...please don't do this,' he said with a grimace.

'It's all right. I'm not going to make a fuss. I just wanted to tell you the way it is. I admit I didn't love you at first. How could I? I didn't even know you. But somewhere along the line—quite soon, I think—I fell in love with you. I'm not sure why. Love, I've come to realise, doesn't always make sense. But you know what? One day in the future, after I've managed to get you out of my system, I'll fall in love with someone else, because that's what I want to do with my life. Whereas you'll just continue doing what you've always done: going from woman to woman, living for nothing but the pleasure of the moment. Till one day you'll suddenly wake up and find that you're a very bored, very lonely old man.'

Warwick's heart squeezed tight in his chest at her declaration of love. He found it strange that hearing Amber say the actual words was much more affecting than he'd have thought. As far as the rest of what she said... He didn't doubt she was quite right. Except in her prediction of his becoming a lonely old man. He would make sure the old part would never happen. As for his being lonely. The truth was he was already lonely. He'd always been lonely, for as long as he could remember.

Only with Amber had he felt less alone. And less… unloved.

That was what she'd given him that he couldn't resist.

Love.

That was why he was having such difficulty in ending their relationship.

But it has to be done, doesn't it, Warwick?

For her sake.

'You're absolutely right,' he said. 'I'm a cold, unfeeling bastard and I have no idea why you would love me. Still, I'm pleased to know that you do want to fall in love again at some stage. Just not with Jim Hansen, please,' he added drily.

'It won't be Jim Hansen. If you must know I can't stand the man.'

'I am relieved.'

Amber rolled her eyes. 'Might I remind you you were the one who contacted him?'

'Yes, but that was when I thought I'd be with you. He wouldn't have dared make a move on you if I'd been around.'

'I can look after myself, Warwick.'

'I hope so.'

'Did you worry about your other dumped mistresses this much?'

'No. But that's because they were real mistresses. You, dearest Amber, were my live-in girlfriend, whom I will continue to worry about until I know you are fit and able to look after yourself properly. So I'm afraid you'll have to tolerate my following the ambulance to the hospital and making sure you're being well taken care of. After all, you can't stop me, can you?' he added, a touch smugly.

Amber was torn between exasperation and resignation.

'I suppose I can't,' she said grudgingly. 'But don't think I'm going back to Sydney with you at any stage, because I won't.'

'I wouldn't ask that of you,' came his honest reply.

She looked surprised by his answer. And just a tiny bit disappointed. She was still in love with him, Warwick realised.

It was a very corrupting thought.

So don't think about it!

The sound of a vehicle pulling into the yard was a welcome distraction.

'That'll be the ambulance,' he said. 'I'll go meet them, tell them you've regained consciousness.'

Amber shook her head at him. 'You are a wicked man, Warwick Kincaid.'

CHAPTER NINE

I WISH I were, Warwick thought as he strode from the room. A wicked man would lie and tell Amber that he loved her too, then ask her to marry him. A truly wicked man might even tell her the truth about himself, taking advantage of her compassionate heart so that he'd have a loving carer when the inevitable finally happened.

'Looks like you're not as wicked as you've always thought you were,' he muttered to himself under his breath as he exited the house.

In the end, Warwick didn't follow the ambulance into Gosford, the paramedics informing him that the rest of the afternoon would be taken up with X-rays or scans and he would just be in the way. They suggested he went in during visiting hours that evening, by which time Amber would have a diagnosis. In the meantime, she did have her cell phone with her so she could ring him if she needed to.

Warwick had no doubt that if Amber's ankle was broken, they would operate. They did that these days, the theory being that strengthening the ankle with steel pins would save the patient from arthritis later in life. A rather wasted prevention where he'd been concerned. But he'd still chosen the operation, because recovery was quicker and you could get around better by wearing a special boot and using a walking frame. Much more convenient that a cast and crutches.

Warwick's only concern was who would perform Amber's operation. He'd had one of the best bone men in the world do his, after which he'd convalesced in a private sanatorium in Switzerland, where he'd been waited on hand and foot. He didn't like the idea of Amber being operated on by some second-rate surgeon, then being tossed out of hospital within a day or two without proper after-care. What he needed to do before visiting Amber tonight was to find out about the best private hospitals in the area, plus the qualifications of the specialists who operated there.

After the ambulance departed, Warwick remained out on the still sunny and almost warm porch whilst he thought about how best he could glean this information, and how quickly. If he'd had a lot of time he'd have contacted his office in London, where his top research assistant could find all the answers he wanted via the worldwide web. His staff there were highly efficient and quite ingenious. But searching the Internet would still take some time. A glance at his watch showed it was getting on for four o'clock. Why do that when there was a local and more immediate source of information?

Turning, Warwick hurried back inside and into the decidedly chilly kitchen where he spotted a phone on one of the kitchen counters and a telephone and address book sitting beside it. He quickly turned to the R section and there it was: Max and Tara Richmond's phone number. First he put the number into the menu of his BlackBerry, then he called.

'Hello,' a female voice answered quite quickly.

'Mrs Richmond?'

'Yes. Who is this?' she asked a little irritably.

She probably thought he was a telemarketer. 'You don't know me personally, Mrs Richmond. My name is Warwick Kincaid. I'm a friend of Amber Roberts, Kate's niece.'

'Ah, yes! Mr Kincaid. I know who you are. Kate mentioned you to us once or twice.'

'Not with any great approval, I would imagine,' he said drily. 'But that's beside the point now. The thing is, Mrs Richmond—'

'Oh, do call me Tara. I can't stand being called Mrs Richmond.'

'Very well, Tara.'

'I suppose you're ringing for the solicitor's name and address.'

'What? No. No, that's not why I'm phoning.'

'Didn't Mrs Roberts pass on my message?'

'What message?'

'That Kate used our solicitor to make her will. He wants Amber to contact him.'

'I see. Well, I'm not sure about that. Amber didn't mention it to me. But that's not important at the moment. The thing is, Tara, there's been an accident at the house. Kate's B & B, that is. When we heard about Amber's inheritance, we came up from Sydney for the day to look at the place. Unfortunately, Amber tripped and fell down the stairs and I'm pretty sure she's broken her ankle.'

'Oh, dear heaven, how dreadful. Have you called an ambulance?'

'Yes. It's just left here to take her to Gosford hospital.'

'I see. So how can I help?'

'Amber explained to me about the shortage of doctors and I am quite concerned about who is going to treat her. As you can understand, I want the very best for her, so I was wondering if you or your husband could advise me as to which private hospital I could have her transferred to?'

'Mmm. Well, there are a few private hospitals on the coast. But I couldn't personally recommend any particular one, because I've never been to any of them, and neither has Max. I actually had my two babies in Gosford hospital, where I was treated wonderfully well. You shouldn't believe everything you read, you know. There are good and bad everywhere. And you'll find that the specialists at Gosford hospital also practise locally in the private sector.'

'Really? The system appears to be just the same here as it is at home in the UK.'

'I wouldn't worry about her standard of care, if I were you. She'll be just fine. Poor thing, though. It's nasty, breaking an ankle. It's going to take weeks before she can walk properly again. I hope your place in Sydney doesn't have stairs.'

'It doesn't.' Not that Amber would be there. But it did beg the question of where she would convalesce. She couldn't stay by herself at her aunt's place. Well, she *could*, if she allowed him to pay for a private nurse to come in every day. But Warwick couldn't see her letting him pay for anything. He supposed she'd have to go home to her family. She wasn't going to like that!

'It just occurred to me,' Tara said. 'If you are only up here for the day, then Amber won't have anything with her for a stay in hospital. No toilet bag or nighties.'

'Well…no. She didn't have anything like that with her.'

'I'd send you out to shop for her, but if you're anything like Max you won't know what to buy. I'd go myself but Jasmine's having her afternoon nap. Why don't I put some things together for you to take in to her? I have nighties I haven't even worn and we have loads of sample toiletries which people try to sell to Max for his hotel chain.'

'That's extremely kind of you,' he said, and meant it.

'No trouble. When do you think you'll be going in to the hospital?'

'The paramedics said not to bother until tonight. By then, Amber should have been X-rayed and we'll know what the situation is.'

'Right. I presume you're ringing from Kate's place?'

'Yes.'

'Okay. Look, Max goes for a jog along the beach every afternoon around five. Our house is only a couple of minutes from you, so I'll send him along with a bag of things.'

'Are you sure? I could always drive to your place and collect it. It's obviously not far.'

'Don't be silly. It's not out of Max's way. He won't mind.'

'I do thank you. And I'm sure Amber will be most grateful.'

'Only too glad to help. She's a lovely girl.'

'Yes. Yes, she is.'

'Give her my best wishes and do let me know what happens. With a bit of luck her ankle might not be broken, only sprained.'

'Let's hope so. Anyway, I'll ring you when I know the diagnosis.'

'Great. Bye,' she said, then hung up.

Warwick glanced at his watch again. Ten past four.

Suddenly, he felt hungry. And damned cold. This kitchen was rapidly becoming an ice-box. He was used to places that were fully temperature-controlled all the time. He hadn't even brought a jacket with him. He spotted Amber's leather jacket draped over the back of a chair but he could hardly wear that. He found a small fan heater in one corner and turned it on, then set about getting himself something to eat.

There were quite a lot of tins in the cupboards and various loaves of bread in the freezer. He made himself some raisin toast and coffee, which he consumed in record time, after which he decided to have a quick look around the house. When he'd been up here for that barbecue at Easter, he'd only come inside once to go to the small washroom under the stairs. Today was the first time he'd been in the kitchen. Certainly the first time he'd been in the old lady's bedroom.

A brief glance into the formal lounge and dining room showed more dark wooden furniture, which some people might think elegant and timeless, but it wasn't to Warwick's taste. Warwick preferred modern and minimalist furniture, hating anything fussy.

Finally he went back upstairs, this time more slowly, and was surprised when he discovered some temperature controls built into the wall at the top of the staircase, indicating that the upstairs *was* air conditioned. He didn't turn it on, however, fully intending to drive back to Sydney after visiting Amber. No way was he going to stay here tonight. Not if all the bedrooms looked and smelled like the one downstairs; lavender and lace were not to his liking!

The bedrooms upstairs, however, came as a pleasant surprise. They weren't at all bad. There wasn't quite so much lace as downstairs, as it was hung only at the windows. And there was no overpowering smell of lavender. He particularly liked the largest bedroom, which had a queen-sized bed, an en suite bathroom, and French doors opening out onto an ocean-facing balcony. Admittedly the décor was still a bit too old-fashioned for his taste—he hated floral quilts and rugs—but he could ignore those.

Maybe he wouldn't drive back to Sydney tonight after all…

Unlocking the French doors, he pushed them open and walked out onto the balcony where a crisp evening breeze sent the scent of the ocean into his nostrils.

Warwick had always liked the sea. He liked the sound of the waves washing up onto the beach, savoured the sharp, salty smell.

That was one memory from his childhood that he still found pleasure in: his summers by the sea.

When he'd been around eight years old, his father had bought a holiday house right on the coast in Cornwall, in a village that boasted one of the best beaches in England. Not that his father had spent much time there. It had mostly just been Warwick and the housekeeper who'd acted as his minder during the holidays. She'd been a very large lady named Phyllis, who'd drunk like a fish and let Warwick pretty well do whatever he liked. He'd spent each summer playing and swimming with the local children, who'd also taught him how to fish and even to ride a surfboard. He'd absolutely loved it, hating it when the holidays were over and he'd had to return to boarding school.

Unfortunately, when Warwick had turned twelve, his father had sold the Cornish house. After that, his summer holidays had been spent in various camps that specialised in teaching adolescent boys how to survive in the wild. He'd hated them, perhaps because his heart had stayed on the beach in Cornwall. He still hated any form of camping, which was perverse given he liked the great outdoors—just not in a tent, thank you very much, or a dank forest.

Nothing beat holidays by the ocean.

In the summer, that is, Warwick amended as a shiver went through him. Not quite so great in the winter time. Especially when one didn't have a warm jacket to wear. Warwick was about to go back inside when he spotted a tall, well-built man jogging along the beach, carrying a sports bag with him. It had to be Richmond, despite it not being five o'clock just yet. Warwick watched as the man made his way across the sand to the street that ran along the lakefront, where he briefly disappeared from view behind neighbouring houses.

Knowing it wouldn't take him long to arrive, Warwick hurried downstairs and along the hallway to the back door, opening it just as the hotel magnate ran into the back yard.

Not that he looked like a hotel magnate. He was dressed in navy track pants and a grey windcheater, and Richmond's close-cut hairstyle and unshaven face projected a tougher, more physical image than Warwick might have expected. As he drew closer, however, he could see the intelligence in Richmond's eyes. And something else…

Disapproval.

'Tara sent these over for Amber,' he said rather abruptly as he handed over the bag.

Clearly, Max Richmond had preconceived ideas about Warwick's character, none of which was good.

Warwick did not blame the man for thinking he was a cad. Because he was. But he was also a gentlemanly cad. If there was one good thing his father had taught him, it was manners.

'It was very kind of her to do that,' Warwick said politely. 'And very good of you to bring them by. Thank you. I'm Warwick Kincaid, by the way.' And he held out his right hand.

Richmond hesitated only briefly before taking his hand and shaking it. 'Max Richmond,' he replied. 'So how is Amber? Are you sure her ankle's broken?'

'Not absolutely. But she can't put any weight on it at all. I should find out for sure when I visit her at the hospital tonight.'

'Let us know, will you? Tara's quite worried about her.'

'I'll do that. And thank your wife again for me, will you?'

'Sure thing. Bye,' he said, a little more warmly than when he arrived.

Warwick watched Max jog off before carrying the bag inside the increasingly cold house. Cold and dark. Turning on the hall light, he closed the door and glanced up the stairs. Should he go up there and turn on the heating? Or should he just get out of here and find somewhere warm and comfortable to have a meal before going to the hospital to visit Amber?

Amber…

A bleak wave of guilt washed through Warwick as his mind returned to Amber. It was no wonder people held a bad opinion of him.

'Shame on you,' her aunt had said to him, only a few yards from where he was standing at this moment.

What would she have said if she'd seen the way he'd acted today? He deserved to be tarred and feathered for chasing after Amber like that. For making her afraid. For making her fall.

And now, because of him, she was in hospital, all alone.

There was no one in there with her, holding her hand. No one to reassure her that everything would be all right, no one at all.

Not that Amber wanted him in there holding her hand. He was good for nothing in her opinion. Which wasn't totally true, Warwick thought a tad caustically. He *was* good for looking after her financially, if she'd let him.

By the time Warwick locked up and left the house for the drive into Gosford, he vowed to do everything in his power to persuade Amber to accept his help with her convalescence. Considering she'd been going to accept a five-million-dollar apartment, surely she'd accept a few measly thousand towards paying for a private nurse.

Warwick could not possibly have anticipated that fate would present another alternative for Amber's convalescence, one that would tempt him anew, then test him to the nth degree…

CHAPTER TEN

WITHIN one minute of her mother having answered the phone, Amber was regretting making the call. She'd been feeling terribly low and a little frightened as she'd never been in hospital before, let alone been faced with an operation. On top of that, the evening's visiting hours had begun, and Warwick hadn't arrived. The other three patients in the ward, however, all had visitors, making her feel unloved and horribly alone.

It had seemed the natural thing to do to ring home and tell her parents about her broken ankle. When her mother sounded genuinely concerned and sympathetic, Amber even momentarily considered telling her that she'd split up with Warwick.

Till she realised what she would be setting herself up for.

'I'll be fine, Mum, honest,' Amber said, squeezing her eyes shut in frustration. Why, oh, why hadn't she foreseen how her mother might react to her news? 'The doctor said the operation's a very simple one. And that I'll be out of hospital the day after tomorrow. There's absolutely no need for you to drive all the way up here.'

'But what about when you leave the hospital? How will you cope?'

'I'll be fine, Mum. Warwick will look after me.'

'Hmph!' Doreen snorted. 'I know exactly what he'll do. Hire some snooty nurse to stay home with you in that fancy apartment of his whilst he swans off, looking for mistress number twenty-five! No, no, my girl, you'll be coming home here where you can be looked after properly.'

Full-on panic set in. She wasn't going to go home, no way!

'You are so wrong about Warwick, Mum,' Amber defended in desperation. 'He's already offered to look after me personally. And not in his apartment. We're going to be staying up here in Aunt Kate's place.'

'Don't be ridiculous!' Doreen exclaimed. 'That place has stairs—steep ones! You should know that since you fell down them today.'

'I don't need to go upstairs,' Amber pointed out. 'I can sleep in Aunt Kate's bedroom. It has a bathroom attached, a TV and everything else I could possibly need.'

'Oh, yes. I'd forgotten about that room,' Doreen said grudgingly. 'But what about meals? I can't see Warwick Kincaid being able to cook.'

'Of course he can cook. Warwick can do anything he sets his mind to,' Amber added, sucking in sharply when she opened her eyes to find the man himself standing at the foot of her hospital bed with a frown on his handsome face.

Amber winced at the realisation that he must have overheard at least some of her outrageous lies. Still, she'd straighten everything out with him when she finally got off the phone. In the meantime she had to prevent her mother from driving up and seeing for herself that her relationship with Warwick was over.

'What about your washing?' Doreen kept on with

relentless logic. 'I'll bet he's never operated a washing machine in his life.'

'One doesn't have to be a genius to operate a washing machine, Mum.'

'You don't want my help,' Doreen replied, sounding rather wan all of a sudden. 'Do you?'

Now Amber felt guilty. 'It's not that, Mum. But I'm not a child any longer. I have to learn to cope with my own problems.'

Her mother sighed. 'You will ask, if you ever need me, won't you?'

'Yes, yes, of course I will.'

'It's not that far to Wamberal, you know. I could drive up during the day and still be back by the time your father gets home from work.'

Which would be the extent of her help if I stay up here, Amber thought bitterly. No way would she offer to leave everyone down there and stay with me for the next few weeks. That would mean putting me first for once. Couldn't do that, could you, Mum?

'Must go, Mum,' she said a bit abruptly. 'Warwick's just arrived.'

Another sigh wafted down the line.

'I hope everything goes well tomorrow, dear,' she said. 'I...I'll be in touch.' And she hung up.

'What was all that about my offering to look after you personally?' Warwick asked immediately.

Amber didn't see any point in lying. Clearly, he'd overheard everything.

'Mum wants me to go home with her after the operation,' she said with a weary sigh. 'As you can imagine, I don't want to, so I said you were going to look after me.'

'Right down to doing all the cooking and washing?' he said, sounding almost amused.

Amber shrugged. 'Yes, well, she made some crack about you hiring a snooty nurse to stay with me in your fancy apartment whilst you…er…um…' Amber broke off, suddenly realising that he couldn't have overheard her mother's part of the conversation. So there was no need for her to be *that* honest.

'Whilst I what?' he demanded to know in that uncompromising way he had at times.

Amber finally decided that honesty *was* probably best after all.

'Whilst you were out looking for your next mistress,' she told him bluntly.

'Charming,' Warwick bit out. 'Absolutely charming.'

Amber found his condemnation of her mother's words somewhat hypocritical. 'You can't blame her for thinking that.'

'I don't. But don't blame me if I find everyone's poor opinion of my character just a fraction irritating.'

'Who's everyone?'

'Max Richmond, for starters.'

'You met Max? How come?'

'Only very briefly. I found his number in your aunt's address book and rang to make some enquiries about private hospitals in this area. His wife answered and told me that they'd look after you just as well in this hospital. Not sure if I should have believed her,' he said, glancing with disapproval around the rather crowded four-bed ward. 'Are they looking after you?'

'I have no complaints. The food isn't so great but I'm not very hungry. Have you eaten?'

'I had a meal of sorts at a club not far from here. The Leagues' Club, I think it was called. I wasn't all that hungry, either. I was too worried about you. So what did the tests show? Is your ankle broken?'

'Yes, you were right. It's well and truly broken. They're going to operate first thing in the morning.'

'And the doctor? What did you think of him?'

'The nurses say he's very good. A top specialist who moved up from Sydney not long ago.'

'What's his name? I'll check him out.'

'You'll do no such thing,' Amber said sternly. 'Warwick, you have to stop this. I'm not your responsibility.'

'That's not the way I see it. I caused your accident, Amber. If it wasn't for my chasing you up those stairs and frightening the life out of you, you would never have fallen.'

'Please...I...I don't want to talk about that any more. What's done is done.'

Warwick hated seeing the vulnerability in her eyes, and the pain.

'So when will you be getting out?' he asked gently.

'The day after tomorrow.'

'Oh, I almost forgot,' he said, and lifted a bag up onto the foot of the bed. 'Tara Richmond sent some things for you. A couple of nighties and some toiletries. That's how I actually met Max Richmond. He brought them to the house.'

'That was very kind of her.'

'She sounded like a nice lady.'

'She is.'

'They asked me to let them know how you were.'

'Maybe I should give them a call,' Amber said, and picked up her phone once more.

'Can't you do it later?'

'No. No, I think I should do it now,' she said. 'I have their number in my phone. I was supposed to ring them anyway about seeing their solicitor. Something to do with Aunt Kate's will.'

Max tried not to feel put out whilst Amber called the Richmonds. He wasn't used to being less than number one with Amber. He certainly wasn't used to her looking at him in the way she'd looked at him a moment ago—as if he was no longer a part of her life.

Which he wasn't, of course.

Clearly it was Tara Richmond who answered Amber's phone call. The two women made girl-talk whilst Max wandered over to stare through the window by Amber's bed.

He wasn't looking at the town below. He was thinking.

Finally, he turned from the window and returned to the bed, just as Amber finished her chat with Tara.

'You didn't tell Tara or Max that we'd broken up,' she said straight away.

'You didn't tell your mother, either,' he countered.

'If I'd done that, she would have insisted I go home with her. This way, I can still be the boss of my own life.'

'You won't be able to manage on your own when you get out of hospital,' Warwick told her. 'I know that for a fact. You'll need someone with you all the time till you're properly healed.'

Amber hadn't thought that far ahead. Till now…

'I guess I'll have to pay someone,' she said.

'Private nursing costs a small fortune, Amber. I know you said you had money but you won't have much left in six weeks' time.'

'Six weeks!'

'That's how long it's going to take to mend.'

'I…I didn't realise…'

'Well, I do. So this is what I propose: I'll do exactly what you told your mother I was going to do. Look after you up here at your aunt's place till you get better. No, no, don't say a single word till I've finished. Initially, I was going to offer to pay for a private nurse to stay with you, but just now I realised that, even if you agreed, your mother would eventually find out what was going on and you'd have to tolerate all sorts of recriminations and criticisms, which you do not deserve. I know you're going to think I have a hidden agenda in making this amazingly generous offer. No doubt you'll imagine I'm just waiting my chance to have my wicked way with you again. But I give you my solemn word that that isn't the case. This is me doing what is right for once. This is me making amends for my totally selfish behaviour in the past. I want to look after you, Amber. Not as your lover but as a friend. There will be no sex. Then, when you're totally better, we'll part as friends. Not the way we parted today, in bitterness and anger. So what do you say? Will you trust me to do this for you?'

Amber just lay there, absolutely stunned. She found it difficult to know what to say. Because of course she wanted him to stay up here and look after her. It was a dream come true.

Though not quite. A dream come true would be his saying he was doing it because he loved her and could not bear to lose her. Amber knew that Warwick's amazingly generous gesture was inspired not by love but by guilt.

'I take it you're not too thrilled with my offer?' he asked.

'I'm just…surprised, that's all.'

Warwick's smile was wry. 'I can imagine. But you have only yourself to blame.'

'Me?'

'Yes. When I heard you telling your mother that I could do anything I set my mind to, I began thinking that maybe I *could*, even down to doing the cooking and washing. I admit it's going to be a challenge. But I'm game if you are.'

Down deep, Amber knew that to agree to what Warwick was proposing was probably not a good idea. But she didn't have the emotional—or the physical—strength to refuse. Today had been hell. Tomorrow didn't promise to be any better. Then there was the reality of how *would* she cope on her own?

Not very well.

'All right,' she said somewhat wearily. 'I accept your offer.'

'That's good. Now, before I forget, I need to know what you want me to collect for you from the apartment. I'm driving back down to Sydney tonight after I leave here. And before you tell me you don't want anything, just remember that you *will* need something to wear. You can't spend the next six weeks borrowing stuff from Tara. And you can hardly go shopping for more clothes just at the moment.'

Amber decided the time for excessive pride was not right now.

'Okay. But I don't want too much. Just some casual things, plus nightwear, undies and toiletries. Oh, and the towelling robe hanging on the back of the bathroom door.'

'Will do. Look, perhaps I'd better get going. What time is your operation tomorrow?'

'I'm one of the first in the morning. I can't drink or eat anything after midnight.'

'I'll ring the hospital mid-morning to find out how

things went and I'll be back to see you after lunch. You should be ready to face visitors by then. You're not allergic to anaesthetic or anything like that, are you?'

'I…I don't know,' she said, a bit shakily. 'Like I said, I've never had an operation before. I've always been disgustingly healthy.'

'In that case you'll be just fine,' he said, and bent forward to give her a peck on the forehead. 'Try to sleep, sweetheart. Oops. I mean, Amber.' He smiled as he straightened. 'Bad habits die hard. You might have to be patient with me. But I will do my level best to behave.'

'And to keep your hands off,' she reminded him.

He lifted his hands high into the air. 'You already have my solemn oath.'

Amber rolled her eyes. 'Oh, just go, for pity's sake, before I change my mind and tell you not to come back.'

'Methinks you won't be doing that. Not unless you want to go home with Mummy Dearest.'

Amber grimaced. 'Don't remind me.'

'I will, if you turn into one of those impossible patients who can never be pleased.'

'Are you talking from experience here?'

'I have to confess I was not the best patient in the world when my ankle was broken. I trust you will be much more…amenable. Now I really must go. I'll see you tomorrow.'

The moment Warwick disappeared from sight, Amber was besieged by doubts over her decision to accept his offer. What good could come of it? She wanted to get over the man, not fall even more in love with him. Which she might, if he showed her more of this noble side that he seemed to have suddenly acquired.

The only positive she could find about the prospect of living with Warwick as a friend rather than as a lover was maybe she would discover that, without the magic spell of his lovemaking, her so-called love for him would disappear like a puff of smoke. It was a vain hope but remotely possible. Sex had been a dominant part of their relationship up till now. It might have coloured her thinking. She'd read somewhere that it was common for young people to confuse lust and love. If that didn't prove to be the case, and she remained hopelessly in love with him, then maybe being with her without sleeping with her would make Warwick see that there was more to her than just being his penthouse pet. Maybe he would finally fall in love with *her*.

Wow! She hadn't thought of that.

For the first time since the accident Amber's spirits lifted.

'Now that's much better,' the ward nurse said when she came in to take Amber's blood pressure.

Amber blinked up at her. 'What do you mean?'

'You're almost smiling,' the woman replied. 'Must be because of that handsome fellow I saw by your bed just now. Is he your boyfriend?'

Amber almost told the truth, but decided a little white lie couldn't hurt. 'Yes,' she said. 'Yes, he is.'

'Lucky girl.'

'We've been living together for nearly a year,' Amber found herself adding.

'Even luckier.'

'He's English.'

The nurse laughed. 'He's a right hunk, that's what he is.'

'That too,' Amber agreed, smiling.

'I'd be hanging on to him, dear, if I were you.'

'I intend to,' Amber said, finally accepting it was worth the risk of more heartbreak to give her hopes and dreams of a future with Warwick one last chance.

But she had no idea, as she began actually looking forward to her convalescence, that there might be no hope of a future with Warwick Kincaid. No hope of anything but heartache and unhappiness...

CHAPTER ELEVEN

BY THE time Warwick let himself into his Point Piper apartment, he'd totally come to terms with his decision to look after Amber himself. There were no longer any doubts and definitely no recriminations. It was the right thing to do. The *only* thing to do, if he was going to live with himself after they parted.

Okay, so there were going to be some difficult moments. He hadn't gone six weeks without sex since he'd left boarding school at eighteen and entered Oxford University, not even when he'd broken his own ankle a few years back. There was nothing like physical inactivity and boredom to raise a man's testosterone levels. Within a couple of weeks of entering the rehabilitation clinic he'd been climbing the walls. Figuratively speaking, that was. He hadn't been climbing anything with that damned boot on. Fortunately, there'd been one very pretty nurse who hadn't minded going that extra mile for her patient, especially when that patient was presentable and single and very, very rich.

So, yes, Warwick wasn't in the habit of doing without.

But he was sure he could manage. How hard could it be?

Very hard, he accepted when he started packing

Amber's things. Damn, but her nightwear was sexy: no flannelette nighties for her. Everything was made of satin, silk and lace, something he should have realised since he'd bought most of the garments for her. Of course, he always kept the temperature in this apartment at a very pleasant level. Even in the winter, Amber had been able to swan around in flimsy lingerie without fear of catching a chill.

And he'd liked her swanning around in flimsy lingerie.

Bad train of thought, Warwick. Very bad train of thought!

Grimacing, he pushed the lingerie drawer firmly shut before emptying her underwear drawer into a bag without further inspection, knowing it would be just as sexy. After that he proceeded into the bathroom where he scooped all of her skin and hair care products into a large toilet bag, grabbed her bathrobe off the back of the door, then went back out into the bedroom where he stood, glaring at the bottles of perfumes sitting on her dressing table. They were all extremely expensive, exotic scents that he'd personally chosen for her and which turned him on.

'She never said anything about bringing her perfume,' he muttered. So he left them there, the same way he'd left the sexy lingerie behind. Tomorrow he'd go buy her some more modest nighties, which wouldn't make him wish he'd never suggested this crazy idea in the first place.

Her casual clothes didn't present any visual stimulation problems. But Warwick quickly realised that all Amber's skinny jeans were unlikely to fit over the rather bulky boot she'd have to wear to support her broken ankle. He recalled how he'd lived in roomy tracksuits during his recovery, ones where the pants had elastic around the ankles or zippers up the sides.

Amber didn't have any tracksuits. She didn't like them. She wore shorts or leggings to the gym.

He still threw all her jeans in with her other casual clothes, but he put a couple of pairs of jogging bottoms on his mental shopping list. Warwick recalled passing a large shopping centre between Gosford and Wamberal, which should have anything he needed to buy.

When he'd finally finished packing Amber's things, he filled a suitcase with some clothes for himself, after which he took a long hot shower and tried not to worry about how he would cope, living the life of a monk. By the time he climbed into bed, he was so darned tired that his mind shut down immediately.

His dreams, however, were not quite so kind. Like most dreams they were rather jumbled, but still vivid and unfortunately very erotic, and about Amber. In the dream just before he woke, she was lying naked in her aunt Kate's bed. He was standing by the bed, staring down at her, dying to climb in with her, but he couldn't seem to move. Then another man came into the room: it was Hansen. Warwick recognised the smarmy smile on his face. When Amber lifted the bedspread to invite him in with her, Warwick went to cry out. But no sound came out of his mouth, even though he was screaming in his head. When Hansen started kissing Amber, he shot awake and upright, his hands balled into tight fists by his side.

The realisation that it was only a dream brought some relief. But only to his mind, not his body. Warwick sighed, then climbed out of bed and headed for a decidedly cold shower, after which he returned to bed and just lay there, thinking about Amber and all that she'd said to him the previous day.

Despite being a man of considerable intelligence, Warwick wasn't used to deep and meaningful thinking. He'd given it up soon after he'd found out what the future held for him, making a conscious decision to live his life in the here and now, seeking pleasure and satisfaction in whatever took his fancy for as long as it lasted. He didn't let himself worry about what other people thought or felt. He didn't worry about outcomes, even with his many and varied investments.

Knowing what awaited him had been strangely liberating in that regard. What did it matter if he lost all his money, when compared with the inevitability of losing his mind?

Perversely, his disregard of risk had made him an even wealthier man than he'd been when his father died. He'd plunged into deals that a more careful man would not have considered, most of which had returned a profit. On the other hand, he'd never been greedy, taking his money out of the stock market when it had still been on the rise, just before the disastrous crash in 2001. Not because he'd foreseen the future. Warwick didn't think about the future. He just knew he'd already made good money and enough was enough.

People often said he was lucky. That always made him laugh. Lucky, he wasn't. But as the saying went, fortune did seem to favour the brave. Not that he would call himself brave, either. He was impulsive and reckless and, at times, downright foolish. On the other hand, however, he did have a good brain—a brilliant brain, one of his teachers had once said.

One day, however, that so-called brilliant brain would begin to stop functioning. When this would happen,

Warwick could not be absolutely sure. But given his family history, it seemed likely that the age of fifty would be his deadline.

So what are you planning to do for the next ten years, Warwick, my man? he asked himself as he lay there in the darkness, waiting for the dawn. More of the same? Or something different. Something a little more… worthy.

'An odd word, that,' Warwick muttered to himself. 'Worthy.'

What did it mean?

Suspecting that sleep was not likely to claim him now, Warwick climbed out of bed and padded, naked, out to the kitchen, where he set about making himself some coffee. The clock on the wall said it was ten past six. Soon the dark of night would lift and the sun would slide up over the horizon, heralding another day.

'What does it mean to live a worthy life?' he asked himself aloud as he waited for the electric jug to boil.

Warwick frowned. A year ago, he would never have been having this conversation with himself. He certainly wouldn't have been questioning his lifestyle or searching his soul for enlightenment over how to live what was left of his life.

But then, a year ago, he hadn't met Amber.

A year ago, he hadn't been loved.

Warwick didn't want Amber to ever look at him the way she'd looked at him yesterday. He wanted to see, if not love in her eyes, then at least admiration. He wanted her to be proud of him.

Which she might be, if he looked after her the way he'd vowed to last night. With his own two hands—those same two hands that had to be kept firmly off her delectable and highly desirable body.

Warwick's mouth twisted to one side as he envisaged all the intimate things he might have to do for her: help her dress and undress; help her in the bathroom; help her into bed. The list contained nothing but endless torment.

He had to be the worst masochist in the world to suggest it. Or a saint.

Unfortunately, he was neither. The next six weeks, he realised, were going to be sheer, unadulterated hell!

Shaking his head, Warwick took his coffee into the living room, where he settled down on the sofa that faced the water. There he sat, slowly sipping the steaming liquid whilst watching the dawn, at the same time making a mental list of all the things he had to do that day.

Inform the cleaning service that he was going away for six weeks. Visit the club and tell the construction manager that he would be liaising with him by phone and email for a while. Ring the hospital to see how the op went. Drive up to Gosford. Buy flowers. Visit Amber. Then go to that shopping centre.

There were several items in the B & B that would have to be replaced. That crocheted bedspread for one. No way was that staying! He'd buy a new quilt for the upstairs bedroom as well, the one he'd liked the most and in which he'd be sleeping. Because of course he wouldn't be sleeping in the same room as Amber.

Then there was the question of some air conditioning in the old lady's bedroom. And a new TV for Amber to watch. The ancient one in the corner didn't shout digital to him.

It was a lot to do in one day, but Warwick had no doubt he'd manage. It was amazing just how cooperative sales people could be when you threw in a cash bonus. He was determined that by the time Amber arrived home tomorrow everything would be ready for her!

CHAPTER TWELVE

An excerpt from Amber's new diary, written two weeks after her discharge from hospital:

Another long, wretchedly frustrating day! I can't stand not being able to get around without wearing that damned boot and pushing that hideous walking frame. Although it's the Rolls Royce of walking frames. Trust Warwick to only hire the very best. It even has a tray top and a basket underneath that I can carry things in, like books and stuff. But I can't seem to read. I used to like reading but not during the past two weeks. Warwick bought me a fancy iPod and downloaded lots of games on it, which was thoughtful of him, I suppose. But not what I wanted when I complained I was bored. The truth is I wanted Warwick to play games with me, not leave me alone to amuse myself. I'm sick of watching television, even if it is the latest flat-screen model which must have cost Warwick a tidy sum. When I first came home and saw all the things he'd bought—including an air conditioner for my bedroom—I told him that he shouldn't have. But he took no notice and hasn't stopped buying me things. I've given up objecting.

One thing I did do for myself was ring an agency and hire a woman to come in and help me shower and dress every morning. I knew I wouldn't be able to stand Warwick doing that for me. And he probably would have. He's been quite amazing, really. He's taught himself how to cook by following Aunt Kate's handwritten recipe books. Not that he doesn't occasionally order takeaway. We've had the odd Chinese and a pizza or two. Washing clothes hasn't presented any problem for him, either. Still, Aunt Kate installed a well-equipped laundry, including a tumble-dryer, with a list of simple instructions for guests taped to the wall near them. I know I shouldn't complain. He's doing everything he said he would. But I hate it. I hate his treating me like a flatmate he's mildly fond of. I hate it that he talks to Max more than he talks to me. But most of all I hate sleeping alone. Not that it bothers Warwick. It didn't even bother him when he came into my room last week and caught me sitting up in bed with nothing on. I was changing nighties at the time. But he didn't turn a hair. Didn't even really look. Which irritated me to death. He used to say I had the most beautiful breasts in the world. Suddenly, they don't even rate a second glance. So yes, maybe my frustration is sexual. Who knows? Have to go now, Diary. Warwick's at the door. You'll hear from me later.

WARWICK ALWAYS tapped on the door nowadays before entering Amber's bedroom, ever since he'd walked in one day last week and caught her in the act of changing her nightie. Seeing her sitting up in bed, naked from the waist up, was not helpful with his resolve to keep his hands off. He'd spent the rest of the day feeling frustration, which had only eased after he'd gone swimming in the sea, in a freezing cold surf.

When he came into the room this time, she was sitting in the armchair that faced the television, fully dressed in a velour maroon tracksuit, her long blonde hair twisted into a knot on top of her head. Despite not wearing make-up, she looked utterly beautiful but decidedly unhappy. Warwick wondered what she'd been writing in the diary that she'd asked him to buy for her the day after she'd left hospital and which was presently resting on her lap. A pen was still in her right hand.

'Dinner's ready,' he announced. 'Do you need any help getting out of that chair?'

Amber sighed as she put both the diary and pen down on the small side table. 'No, thanks. I'll be along shortly.'

Warwick's teeth clenched down hard in his jaw. He could understand her wanting to be independent. But he hated seeing her struggle to do things. Hated not being able to do what he thought was natural for a man to do for his woman.

'Damn it all,' he suddenly muttered and strode over to the chair, where he swept her up into his arms. 'Yes, yes, I know I'm supposed to keep my wicked hands off,' he growled as he carried her from the room. 'But there's a limit to any man's patience.'

She hooked her arms around his neck and stared up at him with her big lustrous blue eyes.

'I...I thought you didn't want me any more,' she choked out.

He ground to a halt in the hallway. 'I'm not carrying

you off to my bed, Amber,' he informed her brusquely. 'Just to the kitchen table for dinner.'

'Oh.' She flushed a dark red and dropped her eyes from his.

'Do you *want* me to take you up to my bed?'

Her eyes lifted back to his, their expression confused and uncertain. 'I don't know.'

She didn't know. Hell on earth, but she'd try the patience of a saint!

'Then let me do my best to make up your mind for you. If you say yes, then I'll quite happily make love to you. All night long if you wish. It hasn't been easy for me being here with you like this. Celibacy does not come naturally to me. But let me warn you, Amber, I will still leave when you're better. It won't change anything. Do not think that sleeping with me will make me stay, because it won't!'

Amber wished he hadn't added that last bit. Wished he'd stopped at how glad he would be to make love to her all night. Then she could have surrendered to the wild, rapturous heat that was racing through her veins and not worried about the future. She could have tried living the way he'd always lived: for the pleasure of the moment.

But, no, he had to tell the cold, hard facts, didn't he? Had to make her face the reality of his offer. Had to put the ball squarely back in her court.

Dear God, but he was cruel!

'In that case, take me to the kitchen,' she said with stiff pride.

'Fine,' Warwick bit out and did just that, depositing her in one of the kitchen chairs before swinging away to see to the food, grateful for the opportunity to collect himself.

For a split second there, he'd almost ignored her not very convincing 'no' and carried her upstairs to bed. Because he'd seen the truth in her eyes. Seen the yearning. She wanted him to make love to her, no doubt about that.

And damn it all, he wanted to make love to her!

But he hadn't come this far to fall at the first hurdle. He had to stay strong. Because it was obvious that Amber couldn't. The accident had made her vulnerable and weak. He would have no trouble seducing her, no trouble at all.

But seduction was not on the menu for tonight. Or any other night.

'I've cooked your aunt's recipe for Hungarian goulash,' he said as he returned to the table with their meals. 'Right down to the dash of Worcestershire sauce. But I didn't cook potatoes with it, just rice.'

'It looks very nice,' Amber said rather dully as she picked up her fork.

'Do you want a glass of red with it?' he asked as he picked up the bottle he'd bought earlier and placed on the table along with two of her aunt's very elegant wine glasses. 'I know you're not mad about red but you can't really drink white with this. And the Merlot is particularly good. Very soft on the palate.'

'Whatever,' she said with an indifferent shrug.

Warwick quickly saw that dinner was going to be a sombre affair. And he was right: Amber didn't speak, just forked the goulash into her mouth like an automaton. She ate it all, though, which was some consolation for the effort it had taken to make the darned food. He'd been in the kitchen for hours. Not that he really minded. Strangely enough, Warwick had found that he quite enjoyed cooking, even if he did take ages to do everything.

But he hated the cleaning up afterwards. Actually, he hated cleaning in general. To put it bluntly, cleaning sucked. He would have hired a housekeeper if he hadn't needed as many activities as possible to distract and tire him, firmly believing the adage about the devil and idle hands. So, along with the housework and the shopping, he ran along the beach twice a day, in the morning by himself and every afternoon with Max, who seemed to have warmed to him at last. Max had actually come to the house last evening after dinner with a bottle of port and they'd drunk it together whilst they chatted away about business, mostly the hotel industry.

They didn't touch upon personal affairs, for which Warwick was grateful. It would have been awkward to explain about his situation where Amber was concerned without coming out looking the baddie. Which he was, of course. But he liked Max and didn't want the man to begin thinking badly of him again. So when Max invited them both to a barbecue at his house this coming weekend, as one would any normal couple, he'd said yes.

But he hadn't told Amber yet, something he would have to remedy since Tara occasionally dropped in to see Amber and would probably mention the invitation herself.

'By the way,' he said as soon as Amber put her fork down. 'Max and Tara have invited us to a barbecue at their place this Saturday. Not in the evening. At lunchtime.'

'Oh?' she said archly. 'And when did this happen?'

'Last night.'

'Really. And what did you say?'

'I said yes.'

'Without asking me first.'

'Yes.'

Amber tried not to explode. But really, he was incorrigible.

'I don't want to go,' she lied. In truth, she was dying to get out of this house for a while.

'If you don't, I'll have to tell them the truth.'

'Then tell them the truth!'

'To what end? They'll feel uncomfortable and so will we.'

'*You're* the one who'll feel uncomfortable,' Amber snapped.

'True. But I'm thinking of you as well. Max and Tara are good people. Good friends. You'll need them after I leave. Why jeopardise their friendship by airing all our dirty linen in front of them at this stage? Far better that we go on pretending that we are what they think we are: lovers. That way, when I finally leave, they're sure to rally around you and give you all the support you need.'

'So this has nothing to do with your new best mate realising that Aunt Kate was right about you being a cold-blooded bastard?'

Warwick had to smile. Amber was one smart cookie. But then, he'd always thought that. She was the one who underestimated herself.

'That could also be a factor,' he admitted, and refilled his wine glass.

'A very big factor. Oh, all right. We'll go to the stupid barbecue, then. Though goodness knows what I'm going to wear.'

'You have four days before the weekend. We'll sort something out. Now, are you going to drink some more of this wine or not?'

'No. I don't much like it.'

'Fine,' he said with a slightly weary sigh. 'I'll carry you back to your room, then.'

'No, you won't. I'll make my own way back.'

His face reflected his exasperation. 'And how, pray tell, are you going to do that? The walking frame's still in the bedroom.'

'I'm sure you wouldn't mind getting it for me.'

'Then you'd be wrong,' he said sharply, and lifted his wine glass to his lips. Damn the girl, but he was not some lackey to be ordered around without any manners.

'*Please*, Warwick,' she said.

'You haven't thanked me for dinner.'

Amber rolled her eyes. 'Thank you for dinner.'

'Fine,' he said, and put down his glass. '*Now* I'll go get the walking frame.'

As Amber watched him stand up and walk from the room she could not help noticing how well Warwick was looking. His face was nicely tanned from all the running he'd been doing and his body looked extra hard and lean, especially his butt. Not that she needed any imagination to envisage what lay beneath the tight-fitting jeans he was wearing. She knew every inch of Warwick's body, and she loved every single part of it.

But it was what he did with that body that she loved the most. His lovemaking technique was superb. Amber had had limited lovers in her life. But she felt sure she could have had a hundred sexual partners and none of them would have compared with Warwick.

By the time he re-entered the kitchen with the walking frame Amber found herself staring at him shamelessly. Thankfully, Warwick's eyes were firmly on the floor and did not witness her shocking lack of decorum, not to mention common sense. Hadn't she learnt her lesson earlier on? She'd been so close to giving in and saying, yes, please, shag me all night and we won't worry about tomorrow! Which was insane, since she wasn't on the pill any more. She'd stopped taking it on the day of the accident, thinking it was a total waste of time.

To climb back into bed with Warwick would have been silly enough. To risk an unwanted pregnancy was beyond the pale. And she might have done just that, because once back in his arms she'd have been so turned on that she would not have wanted to stop proceedings by mentioning her lack of protection.

Heaven help her, but she was a fool!

A severely self-chastened Amber had cooled her lust-filled eyes by the time Warwick glanced up.

'Thank you again,' she said a bit stiffly.

'My pleasure,' he returned in that wonderfully polite and cultured British accent of his. 'I'll leave you to it, then, shall I?'

'Yes, please.'

'In that case I might take myself out for a walk. Try not to fall over whilst I'm gone, will you?'

Their eyes clashed. His were wryly amused, hers, instantly rebellious.

Amber tried to think of something witty to shoot back at him. But before anything came to her mind, Warwick had whirled on his heels and left the room.

'Damn it!' she muttered, hating it that he had had the last word.

His banging the back door shut with a degree of venom showed her, however, that he was not as coolly composed as he liked to pretend. She went to bed, pleased by the notion that Warwick was as frustrated as she was.

Sleep would not come, however, her mind as agitated as her body.

It had been a mistake, she finally accepted, having Warwick look after her. She should have gone home to her mother. She could still do that, she supposed. Her mother was in regular contact, ringing her at least every second day. Though she hadn't been up to visit her daughter as yet. She claimed she'd caught the flu the day after Amber's accident and hadn't felt up to the drive.

Amber wasn't entirely convinced of this. Doreen didn't sound all that sick. But perhaps she was being paranoid.

Even so it was enough to make Amber reluctant to ask her mother for help. Under the circumstances, there was no alternative but to see this nightmare through.

Three and a half more weeks she had to endure. What a ghastly thought!

CHAPTER THIRTEEN

FOUR days later, Amber woke, feeling marginally better at the prospect of actually going out that day, dressed in something really nice for a change. Tara had been kind enough to go shopping for her, bringing back several outfits from a local boutique for Amber to have a look at.

One had stood out as both practical and beautiful, a pale blue woollen trouser suit with flared trousers that totally hid the ugly boot she had to wear. It had a long cardigan-style jacket, which was both stylish and contemporary, and a cream silk cami to wear underneath.

Amber had known without trying it on that it would be perfect.

The only trouble was getting it on. Judy was away for the weekend and couldn't come in to shower and dress her as usual.

'I think you can manage on your own now,' Judy had said the day before. 'Or you can get Warwick to help you.'

Amber had agreed to the woman's face, but privately resolved that she would manage on her own, even if it killed her.

Admittedly, she was much steadier on her feet these days. It was three weeks now since her fall, the wound from the operation had healed and the stitches were out. But it was still painful to put her weight on her ankle without the boot. She could manage to take herself to the bathroom easily, though she couldn't leave the boot on in the shower as it would get very wet indeed. There was a stool in the corner for her to sit on, but Amber doubted she could get in and out of the shower stall without help. Which meant she would have to ask Warwick.

Not a good idea!

In the end she managed by wrapping the whole boot in cling-wrap. But it took her ages. Drying herself afterwards was particularly awkward, since she had to hold on to the towel rail whilst wiping herself down single-handed. Drying her hair wouldn't be so bad as she'd thought ahead and set up her dryer on the bed, along with her underwear.

Possibly it was the noise of the hair-dryer that masked Warwick's knock on the door. Whatever, suddenly, without warning, the door opened and he strode in, grinding to a abrupt halt when he saw that Amber was sitting on the side of the bed, stark naked.

'Oh!' she gasped, and snatched up a pillow to hold in front of her.

He laughed. 'A bit late for that, don't you think? I did knock. Obviously you didn't hear me. I just wanted to see how you were getting on. It's a quarter to twelve. I said we'd be there around twelve.'

Amber pulled a face. 'I'm sorry but I won't be ready for at least another fifteen minutes. I haven't any make-up on and I'm not dressed yet.'

'Um, yes, I did see that,' he said.

Warwick could not believe it when she blushed. How many times had he seen her naked?

So why, Warwick, old man, did the sight of her sitting sweetly like that turn you on instantly?

'It took me for ever in the shower,' she said, clearly flustered by his presence.

Maybe she could see that he was excited. His jeans were fairly fitted.

'I'll give Max a call and tell him we'll be fifteen minutes late,' Warwick said, turning to walk quickly from the room. No point in embarrassing both of them further. Or in wanting what he could no longer have.

Fifteen minutes later he knocked on the bedroom door again.

'Yes, you can come in,' Amber replied. 'I'm ready.'

Warwick did his best not to let the sight of her affect him this time, but she looked achingly beautiful.

'You look lovely,' he said. 'Blue suits you.'

'Thank you. You look very nice too.'

'Nice?' he repeated drily. 'I'll have you know I spent a small fortune on this outfit!' A total lie. The black jeans and black and grey striped shirt had cost him around two hundred dollars in a menswear shop at Erina Fair, and the black leather jacket had been on sale for two-fifty at the same place.

He'd seen the complete outfit in the window, liked it, walked in and bought the lot, a most unusual thing for him to do. A few weeks ago he would never have purchased ready-to-wear clothes. He'd always had everything tailor-made. But since coming to Wamberal he no longer cared about such things. They seemed… unimportant.

Neither did he care about arriving at Max's in Aunt Kate's car rather than his made-to-impress Ferrari. All he cared about was Amber's comfort.

'I've never actually been here before,' Amber said

when they arrived at Max's address, which was less than a kilometre away from the B & B. Even from the street, it looked impressive: a multi-level cement-rendered house right on the beach. But what else would one expect? Max was a seriously wealthy man.

Amber and Warwick were stopped in front of the high-security gates for little more than ten seconds before they slid open to reveal an enclosed courtyard graced by tall palm trees and a fountain in the middle. Warwick drove in and followed the paved circular drive, bypassing a large garage complex on their left before pulling up in front of an elegantly columned portico. One of the two massive wooden front doors opened as soon as he turned off the engine, Max emerging with a welcoming smile on his face.

The two men helped Amber out of the car, Amber having refused to bring the walking frame along.

'You're just in time,' Max said to them both as they made their way slowly up the steps. 'I opened a bottle of simply marvellous red ten minutes ago and it should be ready to drink by now. But you don't have to worry, Amber. Warwick told me you're not a red girl, so I've put a couple of bottles of Sauvignon Blanc on ice for you.'

'A couple of bottles!' she exclaimed. 'I'll be under the table before I'm finished.'

'I wouldn't think so. Tara prefers white as well. She'll help you drink it. This way…'

'What a lovely home you have,' Amber said as she was led through the spacious foyer into the body of the house.

She'd been expecting something way different from the décor that greeted her. In the time she'd spent with Warwick in Sydney, she'd gone to a lot of dinner parties in the homes of the rich and famous. Amber had found that she could divide the décor of these houses into two types: those that were filled to the rafters with chandeliers, antiques and more marble than the Vatican; and then there were the ones whose owners invariably had a penchant for black and white, plus the kind of stylistic minimalist furniture that looked good in a photospread but lacked both warmth and comfort in reality.

Tara and Max's home was filled with both warmth *and* comfort, without an antique or a chandelier in sight. The main living area was open-plan, with recessed lighting and polished wooden floors covered by lush cream rugs, the same colours as the walls.

Everything was modern, yet casual: the soft-looking leather lounge suite in a lovely buttery yellow; the kitchen with its cream cupboards and stone bench tops. There was a play area for the children to one side, an informal eating area on the other, and a huge flat-screen television built into the back wall, on either side of which were floor-to-ceiling glass doors, beyond which Amber glimpsed a decked terrace and a pool.

'Tara's just getting Jasmine dressed after her morning nap,' Max said, explaining his wife's absence. 'But she won't be long.'

'That's all right,' Amber replied. 'Take me out to that table on the terrace and I'll just sit in the sunshine.'

'Good idea. I'll pour you some wine in a jiffy but first I want Warwick to come and meet Stevie. He's outside playing in the sandpit as usual.'

Warwick had forgotten about Max's children when he'd accepted the invitation to this barbecue. He wasn't good with kids, perhaps because he knew he would never have any. He was often impatient with them, and indifferent to the many qualities their parents proudly pointed out.

But it was impossible not to like Stevie. Not only was he a good-looking child, he was totally lacking in that annoying energy that small children seemed incapable of harnessing. He also didn't seem to need to be constantly entertained, being perfectly happy playing in the sandpit by himself, making roads and garages for his toy cars.

'What a great boy you have there,' Warwick said as the two men returned to the house.

'We think so. He's nothing like I was as a child,' Max said as he went about getting everyone a drink. 'I was a right little pain in the butt. Always wanting attention, always wanting to be first. Stevie's extremely self-contained and very easy-going. He takes after my kid brother, who had the most wonderfully placid nature. His name was Stevie, too. Unfortunately he died young, of testicular cancer.'

'What rotten luck.'

'I don't think it was totally a question of luck. Mum said he probably inherited the gene which caused it.'

Any talk of inheriting bad genes always got Warwick's attention. 'Aren't you worried you might have inherited it as well?'

'Nope. Stevie and I have different dads. Stevie's father died young of cancer. My dad's still going strong. He did have a stroke a few years back, but he's recovered well.'

'Your mother married twice, did she?'

When Max hesitated to answer Warwick knew he'd possibly touched a nerve.

'No,' Max said eventually. 'Mum had an affair.'

'Ah...'

Max shrugged. 'It wasn't entirely her fault. My dad was away from home a lot. I guess she was lonely.'

'Does your father know about your mother's affair, and your brother's paternity?'

'He didn't at first. When he found out, he did what most men do when faced with something unthinkable. He ran away. Well, not literally. But he travelled even more than he already did.'

Which is what I do, Warwick conceded. Travel a lot. Go from place to place, business to business, woman to woman.

And it had worked well for him up till now. He hadn't allowed himself time to think. Thinking inevitably led to depression and other more terrible thoughts. He felt genuinely sorry for Max's father and understood fully his methods of dealing with his wife's infidelity.

'It must have been a very difficult time for him,' he said sincerely.

'It was a very difficult time for me, too,' Max said a bit sharply. But then he shrugged. 'But that's all past. No point in living in the past.'

'No point at all,' Warwick agreed. It was the future that was the worry.

'Here. Take this glass of white out to your girl. I'll go see what's keeping Tara.'

Warwick stood for a long moment after Max disappeared. Finally he gave himself a mental shake and headed for the terrace.

'It *is* good to get out of that bedroom for a while,' Amber said as he handed her the glass of white.

'Max has gone to see what's keeping Tara,' he told her, and took a sip of his own wine. 'Mmm. This is a *very* good red.'

'Oh, you men and red wine,' Amber said somewhat

impatiently. 'I don't know what you see in it. Give me white any day.'

'You'll change your mind when your taste buds mature. Ah, here's Tara now. With little Jasmine, isn't it?'

How strange, Warwick thought as he looked Max's wife up and down. She was a really stunning-looking blonde, and had a great figure, shown to advantage in tight white jeans and an emerald green mohair jumper that matched her green eyes.

But she didn't make his heart race the way Amber could, which perhaps was just as well.

Warwick soon saw that Max's three-year-old daughter was absolutely nothing like her older brother, either in looks or in nature. Whilst Stevie was an attractive enough child, Jasmine promised to be a great beauty, with her mother's heart-shaped face, soft blonde hair and striking green eyes. On top of that, where Stevie didn't like attention, Jasmine lapped it up. She quickly demanded that 'Uncle Wawie' pick her up and hold her whilst her daddy attended to the barbecue.

Amber had already gone back inside with Tara so Warwick could find no reason to refuse.

'Jasmine loves to watch me do the barbecue, don't you, princess?' Max said indulgently after Warwick had hoisted Jasmine up high into his arms.

'Daddy sometimes burns the meat,' his daughter said, somewhat precociously for a three-year-old. ''Specially the sausages. That's why I have to watch. You can watch too, Uncle Wawie.'

Max rolled his eyes. 'What say Uncle Wawie looks after the sausages whilst I do the steak?'

Jasmine pouted her already pouty lips. 'He can't do

that, Daddy. He only has two hands and they're both busy.'

'Yes, Max,' Warwick said. 'Very busy.' And he picked up his wine glass with his free hand and took an appreciative swallow.

Max shot him a droll look. 'I tell you what, Jasmine. Why don't you go over and play with Stevie in the sandpit? He must be lonely there all alone.'

'Stevie likes playing 'lone, Daddy. I want to stay here.' And she batted her eyelashes shamelessly at Warwick.

Suddenly, it killed him, the fact that he would never have a gorgeous little girl of his own like this. Or a great son like Stevie.

If only he hadn't been his father's son, he could have married Amber, and had a family like Max's. He could have lived up here in a house just like this. Could have grown old with Amber the way Max would probably grow old with Tara. Could have become a grandfather, even.

But that would never be.

Max was so right. It was all a matter of inheritance.

Warwick knew then that he could not bear to stay with Amber much longer. He had to go back to the life he'd had before, where nothing and no one mattered to him. This was much too painful.

Maybe he'd be able to last another three weeks, but he seriously doubted it.

'Is anything wrong, Warwick?'

Max's query snapped him out of his increasingly dark thoughts. 'No. Why?'

'You were looking a bit bleak there.'

'What does bleak mean, Daddy?' Jasmine asked.

'It means sad.'

'Are you sad, Uncle Wawie?'

'I think I just need to eat,' Warwick said by way of an excuse. 'This is great wine but it packs a powerful punch.'

'Well, the meat's just about done. And not at all burnt, missie,' Max added, giving his little girl a narrowed-eyed glare.

She just giggled.

'Tara!' he called out. 'How's that salad coming along?'

'Everything's on the table, waiting for you,' she called back.

'In that case, the meat is on its way. And so are we! Stevie, go wash your hands. Lunch is ready.'

CHAPTER FOURTEEN

'IT's been a lovely day,' Amber said to Tara shortly after four-thirty. They were alone in the kitchen, the men having taken the children for a walk along the beach. 'Thank you so much for inviting us.'

Tara straightened up from where she'd been stacking the dishwasher. 'Thank *you* for coming,' she said. 'It's not often we entertain these days. Other than family, that is. Children have a way of putting a stop to your social life. Not that I mind. I like being a homebody.'

'And Max?' Amber asked. 'Does he mind?'

Tara smiled a soft smile. 'I used to worry that he'd miss the jet-setting lifestyle he had before we got married. But he doesn't. Of course we do still travel quite a bit. But it's always as a family. Max never goes alone any more.'

'You both do seem very happy.'

'We are. And you, Amber? Are you happy with Warwick?'

Amber almost confided in her. But only almost.

'Very,' she said, and forced a smile to her mouth.

'Do you think you might get married at some stage?'

Amber decided not to carry her lies too far. 'Warwick's not keen on marriage.'

'Um. Yes, so I heard.'

'From whom?'

'Kate.'

'What did she say, exactly?'

Tara pulled a face. 'I don't think I can repeat it.'

'As bad as that, eh?'

'Look, men can change,' Tara said kindly. 'When I first met Max, he told me marriage wasn't on his agenda. At the time, he was in charge of over a dozen international hotels and spent half his life on planes.'

'So what changed him? From what I can see he's the perfect family man.'

Tara's laugh was soft and melodic. 'Having little Stevie changed him.'

Amber's heart sank. 'Unfortunately, Warwick doesn't want children any more than he wants marriage.'

'A lot of men say that, till they have them. Max said he didn't want children either, but when I fell pregnant he soon changed his mind and asked me to marry him.'

'That's because he loves you.'

Tara frowned at Amber. 'You don't think Warwick loves you?'

Amber bit her bottom lip. Now she'd done it. 'Well, I…er…he's never said that he does.'

'That doesn't mean anything much with men like Warwick. I can see what type he is.'

'What type is that?'

'Reserved and a bit uptight. You know, typically British.'

Amber had to laugh. 'Warwick's not at all like that. He's the most impulsive, reckless, crazy man I've ever met.'

'Really?'

'Yes, really!'

'Heavens, I would never have guessed. He seems so… conservative. How is he in bed? Or shouldn't I ask?'

Amber flushed. 'I have no complaints.'

Tara laughed. 'Now who's being reserved and uptight?'

Amber laughed as well.

'Man, but it's getting nippy out there!'

Amber swung slowly round on the kitchen stool at the sound of Max's voice. He was standing on the mat just inside the sliding glass door, wiping his feet and rubbing his hands vigorously together. Warwick was still outside on the terrace, Amber saw, brushing the sand down from Jasmine's clothes. When Stevie followed his father inside, Max took his son's hand and led the boy over to his mother.

'You should have seen the sandcastle Warwick and Stevie built together,' Max told Tara. 'It even had a moat.'

'I used a cuttlefish bone I found as a drawbridge,' Stevie added proudly.

'What a clever boy you are,' Tara said.

Stevie beamed with pleasure at his mother's compliment. 'Uncle Warwick said he'd help me build another one soon.'

'That's kind of him,' Tara replied. 'But not right now. Now, it's bath time.'

'And time we went home,' Warwick said as he came inside, carrying Jasmine.

'I don't want Uncle Wawie to go home,' Jasmine said with her by-now-familiar pout.

'I don't want to either, sweetie,' he said. 'But Aunty Amber has a broken ankle and gets tired easily. I should take her home and put her to bed.'

'She has to have a bath first,' Jasmine pointed out.

'She had a shower this morning.'

'Mummy won't let us have showers,' Jasmine said. 'Not till we're older.'

'Baths are much better,' Stevie piped up. 'You can play in the bath.'

'Here, I'll take Jasmine,' Tara said, and took Jasmine out of Warwick's arms. 'Max, you give Warwick a hand with getting Amber down those front steps, will you? Sorry to love you and leave you. But these two darlings are very much children of routine. Get out of it and it's bedlam.'

Was it fate that Max should accompany them outside?

Whatever, it was certainly Max who said the fatal words that put the idea into Amber's head.

'Thanks for your help with the kids, Warwick,' Max said as both men helped Amber down the steps. 'You were incredibly patient with Jasmine. You know, you'd make a great father.'

Warwick said something offhand in return but Amber didn't quite catch it. Her mind was already elsewhere.

Warwick *would* make a great father, she'd begun thinking. She too had noticed how good he was with Max's kids, especially Jasmine. His patience and gentleness had surprised her.

Okay, so he was wary of fatherhood. Probably because of his own neglectful father, plus the abandonment of his mother. He hadn't exactly had good examples of parenthood.

But basically he was an honorable man, despite the rather decadent life he'd chosen to live so far. A decent man: look how he'd stayed to look after her. *And* he'd kept his hands off as promised.

But he wouldn't, if she gave him the green light. He'd

pretty well admitted the other night that celibacy was proving difficult. A highly sexed man like Warwick wouldn't take much seducing, provided she could convince him that all she wanted from him was sex. That might be a bit tricky, but she'd think of something.

Of course, he had no idea she'd gone off the pill. She hadn't told him. There'd been no reason to. If they went to bed, he would not imagine for one moment that she'd be trying to conceive his child.

Heavens, just the thought of doing such a bold thing took her breath away!

'Something wrong?' Warwick asked.

'What?' Only then did Amber realise they were on the road driving home. She couldn't even remember saying goodbye to Max.

'You made a sort of gasping sound. Like you'd had a fright.'

'Oh, that,' she said. 'I moved my foot and it hurt.'

'You've done too much today,' he chided, though gently. 'You should have let me bring the walking frame.'

'Warwick, don't fuss. I'm fine. It was just a twinge.'

'It sounded like more than that.'

'I'll take some painkillers when I get home.'

How was she going to seduce the man when he thought she was in pain?

Yet she would have to seduce him if she wanted to have his baby. And she did—more than anything else in the world. So why shouldn't she try to make it happen? Why should she lose *everything*? And who knew? If she was successful, if falling pregnant became a reality, Warwick just might do a Max and change his mind about marriage and children. He might even realise he loved her after all.

There again, he might not. Which meant she would have to raise his child all by herself…

It was a possibility that had to be faced.

Her mother would be furious with her. But Aunt Kate would have understood. Amber knew all about the baby Aunt Kate had once conceived and which she'd terminated when the father of the child became abusive to her. Even so, the poor woman had always regretted what she'd done. She'd once told Amber that if *she* became pregnant when she was still single, she should keep her child, no matter what. Kate'd said she would help her if the father wouldn't.

Well, Aunt Kate had already helped her, hadn't she? She'd left Amber her lovely house and her car. And a legacy of self-esteem and independent thinking.

I can do this, Amber decided by the time they arrived back at the B & B. I *have* to do this. It's not wrong, it's right. For both of us.

CHAPTER FIFTEEN

WARWICK parked the Astra as close as possible to the back porch, unlocking and opening the back door of the house before returning to the car to help Amber out.

'If you don't object,' he said, 'it will be much quicker if I carry you inside.'

Surprise flickered in her big blue eyes. Surprise… and something else.

Damn, but he could usually read her like a book. This time, however, her thoughts remained hidden to him. She'd been very quiet since leaving Max's house. Clearly, her ankle was aching badly, which was another reason for him to carry her inside.

'I suppose it's all right,' she said with a resigned-sounding sigh.

'Trust me, I wouldn't do this if it wasn't necessary,' he ground out as he scooped her up into his arms.

Masochism had never been his style. Till these last three weeks, that was. Living with Amber on a platonic basis was masochism in the extreme. Holding her close like this was the icing on the cake of his self torture.

Warwick swallowed hard when her arms tightened around his neck, bringing his head forward slightly and pressing his nose and mouth against the fragrant softness of her hair. She smelled wonderful, *felt* wonderful.

His own arms tightened around her, his resolve not to make love to her wavering in the face of emotions that carried even more temptation than the fact that he was fiercely frustrated.

It wasn't the need for sex that would be his downfall, Warwick realised as he carried her inside. There were other feelings—other needs—much more powerful, the main one being the need to see her eyes light up with desire for him one last time.

'Amber,' he said, grinding to a halt in the hallway outside her bedroom door.

Her eyes lifted to gaze up at him. 'What?'

'I'm sorry,' he said.

'Sorry for what?'

'For this…'

The moment his lips crashed down on hers, something happened inside Warwick, something he'd never experienced before. His heart felt as if it had exploded, a hot mushroom cloud of emotion bursting up through his chest and into his head, leaving him feeling dizzy and disorientated.

But as the kissing continued it wasn't long before Warwick's responses changed from the emotional to the physical. Desire kicked in, fierce and urgent, his tongue diving deep into her gasping mouth till he had to wrench his mouth away and drag in a badly needed lungful of air.

'Don't tell me to stop,' he bit out harshly.

She didn't say a single word. Maybe she couldn't. She looked stunned.

He didn't wait. He carried her up the stairs, taking them two at a time. Once in his bedroom he laid her down on the bed before gathering her back up into his arms and kissing her over and over till he was sure she wouldn't change her mind and say no.

Only then did Warwick start to undress her, confident enough by then to take his time. Which was what he'd always liked to do with her. Take his time.

Slowly, gently, he removed her cardigan, then the rest of her clothes till she lay there in nothing but her impossibly sexy underwear, and that most unattractive boot.

'You won't be needing this on for a while,' he said as he undid the straps, carefully easing the boot off her foot.

'Am I hurting you?' he asked, glancing up at her face.

'No,' she replied.

And in truth he couldn't see any pain in her eyes. Just the most beguiling excitement.

'Please don't talk,' she suddenly choked out.

Her request startled him, then worried him. Underneath her obvious excitement, was she upset over doing this?

Yes, of course she was, he accepted. But it was too late now, way too late.

Once the boot was removed, he took her hands and pulled her up into a sitting position so that he could undo her bra. Her shoulders stiffened once the fastener gave way, a shiver running down her spine as he slowly pushed the bra straps down her arms. He doubted it was a shiver from being chilled. He'd left the heating on all day, not wanting to return to a cold house.

No, it was a shiver of erotic anticipation.

Once the bra was dispensed with, he ran a fingertip up and down her spine, building on the delicious tension he could feel in her body. When a more fierce shudder ran through her he eased her back onto the bed, arranging pillows behind her head till she looked comfortable.

The temptation to play with her beautiful breasts was acute. But he didn't want to do that just yet, not whilst he was still dressed. He wanted to be ready when she was ready. Which he suspected would not be far off if he kept up the foreplay. Her eyes were clinging to his the way they often did when she was hopelessly turned on.

Leaving her panties in place—to have her lying before him totally nude at this stage would be a mistake—he set about slowly undressing himself, using the time away from touching her to regain some control over his own wildly clamouring flesh. Maybe her ankle wasn't giving her any pain, but some parts of *his* body certainly were. Women didn't realise just how uncomfortable some erections could be. The one he had at this moment was nothing short of cruel. It was to be hoped that it didn't look as angry as it felt. He didn't want to frighten her.

Amber could not believe how incredibly exciting it was, watching Warwick undress like this. He'd never done a slow strip for her before. It was a relief to be able to look at him openly and not feel guilty about it.

He was a hunk all right. That nurse had been so right about that. A gorgeous hunk, and all hers. At least for tonight. What tomorrow morning would bring Amber did not know. All she could be sure of was the here and now. And that promised the kind of pleasure that only Warwick could give her—the kind of pleasure that no girl could resist.

For a brief moment, whether she fell pregnant or not no longer seemed crucial: she wanted to be here with him no matter what.

When Warwick finally slipped off his underpants he saw her eyes widen a little but not with fear. Flattered by her reaction, he stretched out beside her on the bed and began caressing her nipples in the way he knew she loved him to, first with his fingers and then with his mouth. When her back started arching from the bed, he moved on, trailing his mouth down past her navel till he encountered the top edge of her satin panties.

She trembled uncontrollably when he ran a hand up her thigh and slipped it under the leg elastic.

She was wet down there, *very* wet.

Removing his hand, he then removed her panties, sliding them slowly down her legs, holding her dilated eyes with his at the same time. Once the panties were dispensed with, he eased her legs apart then bent them up at the knees. Carefully, so that he didn't bump into her damaged ankle, he settled himself between her thighs and slowly, very slowly, pushed himself into her.

It was then that it happened again, that overwhelming rush of emotion that flooded his body and tightened his chest till he thought he might be having a heart attack.

'Dear God,' he actually cried out.

'What is it?' she said immediately. 'What's wrong?'

Nothing was *wrong*, he finally realised as enlightenment hit.

For a long moment he just stared down at her, at her lovely face, her lovely body and her even more lovely soul.

So *this* was what falling in love felt like.

'Nothing's wrong,' he replied, his voice husky. 'You just take my breath away.'

The compliment brought tears to Amber's eyes, and hope to her heart.

'Don't you dare cry,' he said thickly.

She blinked madly. 'I won't. I promise.'

'Let's just enjoy each other tonight, the way we used to.'

'All right,' she agreed.

But down deep, in that place where guilt festered, Amber knew that tonight was different from what they used to do. Tonight she was deceiving Warwick, big time. Tonight she had a secret agenda.

And whilst she had no intention of telling Warwick the truth, it struck Amber that maybe her troubled conscience would stop her from enjoying the sex the way she used to. Perhaps she would have to fake an orgasm or two, something she'd never had to do with Warwick before.

It was a worrying and slightly depressing thought.

'Good girl,' he said, and began to move, using that tantalising but powerful rhythm where he would almost withdraw before plunging back into her like a sword filling its scabbard to the hilt.

Soon, all worry had ceased, all her thoughts focusing on the exquisite sensations he was evoking. She knew, well before it happened, that she would not have to fake her orgasm. How silly of her to imagine that could ever be the case!

Her hands gripped handfuls of the quilt, trying to hold on to the pleasure, trying to make it last.

A futile exercise!

She cried out as she came, her bottom lifting from the bed at the same moment that he reached release. He cried out too, as his seed shot, hot and strong, into her womb. Only then, as he shuddered into her, did she think of the child whom this mating might produce. Just the thought of it brought an elation—and an emotion—which was difficult to control. She wanted to laugh and to cry at the same time. It was the strangest feeling, both joyful and sad.

She turned her head away and closed her eyes tightly shut, afraid to look up at him, afraid of what he might see.

'I'm sorry, Amber,' he said, and stroked a gentle hand down her cheek. 'I know this was not what you wanted.'

She could not bear to let him think that. Could not *bear* it!

'Don't be silly!' she exclaimed, her eyelids flying upwards as her head turned to face him. 'It's exactly what I wanted. I haven't liked being celibate any more than you have.'

His eyebrows lifted at her words. 'Does that mean I'm not going to have my wrists slapped for seducing you?'

'For pity's sake, Warwick, you didn't seduce me. I'm as responsible for what happened just now as you were. I could have said no at some point but I didn't. I *chose* to let you make love to me.'

'And will you choose to let me make love to you some more?' he asked, a sudden movement of his hips reminding her that he was still deep inside her and not totally spent, by the feel of him.

A memory popped into her mind, of a television programme she'd once seen about fertility problems, where it had been explained that too much sex was not conducive to conception. It was more a matter of quality rather than quantity, and of timing.

The trouble was Amber wasn't quite sure when she might ovulate.

Was more than once a night too much? she wondered.

'I'll take your silence for a yes,' Warwick said, and started to move, rocking backwards and forwards in a slow, sensual rhythm.

Amber caught her bottom lip with her teeth in an effort not to moan. But it felt so delicious. *He* felt delicious.

She couldn't tell him to stop now. She just couldn't.

Tomorrow she'd be more in control.

Tomorrow she'd come up with a plan…

CHAPTER SIXTEEN

Excerpt from Amber's diary two weeks later.

Haven't been writing much in you lately. Guess I didn't really want to think too hard over what I've been doing. It's not in my nature to deceive anyone. I hate dishonesty. But really, what else can I do? I simply can't face the rest of my life living alone, like Aunt Kate did. I need a child to love. I need Warwick's child. It worries me though that we've been doing it too much—way, way too much. If that show I saw on television is right, then that's not the best way to conceive. And I'm running out of time. Warwick's still going to leave when the six weeks are up. He tells me so every now and then, usually after he's made mad passionate love to me, sweet sensitive man that he is. Not! Lord knows what I'm going to say to Mum and Dad when he goes. They came up to visit me last Sunday and you know what Warwick did? Cooked them a baked dinner. I tell you, they were dead impressed. Mum even admitted to me that she was wrong about him, that it was obvious he loved me and would marry me in the end. I have to confess she did put ideas into my head. So I asked

Warwick why he went to all that trouble, and do you know what he said? He said it was because he wanted my parents to see that he did care for me, and that I wasn't a total idiot to give up a year of my life to live with him. Which was not quite what I was hoping for, as you can imagine. I didn't cry, though. I haven't cried ever since Warwick said I was a cry baby, not even when my ankle hurt like hell. By the way, my foot's feeling great now. I've given up the walking frame and am just using a walking stick to get around. Warwick still carries me up and down the stairs, though, which I find very romantic. He helps me in the shower as well. Naturally, I told Judy she was no longer needed. Warwick's out shopping at the moment but he'll be back soon. I'm down in Aunt Kate's room whilst he's gone. Warwick says he'd worry about me if he left me upstairs. I think I just heard him drive in. Must go.

WARWICK CALLED out to Amber as he carried the first of the shopping bags inside. She didn't answer.

Frowning, he dumped the bags onto the kitchen table and walked across the hallway to the bedroom where he'd left her. She wasn't there. The bathroom door, however, was shut.

'Amber! Are you in there?' he called out from the doorway.

'Yes,' came a rather feeble reply through the bathroom door.

'Is everything all right?'

No answer this time.

Instant alarm had him striding over to the bathroom

door and knocking on it. 'Amber, what's going on in there?'

'Nothing,' she choked out.

He wasn't having any of that. But when he went to open the door he discovered that it was locked.

'If you don't tell me what's going on,' he ground out, 'I'm going to break this door down.'

He was about to do just that when the door opened and there stood a devastated-looking Amber, her lovely blue eyes awash with tears.

'Dear God, what is it? What's happened?'

'I can't tell you,' she cried.

'Why not?'

'I just can't!' she blurted out, then broke down entirely, almost falling over when her head dropped into her hands.

Warwick scooped her up into his arms and carried her over to the bed, where he laid her gently down on top of the quilt. There, she gave him one last traumatised look before she rolled over onto her side and curled up into the foetal position, her eyes squeezing shut as deep sobs racked her slender body.

'Go away!' she choked out when he bent to stroke her hair. 'Just go away!'

Warwick had never in his life felt so helpless, or so guilty. Because he didn't have to be told what was behind Amber's distress.

He was, somehow.

He didn't go away; he couldn't. He pulled up a chair by the bed and sat watching over her till her weeping subsided. Even so she didn't speak, just lay there staring blankly into space.

'It's me, isn't it?' he said bleakly at last. 'I've caused this.'

A deep sigh reverberated through her as she slowly straightened and looked up at him.

'I wish I could blame you but I can't,' she said in a dull, flat voice. 'It's all my own fault. I'm the one who did the wrong thing. And now I'm being punished.'

Warwick had no idea what she was talking about. 'What do you mean, punished? For what?'

Her eyes searched his face, her expression half guilty, half regretful.

'Shortly after I broke my ankle,' she said brokenly, 'I stopped taking the pill. No, please don't say anything. Let me finish first. Let me try to explain.'

Warwick's stomach had already fallen into a deep dark pit. For she didn't really have to explain. He knew why she hadn't told him she'd gone off the pill. And he knew exactly what had just happened.

Poor darling, he thought as a tidal wave of remorse washed through him, poor, poor darling.

'At first, I did it because I thought we were finished. Then I realised I wanted a baby,' she blurted out. 'No, that's not totally true. I wanted *your* baby. And I knew you'd never give me one willingly.' Her face twisted with raw emotion, her throat convulsing as she swallowed several times. 'Believe me when I tell you I wasn't trying to trap you into marriage or anything. I would never do that. I just wanted a small part of you to love after you left me. I knew all along it wasn't right. But you do dreadful things when you're desperate. Still, you don't have to worry,' she added, her voice turning bitter. 'As I'm sure you've gathered by now, I got my period just now. So I'm not pregnant. I'm sure you're relieved to hear that.'

Warwick sighed a deeply unhappy sigh. He'd been hoping to extricate himself from Amber's life without leaving behind too much hurt, and without revealing the wretched truth. But he could see now the extent of his delusion. He knew Amber loved him. How could he possibly think that staying all this time and making love to her as much as he had would not give her more pain?

'I'm not at all relieved, Amber,' he told her truthfully. 'I would dearly love you to have my child.'

She sat bolt upright in surprise, eyes blinking wide. 'You would?'

'Yes. But it's never going to be, my love.'

His *love*? Had she heard that right?

Amber frowned as she struggled to make sense of the rest of what he'd said. Was he sterile? Could that be the answer to his distancing himself from any form of commitment?

'What I'm about to tell you will come as a shock.'

Amber was all ears.

'You could not become pregnant by me because I have had a vasectomy…'

CHAPTER SEVENTEEN

'A VASECTOMY!' Amber exclaimed, her eyes rounding.

'Yes.'

Warwick saw her shock turn to confusion.

'But why...why would you do something like that?' she asked in disbelieving tones. 'And when? When did you do it?'

Warwick sighed. 'I had it when I was twenty.'

Amber's mouth fell open as her face registered, not just shock, but total disbelief.

'I have this gene,' he went on whilst she just sat there, staring at him with stunned eyes. 'All the men in our family have it. Actually, now that I come to think of it, there are only men in our family. Except for their wives, of course. But they don't carry the same blood.'

She blinked. It was the first movement he'd noted since he told her how long ago he'd rendered himself sterile. Clearly, she was in deep shock.

Good, he thought. It would give him time to explain.

'My father didn't commit suicide because of gambling losses,' he went on. 'I believe he did it because he'd begun experiencing the first signs that his mind had begun to deteriorate. That's what this gene causes. Early onset dementia, or Alzheimer's, if you want the more technical term. I found out the truth not long after my father died. My aunt Fenella told me. She was married to my dad's older brother. I knew my uncle had suffered from dementia before he died but I had no idea that it ran through the family tree the way it did. My grandfather also had it, apparently, and my great-grandfather. Aunt Fenella did some research and discovered that they all had begun to lose it around fifty years old. She said she was only telling me to stop me from having children and passing on the gene to another generation. She said it was a shame that my father hadn't realised the situation before he'd had me. Apparently, Uncle George had had his suspicions and had refused to have kids. Unfortunately, he and my dad were always at loggerheads with each other and hadn't spoken in years. She said she was sorry to have to tell me such bad news but felt it was her duty.'

Warwick dragged in some much-needed breath before continuing his harrowing tale. 'I have to confess I wasn't too happy with her at the time. I'd never suspected a thing, you see. My grandfather died when I was a very small boy so I never knew what ailed him. To me he was just an old man in a wheelchair. My grandmother never enlightened me. Maybe she didn't know back then that it could be inherited. She died when I was eight, leaving me a whole heap of money in trust because she didn't approve of my father's hedonistic lifestyle. I used to disapprove of his amoral behaviour as well, till I found out why he'd gone off the rails the way he had. Down deep, he must have suspected what might happen to him. Like they say, you shouldn't judge a man till you've walked a mile in his shoes. Well, I've walked in my father's shoes for the last twenty years and, I can tell you, it's not a very pleasant experience.'

'Oh, Warwick...'

'Please don't cry. I couldn't bear it if you cry.'

Amber struggled to fight back the tears. And she managed, on the surface. Inside, she was still weeping. But not for herself—for him. How dreadful it must have been to have found out at twenty that you had no hope of living a long happy life; that you were condemned to a future where you knew nobody and remembered nothing. Bad enough at seventy, or eighty, but at fifty? It didn't bear thinking about.

But she *had* to think about it. She had to find a way to make what life Warwick did have left be filled to the brim with happiness.

'If you didn't have this gene,' she said, 'would you have got married and had children?'

'I don't believe in what ifs, Amber. I do have this gene and nothing can change that.'

'Are you sure? I mean, are you absolutely sure? Have you been tested? They have tests for such things, don't they? I know they do.'

Warwick frowned at her questions. In actual fact he hadn't been tested. There hadn't been an accurate test twenty years ago. But he'd known the truth, as his aunt Fenella had known the truth. With some further research he'd found out that there were others in his family line who had gone the same way.

In view of this cast-iron evidence, he'd taken what actions were necessary to make sure he never passed on the flawed gene. When a test had become available in more recent years, he'd thought about having it, then dismissed the idea as a total waste of time.

'You haven't been tested, have you?' Amber swept on.

'No.'

'Good heavens, why not?'

Warwick shrugged. 'By the time a test became available, it seemed…pointless.'

'How can you say that? Genes are known to skip generations. Or become recessive. Or whatever it is genes do!'

'In my family this gene has not skipped a single generation.'

'Maybe not, but miracles do happen, Warwick. I thought you would never fall in love with me,' she said. 'But you have, haven't you?'

How could he lie? If nothing else, she deserved the memory of his loving her.

'Yes,' he said, and for the first time in twenty years he felt tears well up in his own eyes. But to start weeping was unthinkable.

'I must go,' he said, and stood up abruptly.

'But you can't go!' Amber cried, and swung her legs over the side of the bed, wincing when she tried to stand up without the walking stick.

'For goodness' sake, woman,' he ground out as he settled her back on the side of the bed, 'I'm only going out to the kitchen. The ice cream's probably melted by now.'

'I don't give a hoot about the ice cream. I'm not letting you leave this room till you promise me to go and have that test.'

He sighed. 'Amber, I—'

'If you love me at all then you'll promise me.'

'And when it comes back positive?'

'Then we'll know for sure and we'll deal with it. *We*, Warwick: you and me together. That's what love is all about. Being there for the person you love, through good times and bad.'

'But all I can offer you is bad.'

'That's not true. We could still get married and have a child. We could adopt. You're wealthy. We could get a baby from Asia without waiting too long. An orphan in need of a good home. You're only forty, Warwick. You have years and years of good life ahead of you.'

'No more than ten, Amber,' he reminded her harshly. 'And what then? You'd nurse me until I wouldn't even recognise who you are? I know you. You wouldn't put me in a nursing home. I'd be like a millstone around your neck until the day I died. Sorry, Amber, but I love you too much to put you through that. You deserve better out of life. You deserve a man who's going to be there for you and your children until they grow up, a man who can make love to you and make you happy.'

'Please don't do this, Warwick,' she sobbed. 'Please don't leave me.'

'I have to, Amber.'

'No, you don't. Not yet. Look, forget marriage and children. We could still have a lot of good years together. We could travel and make love and…and…'

'No, Amber. Trust me to do the right thing here at long last. I have to leave and let you get on with your own life.'

'No, no, no!' she cried, shaking her head violently from side to side. 'You don't understand. I won't get on with my own life. I'll never love anyone else the way I love you. I'll never get married. I'll die in this place a lonely old maid, just like Aunt Kate.'

Warwick ached to take her in his arms and say he would do whatever she wanted. But he knew he would hate himself in the end if he weakened.

'That's your choice, Amber. But you don't have to die lonely. I'm sure there are plenty of men out there who will happily give you what you want. Though, for crying out loud, don't try Jim Hansen! Find someone nice, a man who comes from a good family. Check out what kind of man his father is. That'll give you a good guide. And make sure he's healthy.'

Amber clamped her hands hard over her ears. 'I'm not listening to any more of this. You're not going to leave, you're going to stay, and we're going to work something out.'

Gently, he took her hands away from her ears and looked her straight in the eye.

'I'm sorry, Amber,' he said firmly, even though his heart was breaking, 'but I *am* going to leave. I *have* to. There's nothing you can say to change my mind, I'm afraid.' He let go of her hands and stood up. 'I'll go and put away the food first, then I'll pack my things and make my way. You should be able to manage here on your own now, if you use your common sense and be careful, and move back into this room. I'm sure Tara and Max will help. And your mother, too, if you ask her.'

'No!' she cried. 'Don't leave me, Warwick. Please don't leave me.'

'Amber,' he said, his eyes tormented, 'don't make this any harder for me than it is.'

She saw, then, that there was nothing she could say to make him stay. Saw, also, how much he loved her. So much so that he was prepared to sacrifice his own happiness for hers.

It was a humbling realisation but a strangely empowering one. If he could do this for her, then the least she could do was accept his decision with dignity and grace.

'Promise me one thing before you go,' she said softly.

Warwick frowned. 'What?'

'You'll have that gene test.'

'Amber, I—'

'It's not too much to ask, surely.'

'Very well,' he agreed, if somewhat reluctantly.

'Give me your solemn word,' she insisted.

'You have it. Now I really must go.'

CHAPTER EIGHTEEN

'HAVE you heard from him?' Tara asked.

'No,' Amber replied.

They were sitting out on the terrace of Tara's house, having coffee. They were alone, Max having taken Stevie and Jasmine for a walk along the beach. The strong winds of the day before had abated, and the sky was blue and the sun was out.

It had been two weeks since Warwick had left. Two weeks during which Amber had done a lot of thinking and talking.

Confiding in Tara and Max had been a very wise decision. They'd stopped her from becoming too depressed or maudlin. She hadn't, however, told her mother yet that her relationship with Warwick was over. Whenever Doreen rang, Amber pretended everything was fine. That was easier than launching into the explanation of why he'd left. One day, she would explain, but not right now.

'He should have had the results of the gene test by now,' Tara pointed out.

'I would imagine so,' Amber replied with a jagged twist to her heart. 'Obviously it came back positive.'

Tara sighed. 'I know it's hard to accept, Amber,

loving the man the way you do. But perhaps it's all for the best that he's gone.'

'No, it's not,' Amber replied with a fierceness that betrayed how upset she still was. 'I could have made him happy, if he'd let me.'

'You already made him happy. You showed him what love was and taught him how to love in return.'

'Maybe. But I'm afraid, Tara. Afraid of what he's going to do when things start to go wrong and there's no one there to love him and look after him.'

'You don't think he's going to commit suicide like his father did?'

'I *know* he will.'

'Oh, Amber...'

Amber stood up abruptly. 'I have to go to him. I have to make him understand that when you love someone you can't just forget them like that. I...Oh, my God!' she gasped. 'Warwick!'

Tara's eyes whipped up to see the man himself walking across the sand towards them. Max was with him, carrying Stevie, Jasmine having bolted on ahead. She burst through the back gate and ran up onto the terrace, her pretty little face highly animated.

'Uncle Wawie's come back!' she cried. 'You were *wong*, Mummy. He hasn't gone.'

'So it seems, darling,' Tara replied.

Despite her heart having leapt up into her mouth, Amber tried not to read too much into Warwick's unexpected visit.

Maybe he'd just come to say a last goodbye before leaving Australia. Maybe he'd brought her the rest of her things from his Sydney apartment. Maybe he...

No, no. She dared not hope that that test had come back negative. That would be nothing short of a miracle.

Her eyes went to his as he came into the backyard. There was no great joy in them, she noted. He actually looked very tired. Her heart sank again, that foolish heart that couldn't seem to stop hoping for miracles.

'Hello, Amber...Tara,' he said as he stepped up onto the terrace. 'Sorry to drop in on you like this. But I needed to talk to Amber and I didn't want to do it over the phone. When you weren't at home,' he directed straight at Amber, 'I guessed you might be here.'

'She drops in most afternoons,' Tara said.

Warwick frowned at Amber. 'I sure hope you didn't get here by way of the beach. Walking across that soft sand would be much too hard on your newly healed ankle.'

Amber had to smile. He really couldn't get out of the habit of running her life for her.

'No, Warwick, I didn't walk, I drove. And before you say anything more, I am allowed to drive.'

'Tara,' Max said as he joined them. 'Warwick wants to have a private word with Amber, so what say we take these kids upstairs for a bath and leave them to it?'

'But I don't *want* a bath,' Jasmine wailed when her mother scooped her up. 'I want to stay with Uncle Wawie.'

'It's all right, sweetie,' Warwick told her. 'I'll still be here when you've finished your bath.'

'You will?' a stunned Amber said once the others had gone.

'Yes,' he said and sat down beside her.

Amber swallowed. 'I'm not sure I understand. Did your gene test come back negative? Is that why you're here?'

'No. This has nothing to do with any gene test.'

'You did have it, didn't you? You gave me your solemn word.'

'Yes, I had it done last week. But I haven't received the results yet, though they should be through any time now. They did say, however, not to get my hopes up. Not with my family history. Frankly, I only did it because you asked me to.'

'I see.' Amber was beginning to feel confused. 'So why *are* you here, then?'

'Well you might ask. I really was determined to leave you, my darling. Quite determined. Determined to leave Australia as well, never to return. I've already put the apartment up for sale. But then I had this telephone call from Max last night, and he asked me what I'd have done if I had been perfectly well and it had been *you* who'd had the bad gene. He set me thinking. Actually I stayed up all night. And I finally realised that my so-called noble sacrifice in leaving you was not so noble after all. I mistakenly thought I was saving you from unhappiness in the future,' he said. 'Instead, I was condemning you to unhappiness right now, and possibly for the rest of your life. I knew if our situations were reversed I would not want to leave you. So, if you still love me, my darling,' he said, taking her hands in his and lifting them up to his lips, 'if you still have the courage…would you do me the honour of becoming my wife?'

Amber could not stop the tears from flooding her eyes.

This time, he didn't tell her not to cry. Instead, he gathered her close and held her whilst she sobbed quietly against his chest. And it was whilst he was holding her that Warwick heard the sound of his phone ringing.

'Damn it,' he muttered. 'Sorry, darling.' He disengaged himself from her arms and reached for the handset in his back pocket. 'It's probably my estate agent with an offer. He was showing a few people around the apartment today. I really should answer it and tell him I'm not selling after all.'

It wasn't the agent. It was the professor who'd taken charge of his gene test and who'd been extremely interested in Warwick's case.

'The results have just come in,' the professor said. 'You left your phone number so I thought I should ring you straight away.'

'That was most considerate of you.' Despite knowing what he was about to say Warwick couldn't help the tightening in his chest.

'It's negative, Mr Kincaid. You do not have the early onset Alzheimer's gene.'

'*What?* Are you sure? There couldn't have been a mistake made?'

'There have been no mistakes. I double checked everything. Of course this doesn't mean you won't get dementia at some stage in your life. But the risk is no greater than for anyone else.'

'I can't believe it.' And he couldn't: his heart was pounding and his head was spinning.

'I have to admit that I was surprised after the family history you gave me. I can only think that perhaps the man you thought was your father is not really your biological father. Such things do happen, you know. In any case, it's good news, isn't it?'

'Very good news. Thank you so much for calling me.'

'My pleasure.'

The professor hung up and Warwick turned his eyes to look at Amber.

'I still can't believe it,' he said, only just managing to hold on to his emotions.

'What is it?' Amber asked. 'What's happened?'

'That was Professor Jenkins, from the laboratory where I had my gene test done. The result was negative.'

'Oh, my God! Oh, Warwick. Is he sure? They couldn't have made a mistake, could they?'

'That's the first thing I asked him. But no, he said he double checked everything and he's quite sure.'

'Oh, Warwick, oh, dear, I know I'm going to cry again.'

'That's perfectly all right, my darling,' Warwick choked out as he pulled her into his arms. 'I think I'll join you.'

By the time Max returned downstairs, all weeping had stopped and two joyous faces turned to meet his enquiring eyes.

'Clearly she said yes,' Max said to Warwick.

'Yes,' Warwick replied, smiling.

'Sounds like a good excuse to break out a bottle of my best champagne.'

'Before you do that I have some other good news,' Warwick said.

'Really? What?'

'The results of my gene test came back negative.'

'You're kidding me. Wow. This is truly great news. I'll have to go tell Tara straight away. Tara?' he called out as he raced back into the house. 'Guess what?'

'You do realise what my negative result means, Amber,' Warwick said whilst waiting for their friends to reappear.

'Not really. What do you mean?'

'The professor suggested it's highly likely that the

man I thought was my father is *not* my father. That's got me thinking. Under the circumstances, I feel I should go to London and ask my long-lost mother a few questions. I know she lives there somewhere. Would you like to come with me?'

'Just try and stop me.'

'And whilst we're in London, I'll make enquiries about who's the best man for the job of reversing my vasectomy. I know it's possible because the doctor who did my original operation thought I might change my mind at some stage so he made sure that it could be reversed.'

'In that case, why can't *that* doctor do the reversal?'

'Darling, that was twenty years ago. He's probably an old dodderer by now with shaking hands and bad eyesight. No, I'll find a younger man, an expert in the field. We don't want anything getting between you and your babies, do we?'

Till the day he died, Warwick would always remember the look on her face at that moment.

CHAPTER NINETEEN

LESS than a week later, Amber and Warwick were standing on the doorstep of his mother's very smart town house in Kensington, waiting for someone to answer the doorbell. They had telephoned beforehand, having received the address and phone number from the private investigator Warwick had hired a week earlier. His mother had sounded agitated at the prospect of her long-estranged son visiting her, but had agreed in the end when he'd said it was a matter of some importance, though he hadn't elaborated further.

'How old would she be now?' Amber whispered to him as they waited, hand in hand.

'Sixty,' he replied. 'She was twenty when I was born. Twenty-one when my father divorced her.'

Amber frowned. 'Goodness. That was very young to be married and divorced.'

The woman who answered the door didn't look sixty. She didn't even look fifty: she could have easily passed for forty-five, her handsome face unlined, her figure superb, her obviously dyed red hair exquisitely groomed. But, despite her striking looks, Gloria Madison had never made it big in the acting world, her career having been relegated to minor roles in lesser movies. Nowadays, she rarely got a part at all.

For a long moment she just stared at Warwick.

'My goodness,' she said, a red-nailed hand lifting to rest at the base of her throat. 'You're the spitting image of him.'

'Of whom?' Warwick returned coldly.

Gloria blinked, her gaze shifting abruptly to Amber before returning to Warwick.

'Your father, of course,' she said somewhat brusquely.

'And who, exactly, was my father?' he shot back.

'What? What kind of strange question is that? You know very well who your father was!'

'I know who I *thought* he was.'

Heat reddened Gloria's already rouged cheeks. 'What are you suggesting? If you think I cheated on your father when we were married, then you'd be very wrong indeed. I wouldn't have dared.'

Warwick's hand tightened around Amber's. Suddenly, it worried him that somehow that test result might have been wrong. Mistakes did happen, no matter what the professor said.

'Can we come inside, Mother? I really don't want to discuss what is a highly personal situation out in the street.'

'Oh, very well. But you will have to be quick. I'm expecting a visitor in half an hour.'

A man, no doubt, Amber thought as she looked Warwick's mother up and down. You didn't wear an outfit like that for a woman friend.

Gloria led them into an elegantly furnished reception room where she waved them over to the cream sofa that sat beneath an elaborately dressed bay window. She then lowered herself stiffly into a matching armchair that faced them. Warwick introduced Amber, but Gloria didn't say anything to her.

Amber could see the woman was very nervous. Why be so, unless she was lying?

'Warwick wants to have a DNA test done,' Amber invented suddenly, despite knowing that was impossible, since there was no one on his father's side left alive to get samples from. 'That way it can be confirmed that his father really was his father.'

Alarm flashed into the woman's face. 'But, why, for heaven's sake?'

Amber leaned in to Warwick. 'I think she's lying about having cheated during her marriage,' she murmured.

Warwick was beginning to think so too. Maybe if he told her the truth…

'You probably don't know this, Mother, but there is a gene in the Kincaid family which produces early onset Alzheimer's. Dad inherited it. But I don't think he realised this fact till after I was born. It's the real reason he committed suicide. The symptoms usually start around fifty.'

'Good Lord!' Gloria gasped. 'Oh, how awful! No, I never knew. Honestly.' A frown gathered on her high forehead, her blue eyes clouding with real distress. 'But I…I think you're wrong about James not knowing this before you were born, Warwick. He must have known. It's why he did what he did. Why he—' She broke off, her feelings of being flustered filling her face.

'What did he do?' Amber jumped in immediately.

Gloria stared at her before her eyes swung suddenly to Warwick's. 'Are you saying you've believed all this time that *you've* inherited that dreadful disease?'

Warwick's heart skipped a beat as he heard the

inference behind his mother's words. 'Are you admitting that James Kincaid wasn't my biological father?'

'I…I promised to never say anything,' Gloria cried. 'I signed a legally binding contract. James paid me a lot of money to do what he wanted me to do.'

'And what was that, exactly?'

'To marry him and have you, but then to divorce him and give you up. He said he wanted a child, but not a wife.'

Warwick's confusion was acute. 'So James Kincaid *was* my biological father.'

'No, no, he wasn't!' she confessed. 'I didn't even meet James till I was four months pregnant with you.'

Amber and Warwick just stared at her.

'I'm so sorry,' Gloria blurted out, 'so terribly terribly sorry. But how was I to know? James never said a word about inheriting Alzheimer's to me.'

'I see,' Warwick bit out as shock over her revelations set in. His hands actually began to shake. 'Do you think Mother, that I might have a spot of whisky, or brandy? Whatever you have.'

'Yes, of course.' And she jumped up.

'Me too,' Amber said, her hand tightening around Warwick's.

His mother returned with two balloons of brandy—very good brandy, actually. Considering the lack of success in her acting career she must have received an extremely generous settlement for giving up her son. Strangely, this thought didn't upset Warwick. He wasn't at all bonded with the woman, or the man who'd fathered him.

Though he *was* curious.

'When you said I was the spitting image of him,' he

began after swallowing a reviving gulp of brandy, 'you meant my biological father, didn't you?'

'Yes,' she said with an almost wistful sigh. 'Though you're not unlike James. I was always attracted to the tall, dark and handsome type, usually with blue eyes. So when you were born people readily believed you were James's son.'

'Who *is* my real father, then?' Warwick asked.

'A man called Alistair Johnson. He was an actor…a married actor. I met him when I was only nineteen. He was twenty years older than me and I was crazy about him. When I fell pregnant, I thought I could get him to leave his wife and marry me. When I didn't go through with the termination he'd arranged, he still refused. Said his wife knew he slept around and didn't care.' Remembered distress flickered across her face. 'I didn't want to have a baby by myself. It was hard back then, being a single mother. I knew my family wouldn't help me. I'd run away from home when I was only fourteen to become an actress. They told me to never go back, and they meant it.'

For a long moment, Gloria looked truly sad and regretful. Amber felt a little sorry for her. As much as she had her differences with her own family, she knew they would never do something like that; they would never disown her.

Gloria sighed, then straightened her shoulders in a telling gesture. It reminded Amber of Warwick and the way he straightened his shoulders sometimes.

'I met James at a party,' Gloria continued. 'He seduced me with surprising ease, and it was during the first night we spent together that I confessed my predicament to him. You could have knocked me over with a feather when he said he would marry me and raise my baby as his own. But only if I took myself totally out of the picture. He said he wanted a legitimate child whom people recognised as his own, but not a wife.'

Amber took another sip of brandy to hide her shock. What kind of man made a proposition like that?

'He told me that he'd had cancer as a young man, and several bouts of radiation therapy had rendered him sterile,' Gloria elaborated. 'Which I totally believed. But now that I know the truth, I suspect James might have already got himself a vasectomy so that he couldn't have children. The man I married would not have risked passing on that horrible gene you told me about. James was too intelligent to let that happen.'

Warwick could only nod in agreement. It was, after all, what he had done himself.

'I know you probably both think it was terrible of me to take money to give up my baby, but back then it seemed the best solution. I was only young and silly and, yes, ambitious. If it means anything to you,' she said, looking directly at Warwick with sad eyes, 'then I have thought of you often.'

'And I you,' he returned, not at all warmly.

'Oh, dear,' she said somewhat brokenly. 'I suppose it's too late to ask for your forgiveness.'

'Much too late,' Warwick bit out.

'It's never too late for forgiveness,' Amber piped up beside him. 'This is your mother, Warwick. The grandmother of your future children. I refuse to leave this house till you've made peace with each other.'

Both of them stared at her, Gloria with surprise and Warwick with irritation. Till he remembered that this was why he'd fallen in love with Amber. Because of her kind heart and warm, loving nature. Not to mention her stubbornness. Even when she was being stubborn, she was endearing.

His sigh carried resignation. 'If I must…'

'You must,' Amber insisted.

'All right. I forgive you…Mother.'

Strangely, when he said the words, Warwick felt better. Not that he'd ever been overly bitter about his mother abandoning him. After all, he'd never known her.

Gloria tried not to cry. She'd been trying not to cry ever since she'd opened the door and seen her son for the first time in over thirty-nine years. For most of those years, she'd deeply regretted the deal she'd made with James. The guilt had eaten away at her very soul till she was little more than an empty shell.

No wonder she'd never really made it as an actress. It must have shown up on the screen, the emptiness inside, the lack of love.

Not that she was lacking in love at this moment. It came rushing back, the fierce love that she'd felt for her baby the day he was born, but which she'd quickly buried beneath her selfishness and greed.

'Thank you,' she choked out. 'And thank *you*,' she directed at the lovely girl her son had brought with him.

The girl smiled, first at her, then up at Warwick. It was the most beautiful smile Gloria had ever seen: full of love and joy. A smile she hoped to see often in the years to come.

If fate would be that kind…

'We should go now,' Warwick said, taking Amber's arm and standing up. 'Your visitor will be arriving shortly.'

Gloria stood up, too. 'There is no visitor. I lied about that.'

Amber swiftly realised that the man Gloria had dressed for had been her son.

'Why don't we take Gloria out for lunch, Warwick?' she suggested. 'It's high time we got to know one another. After all, she is going to be my future mother-in-law.'

'You're getting married!' Gloria gushed. 'How wonderful. But you're not wearing an engagement ring?' she directed at Amber.

'She will be by tonight,' Warwick said brusquely.

'So when is the wedding to be?'

'This summer,' Warwick replied firmly. 'On a lovely little beach just north of Sydney.'

'I thought I detected an Australian accent,' Gloria said, smiling at Amber. 'I've always wanted to go to Australia.'

Amber glanced up at Warwick, who shrugged his resignation over what he had to do.

And so it was, that on a brilliantly sunny day in the first week in November on Wamberal Beach, Amber Roberts became Mrs Warwick Kincaid, the simple ceremony watched by only a small group of family and friends. Max was the best man, of course, with Tara a stunningly beautiful matron of honour. But not as beautiful as the bride, in Warwick's opinion. Amber shone that day with a radiance and joy that transcended her physical beauty. He was so proud of her.

They didn't have a traditional sit-down reception afterwards, choosing to celebrate with a more informal pool party at Max's home.

Gloria, whom Warwick had flown over for the occasion, said it was the best wedding she'd ever been to.

Still, by the time Warwick and Amber flew off on

their honeymoon—they'd chosen a secluded and exclusive island resort up in the Whitsunday passage—both of them were happy to be alone. The last few months had been a rather stressful time, what with Warwick having had his vasectomy reversed, then having to wait to see if it had worked. Amber had not yet fallen pregnant and it worried Warwick that he would not be able to give her what she wanted most in the world—and what he wanted too.

So it was a highly concerned Warwick who awaited the result of another pregnancy test, which Amber took on the last day of their three-week honeymoon. Her period was only a week late, so it was possibly too early to have a definitive result.

Still…

His heart was thudding loudly in his chest by the time she emerged from the bathroom.

'Well?' he asked, unable to read the somewhat blank expression on her face.

'It went blue,' she said. 'Very blue.'

'Which means?'

'I'm pregnant, Warwick. We're going to have a baby!'

Warwick couldn't speak, a huge lump forming in his throat. Amber hurried over to where he was standing by the bed and wrapped her arms around his waist.

'You don't have to say anything,' she murmured, and laid her head against his chest. 'I know exactly how you feel…'

EPILOGUE

Excerpt from Amber's new year diary, started late in her twenty-sixth year, well after she became Mrs Kincaid, and the mother of a girl.

I haven't had much time to write in you lately, diary. Having a baby is very...time-consuming. You know, I thought I'd be able to handle being a mother just fine. I was so organised. By the time I went into labour, we'd finished redecorating the B & B at Wamberal into the most beautiful family home, with one of the guest bedrooms upstairs being turned into the prettiest pink nursery—we knew we were having a girl. But shortly after I brought little Kate home from hospital, I found myself crying one day and unable to stop. Poor Warwick didn't know what to do. He rang Tara, who had a new baby of her own. Another boy, named Lachlan. She said what I needed was some temporary help with the baby, but not a professional nanny: someone who cared about me. She suggested my mother. I was doubtful, but Warwick rang Mum anyway and she was up here in a flash. Turns out I had a mild case of post-natal depression. Mum recognised it straight away because she apparently suffered from it very badly after having me. She told me that she'd been totally unable to care for me and that Aunt Kate had taken me right away to her place for almost three months. Fortunately, I wasn't as bad as that. Still, it explained to me why Mum didn't have the same bonding with me that she had with my brothers. But you know what? During the last month of her staying here and helping me with Katie, we've become so close. Warwick's opinion of her has gone full circle, too. He thinks she's marvellous and says so all the time. Of course, Mum goes to mush and even blushed once or twice. If I hadn't witnessed it for myself I wouldn't have believed it. She's going home tomorrow and I'm going to miss her heaps. But it will be nice to have my darling Katie to myself again. She's just so adorable. Warwick says she's a clone of me but I can see him in her eyes. And she's much longer than I was as a baby. Or so my mum says. She's going to be tall—and very smart. She's already smiling and I'm sure it's not gas! Warwick said he's not going to spoil her, but you only have to see all the toys he's already bought to know that he's going to be putty in her hands. I thought Max loved his children but when I see Warwick hold Katie there's something extra special in his eyes, something miraculous.

That's what he always calls her: his little miracle.

When I think about all that's happened, I'm sure he's absolutely right…